HIDDEN THINGS

WHERE THE PAST MEETS THE PRESENT— HEAD ON

ANDREA BOESHAAR

BARBOUR
PUBLISHING

HIDDEN THINGS

© 2003 by Andrea Boeshaar

ISBN 1-58660-970-X

All Scripture quotations, unless otherwise noted, are taken from the King James Version of the Bible.

Scripture quotations marked NKJV are taken from the New King James Version. Copyright © 1979, 1980, 1982 by Thomas Nelson, Inc. Used by permission. All rights reserved.

This book is a work of fiction. Names, characters, places, and incidents are either products of the author's imagination or used fictitiously. Any similarity to actual people, organizations, and/or events is purely coincidental.

For more information about Andrea Boeshaar, please access the author's Web site at the following Internet address:
www.andreaboeshaar.com

Acquisitions and Editorial Director: Rebecca Germany
Editorial Consultant: Susan Downs
Art Director: Robyn Martins
Layout Design: Anita Cook

Published by Barbour Publishing, Inc., P.O. Box 719, Uhrichsville, OH 44683,
www.barbourbooks.com

*Our mission is to publish and distribute inspirational products offering
exceptional value and biblical encouragement to the masses.*

Member of the
Evangelical Christian
Publishers Association

Printed in the United States of America
5 4 3 2 1

I believe God uses the hidden things of life to bring us to Him or closer to Him. About thirteen years ago, shortly after I became a Christian, I received a phone call from a man who said he'd like to help me with the foreclosure of our home. I refused to believe our home was pending foreclosure; however, the gentleman on the other end of the line gave me information that proved otherwise. Soon I discovered my husband, Daniel, had been gambling away the mortgage money for months—and I never had a clue. When I finally found out, I was devastated .

On my knees, pouring out my heart to God, I would pray that He would change my husband. I felt in my heart that marriage was for better, for worse—for keeps, so divorce was out of the question. I thought I was being ever so sacrificial, but instead of changing my husband, God worked on me some more! That really didn't seem fair; however, as I tried to become a godly wife, my husband soon made decisions that honored Christ, which, in turn, changed his life—and the lives of his family.

Today, Daniel is free from the bondages of alcohol and gambling. Jesus Christ set him free. Our sons saw the power of God in their father, and one of them, Benjamin, is now in full-time ministry. I shudder to think where my family would be today without the Lord in our lives.

So if you're battling some recently uncovered hidden things, please know that there is nothing on earth that can knock God off His heavenly throne. He knows what you're going through. He sees your problems and feels your pain. He is with you, and you are loved.

" 'I will give you the treasures of darkness
And hidden riches of secret places,
That you may know that I, the LORD,
Who call you by your name,
Am the God of Israel.' "
ISAIAH 45:3 NKJV

PROLOGUE

The skeletal limbs of barren treetops cast eerie shadows on the snow-covered driveway as Kylie Rollins made her way back to the house with today's mail in hand. She barely noticed the sunshine or blue sky on this Saturday afternoon. In her heart, it was a dark, gloomy day. A bad day. Kylie had them off and on since her mother's recent death. Oftentimes, it seemed like a storm cloud hung over her and shadowed her every move. That storm cloud had a name. Mourning.

Entering through the back door, Kylie kicked off her boots, hung up her jacket, and walked into the kitchen. She collapsed into a chair at the white, wooden table and sifted through the envelopes, inspecting each one. Most contained bills, but some appeared to hold belated sympathy cards. The latter she set aside for another time when she felt stronger.

Mom's death still seems so unreal.

Her mother, Wendy Rollins, had been her best friend. After Kylie's father, Dr. Joshua Rollins, died more than seven years ago, she and her mother had drawn strength from each other. Now Kylie felt she had no one. Well, except her fiancé, Matthew Alexander. She loved him with all her heart, and she had him to lean on. She had his mother, Lynellen, and a host of other friends. She had her church family. . . .

So why do I feel so alone?

An oversized brown envelope at the bottom of the stack suddenly caught Kylie's eye. Lifting it, she inspected the return address. It came from someone in Oakland Park, Illinois. Kylie didn't know anyone in Illinois and didn't recognize the sender's name either. Allison Drake Littenberg.

Kylie tore open the envelope and extracted a faded photograph that had been copied and enlarged. The date printed on the bottom of the snapshot read March 1969. She stared at the photo, trying to understand its significance. Pictured were three young ladies who stood on either side of a policeman whose arm was draped possessively across the shoulders of one female in particular. The word *Me* was written in marker with an arrow pointing to that woman, so Kylie assumed it was the sender. Then she saw the other names. Blythe. Jack. Wendy.

No way! That's Mom?

Kylie held it nearer, for better inspection. It was a close-up shot of the four, only their upper torsos in view, although the original photo must have been somewhat damaged because the copy was speckled and blurred in areas. But Kylie could make it out and. . .sure enough, her mother was one of the women in the photograph. Except it couldn't be. Wearing a tie-dyed smock top, a beaded band around her forehead, large loopy earrings, and her chestnut brown hair hanging long and straight, her mother resembled one of those infamous protesters that Kylie had glimpsed in history books, documentaries, and movies. The fact that she held a picket sign over her shoulder, stating, "WAR Is Not Healthy For Children And Other Living Things!" only enhanced the stereotypical image in Kylie's head.

She blinked. No. This woman couldn't be her mother. Wendy Rollins had been a conservative Christian all her life.

Kylie's heart quickened with indignation. Surely this was a joke. She had heard about people who read the obituaries, then swindled grieving families. Was this some sort of scam?

As she imagined the worse, a folded letter fell from the package and into her lap, along with what appeared to be a wedding invitation. Kylie opened the missive first and read the neat penmanship on the flowered stationery.

Hi, Wendy,

Look what I found when I was moving last summer! If I remember correctly, the photo was snapped right after the antiwar demonstration you talked Blythe and me into joining. We marched in front of Oakland Park's City Hall with about fifty other kids. Jack and I had been dating for six months, and he threatened to haul us off to jail, but of course, he didn't. Seems like a lifetime ago—what am I thinking, it was a lifetime ago!

Kylie turned to the second page.

Last August I returned to Chicago on business. I met up with Jack Callahan and, you might not believe this, but after thirty years, we have renewed our romance and now we're getting married! We're planning a small

wedding ceremony on April 21, right before we leave on
a cruise. At the end of May, we'll host a reception upon
our return. I've enclosed an invitation. I hope you can
come. Jack and I would love to see you again. Give me
a call or drop me a line. Here's my phone number and
E-mail address. . . .

Shocked and confused, Kylie studied the strange, yet familiar, image of her mother in the photograph again.

"This can't be Mom," she murmured aloud. "March of 1969. . . ?" Kylie quickly did the math. Her mother would have been nine months' pregnant at the time. Kylie was born April 10, 1969. Why would her mother join a demonstration when she was expecting a baby any day? And where was her father? Had he been the one who'd taken the picture?

Tingles of foreboding wound their way up Kylie's spine. Something was wrong. She stood and left the kitchen in search of the portable phone. Finding it on the polished coffee table in the living room, she lowered herself onto the floral-upholstered sofa and dialed the number printed in the letter.

"Hello?"

"Um. . ." Words suddenly clogged her throat. She hadn't expected to reach a real person. She had intended to leave a message.

"Hello?"

"Um. . .hello. Is this Allison Drake Littenberg?"

"Yes, it is. Who's this?"

She cleared her throat. "My name is Kylie Rollins and, um. . .I'm Wendy's daughter. I received the picture you sent today."

A pause. "You received it?"

"Yes. . .I mean, well. . .I know it was addressed to Mom,

but. . ." Kylie's eyes teared. "Mom died at the end of January."

"Oh, I'm so sorry!" the female voice at the other end replied. "I had no idea. . . ."

Kylie swallowed the sadness. She'd been thinking of her mother all day today as she tidied the house.

"I. . .I feel awful. I wish I could have contacted Wendy sooner, but it took several months to locate her." Another pause. "How did she die. . .if you don't mind me asking?"

"No, I don't mind." Kylie had told scores of people how it happened, at the visitation at the funeral home and, later, after the memorial service. Oddly, relaying the news of the tragedy again would be almost comforting. "It was sort of a freak thing. Mom and I were cleaning, and she tripped on the edge of the bedroom rug and struck her head against the corner of the footboard. She had a gash, but we didn't think too much of it. Mom washed it and put on a bandage. We even laughed about how funny she looked with a Band-Aid on her forehead.

"That night we had supper, watched some TV, and went to bed. Just like normal. But Mom. . ." That familiar dark cloud of gloom converged on her again. ". . .Mom never woke up the next day. Apparently, she had ruptured something in her head and we never knew it."

"How awful. Please accept my deepest sympathies." The woman's voice sounded kind and compassionate—even soothing. "My own mother died of something similar. A brain aneurysm, although it wasn't from an injury."

Walking back to the kitchen, Kylie nodded a reply, even though she knew the woman on the phone couldn't see it. She reached the table and lifted the photograph, staring hard at it. Dozens of questions buzzed in her brain. "I'd like to ask you about a few things. Do you have some time?"

"Yes, of course."

"Will you tell me how you met my mother?" Inhaling deeply, she sat down, one leg folded underneath her. "Tell me about how the two of you became friends, and. . .was this picture really taken in March of 1969?"

CHAPTER ONE

Kylie dressed for church the next morning, pulling on a black skirt and French blue silk blouse. She mentally replayed her conversation with Allison Littenberg, or "Allie," as the woman preferred. If Allie told the truth, Kylie's mother had lied—but how could that be? Kylie and her mother shared everything, or at least Kylie thought they had.

Throughout the years, Mom maintained that she was an only child, but Allie said Wendy had a brother named Rob. The two of them had planned to travel from state to state, going all the way to the Pacific Coast, joining war protests everywhere. After that, their intentions were to go into Canada so Rob could dodge the draft, but he was tragically killed in a riot during the 1968 Democratic National Convention before they ever left Illinois.

Maybe that's why Mom didn't tell me. Maybe she'd been so

devastated to lose her brother. . . .

Even so, the inconsistencies didn't end there. Mom said she'd grown up around here, Basil Creek, Wisconsin. But Allie said she hailed from Charleston, South Carolina.

Kylie shook herself mentally. *I can't think about this now. I'm going to be late for church.*

Grabbing her Bible off the bedside table, she left her room and dashed down the beige carpeted steps. But even in her haste, she remembered the photograph and Allie's letter. She'd forgotten them last night when she went over to Matt's for supper. She had felt so confused that she didn't say anything to him or his mother—who happened to be Wendy Rollins's best friend, next to Kylie.

Lynellen will know if Allie is lying, she thought, climbing into her forest green Subaru Outback. Kylie turned the key, started the engine, and rolled down the snow-packed driveway. Reaching the road, she made a left and proceeded to church.

As she drove the two-mile journey, Kylie figured she had probably been down this rural stretch of highway too many times to count. She'd been born and raised in Basil Creek, a nothing little town near the Mississippi River. She'd known Matt all her life. A grin tugged at her mouth as Kylie recalled how she couldn't stand him in grade school. Three years older, he used to call her "china doll" because of her black hair and porcelain-white skin. Over the years, Kylie had learned to deal with her paleness, using foundation, a bright shade of lipstick, and an occasional visit to the tanning booth in the neighboring city of La Crosse. But with the way in which her mother cut Kylie's thick, ebony hair when she was a girl, chin length all the way around and bangs, she supposed she did resemble a "china doll." Except, at the time,

Kylie abhorred the name whenever Matt teased her. She was only too glad when he went off to high school, became involved with football and girls, and left Kylie alone. But since his mother and Kylie's mother were always on the phone or at each other's house, she saw him more than she cared to. . .back then.

My, how time changes things, she thought, cranking up the heater on this chilly morning in March.

After high school, Matt had attended the University of Wisconsin–Madison and earned a business degree. He got married, and Kylie and her parents attended the elegant affair. After five years of trying to have a child, Matt's wife, Rochelle, finally gave birth to a boy, Jason, and Kylie could still hear Lynellen's voice ringing with happiness each time she brought over pictures of her grandson.

But then. . .the accident. . .

Rochelle had been a nurse in Madison and worked the night shift. Matt, employed at a large corporation at the time, worked during the day. Their arrangement was that after her shift at the hospital, Rochelle would meet Matt in his company's parking lot, they'd do a "baby exchange," and then Rochelle would take Jason home. When the baby went down for his naps, she slept. After five, when Matt arrived home, Rochelle would catch a few more hours of sleep before going back to work.

But that day, as she drove home on a lonesome ribbon of road, Rochelle fell asleep. Her car plowed into a tree. Neither she nor their baby survived.

Matt, of course, had been devastated, as was Lynellen, his mother. In fact, most of the Basil Creek population grieved right along with the Alexander family—just as they grieved with Kylie now over the loss of her mother.

Pulling into the churchyard, she managed to find a space in the crowded lot. She parked and ran for the front door of the quaint country structure. Built in the early 1900s, the little white church had seen its share of tears.

Strains from the pipe organ reminded Kylie of her tardiness. As she stepped into the foyer and hung up her coat, she couldn't help but smile at Martha Finski's enthusiastic rendition of "Onward Christian Soldiers." It sounded like something out of *Phantom of the Opera.* Nevertheless, Kylie thanked God that the congregation had stood so she was able to make a fairly unnoticed entrance. Pausing at the third pew from the front, she slipped in beside Matt.

He gave her a wide-eyed look.

She replied with a single shrug.

He switched hands and held the songbook out so they could share. Kylie finished singing the last part of the hymn. "With the cross of Jesus, marching on before."

Hymnals slapped shut, and Pastor Hanson stood at the pulpit, wearing a white robe and somber expression. "You may be seated."

Lowering herself into the pew, she saw Matt tap his wristwatch. She slid her gaze up the arm of his navy suit coat and met his curious stare, then shrugged again.

Matt looked away, but Kylie thought she saw a hint of a grin.

"Hi, Sweetie," Lynellen whispered, reaching over her son to give Kylie's hand an affectionate squeeze.

Kylie smiled and returned the gesture.

Pastor Hanson read the announcements, and while she listened, she studied the back of Matt's strong, weather-beaten hand. Her gaze traveled higher, to his clean-shaven jaw, straight nose, and neatly combed blond hair.

He suddenly looked at her, his German-Norwegian baby blues darkening with curiosity. He leaned close and whispered, "Everything okay?"

She nodded for lack of a better response. She couldn't exactly go into detail at the moment about how skewed her world had become since she received that photograph yesterday. Even so, she hoped Matt would understand when she finally did tell him. He had a tendency to still see her as that fragile china doll without a brain in her head.

On the contrary, Kylie had earned her bachelor's degree, and now, at thirty years of age, she had worked her way up to the prestigious position of head librarian at Basil Creek's brand-new facility. Kylie remembered when the building first opened. It was just after Matt had returned.

A year after his wife's death, he sold their home in Madison and moved back in with his mother. His dad had succumbed to prostate cancer, so Matt took over his family's dairy farm. As the youngest son, whose siblings were settled with families of their own, he felt an obligation to his mother. He also thought, with his business skills, he could revive their ailing farm. In the past eighteen months, Matt had made some progress, but Kylie still recalled how she felt when she first saw him shortly after his return to Basil Creek. His eyes looked so pained and dull, and she thought she'd do just about anything to wipe the misery off his handsome face.

Then their mothers joined forces and launched their grand campaign. Lynellen began to ask Matt to drop off her library books anytime he was headed into town. Kylie's mom would tell her woebegone tales, ending with, "It's going to take the love of a good woman to heal that poor man's heart."

Kylie started thinking she might like to be that "good woman," and one day when Matt stopped in with his mother's books, she made a point to say hello.

His blue eyes widened, the way they always did whenever he was caught off guard. "Kylie? Kylie Rollins? Is that really you?"

"Yes." She had laughed at his incredulousness.

"When did you grow up?"

"Probably the same time you did." She had always heard men matured slower than women, but her quip was lost on Matt, who continued to gape at her.

"How long have you been working here?"

"At the library? Ever since it opened."

"How come I've never noticed you before?"

She shrugged. She had noticed him plenty of times.

Two days later, Matt came into the library and asked Kylie out for Saturday night. She accepted, and just this past Christmas, he had asked her to marry him. Kylie accepted that offer, too, although she often wondered if he still loved Rochelle. . . .

Well, of course he did. Matt couldn't just sever all the love he had for his wife any more than Kylie could sever the love she had for her mother. She had learned that cold, hard fact firsthand. Death couldn't separate conjoined hearts!

Matt nudged her with his elbow, and Kylie snapped from her reverie.

"That's Jeremiah thirty-two," Pastor Hanson said, "and let's read verse twenty-seven together in the New King James Version."

She flipped open her Bible and found the passage in time to read along. " 'Behold, I am the Lord, the God of all flesh. Is there anything too hard for Me?' "

The pastor began to expound on the Scripture verse, and Kylie realized she'd known the reverend and his wife, Sarah, for at least half her life. She'd gone through school with their children—she'd even dated their oldest son.

"And there's nothing too hard for God. He's the One who fed five thousand with a few fish and a loaf of bread. . . ."

With her mind taxed from thinking all night instead of sleeping, Kylie couldn't focus. She glanced across the aisle and saw her friend Dena Hubbard sitting between her two children. It was hard to believe Ryan was thirteen already and Amber just eighteen months younger than he. It made Kylie feel old, but then again, Dena had gotten married right after high school. Unfortunately, her friend's marriage ended in disaster. Todd drank too much and became physically abusive. After he beat her up one too many times, Dena packed up Ryan and Amber and returned to Basil Creek, where she bought a mobile home north of town in the new trailer park subdivision. As for Todd, he had since remarried, and rumor had it that he didn't treat Wife Number Two any better than he had Wife Number One.

As if sensing Kylie's stare, Dena turned. They regarded each other the way they always did—ever since they were four years old—all smiles and impish gleams in their eyes.

Suddenly Dena leaned forward so Pastor wouldn't see, and she stuck out her tongue. Kylie's jaw slackened; her eyes grew wide. She couldn't believe what Dena had done! Averting her gaze in one quick motion, Kylie willed herself not to laugh.

What a nut.

"And so, in the face of our trials," Pastor Hanson concluded, "we can boldly and triumphantly say that nothing is too hard for our God." A dramatic pause. "Let's bow for prayer."

Lowering her head, Kylie tried to pray, but she couldn't

seem to concentrate. God seemed so far away since her mother's death.

"Wasn't that a touching message?" Lynellen said after the service.

Kylie nodded, feeling a pang of guilt for her inattentiveness. She rose from the pew and took a step into the aisle. At that moment, Dena passed by and purposely bumped Kylie's shoulder, sending her into Matt's broad chest.

"Oh, excuse me," her friend drawled.

Kylie laughed and glanced up into Matt's eyes. Yes, she loved him. Did he even know how much?

He sent Dena a look of irritation but then smiled at Kylie and tweaked her nose. "Let's go eat. I'm starved."

*   *   *

Kathryn Chadwyk wished she hadn't missed church this morning, except she'd awakened with one of her sick headaches and couldn't muster the strength to get out of bed. But now that the throbbing pain in her temples had ebbed, the waves of the Atlantic gently washing up to shore outside her window seemed to beckon her as she lay in her bed.

Rolling onto her side, she glanced at the alarm clock. Eleven-fifteen. Lee and TJ wouldn't be back until at least noon. A stroll on the beach might be exactly what she needed. Fresh air. Sunshine. And she didn't have to worry about fulfilling her hostess responsibilities because, at the present, there weren't any guests staying in their modern beach home, which she and Lee had converted into a bed-and-breakfast.

Slipping out from beneath the bed covers, Kathryn padded to her closet and dressed in blue jeans and a white, cotton button-up shirt. She glanced in the mirror and thought her hazel eyes seemed puffy, but the headache medicine tended to have that effect.

Kathryn walked to the bathroom and brushed out her short, reddish-brown hair that she refused to let become gray. She decided, for someone who had just turned seventy-five, she appeared quite "well preserved," as TJ would say. He was such a tease. He thought he was funny. However, Kathryn knew of younger women who looked much worse than she did—and who weren't as healthy either.

Lord, You are so good, she prayed as she made her way through the house and exited by way of the back door. Out on the deck, she slipped her feet into worn canvas tennis shoes before she began her trek down the long, wooden boardwalk that led to the beach.

As she ambled along the shoreline, she was suddenly reminded of the day she and Lee first came here to Sabal Beach. Perhaps it was the way the sun shone above the eastern horizon and sparkled on the blue-green sea or the way the sand gave way beneath her feet. Whatever it was, something triggered the memory. Had it really been thirty-two years ago?

Kathryn worked the numbers in her head. Yes, they'd bought their first home in '67. They'd moved here from Maine. Wendy had been fifteen and Rob, seventeen. Those two had been rabble-rousers, bringing the police to the Chadwyks' door almost daily. Accepting a job in Charleston, Lee had thought the change in locale would make a difference. He thought the kids would straighten up.

They didn't.

Tears blurred Kathryn's vision. Her mother's heart had never healed from losing her two precious children. Not a day went by that she didn't think about them, and she still harbored hope that she'd see them again.

Wendy and Rob had both run away from home during their teenage years. Rob, nineteen at the time, was determined to dodge the draft, and Wendy, only seventeen, was equally as determined to help him. At first, Kathryn had persuaded her husband to "let them go," so Lee didn't phone the police and report Wendy, a minor, missing. Kathryn and Lee enjoyed a bit of respite from their troublesome teens but felt certain that as soon as the pair needed money, they'd call or return home.

And that's exactly what happened. Wendy phoned from Pittsburgh asking for a handout, which Lee refused to give her. Weeks later, she called from Cincinnati with a similar request. Again, Lee declined, but he offered her a plane ticket home so she could finish high school. Wendy didn't want it.

Then Rob called from Detroit, and he and Lee had a terrible argument. Lee had been—and still was—a very patriotic man who had fought in World War II. He felt disgraced that his son wouldn't follow in his footsteps and aid his country's war efforts in Vietnam. But Rob insisted he wouldn't fight. Instead, he vowed to seek political asylum in Canada or another country.

As far as Kathryn knew, that's where he was today.

And Wendy. . .after that last horrid phone call she'd made, she all but vanished off the planet. Even the private detectives Kathryn and Lee had hired over the years couldn't locate her— or Rob either. Of course, back then the technological resources hadn't been nearly as advanced as they were today.

Stooping to pick up a uniquely shaped seashell to add to her collection in the yard, Kathryn wondered if maybe it was time to try again, although she knew her husband would balk at the idea. His hurt ran as deep as the Atlantic, and Lee had grumbled more than once about spending money trying to find people who didn't want to be found. Kathryn supposed he had a point. However, it didn't lessen her sense of loss.

Having ventured half a mile down the beach, she turned around and walked back to the bed and breakfast she and Lee built almost fifteen years ago. There was a lot to do before the next influx of guests checked in this evening. Spring break was upon them, and then the Easter holiday would arrive. But for the next hour, Kathryn would sit in the sunroom with a cup of herbal tea, read her Bible, and pray. She wouldn't forget her First Love in all her busyness. She only wished she would have known Jesus Christ when she was raising her children. Kathryn had no doubt that His love would have transformed their home.

There are just some things in a Christian's past she can't change, aren't there, Lord? And if I keep looking back, I'll end up like Lot's wife—a pillar of salt.

Breathing in the fresh sea air, Kathryn reluctantly set her worry and despair in God's loving hands and determined once more to trust Him with her future.

CHAPTER TWO

J ack, I feel just awful!"

"Why? You had no idea Wendy died."

Walking beside him as they made their way across the crowded church parking lot in Schaumburg, Illinois, Allie did her best to keep up with Jack's long strides.

Finally, she threaded her hand around his elbow and gave it a tug. "Slow down, will you? I'm wearing heels today and the pavement is slippery."

He did as she asked. "Sorry. Guess I wasn't thinking."

Allie heaved a dramatic sigh and Jack chuckled.

"Old habits die hard. I've been in a hurry most of my life."

"Well, now that you're retired—"

"Retired? What are you talking about? You keep me busier than the Oakland Park police chief ever did!"

Allie had to laugh as she clung to Jack's arm. It was true.

With his law enforcement background and her consulting expertise, they made a dynamite consulting team, and they'd just finished their first assignment together. Working fifty-hour weeks for the past four months had become the norm. They both needed a break.

"All right, now that the job is over at Lakeland Enterprises, I'll cut you some slack."

"Promises, promises," Jack groused.

They reached his black Ford Explorer. Pulling his keys from his overcoat pocket, he unlocked the passenger door for her.

"I wish I would have tried to contact Wendy when I first found that old photograph. Maybe I could have seen her before she died."

"Allie, don't torture yourself." Jack set his forearm on top of the vehicle's door and leaned against it. As always, his short dark hair, sprinkled with gray, was neatly parted to one side, but this morning his cocoa brown eyes were shielded behind dark sunglasses. "Wendy wasn't easy to locate, and after what you've told me, I suspect there was a reason for it. If you would have contacted her months ago, she might not have wanted to see you."

"I know. . . ."

"So don't play that 'what-if' game."

"But, Jack, Wendy's daughter kept asking me if her mother was really nine months' pregnant at the time the photograph was taken. I didn't know what to say. I didn't want to lie, but—"

"It's none of our business. You did the right thing by skirting the issue."

"Did I?" Allie felt so uncertain. Had she been in Kylie's place, she would want to know the whole truth.

"Let me say it again." Jack reached out and brushed several strands of hair off her cheek. "You did the right thing."

"Okay, okay, I might even believe you this time."

Wearing a smirk, Jack glanced at his wristwatch. "Hop in. We'd better get going. Steve and Nora are expecting us for lunch."

At the mention of Jack's brother and sister-in-law, Allie smiled as she climbed into the SUV. It was fast becoming a routine to spend Sunday afternoons at the Steve Callahan home.

"All set?"

She gave him a nod. Jack removed his hand from her elbow and closed the door. Pulling the seat belt across her slender frame, Allie watched the man she loved so much walk around the vehicle to the driver's side.

Jack Callahan had come a long way, both spiritually and emotionally, in the last six months. Allie respected him for being so willing to allow the Lord to change his heart. What's more, Jack offered her the kind of love, companionship, and protection she'd once thought possible only in fairy tales. With Jack, she felt cherished by a man who feared the Lord and desired to grow in His Word. Allie sensed God would use both of them in mighty ways. The very idea was exhilarating.

Jack opened the door and seated himself behind the wheel. Allie shivered as a blast of cold March wind followed him inside.

"I can't wait to be warm again. Sunny Saint Thomas, here we come."

"Just a little more than five weeks, Allie." Sticking the key into the ignition, Jack started the engine. "I'm counting the days—thirty-nine, to be exact."

She smiled and gave him a long look. She couldn't wait to become his wife.

꿈　　꿈　　꿈

Sitting in the restaurant as they waited for their lunch to arrive, Kylie tried to gauge Lynellen's reaction to the photograph and Allie's letter. "So what do you think? Is that woman lying? And, if she is, what's her motive?"

Lynellen raised her head and gave it an inconclusive shake. At sixty-three years old, she didn't look a day over forty-nine. Outspoken and spunky, Lynellen always had an idea up her sleeve and a quip on her tongue.

"It sure looks like Wendy." She chuckled. "I'm sorry to laugh, but I can see your mother doing something like this."

Kylie raised her brows. "Protesting? When she was nine months' pregnant with me? You could see her doing something like that?"

"When Wendy was nineteen? Sure. Except. . ." Lynellen's russet brows pulled together as she inspected the snapshot again. "Wendy doesn't really look pregnant, if you ask me."

Kylie frowned. "What do you mean?"

"Well, usually women look sort of. . .filled out."

Wearing a frown, Matt reached for the photograph. "Let's not speculate. This probably isn't even Wendy. It wouldn't be hard to alter a photograph with the aid of a computer. Could be this is Wendy's face superimposed into the snapshot."

"I suppose you're right, Son." Lynellen took a sip of her coffee.

Kylie shook her head. "Why would Allie go through all that trouble?"

Matt lifted his shoulders in a smooth up-and-down motion. "I don't know. Maybe she thinks she's entitled to a portion of your inheritance. Working for Heritage Mutual in Madison really opened my eyes. Weirdos come out of the woodwork when they smell life insurance. They want a piece of the pie."

"But Mom didn't leave me that much. Besides, Allie didn't even know Mom died until yesterday."

"So she said. . ."

"Hmm. . ." Now Kylie had to wonder. There had to be some explanation. Her mother wouldn't have lied to her.

"Who is this other woman?" Lynellen asked. "The dark-haired one?"

"I don't know." Kylie sipped her diet cola. "The name underneath says Blythe—and it's so odd, but I have this strange feeling I've met her somewhere."

"Could be. But I don't recall your mother ever mentioning a woman named Blythe."

"What about her brother? Do you know anything about him, Lyn?"

"Nope. But I would buy into your theory about Wendy being so overcome with grief that she refused to broach the subject. There were some areas of your mother's life that she kept private. Even from me."

"Like what?"

"Like. . ." Lynellen pursed her lips as she seemed to search for an answer. "Like her childhood, for instance. Wendy never liked to talk about it. I always thought maybe something awful happened to her when she was young. So we stayed clear of that topic of conversation."

"Something awful. . .what do you mean?" Kylie persisted.

Lynellen's voice was but a whisper when she answered. "I wondered if maybe she'd been a victim of rape or incest."

Kylie sucked in a breath. "My mom?"

"Will you two knock it off?!" Matt gave them both an

annoyed glance. "I think you've been watching too many day-time dramas."

"Oh, yeah?" Kylie replied. "Who has time for that with an eight-hour-a-day job?"

Matt smirked at her comeback. But Kylie had made a mental jump back to the topic of her mother. She rummaged through her memories and realized her mom really hadn't spoken about her childhood, other than to say she had no living relatives. If she ever mentioned her parents, it was a passing remark and nothing detailed. *"My church family is the only family I need. There I have dozens of brothers and sisters. Here at home, I have a wonderful husband and sweet little girl. . .what more could a woman ask for?"*

"Kylie?"

Matt's voice prevailed over her mother's, and she shook off the remembrance.

"Ky, are you okay?"

She blew out a sigh. "This photograph thing has me upset and confused."

"Well, there's your answer." Matt stuffed the picture and Allie's letter back into the brown envelope and set it aside. "God is not the author of confusion, right? That's what the Bible says. I think this photograph is a farce."

"But what if it's not?" A horrible thought struck Kylie. "You don't think that I'm the product of. . .something awful, do you?" She looked from Matt's wide-eyed expression to Lynellen's frowning countenance.

Matt recovered first. "Honey, your imagination is running wild. Rein it back in."

She drew in a deep breath. She loved to read, and she supposed she had indulged in a few too many mystery novels. "Maybe you're right."

Matt grinned. "I'm always right."

Kylie rolled her eyes.

"Listen, honey bunch, you're not the product of anything but a sweet union between your parents," Lynellen told her, lifting her coffee cup. "Your mother would have said otherwise. That she would have talked about. I'm certain of it. If it would have harmed you, Kylie, she would have spoken up."

"See?" Matt lifted his glass and took a drink of his cola. "No need to fret another second, okay?"

Kylie managed a smile, but deep inside she felt curiously unsettled. . .and somewhat betrayed. It just didn't seem right that her mother would lie or keep secrets from her. They'd shared their hearts on several occasions, even discussing painful matters, such as Kylie's father's death and the previous deaths of his parents, to whom Mom had been very close. It just didn't make sense.

The waitress brought their lunches. Lynellen had ordered a cup of soup and the club sandwich, Matt chose a huge hamburger smothered in Swiss cheese and onions, and Kylie had selected a grilled chicken salad with shredded provolone and sliced tomatoes.

"Is that all you're eating?" Matt opened his napkin and placed it in his lap.

Kylie couldn't help a grin. "Yes, this is all I'm eating. I want to fit into my wedding dress come September."

Matt's glance was subtle but appraising, and it spoke volumes, although he didn't say a word. He didn't have to; Kylie knew exactly what he was thinking. Matt said, at five feet five inches tall, she looked just right in a size fourteen—not too thick, not too thin. Matt told her he didn't appreciate skinny women. But what he didn't know was that she could gain weight just thinking about food.

"Matt, if I gave in to my urges, I'd resemble one of your heifers."

He chuckled and sent her a doubtful glance. "Listen, I can think of plenty of ways you can work off a few extra calories."

"Not the E-word again." At Lynellen's confused frown, Kylie explained. "Exercise."

"Oh!" Lynellen laughed. "And here I thought Matt had a backward way of asking if you'll help him with his chores tonight."

Smiling, Kylie looked at him askance. "I'd help Matt in a minute. He knows that." She'd do about anything in order to spend time with him.

"Yeah, I know." His eyes darkened with sincerity. "I don't deserve you, Ky. You're too good for me."

She narrowed her gaze. "I wish you'd stop saying that. You're beginning to worry me."

"Oh, he just knows what a great catch you are, Kylie." Lynellen grinned at her son. "You're perfect for each other."

"I think so." Kylie watched Matt's expression for any sign he felt the opposite.

Meeting her gaze, he gave her an affectionate wink before extending his hand. Kylie pressed her palm into his, while Lynellen clasped Matt's other hand.

He bowed his head. "Let's pray."

❧   ❧   ❧

"Good news. Kathryn's headache is gone. She's up and about and has even made us some lunch."

From behind the wheel of the Chadwyks' fawn-colored Toyota Avalon, TJ McGwyer couldn't stifle his grin. "What sort of lunch did she make?"

Lee chuckled from the passenger seat as he slipped the cell phone into his shirt pocket. "I know what you're thinking,

TJ. But I'm sure she's put together a more substantial meal than those miniscule tea sandwiches she serves the ladies in her book club."

TJ laughed. Funny how Lee knew him so well. Then again, theirs was a special relationship. Ten years ago, TJ had been a ramblin', gamblin' drifter who'd come to the end of the road—and the end of his luck. The Chadwyks had taken him in and hired him as their handyman. Over the years, they showed him Christlike love, and in 1992 TJ believed and became a Christian.

He'd also become like a son to the Chadwyks. Even at age fifty-two, TJ felt blessed to have been adopted into their family, particularly since Lee and Kathryn were estranged from their natural-born children. In essence, he and the Chadwyks needed each other.

"Beautiful day."

TJ glanced over at Lee and noticed the older man's thick white hair seemed even brighter with the sunshine spilling over it. TJ smiled. "It'd be a perfect day if a thunderstorm were brewing."

Lee chuckled. "You and that storm-chasing nonsense. But, I will admit, I've enjoyed your pictures of those dark, ominous clouds and sharp bolts of lightning. You're a talented photographer."

"Thanks." TJ felt it was a God-given gift, and he treated it as such. "If I can keep selling a few photos and videos to the local media, I'm a doubly blessed man."

Lee nodded, and seeing the approving expression, TJ decided his storm-chasing practices were worth it. As a kid, he had longed for praise from his own father. Never got it, though.

"TJ, let me ask you something."

Pulling himself from his thoughts, he grinned. "Sure."

"It's about Kathryn. . . ."

He felt a frown tug at his brow. "What about her? She's not ill, is she? It's not more than just a headache?"

"No, no, nothing like that. Don't worry." Lee chuckled. "You're more of a worrywart than Kathryn."

Embarrassed, TJ pressed his lips together.

"But what I'm about to ask you does concern Kathryn," Lee continued. "She's been. . .well, hinting again about hiring someone to find Rob and Wendy. As you know, I've adamantly refused ever since that last disastrous investigative procedure. Cost me thousands and opened old wounds that still haven't healed."

"Yeah, I know." TJ's heart went out to the man. For all the past trouble TJ had had with his folks, the Chadwyks had it twofold with their children.

More's the reason TJ and the Chadwyks needed each other.

"Wendy's fiftieth birthday is coming up," Lee went on. "I'm sure that's what has sparked Kathryn thinking along the lines of finding her—and Rob, too. Kathryn went through something of a funk a few years back when Rob turned fifty."

"I remember." TJ recalled the proverbial cloud of gloom that seemed to hang over the Light House while Kathryn mourned her runaway children for the umpteenth time.

"Maybe I'll have to take her on a little vacation."

"That's not a bad idea. A little getaway would do you both some good. You work too hard."

"Bah!" Lee paused, obviously lost in thought. "Back to my question. . .what do you think about hiring another investigator?"

TJ blew out a long breath. "That's your call, Lee."

"I know it's my call. I just want your opinion."

"Well, I don't know if I have one." And he sure didn't want to be pinched between the Chadwyks if some feud should arise. "I can see your point of view about not wanting to waste the time and money on people who don't seem to want a relationship with you, but I understand Kathryn's desire to find Rob and Wendy. Guess I'm not much help."

Lee snorted. "You should be a politician, what with those diplomatic skills."

TJ laughed and braked for a stoplight, but the car ahead of him sped through the intersection. His smile turned to a grimace as the other vehicle narrowly missed being broadsided. The nice weather drew the mainlanders, resulting in traffic jams and crowded parking lots at the bait and tackle shops and stores selling windsurfing paraphernalia.

"Basketball game on this afternoon," Lee said, changing the subject, much to TJ's relief. "I think North Carolina plays Stanford."

"You're right." TJ grinned and pressed on the accelerator after the light turned green. "March Madness. Gotta love this time of year!"

CHAPTER THREE

Kylie dusted off her blue jeans after helping Matt in the barn. While he hauled out equipment and milked the cows, she had cleaned the feed mangers and mixed new feed for tomorrow.

"Thanks for giving me a hand with the chores tonight." The night was so brisk that Matt's words came out in little white puffs, illuminated only by the yard light.

She smiled. "You're welcome. Are you sure I can't help you with anything else?" She could only hope. She wanted to stay with him a little longer.

"No. All I have left to do is to bed the cows. I'd rather you get a good night's sleep. You have to work tomorrow."

"Matt, it's only eight o'clock."

"I know, but by the time you drive home and do what you have to do to get ready for bed, it'll be eleven o'clock."

Kylie gave him a disbelieving stare. "It doesn't take me that long to get ready for bed. But, okay, okay, if that's what you want, I'll go. . .home."

That old familiar cloud of gloom settled over her. She hated going home now, since her mother was no longer there.

"I'm just thinking of you."

"Thanks, but I'm not a child."

"I've got two eyes. I'm well aware of that fact."

Kylie rapped him on the arm for the smart remark.

Chuckling, Matt walked her to her car, and leaning forward, he placed a quick kiss on her lips. "Ring the phone once so I know you got home all right?"

She smiled. "You are such a worrywart."

"Hey, that's my job."

In spite of Matt's remark, Kylie sensed something between them—an undefined chasm that only seemed to be growing by the day.

"I'll see you tomorrow," he said, spinning on his heel and walking away.

"I love you, Matt," she called after him.

He swung around. "Love you, too. Call me on your lunch break tomorrow." After walking backward a few paces, he pivoted and, moments later, disappeared inside the barn.

A sense of trepidation trickled down her spine as Kylie climbed into her Outback. Was Matt having second thoughts about marrying her? No, that couldn't be. He said he loved her. He was just. . .busy.

Starting the engine, she drove off the Alexander property via the winding road that led to the main highway. The twilight around her was like enveloping loneliness, and it was all she could do to keep from turning the vehicle around. Maybe if she had confessed her despair to Matt, he would have let her stay. Maybe if she'd stayed, she would have mustered the courage to ask Matt what was wrong.

Again, she fought the urge to go back. . . .

"Oh, come now, you and Matt are perfectly fine. He loves you. You love him. You're a big girl," she scolded herself. "You've got to be strong. Your mother didn't raise you to be such a wimp!"

The self-chastening didn't help. She still felt sad and alone.

When Kylie arrived home, the two-story, white vinyl-sided house was cold and dark inside. She squelched the urge to call out, "Mom? You home?" Lifelong habits were hard to break.

After turning on the kitchen light and two lamps in the living room, Kylie picked up the phone and dialed Matt's number in the barn. But, instead of hanging up, she allowed the phone to ring more than once. She just wanted to hear his voice. But after almost a minute, it seemed apparent he wouldn't answer.

"Ring the phone once so I know you got home all right. . . ."

Confusion and frustration surged through her. Mom. . . Matt. . .didn't people mean what they said anymore? Kylie slammed down the receiver of the wall phone. The clamor of hard plastic as it met metal echoed through the lonesome hallway.

Collecting herself, she dialed Matt's home phone. Lynellen answered.

"He's still in the barn. Call him out there."

"I tried already."

"Oh. Well, do you want me to get dressed and go fetch him? Won't be too much trouble. I'm just sitting here knitting and watching a little television."

"No, no. That's okay. I'll, um, talk to Matt tomorrow."

"All right. . .if you're sure."

"Yes, I'm sure," Kylie fibbed. But she couldn't ask Lyn to redress and go out to the cold barn just because she was acting like a kindergartener at the classroom doorway on the first day of school!

"You sound upset."

Kylie swallowed down the lump of emotion in her throat. "I guess I'm feeling a little blue, and I just wanted to talk to Matt."

"You seemed fine this afternoon."

"I felt fine, but it's so hard to come home at night. Mom's gone. I'm alone."

"I understand. But you know what you need to do? Turn on the TV. There's a funny show on channel eleven."

Kylie didn't feel like watching TV. She wanted to talk— and she wanted to talk about her mother.

"Or you could take a nice hot bath and go to bed. That's what I do when I miss John," Lyn said about her deceased husband. "I don't dwell on it. I get my mind on something else."

"Thanks," Kylie said out of politeness. In truth, the advice didn't help her a bit. "Good night, Lynellen."

"Sleep tight, honey bunch."

"You, too."

Kylie hung up the phone again. She couldn't help wondering how many times in the past she'd let the phone ring once and Matt had never heard it—or he ignored it. Leaning against the smooth plaster wall, she tried to stave off her tears of dejection.

Oh, God, I just need someone. . . .

Kylie lifted the phone and called Dena.

"Hey, can you talk?"

"Oh, Ky, the kids came down with the stomach flu right

after church. I'm up to my elbows in you-know-what."

Kylie wrinkled her nose as she imagined the scene. "Do you want me to come over and help?"

"No, my mom's here, and I don't want you to get sick. But let's do lunch this week, okay?"

"Okay. . ."

"Love you." Dena made smooching noises into the phone, then hung up.

Kylie leaned against the wall again, feeling more alone than ever. Moments later, the faded photograph in yesterday's mail came to mind, along with Allie Littenberg's soothing voice. Kylie wasn't exactly thrilled with what Allie had told her, but they'd talked for nearly an hour and had a rather meaningful conversation. The woman seemed compassionate—even motherly.

Finding the letter tucked into her purse, Kylie wandered into the den and picked up the cordless phone. She called the number neatly printed on the flowered stationery and then dropped into a nearby armchair.

"Hello?"

"Allie?"

A pause.

"This is Kylie Rollins again."

"Well, hi, Kylie. What can I do for you?"

"Are you busy? I wondered if we could. . .talk."

❧   ❧   ❧

Standing in the living room of the house that she and Jack recently purchased, Allie cringed. Boxes needing to be unpacked lay everywhere, and she'd just arrived home from evening service. What's more, she didn't want to divulge any secrets she shouldn't share, but something in Wendy's daughter's voice made Allie decide to give her a few minutes.

She shrugged out of her winter coat and set it over a stack of cardboard boxes. "No, I'm not too busy. What's on your mind?"

"Well, I'm just feeling particularly alone tonight. I hate coming home to this empty house now that Mom's. . .gone."

"Very understandable. Is there anyone you can stay with tonight?"

"No. One of my close friends is busy with sick kids. My other friends have families, too. My fiancé is. . .working. But I'll be okay. I just needed somebody to talk to. . .somebody who knew my mom."

Me? Allie blinked, thinking over what Kylie had just said. "I knew your mother a long, long time ago."

"What was she like. . .back then?"

"Um. . ."

"Please? I want to know. I'm trying to make sense out of everything you told me yesterday."

Allie glanced around for a place to sit, but the new furniture for this room had not yet arrived. She ambled down the hallway of the ranch-style home and entered the master bedroom, where she could recline on her lovely new queen-sized bed and gaze at the two gorgeous, matching cherry dressers while she chatted with Kylie.

"Your mother. . .let me think." Flashes from the past flittered through Allie's head. "Wendy and I were a lot alike in that we were both estranged from our parents. My mother had died when I was a senior in high school, and I didn't get along with my stepdad. Wendy said her parents didn't understand her either, so the two of us hung out at Blythe's house a lot. Blythe's parents were 'hip,' you see." Allie grinned at the '60s lingo. "They let us come and go as we pleased. Wendy's brother, Rob, stayed there a lot, too, because he and Blythe were. . ."

Allie paused, guarding her words. Shortly after Rob's death, Blythe discovered she was pregnant with his child. Allie recalled that her friend's intentions were to give up the baby for adoption. Blythe struggled with the decision, but back then single mothers didn't have the options they did today, and Blythe wanted Rob's son or daughter to have as many opportunities in life as possible. Allie had no doubt in her mind that Kylie Rollins was that child! She'd put all the facts together, and it explained Blythe's disinterest in helping to locate Wendy. It also explained Blythe's aloofness. Even so, Allie didn't feel she had a right to divulge such information.

"Were they in love or something?" Kylie asked.

"Yes, Rob and Blythe were very much in love."

"That must have been terrible for her when he was killed."

"It was. Blythe was beyond consolation. Your mother was, too."

"Do you know anything else about my mom's parents?"

Allie stretched out on the bed. "All I know is they lived on a beach in South Carolina."

"Myrtle Beach?"

"Maybe, I don't remember."

"Would their last name be Wick?"

Allie frowned. "Wick?"

"Yeah, my mother's maiden name."

Allie worked her lower lip between her teeth in consternation. "Kylie, your mother's maiden name was Chadwyk—at least, that's what Wendy told me and all the rest of us. But maybe I'm wrong and it was Wick. Could be your mom didn't want us to know her real name."

"Chadwyk?"

Hearing the incredulousness in the younger woman's voice, Allie felt awful. She hated being the bearer of such news.

Why had Wendy lied to her daughter? Hadn't she realized the past would catch up to her eventually? It always did. . . .

"I feel so confused. My mother was my best friend—or so I thought. But now I feel like I never even knew her. I feel so. . .deceived."

"I'm sure your mother never meant to hurt you. Knowing Wendy, she loved you more than her own life."

"But she lied to me. . .either that or you're lying to me."

Allie didn't know what to say. She had already marred Kylie's memories, and she didn't want to inflict any more pain on her, and yet she wasn't going to compound the mess by telling more untruths.

"You're not lying, are you?"

"No, I'm not."

"I've had a hunch all along that you weren't." Kylie blew out a breath. "Did you know my dad?"

Allie most certainly did. He'd been killed in a riot in the streets of Chicago. But that's not who Kylie was referring to. "No, I never knew your dad."

"But if Mom was nine months' pregnant when that old photograph was taken, how could you not know my dad?"

Allie skirted the question. "Kylie, the summer you were born, I was very much into myself. I lived a selfish existence. The world revolved around me. I even left the man I loved in pursuit of what I thought would bring me happiness. But I found more heartache instead. If I met your father, I don't remember him."

"He died about seven years ago. He was a wonderful man."

"I'm sure he was."

"Dad was a family practice doctor. He ran the clinic in town and worked at the hospital in La Crosse."

"Sounds like he was a busy man."

"He was. He loved to help others."

"Hmm. . ." Allie had a feeling Blythe would know the man and how Wendy met him. But far be it for Allie to inquire. She was in enough hot water, and Jack had warned her not to stir the pot.

"I probably shouldn't take up your time like this."

"No, it's quite all right." Allie sat up and combed her fingers through her hair, then went in search of her Bible. She knew firsthand that nothing soothed the spirit like God's Word. "Kylie, may I ask you a personal question?"

A brief hesitation. "Sure."

"Are you a Christian?"

"Yes."

"I remember when your mother became a Christian. Around Christmastime 1968, Jack explained how she could enter into a personal, one-on-one relationship with Jesus."

"Wait a second. My mother said she'd been a Christian all her life!"

Allie winced. "Oh dear. . ."

"Another lie!"

"Well, maybe not." Allie wanted to at least try to give Wendy the benefit of the doubt. "Let's think about this a minute. Perhaps your mother was so ashamed of her rebellious past that she discounted it and everyone who had a part of it. That's what I did. I burned many bridges in my younger days. Maybe your mother wanted to do the same."

"I don't know what to think," Kylie admitted. "I'm so confused."

"May I read you a few Scripture verses? I guarantee they'll make you feel better."

"I. . .I guess so."

Allie located her Bible in the cluttered living room.

Opening to the front inside flap, she scanned the passages she'd jotted down over the years—the ones that brought her the most comfort and strength—and began to read.

๛ ๛ ๛

As Kylie listened to the selected Scripture passages, tears filled her eyes. The words touched her heart.

"Here's my life's verse," Allie said. " 'And we know that all things work together for good to those who love God, to those who are the called according to His purpose.' Romans chapter eight, verse twenty-eight" [NKJV]

"What's a 'life's verse'?"

"A passage of Scripture I turn to when life gets tough. It lifts me up and helps put things into perspective."

"I don't have a life's verse," Kylie admitted as she swatted an errant teardrop from her cheek.

"Perhaps you'll find one as you walk through this trial. But remember, Kylie, you're not alone. If you're a believer, and you said you are, then Jesus is walking alongside you. I know how much you miss your mother because I still miss mine, and I turn fifty this year."

Kylie smiled. So she wasn't acting infantile after all.

"May I suggest that you allow yourself to feel the hurt and sadness over your mother's death? I know it sounds like an oxymoron, but giving in to the pain, acknowledging it, will lessen it as time goes by."

Kylie thought that made sense. The grieving process was just that—a process. "Thanks for all your advice and for reading the Bible to me. I needed to hear those words."

"I'm glad I could help."

"You did. But. . .but I still feel compelled to find out about my mother's past and why she lied to me. Do you think I should start with trying to locate my grandparents in South

Carolina. . .if, indeed, they're still alive and they're truly my grandparents?"

"Kylie, this journey is yours. I can't tell you what to do."

"Okay. . .but will you help me?"

A heartfelt sigh filled the telephone line, followed by the briefest of hesitations. "Yes, I'll help you—as much as I'm able."

"Thanks." A strange sense of peace filled Kylie's being. "I think you're the only one who understands how I feel."

"Oh, Kylie, I understand more than you'll ever know. . . ."

CHAPTER
FOUR

The next day Kylie spent her lunch break searching the Internet for a place called The Light House Bed and Breakfast. Earlier today, she had phoned directory assistance, and the woman had proved most helpful. There weren't any Chadwyks—with a Y, as Allie had spelled it—listed in Myrtle Beach, but a couple named Lee and Kathryn Chadwyk were listed in Charleston, specifically Sabal Beach, and it appeared they operated a bed and breakfast.

Finding The Light House listed in an on-line directory, Kylie clicked on a link, and a picture of a beautiful home appeared on her screen. Built off the ground for obvious reasons—like hurricanes and floods—the home was erected on what looked like ten-foot stilts. Arched carports had been constructed underneath each side of the home, and a graceful centered staircase wound its way up to the front door. The white, spindled rail of the veranda aligned the first floor. The second floor had two large windows on either side and one majestic window in the middle. "Enjoy a view of the Morris Lighthouse from your bedroom window," read the caption below the picture of the dwelling. "This homey bed and breakfast offers a safe and comfortable night's rest. Buffet breakfast served between 7:00 A.M. and 9:00 A.M., seven days a week."

Staring at the screen, Kylie wondered if the people who owned this inviting establishment on the Atlantic could really be her grandparents.

"Hey, Kylie?"

Turning to her left, she saw Lauren Kendricks standing in the office doorway. The heavyset brunette flicked several strands of her long hair over her shoulder, and the bangles on her wrist jangled.

"Matt's on line one."

"Oh, rats," she muttered. "I forgot to call him."

"Tsk, tsk." Chuckling, Lauren left Kylie's office. "Good thing Matt's a forgiving guy."

Smiling in her coworker's wake, Kylie lifted the phone on her desk and pressed the first of three buttons. "Hi, Matt."

"Hi, yourself. I thought you were going to call me when you took lunch."

"I was. I. . .um. . .sort of got distracted."

"That's been happening a lot the past couple of days."

Kylie winced. "I'm sorry, Matt."

"Apology accepted." There was a smile in his voice. "I suppose I shouldn't complain. I walked around in a fog for almost a year after Rochelle and Jason died."

Kylie nibbled her lower lip, wishing Matt wouldn't have mentioned Rochelle's name. While she knew she shouldn't feel jealous, she somehow couldn't help it.

Whenever Matt mentioned Rochelle, even in passing, Kylie felt as though she were competing for his affection. Competing with a memory. And yet it seemed only natural that Matt would talk about her now and then. In fact, when they'd first started dating, Kylie had listened for hours as Matt poured out his sorrow over losing his wife and infant son. He said he'd never discussed the situation with anyone else, like he'd discussed it with Kylie. She had the impression their conversations were quite therapeutic for him, and for months Kylie felt honored to hold such a position in Matt's life. But now she felt tired of sharing him.

"Hey, Mom told me you were trying to reach me last night and I tried to call you back, but your line was busy. I figured you were checking your E-mail or something."

"Actually, I was talking to Allie Littenberg, the woman who sent the photograph."

The long pause at Matt's end made his disapproval known.

"Did she call you?"

"No, I phoned her."

Another pause and Kylie began to doodle on a piece of scratch paper.

"Mind if I ask why?"

"There are a lot of questions that warrant answers, Matt. As it turns out, I might have grandparents in South Carolina. Allie gave me some more information, and I think I found them on the Internet."

"You're heading for trouble, Ky."

"These people are elderly and they own a bed and breakfast. How much trouble can I get into?"

"Ky, did you ever stop to think that there might be a good reason your mom didn't want you to know about your grandparents—if they even are your grandparents?"

"I thought about that, yes. But thirty years changes a lot of things and a lot of people."

Matt let out a weary sigh.

"If you were in my position, wouldn't you want to know the truth?"

"Nope. I'd leave well enough alone. I'd trust what my mother and fiancé said and I wouldn't listen to strangers."

Kylie slapped down the pen onto the desktop. "Can't you even try to understand the way I feel?"

"I can't when you're being so irrational. Now, look—"

"I've got to go, Matt." Frustration filled her being and Kylie clenched her jaw. She hung up the phone, not wanting to say something she'd later regret.

⁓ ⁓ ⁓

Allie sat down on the sofa and admired the way her living room looked with its new furniture in place.

"What do you think, Jack?"

Arms akimbo, he stood at the doorway wearing black jeans and a tan-and-red-striped sweater. Glancing around the room, he pursed his lips as he made his assessment. "All this pink and purple is kind of feminine for my tastes. But if you like it, I'm happy."

"Pink and purple? The color in the sofa is mauve, Jack. And the two armchairs are navy blue."

He grinned. "Like I said, if you're happy, I'm happy."

Allie laughed. "Just keep thinking that way, Jack."

Chuckling, he strode to the couch and sat down beside her. "Well, it's comfortable, anyhow."

Allie arched a brow. "Anyhow?"

"In spite of all these flowers," Jack said, rubbing his hand over the floral-patterned material.

Allie shook her head at him. "You're such a guy—hey!

they planned to spend some time in Long Beach, where Allie owned a condominium. She and Jack had to figure out whether to sell it or use it, as Allie suggested, as their winter getaway. But Jack wasn't certain they could afford to maintain both a house in Illinois and a condo in California. Decisions would have to be made, and Allie had a hunch difficult choices lay ahead. Knowing she had a place in sunny California served as something of a security blanket during this past long, gloomy winter. Giving it up, selling it, caused her to feel trapped with no way out—just like she'd felt thirty years ago when she left Illinois the first time and left Jack.

But things are different now, aren't they, Lord? I can be happy in Oakland Park just as easily as I can be happy in Long Beach. Allie sighed, but she acknowledged the fact that at least Jack loved her enough to understand—or he tried to understand. The poor man.

"What are you grinning about?" Jack asked, wearing a hint of a smirk.

"You. And I'm thinking you have no idea what you're getting into by marrying me."

He blew out a sigh. "I suppose I could say the same thing. But the way I see it, we deserve each other."

Allie laughed.

"And speaking of deserving each other, which I guess is the million-dollar question at this point. . . ." Jack rested his head against the back of the couch. "I heard from Logan that Marilee's concerned our reception is going to be too close to their wedding."

"Oh, for pity sakes! That was the whole idea! Family members coming from miles away won't have to travel twice." Allie shook her head. "I talked to Marilee about this before I did any planning. It's a little late for her to have concerns now!"

"I agree, and so does Logan," Jack said, referring to his son. "But you know how Marilee has been acting since her car accident. Nothing's ever right. She's crabby and moody. . . ."

"Oh, Jack, this is awful." Allie's heart broke for the young woman. In addition to her physical struggles—a broken leg and a fractured pelvis—Marilee Domotor had been forced to face emotional hardships, too. "So what should we do?"

"Nothing. Our plans stay as they are. I'm not caving in to Marilee's whims the way Logan does." Jack turned and his dark gaze locked with Allie's. "If you ask me, they need to postpone their wedding. Marilee's not ready to take on the role as his wife. She could very well destroy his ministry."

Allie grinned. She couldn't help it. "And this coming from a man who used to tell Logan to 'get a real job.' "

Jack gave her a quelling look. "Yeah, well, I was a very different man when I made that remark."

"Which is precisely my point. With the Lord's help, people can change. Besides, there wasn't a doubt in anyone's mind that Marilee would make a wonderful youth pastor's wife before her accident, so I don't think we should give up on her now. All she needs is time to heal from the emotional injuries she sustained."

"That could take a lifetime."

"With God all things are possible."

A myriad of expressions flittered across Jack's face, the last one being acquiescence. "Can't argue with what God's Word has to say, now can I?"

"Nope." Allie laughed. "Not to change the subject or anything, but are you taking me out for supper? I'm hungry, and since the kitchen appliances haven't arrived, there's no food in this house."

"Nag, nag, nag," Jack replied with a teasing smirk. He

stood. "Sure, we can go eat. Where would you like to go?"

"How about that wonderful deli we passed last week?"

"Yeah, we can try that place."

He extended his hand and helped Allie up off the sofa. Then he playfully yanked her into his arms and placed a soft kiss on her lips.

"I love you, Allie."

"I know." She smiled up into his eyes and touched his stubbly cheek. "I love you, too."

Another kiss and he released her. She strode to the front hall closet where their winter coats hung. Then for some odd reason, she suddenly recalled her telephone conversation with Kylie Rollins.

Jack came up behind her, and Allie handed him his black leather jacket. "Wendy's daughter called me again last night. She e-mailed me today, too, letting me know she might have found her grandparents in Sabal Beach, South Carolina."

Jack shrugged into his jacket, but his narrowed gaze let Allie know he was digesting the information.

"So, what do you think?"

"I think you'd better be careful," he said, taking her red wool coat and helping her into it.

"Do you think we should say something to Blythe?"

"Why?"

Surprised, Allie turned to face Jack. She buttoned her coat as she spoke. "It's obvious that Kylie is Blythe's daughter. I think it's only a matter of time before Kylie contacts her, don't you?"

"Allie, we don't know that Kylie is Blythe's daughter. You're guessing."

"Put the puzzle pieces together. Kylie was born at the same time Blythe's baby was due. It was no secret back then that the father of Blythe's baby was Rob Chadwyk. Blythe was planning to give the child up for adoption. . .so it just goes to figure that Wendy adopted her brother and best friend's baby."

"Allie. . ." Jack cupped her face with his hands. They felt warm against her cheeks. "We have to stay out of this—for Blythe's sake."

Allie frowned, feeling puzzled. "What do you mean?"

Jack let his hands fall away. "I mean, that was a very difficult time for her. Giving up her baby wasn't an easy thing to do." He hesitated. "What you don't know is, Blythe's parents ended up sending her to a sanitarium somewhere in northern Wisconsin. She was there for a year."

"I find that hard to believe." At Jack's protest, she held up a hand. "Oh, I'm sure it was difficult giving her baby up for adoption. That had to be heart wrenching. But I think Blythe is made of sturdier stuff than you're describing. I have an odd suspicion that sanitarium business is part of a grand cover-up that's slowly unraveling."

"Whether it is or isn't, I don't want you tangled up in that mess, okay? What's more, you've overestimated Blythe's emotional stability. I don't want to see anybody get hurt." He touched his nose to hers. "Especially you."

*   *   *

"You didn't have to do this, Ky." Dena took a large bite of her third slice of pizza. "But I'm glad you did. I didn't know what I was going to make for supper tonight."

"Don't talk with your mouth full." Kylie smiled after her friend tossed a piece of green pepper at her. "And no food fights. We need to be good examples to your impressionable teenagers."

"They're in the living room, watching TV and enjoying

this incredible pizza. Oh, and just a bit of a reminder, Amber is only twelve. She's not a teenager yet. . .thank God." Dena took a swallow of her cola. "By the way, do you realize that you sound like more of a mother than I do?"

Kylie laughed.

"So, now, tell me all about the lovers' quarrel that you and Matt had."

Kylie regarded her dear friend, marveling at how much Dena could eat. Tall and reed-thin, Dena could pig out the night before and be down two pounds the next day. Kylie, on the other hand, had to watch every morsel that went into her mouth. Life just wasn't fair. . . .

"Are you and Matt still on speaking terms?"

"We didn't have a quarrel. That's why I'm over here. To avoid any confrontations that may arise just because I want to scout out my mother's past. I want answers. Matt says I'm being irrational."

"Kylie, he's a guy. It's that Venus and Mars thing. He'll probably never understand."

"Oh, great." Kylie eyed the pizza and decided on a second slice, promising herself she'd eat like a rabbit tomorrow. Taking a bite, she ignored her own reprimand. "I'm dying to contact the Chadwyks and find out if they're really my grandparents."

"How do you plan to get in touch with them? E-mail? A letter? Telephone call?"

"Actually, I was thinking of a visit."

"Really? That's pretty gutsy."

"Well, not really. They wouldn't know who I was, and I could sort of scope things out. . .maybe even figure out why my mom would keep them a secret from me."

Dena laughed. "You and your mysteries."

Kylie grinned. "Well, there's just one problem. Matt will never go for it. He thinks I'm heading for trouble and I'm going to get hurt, and maybe he's right. But I'm willing to take the chance in order to find out the truth."

"Well, don't let him know what you're up to. Just say you're off to visit a dying aunt or something."

"Oh, right." Kylie shook her head. "He'll know I'm lying. . .just by looking at my face."

"Yeah, that's true. You're a terrible liar." Dena became suddenly pensive. "What about trying to sweet-talk him into letting you have a little space before you guys get married so you can discover your heritage?"

"Sweet talk doesn't work on Matt."

"Yes, it does."

Kylie arched a brow. "How do you know?"

Dena flushed. "He's a man, isn't he?"

"Well, yeah. . .but I'm as terrible at sweet talk as I am at lying."

"Get out! You sweet-talked your dad all the time. He gave you whatever you asked for, you spoiled little brat."

"I was his only brat," Kylie replied with a grin. "Who else was he going to spoil?"

Dena shrugged her slender shoulders and bit into her pizza. "You're so lucky, Ky. You had great parents and now you've got a great guy. I'm envious."

"Oh, right. And here I'm envious of you!"

"Me? Why? You can take my kids anytime you want."

Kylie laughed. "But I can't wear everything I want. . .like you can. Clothes look fabulous on you. You resemble one of those models in *Vogue* or something."

"Oh, brother!" Dena rolled her hazel eyes. "Aren't you comfortable in your own skin yet?"

Kylie grinned. "When I'm a size six, I'll be comfortable, okay?"

Dena gave her a cynical smile. "Well, look at it this way, Matt obviously prefers women with a little meat on their bones because I sure tried to get something going between him and me."

"You did?" Kylie brought her chin up in surprise.

"You know I did! When he first came back to town. Remember?" Dena shook her head, and brassy curls bounced off her shoulders. "I know I told you about it. I was head over heels in love with the man, but I couldn't even catch his eye."

Kylie didn't recall.

"You probably weren't listening. . .as usual."

Kylie knew that couldn't be true. She would have been plenty attentive if the subject pertained to Matt Alexander. She'd been head over heels in love with the man, too!

Still was.

"You're just trying to goad me. . .as usual." Picking a piece of sausage off her pizza, Kylie whipped it across the table at her friend.

Dena gaped at her. "I see 'Let's be good examples' just went right out the window."

"That's a payback for sticking out your tongue at me in church yesterday morning."

Dena collapsed against the back of her chair in a fit of laughter. "That was the best. You should have seen your face, Ky. I almost lost it right there, in front of God and everyone!"

Kylie laughed, too. Such daring had seemed quite amusing.

The telephone rang, filling the entire mobile home with its demanding shrill.

"Probably one of my many creditors. We're all on a first-name basis." Leaning backward, Dena lifted the receiver from where the phone hung on the wall. "Hello? Oh, hi, Matt." She winked at Kylie. "I knew you'd come to your senses and give me a call."

Kylie watched as the playful expression on Dena's face died away.

"Chill out, Matt. She's here. Just a sec." She covered the mouthpiece. "I don't think he's in the mood for jokes tonight," she whispered. "He wants to talk to you."

With a frown, Kylie took the phone. Dena had the good grace to go and check on her kids. She heard Dena shoo them into their bedrooms to do their homework.

"Hi, Matt."

"Want to tell me what's going on? Mom and I were expecting you for dinner."

Her frown deepened. "I called to say I wasn't coming. I left a message on your answering machine."

A pause. Matt obviously hadn't checked for messages yet.

"I'm sorry you thought I stood you up. I decided to buy pizza for Dena because Ryan and Amber had the flu yesterday and Dena had to work all day today."

"When do you think you'll be leaving?"

Kylie noted the change in Matt's tone, from edgy to amiable. "In a little while. We're not done eating yet."

"Okay, well. . ." He cleared his throat. "Could you stop by on your way home? I think we should talk."

At the thought of going home, an overwhelming sadness descended on her. "Matt, if I stop by your house, I'm not going to want to go home."

Another pause. "What're you talking about?"

"It's lonely, and I feel like there are so many memories in that house that there's no room for me."

"You can stay here, Ky," Dena called from the living room.

Kylie covered the mouthpiece. "Thanks." She thought she might take Dena up on the offer.

"Listen, nobody understands loneliness more than I do," Matt said. "How 'bout I come pick you up and we'll go for a ride? It's a nice night. We can talk in my truck."

"All right." Kylie relished the thought of spending some time with him.

"So, um. . .you're not mad at me? Not trying to avoid me?"

"Well, that depends." With a little smile, she wrapped the curly phone cord around her left forefinger. "Do you still think I'm irrational?"

Matt chuckled. "At the moment? No. You sound quite sane."

She grinned. "Goof."

He laughed. "Sit tight. I'll be there in ten minutes."

Still smiling, Kylie stood and hung up the phone just as Dena reentered the kitchen.

"So. . .what's happening?"

"He's coming to get me and we're going to talk things over."

"Great. Now think sweet. As in sweet talk."

Kylie chuckled as her friend's pink, well-shaped lips formed an incredible pout. Next, Dena batted her long, thick lashes. "Oh, Matt, please understand. . . ."

"You're liable to win an Academy Award, but Matt'll never be persuaded that way."

Dena straightened. "Oh, yeah? You've got a better idea?"

Picking at her pizza, Kylie shrugged. She hated to concede, but finagling and conniving just weren't her style.

"Kylie, you and Matt aren't married yet, and even if you were, he can't control you." She paused. "You know, you've always been a good girl, doing what's expected and wanting to please everyone." Dena smiled, leaned over, and set her hand upon Kylie's forearm. "If you want to go to Sabal Beach and see if those people are your grandparents, Matt can't stop you. No one can."

CHAPTER FIVE

When Matt arrived, Kylie met him at the front door. He swept her into an embrace, and she decided that if she suffocated within the folds of his down jacket, it'd be a death worth dying.

After a quick kiss, he took her hand and led her to his pickup, still running where he'd left it parked right next to Dena's older-model, white van. He opened the passenger door, and Kylie climbed up into the seat. A country/western song played on the radio.

"You're the sweetest escape a guy could know,
   My heart's the arrow and you're the bow.
My soul's sunrise, yours sunset,
   You're the purdiest thing that I've ever met. . . ."

With a grimace, Kylie opened the console between the front seats and selected one of her favorite CDs while Matt walked around to the driver's side. He opened the door and hopped in just as she pressed the play button on the truck's stereo system.

"All set?" Matt situated himself behind the wheel.

"Yes." Kylie fastened her seat belt. "But I hope you don't mind that I put in one of the instrumental CDs you burned for me."

"You know I don't."

She gave him a grateful smile.

"You can't help it that you're a music snob who likes those modern-day Mozarts."

"Oh, please," Kylie said with a little laugh. She liked other music—folk, especially.

"But I'm just a poor farm boy who likes his country/ western tunes."

"Well, I hope to convert you. . ." She gave him a sassy grin. ". . .or die trying."

"You've got your work cut out for you, don't you?" Chuckling, Matt shifted the gears, and they drove out of the mobile home park and onto the highway. "Did you have a good day at work?"

"It was okay. How about you?"

"I had a rotten day."

Somewhat alarmed, Kylie turned to look at him. "What happened?"

"Well, for one, my fiancée forgot to call me on her lunch break, and then she doesn't show up at suppertime. . . ."

"Oh, Matt, I said I was sorry."

"I know." He sent a charming grin her way. "I just thought I'd rub it in." Reaching over, he took her hand. "I look forward to hearing from you, Ky. It breaks up my day. And seeing you at supper is like. . ." He smirked. ". . .the gravy on my mashed potatoes. The ice cream on my pie."

"Good grief." Kylie laughed. "No more country music for you." Glancing to her left, she saw Matt's broad smile. He was trying to tell her he missed her, and that meant a lot.

She worked her fingers between his, and Matt gave her hand an affectionate squeeze.

"Matt, you know I love you, don't you?"

"Sure I do." He took his eyes off the road for the briefest of moments. "I love you, too. You know, just because we have a little misunderstanding once in awhile doesn't mean we don't love each other. They're going to happen, Ky, those petty little arguments. Trust me. Rochelle and I had our share of spats, but they were never serious. We still knew we loved each other."

Kylie's heart did a dive. The woman had a specterlike way of permeating their conversations. Although, to be fair, Kylie had to admit that she and Matt discussed other matters, too. Like their upcoming wedding and what life would be like once they were married. . .

"You're awfully quiet."

Kylie glanced in Matt's direction. "Sorry. I'm just thinking."

"About what? Actually, I'm almost afraid to hear your answer."

She frowned "Why?"

He let go of her hand. "Because you've been so obsessed with that crazy picture you got in the mail on Saturday. And now this business of your grandparents. . .if they really are your grandparents."

Kylie fought down a wave of frustration. "If you must know, I was thinking about us. . .and our wedding."

"Honest?"

"Honest."

Matt didn't say anything more but continued to put the miles behind them.

At last, Kylie chose to lay down her feelings, wear her heart on her sleeve. "As long as you brought up the subject, can we please talk about it?"

"Our wedding? Sure."

"No, the other. . .subject."

She heard him expel a weary-sounding sigh. "Yeah, we can talk about it. I figured it was coming."

"I was thinking about phoning the Chadwyks—that's their last name—the couple in South Carolina."

"I know who you mean."

"Mom must have shortened her name to Wick when she started living on her own."

Matt's silence told Kylie he wasn't buying any of it.

"Anyway, I'd like to go visit the Chadwyks, spend a few days at their bed and breakfast, and scope out the situation. I'm thinking about asking Dena to ask her folks if they'll watch the kids so she and I can make a long weekend of it."

"I don't want you leaving town with Dena."

"Why?"

"Because."

Kylie pulled in her chin at the vague reply. "Because? Now who's sounding irrational?"

Matt dodged the question. "I think if you're bent on contacting these people, you should send them a letter." He slowed at an intersection, then turned left. "It's less intrusive. I mean, you're sort of dropping a bomb, aren't you? 'Hi, you don't know me, but I think I'm your granddaughter.'"

Kylie worked her lower lip between her teeth as she thought it over.

"You could send them some pictures of your mom and you. Then the Chadwyks can decide if it's for real and if they should respond."

"That's a good idea, Matt. . . ."

"Oh, just admit it," he said in an amused tone. "You know I'm right."

Kylie rolled her eyes. "I'll admit to nothing."

Chuckling, Matt pulled into Captain's Café, a restaurant on the Mississippi. It had been established by a riverboat captain, hence its name.

"Thanks for understanding about my wanting to meet the Chadwyks," Kylie said as they made their way to the entrance.

"I don't know if I understand, but I'm trying."

She smiled. "Dena said it's a 'Venus and Mars thing.' "

Matt exhaled a long breath and held the heavy glass door open for her. "You know, I don't think Dena is. . ." He cut himself off. "Oh, forget it."

Kylie frowned. "You don't think Dena is. . .what?"

He motioned her inside. "Let's just drop it, okay? I didn't come here to talk about Dena. I want to spend time talking about us."

Kylie stepped inside the café, but she sensed something was amiss. After they were seated in a booth by a window, she decided to pursue the issue. "What were you going to say about Dena? Tell me."

He glanced outside, a view overlooking the parking lot, and sighed. Kylie noted his clenched jaw and the troubled expression on his face.

"I guess I might as well spill the beans." When he looked back at her, solemnity pooled in his blue eyes. "Dena's not the friend you think she is."

"Oh?" Kylie suddenly felt afraid to hear more, but at the

same time she wanted to know. "How's that?"

He searched her face, all the while seeming to wrestle with something buried deep within. "Don't hate me for what I'm about to say."

"I could never hate you."

"But you love Dena. You'd do anything for her."

"I love you, too."

"Yeah, I know, and that makes telling you this all the harder." Matt reached across the table and took her hand. "I really didn't intend to have this conversation tonight. I wanted the two of us to have some time alone. But. . .well, I suppose now's as good a time as any. This issue has been eating at me for quite awhile."

Kylie wetted her lips, waiting for him to go on.

"There have been a couple of times that Dena. . .well, she's come on to me."

Remembering the dinner conversation, Kylie grinned. "I know about that already."

"You do?" The incredulous note in Matt's voice seemed to ring through the sparsely populated restaurant. Looking embarrassed, he lowered his voice. "What did she tell you?"

"Just that when you first came to town, she fell for you."

"When I first came to town?" Matt drew in a deep breath, then shook his head. "No. Something happened more recent than that."

"Something?" She tipped her head, studying Matt's features. She disliked the mask of guilt he wore all of a sudden. "How recent?"

He looked down at their hands and brushed his thumb across her fingers. "Well, right after we got engaged." He lifted his eyes and met her gaze. "It was that Friday night you weren't feeling good, and I went to the Red Rocket Lounge with Tom and the rest of the gang," he said, speaking of his buddies. "It was the night that live band from Madison was playing. Dena was there with some friends, and we all had a few beers. . . ."

"This is beginning to sound like a confession," Kylie whispered, despite the knot suddenly stuck in her throat.

He stared at their hands again. "It is. My conscience has been bugging me for months now."

She closed her eyes, feeling nauseated. Her best friend and her fiancé?

"Nothing happened, Ky. A kiss, that's it. She was all over me and I. . .I kissed her back."

If Kylie thought she could feel no greater sense of betrayal than she did over her mother's falsehoods, she'd been sorely mistaken. There were no words to describe her present feelings.

Matt's grip tightened. "Kylie, I love you and that's the truth. All I want is for you to be my wife. I want to make you happy and protect you."

She pulled her hand away. "Protect me from what?" she hissed. "You and Dena?"

He took the barb without a word of self-defense. "I don't blame you for being angry. I'd be mad if it was you and one of my friends. I'd lay the guy flat!"

The waitress approached their table, and Matt quickly ordered two cups of decaffeinated coffee. Kylie averted her gaze, regarding the diamond on her left hand. Her vision blurred and then a fat tear rolled down her cheek.

"Honey, I'm sorry. . . ."

Looking up, she couldn't think of a single thing to say, but inside she was seething. She wanted to scream at Matt and slap the apology off his handsome face. She felt like tearing every blond hair out of Dena's head. But Kylie knew her thoughts would never become actions. God hadn't created her with a single violent bone in her body. She didn't like stepping on worms in her driveway or killing spiders in her house. She was known to feed stray dogs and nurse fallen sparrows. However, at present, the sight of Matt made her see red.

"I think I'd better go home," she stated in a surprisingly calm voice. "Will you take me back to Dena's so I can get my car?"

"I'll take you home. I don't want you driving when you're upset."

"I can handle it, Matt," she ground out. "I'm not a child."

"Yeah, that's what Rochelle used to say." He scooted out of the booth and stood. "She didn't need a lot of sleep. She could handle the night shift and a baby."

Kylie tried not to wince at the comparison as Matt threw down a couple of bucks on the table.

Leaving the restaurant, they drove in an impregnated quiet for the first mile, and Kylie tried to figure out how she'd get her vehicle in time for work tomorrow. Matt would have to pick her up in the morning. . . .

"Ky, I know you're angry," Matt said, breaking the silence. "I'm not trying to defend myself by telling you that Dena has a reputation around town as being a—"

"Shut up, Matt!" Kylie didn't think she could stand any more.

He pressed on. "Ever hear the term 'guilt by association'? People will think you're like her. I don't want you hanging around her anymore."

"I don't want you hanging around her anymore either!" Kylie could practically feel Matt's wide-eyed gaze as she continued looking out the window.

"Don't worry. I learned my lesson."

Somehow, that didn't bring Kylie much comfort. Her face burned with controlled indignation. Every muscle in her body tensed with suppressed fury. And yet she tried to remind herself that it was only a kiss.

Only a kiss. . .

Matt maneuvered his truck up her driveway and came to a stop near the walkway to the back door. Kylie climbed out of his pickup and gave the door a good slam. Then she stomped around the front of the truck. Matt met her on the other side and grabbed her coat sleeve as she attempted to pass him.

"I'm so sorry, Ky. Please believe me." He pulled her close.

She squeezed her eyes shut, unable to look at him. It appalled her to think of Dena in his arms.

She started to cry.

Matt cupped her cheeks and kissed away her tears, then wrapped her in his embrace. He murmured more apologies and swore it'd never happen again. He told her he loved her, but Kylie's heart felt like a stone.

Finally, she pushed away from him. "I have to go in," she muttered lamely. She turned for the door, but Matt caught her arm.

"Can you ever forgive me?"

Kylie lifted her gaze. To his credit, he looked as distraught as she felt. "Forgive you?" She figured she was obligated to forgive, according to everything she'd heard Pastor Hanson say on Sundays. "I. . .yeah. . .I guess so."

Matt gave her a little smile. "I'll pick you up in the morning so you can fetch your car."

After she nodded a reply, Kylie walked to the door, fumbling through her purse for her keys. Letting herself into the cold, dark house, she felt more alone than ever.

∽ ∽ ∽

"I'm hardly the villain Matt made me out to be!"

"Lower your voice!" Kylie glanced around the library. Fortunately, only a few patrons were milling about. "Look, I don't want to discuss this anymore."

"Discuss? We never discussed anything. You pelted me with accusations the other morning and never let me have a say."

"A say? There's nothing to say!" Stacking a cart with books needing to be returned to the shelves, she gave Dena a dismissive glance. "I have work to do."

Kylie wheeled the cart to the farthest bookshelf on a hunch that Dena would follow her.

She did. "Whether you want to or not, we need to talk this matter over, and if you won't speak to me here, then you're going to have to answer your phone when I call you tonight."

Kylie didn't reply. For the past few days, she'd been avoiding her so-called friend—until Dena showed up today on her lunch hour.

"I can't believe he even told you. What an idiot! He should have kept his mouth shut."

"I can't believe there was anything to tell!" Kylie shot back, albeit in a whisper. She glared at Dena. "How could you? We've been friends forever!"

"Me? Kylie, it was Matt. He offered to drive me home that night, and he was the one who parked and—"

"What?" Kylie felt the blood drain from her face. The room began to swim. "He parked?"

"I guess Matt forgot to mention that part," Dena said with a toss of her blond head.

Kylie felt like she might be sick. "I was under the impression that it was just a kiss in the Red Rocket Lounge. But

Feet off the coffee table."

He gave her a look that said he wouldn't abide by her female sensibilities for long.

"Can I offer you a compromise? How about if you take that third bedroom and make it your personal den? It's big enough for an entertainment unit on one wall and a sofa or recliner. . ."

"Naw, I've got bigger and better ideas."

Allie resituated herself so she faced Jack. "What sort of ideas?"

"Steve said he'd help me build a rec room in the basement. I want a finished area where I can invite friends over for a game of cards, a Ping-Pong game. . .or both." He grinned. "Down there, us guys will be able to put our feet up on the coffee table, and your nice flowery furniture up here will stay all prim and proper."

Allie swatted Jack's shoulder, a recompense for the wisecrack. However, she had to admit she liked the idea of a finished basement. "I think it's a terrific idea."

He nodded, stretched, then crossed his leg, ankle to knee. "Tell you what, I never imagined you'd agree to buy a house in Illinois."

"I never imagined it either," Allie replied with a little laugh. She'd been a California girl most of her life. "But if we can travel and get out of the cold at least once during the winter months, I'll be satisfied."

Jack nodded his head. When he glanced her way, his brown eyes twinkled. "It's a deal."

Sitting sideways, one leg folded underneath her, she leaned against the back of the sofa and regarded the man she'd marry in a matter of days—thirty-eight, to be exact. After the wedding and once their honeymoon cruise came to an end, now you're saying that you and my fiancé were necking like a couple of shameless teenagers?"

Dena winced. "It never should have happened. Never!" Her voice was but a whisper, but her features strained as she emphasized each word. "I'll admit my part in it, but it wasn't all my fault like Matt told you. I wanted you to know that."

Tears blurred Kylie's vision.

"We both realized what we were doing was wrong and we stopped before. . .Ky, you don't look so good. Maybe I should take you over to the clinic."

"Why?" she choked in reply. "Doctors can't mend broken hearts."

Dena looked like she might cry, too. "I'm sorry. . . ."

Abandoning the cart, Kylie quickly made her way across the blue-green carpet and into her office, where she closed the door. Leaning her back against it, she squeezed her eyes against the heart-twisting pain. Finally, the sense of betrayal became unbearable, and she put her hands over her face and sobbed. In her misery, she paused to wonder how it could be that she had any tears left.

For the past few nights, she'd gone over to the Alexanders' after work. She'd eaten supper with Matt and Lynellen as usual, and last night she even helped with chores in the barn. She tried to put the kiss behind her—forgive and forget. But now, to find out it was so much more. . .

A knock sounded on the door. "Kylie? It's Lauren. Are you all right?"

At her coworker's question, she made the effort to stifle her sobs. "I–I'm fine."

"Okay, well, I'm right out front if you need me."

"Thanks." Kylie stepped forward and pulled several tissues from the box on her desk. She blew her nose and gave herself a pep talk. *Get hold of yourself. You're at work. You're a professional. Be strong. . . .*

One of her mother's well-used lines scampered across her brain. *"When the going gets tough, the tough go shopping."*

A little grin tugged at Kylie's mouth. She and her mother had been serious shoppers. Every November, they'd drive to Chicago—

Chicago.

Where Rob Chadwyk was killed.

Where. . .

Suddenly Kylie remembered where she'd seen the dark-haired woman in the photograph. Blythe. It had been in an antique store in Chicago! Her mother liked to poke around in there. The shop was called Precious Things, although this past November, they hadn't stopped because her mother had felt ill, and they'd driven home earlier than planned.

Kylie frowned. If her mother had been friends with Blythe, why hadn't she said something? Why hadn't she introduced her to Blythe?

Perhaps the woman at the store and the woman in the photograph weren't the same person.

But Allie would know.

Pulling herself together, she left the sanctity of her office for the rest room, where she splashed her face with cold water. Reaching for a paper towel, she patted dry her puffy eyes, and no less than thirty seconds later, she decided she needed to get away from Basil Creek and Matt and Dena. She suddenly understood the term "winter blues" as never before.

When the going gets tough, the tough go shopping. . . .

Kylie closed her eyes, and she didn't think she could ever feel any more miserable than she did now. But it was Friday afternoon, and she could take the rest of the day off. Lauren could manage until the part-time help arrived at four o'clock.

The idea gained momentum. What if she packed some things and drove to Chicago? Maybe Allie could find a few minutes for her. Perhaps they could meet for lunch tomorrow. Maybe Kylie could visit Precious Things. . . .

Squaring her shoulders, Kylie thought she could probably do better than just a long weekend. She could ask Sara Stevens, her boss, for a leave of absence. Sara would understand and grant the request; Kylie felt sure of it. Then, with her job put on hold, she could head to Sabal Beach after a weekend in Chicago. The drive across country would help clear her head. The sunshine and warm weather in South Carolina would heal her heart, and perhaps the Chadwyks could shed light on some things, answer some questions.

As for Matt and Dena. . .

Kylie tried not to burst into tears again. *If ever two people deserve each other,* she thought, *they do.*

CHAPTER SIX

"Oh, Honey, I'm so sorry." Allie felt like crying, too, as she listened to Kylie Rollins pour out her heart. From where she stood in the living room, she could see Jack in the kitchen, talking with his brother Steve.

"I didn't mean to dump all this on you," Kylie said in a broken little voice. "I just wanted to tell you why I decided to take a leave of absence from work and a vacation in Sabal Beach."

"Vacations do wonders to restore the spirit," Allie replied.

"Well, I thought I'd stop in Chicago first. I won't bother you, I promise. But I wondered if you could meet me for lunch tomorrow."

"Um. . ." Allie thought it over. "I think that'll work. Where are you planning to stay?"

"I don't know yet. I'll find a hotel when I get to Chicago."

The plan, or lack thereof, caused Allie a measure of discomfort. As a single woman who had traveled alone for three decades, she was very aware of the dangers. "Say, listen, I have an idea. Why don't you stay with me tonight? I have this whole house to myself right now."

Jack overheard the offer and glanced her way. He frowned. "Who are you talking to?"

"Paul Newman," she answered with a sassy grin.

Steve hooted at the wisecrack, while Jack shook his graying head at her.

"What?" Kylie asked with a confused tone.

"Oh, I'm sorry. I couldn't resist teasing Jack, my fiancé, who happens to be a very bad eavesdropper."

"I wish I had a fiancé to tease." Kylie's voice fell.

Allie sucked her lower lip between her teeth. She hoped she hadn't made matters worse. "Look, I can tell you're upset. Plan to stay here tonight and we can talk."

"Thanks. I'd like that. I'm almost done packing, and I hope to leave in the next hour or so." There was a note of vulnerability in her voice, but at the same time, she sounded determined. "I could be in Chicago by nine or ten o'clock at the latest."

"Very good. I'll be expecting you. Need directions?"

"I know how to get to Chicago."

"You're not going quite that far. We live in a North Shore suburb."

Allie gave her the best route, then made Kylie promise to call if she got lost or had car trouble.

"I've got my cell phone and a AAA card for road service. I think I'm good to go."

"Seems like it." Allie smiled. "But be careful. I'll pray for a safe trip. See you later."

"All right. Bye. . .and thanks."

Pushing the off button on the portable phone, Allie looked at Jack. "Company's coming."

"So I heard. Who and when?"

Allie exhaled a long sigh, suspecting Jack wouldn't be thrilled when he learned the particulars. "Wendy's daughter, and she's on her way. Oh, now, Jack, don't look at me like that," Allie said as a displeased frown dipped one of his dark eyebrows. "She'll be here for the weekend. That's it. She's having a crisis. Her fiancé and best friend cheated on her. She feels like she has no one she can turn to right now."

"So she's coming here to stay with a total stranger? That makes a lot of sense, Allie."

She gave him a perturbed little grin. "We're not total strangers. We've been talking on the phone and e-mailing each other for a week, and Wendy's our connection."

"A woman you haven't seen in thirty years."

"Wendy was once a friend, and now her daughter is hurting. I feel like it's my Christian duty to help her out."

"Give it up, Jack," his lanky-framed brother said with a smile. "Allie collects needy people like some folks take in stray animals."

"Hey, I resemble that remark," she quipped.

Steve chuckled. "You should have bought a bigger house, Jack."

He tossed his younger brother an annoyed glance before looking back at Allie. "Look, I don't think—"

"I love you, Jack." She figured he wouldn't argue with that.

"Oh, now you're really sunk, Brother." Steve laughed again.

His brown eyes widened as he shot a look at Steve. "Hey, I can do without your commentaries, all right? And, Allie. . ." He turned to face her.

"Yes?" Folding her arms, she figured a lecture on practicality was on its way.

But suddenly his stony cop-for-thirty-plus-years façade crumbled. "I love you, too."

    ು   *ು*   *ು*

Kylie had been able to ignore the telephone, but the pounding at the back door set her nerves on edge.

"Kylie, open up!"

Upstairs in her room, zipping her suitcase, she gritted her teeth. Matt had a lot of nerve driving over here and demanding that she talk to him. Dena must have relayed their conversation in the library, and now Matt wanted to tell her more half-truths.

Thinking of Matt and Dena together caused her stomach to turn.

"If you don't open this door, I'm calling the sheriff."

Kylie rolled her eyes at the threat, glad that her closest neighbor lived half a mile away. The way Matt was hollering would surely summon the authorities otherwise.

Glancing down at the diamond engagement ring she wore, Kylie recalled how happy she felt on Christmas Eve when she'd opened the maroon velvet box and found it nestled within the satiny folds. After Matt asked her to marry him and she accepted, he had slipped the ring onto her finger. It was as though a promise between them had been sealed.

But Matt shattered that sacred promise. How could she ever trust him again?

Pulling the ring off her finger, Kylie went to her dresser and opened the top drawer. She found the burgundy-colored box and tucked the engagement ring inside. Then, holding it in her palm, she turned on her heel and, with determined strides, walked to the hallway window that overlooked the backyard. She opened the inner, thick-paned window, then lifted the storm window. When she did, she saw Matt step backward and into her line of vision.

"Kylie. . ." His voice held a note of relief. "Dena phoned me and said you were upset. Come down here and open the door so we can talk, okay?"

"I don't want to talk to you, Matt. Now or ever."

"Ky—"

She hurled his ring at him, and the box would have struck him in the head had he not seen it coming and ducked in time.

He glanced at where the velvet box lay in the last of a melting snow pile. "What in the world. . . ?"

"Go home, Matt. I never want to see you again. *Never!*"

His blue eyes grew wide. "You said you forgave me!"

"Yeah, for an accidental kiss in the Red Rocket Lounge." Kylie's eyes filled with tears. "But I found out more than that transpired between you and my former friend."

"Now, hold on!" He raised both hands high. "I don't know what Dena told you, but—"

"Did you or did you not drive her home that night and. . . and park?"

Matt suddenly looked as though more than a ring box hit him.

"You make me sick."

"It was nothing, Ky. It meant nothing. I swear!"

Little did he know his words meant nothing. "Get off my property. Get off, or. . .or I'll get my dad's rifle and shoot out the tires on that stinking pickup of yours. And then, who knows, you might be next!"

Matt's jaw dropped and he stared at her in disbelief. Meeting his gaze, Kylie fought to keep her lower lip from trembling. The rage she felt frightened her. She'd never been so angry in her life. Even so, she doubted that she'd be able to make good on her threat. She just hoped Matt wouldn't call her bluff.

Unable to bear the sight of him another moment, she closed the windows and returned to her bedroom, where she allowed herself to sob for the second time that afternoon. Minutes later, and to her relief, she heard Matt start the engine of his truck and drive away. Kylie knew then that it was time to go.

⁊⁊   ⁊⁊   ⁊⁊

When Allie opened the front door and peered into the face of her weekend guest, she felt transported back an entire generation. The younger woman who stood before her had Blythe's creamy complexion, dark hair, and ebony eyes, but she resembled Wendy in height and build—at least the way Allie remembered Wendy. What's more, Kylie had obviously inherited her round face, delicately sculptured cheekbones, and full lips from her father, Rob Chadwyk.

Allie gave her a welcoming smile. "You must be Kylie. I'm Allie Littenberg. Please, come in."

"Thanks."

"Here, let me help you with your things."

Kylie lifted the duffle bag from her shoulder and gave it to Allie. Then she pulled her black canvas suitcase into the house by its retractable handle.

"This thing weighs a ton!" Allie exclaimed with a teasing grin.

The younger woman smiled back. "I brought a few photo albums to show you."

"Ahh, that explains it."

Still smiling, she led Kylie down the hallway and into the

guest room she had thrown together. Steve and Nora had lent her an air mattress and sleeping bag.

"I hope you'll be comfortable in here. I'm still moving in."

"Oh, please, don't worry about it. This is fine. I'm just grateful you can put me up for the weekend."

"My pleasure. Here, let me take your coat. I'll hang it in the front closet."

"Thanks."

Allie watched the young lady slip out of her faux suede teal overcoat. She handed it over, and Allie walked back through the house and hung it up.

"You have a charming home."

Turning, Allie found that Kylie had followed her. "Why, thank you. It's just a typical ranch-style, but it has a lot of unique features, like the fieldstone fireplace here in the living room and the modern design of the kitchen." Allie was so pleased with the new flooring in that room and the recently installed carpet in the living room, hallway, and bedrooms. She smiled at Kylie. "I won't bore you with all the details. I'm just excited at the way everything's coming together."

"Oh, I don't think the details are boring at all, and you've got every reason to be excited."

Allie smiled but watched as the young woman's face fell and a shadow of misery crept across her features.

"I couldn't wait to get married, but now—" She swallowed down a sob.

"I'm so sorry your fiancé hurt you."

Kylie's dark eyes glistened with sadness, and the mother in Allie emerged.

"Oh, you poor thing!" She stepped forward and folded Kylie into an embrace. "You've really been through it, haven't you?"

Kylie dissolved into tears. "I'll never forgive him—and Dena. I'll never forgive her either. She was my dearest friend and I trusted her. I trusted both of them!"

"I know. . . ." Allie ached for the younger woman.

Then suddenly a vague remembrance surfaced of Wendy stating something similar about her parents: *I'll never forgive them. . . ."*

Taking hold of Kylie's shoulders, Allie gently drew back and looked into her tear-streaked face. "Let's make some tea. A cup of tea does wonders. It's amazing."

Kylie bobbed out a weak reply and wiped her cheeks with trembling fingers.

"Come on."

With one arm around Kylie's shoulders, Allie led her into the kitchen. The appliances had arrived and she'd bought groceries, including milk and nonfat creamer. She also knew she had herbal tea in the oak cupboards, and the sugar bowl was full.

"Sit down at the table and I'll put the kettle on the stove. While I'm doing that, why don't you tell me about yourself— and your mother. I'm really very sorry to hear about her death."

"Thank you." Kylie appeared to have collected her wits. "When was the last time you saw Mom?"

"Oh, about the same time that photograph was taken."

"The one you sent with your wedding invitation?"

Allie nodded. "The summer of '69, I stayed busy wait-ressing and dating Jack. Wendy was off doing her thing."

"Yeah, having a baby," Kylie said, "and raising me."

Allie smiled and pulled two teacups and matching saucers from the cupboard. She had promised Jack that she wouldn't be a blabbermouth, but she also vowed not to lie. If Kylie asked her a question, she would reply in all honesty and to the best of her knowledge.

"Do you like milk and sugar in your tea?"

Kylie shook her head. "Did my mom and dad live in Chicago when I was born? I know my father graduated from Rush Medical College."

"Did he?" Allie pursed her lips, wondering how Wendy met the guy. Had he been a med student at the time? "Well, I'm afraid I don't know the answer to that one. As I said, your mother and I lost touch. When I didn't see her around, I figured she had left town and decided to continue her trek to the Pacific Coast—but without her brother."

A wistful look crossed Kylie's face. "That must have been heartbreaking for Mom to lose her brother."

"Without a doubt." After pulling out three boxes of different-flavored herbal teas, Allie leaned against the counter and folded her arms.

"I want to visit his grave. Do you know where he's buried?"

"Um. . ." Allie had to think. She'd attended Rob's funeral, cried with Wendy and Blythe; and as the three locked arms, they watched together as he was "laid to rest." But where had that taken place? "Oh, Kylie, I'm afraid I can't remember. His funeral was held in a little chapel, and the burial was in an adjoining cemetery outside of the city, but I can't recall its exact location."

"Would Blythe know? You said she and Rob were in love."

"Yes, I'm sure she'd remember." Allie reminded herself to proceed with caution in this area.

"As long as we're on the subject of Blythe, does she by any chance own an antique store called Precious Things?"

"Why, yes, she does." Allie hoped she adequately hid her surprise. "How did you know?"

"Because I've been going there for as long as I can remember." Kylie pulled the clip from her hair and the dark tresses fell down past her shoulders. Gathering the thick mass, she smoothed it back off her forehead, twisted it around, and repinned it. "Every year when Mom and I made our annual shopping trip to Chicago, we stopped in that little store. . . except this past November, we didn't. Mom thought she was coming down with the flu or something, so we cut our day short."

Allie concealed a knowing smirk. November was about the time she had begun searching for Wendy. Blythe knew it. Had she forewarned Wendy?

Allie tried not to feel hurt that her past friends hadn't wanted to see her again.

"Did you visit Precious Things often?"

"No, just once a year." A mixture of innocence and confusion pooled in Kylie's black eyes. "Allie, I don't get it. If Mom and Blythe had been friends, why didn't Mom just say so? Why didn't she introduce me to Blythe?"

"I don't know," Allie stated in all honesty. She couldn't fathom why Wendy hid Kylie's adoption from her. Perhaps she meant to tell her someday and "someday" never came. On the other hand, the fact that Wendy took Kylie into Precious Things might have been a way of allowing Blythe a glimpse of her daughter over the past few decades.

"Well, that's one of the things I plan to do tomorrow—visit Blythe and ask her two questions: Where is my uncle buried, and why is it such a big secret that she and my mother were once friends?" Kylie smiled at Allie. "Want to come?"

Allie stifled a shocked little laugh. "Oh, I'm sorry. That won't be possible." If she walked into the shop with Wendy's daughter, Allie feared Blythe would blame her for any fallout.

Kylie's expression fell. "I was hoping you'd go with me."

"Why don't you make it another day?" There! She'd done her duty to forestall the inevitable.

Kylie shook her head. "I want to learn as much as I can here before heading to Sabal Beach. I'm sure my grandparents—if that's who they are—will want to know details, and I plan to be prepared to give them."

The kettle whistled out a long shrill, and Allie turned off the stove. "When are you going to Sabal Beach?"

"Monday. I took a month's leave of absence from work. I figured that should give me time to find out about my mother, grandparents, and. . .and get over Matt."

"A month to get over Matt?" Allie raised her brows in question. "Took me thirty years to get over Jack, and even then I wasn't successful."

"Well, maybe I won't 'get over him' in that short period of time," she conceded. "But I hope to at least be adjusted to life without him. I mean, I can't fall apart every time our paths cross—and they will. Basil Creek is a very small community."

Allie sensed more tears were on the way. Walking into the powder room, she fetched the box of Kleenex and handed it to Kylie. "What kind of tea would you like?"

"Whatever you're having."

Allie selected two bags of apple cinnamon and put them into the cups. She poured boiling water into each one. Carrying them to the table, she set one down in front of Kylie before seating herself next to her.

"About Sabal Beach. . .are you flying out of O'Hare?"

"No, I'm driving."

"Alone?" Allie's eyes widened.

"Sure, why not? I'm a careful driver. I don't take any chances, and I'm not in the habit of giving rides to strangers. I'll be fine."

Allie wasn't convinced. "You know, I have a lot of frequent flyer miles accumulated. I could see about getting you a plane ticket."

"Thanks." The tea bag bounced up and down in her cup as Kylie toyed with its string. "But I can afford my own airfare. I just want to drive. I figure seeing the countryside will clear my head."

But it's not safe! Allie swallowed the protest before she could voice it. She had no right to interfere. Kylie was thirty years old. A grown woman. However, Kylie had a naïveté about her that made Allie decide she'd mention Kylie's plans to Jack. If he shared some of his cop stories, he'd sufficiently scare her out of the idea of driving to South Carolina by herself!

Allie only wished Kylie would change her mind about visiting Blythe tomorrow. It sounded as if poor Kylie had experienced enough trauma for one week.

Allie cleared her throat. "Downtown Chicago on a Saturday is going to be a madhouse. How about waiting until Monday and I'll drive you to Blythe's shop. . .on the way to the airport?"

For the first time, Allie saw the younger woman laugh. "Now you sound just like my mother!"

CHAPTER
SEVEN

"Y ou've got your directions, right?"

With her hand on the front doorknob, Kylie nodded. In spite of her upsetting day yesterday, she'd had a surprisingly good night's sleep. Then, this morning at breakfast, Allie had sketched out a map to Blythe's shop.

"And you've got my cell phone number," she told Allie, "so if you have to leave or something else comes up, you can call me."

"Yes, I have it. But I'm planning to be here all day." Allie smiled and rubbed her palms together. "My washer and dryer are being delivered this afternoon."

Kylie laughed. "You look like a kid on Christmas morning."

"Oh, does it show?"

Allie batted her lashes, causing Kylie to chuckle. Standing there in her fluffy pink robe, Allie appeared so happy, well-adjusted, and wise. And, similar to Lynellen Alexander, Allie was always willing to earn a smile with one of her sassy replies.

Tall and slender with silvery-blond hair, Allie Littenberg looked at least ten years younger than her true age, Kylie decided. A thin white scar marred her cheek, from the corner of her right eye to her chin. But it was hardly noticeable, and after Kylie heard last night how Allie had received it, she felt in awe of the older woman. Kylie couldn't imagine ever living with an abusive husband, as Allie had. How could she have been so strong and brave. . .so forgiving?

Wishing her hostess a good day, Kylie walked to her Outback. She decided she liked Allie—she liked her a lot. Allie was kindhearted, generous, concerned; and there wasn't a doubt in Kylie's mind that everything she'd said was true.

Now, if only Kylie could find out the whys behind those pieces of truth. She knew her mother had loved her, and Kylie could only imagine that she'd lied to protect her from something—or someone.

Unlocking the door, she climbed behind the wheel of her vehicle. After starting its engine, Kylie figured it might be smart to turn on her cell phone. A moment later, a series of bleeps alerted her to unheard messages. As her car warmed up, she pressed the appropriate buttons on her phone.

"You have three unheard messages," the computerized voice announced.

Three? Kylie frowned.

"First message, sent yesterday at 9:58 P.M."

"Ky, it's Matt. . . ."

She grimaced.

"I'm sitting here in your driveway, wondering where you are. I've looked all over town for you. I've checked with your friends. No one's seen or heard from you." A pause. "Honey, we have to talk. Give me a call and let me know where you are."

Beep!

Kylie held the phone away from her ear and glared at the thing as if it had committed an offense. Then it gave her a small measure of satisfaction to press the delete button. Matt's message disappeared. *Too bad life's not that simple,* she thought as she went on to message number two.

"Ky, it's Matt again. It's after midnight and you're still not home. I'm getting worried. Give me a call."

Beep!

"Yeah, ring the phone once to let me know you got home okay." She deleted that recording also.

Message number three was from Lynellen. "Hi, honey bunch, it's after nine o'clock and Matt says you never came home last night. He's worried sick and so am I. Please call us and let us know you're all right."

Beep!

Kylie's conscience pricked her. While she felt little to no remorse over Matt being "worried sick," she did care a great deal about his mother. Glancing at the clock on her dashboard, she saw that it was nearing ten-thirty. Matt would probably be at the house if she called now, and she didn't want to speak to him.

She put her car in gear and began her trip to downtown Chicago. Within minutes, she came up with the idea to phone the Hansons and ask either Pastor or his wife, Sarah, to call Lynellen. After all, they would both know something was amiss when Kylie wasn't in church tomorrow morning. It wouldn't hurt to forewarn them.

Braking at a stoplight, she quickly pressed the Hansons' number into the keypad on her cellular phone. It was a number she knew well; she'd dated Trevor Hanson for two years during their junior and senior years in high school. But their relationship never evolved into more than friendship. After graduation, she and Trevor went off to different colleges, and now he was an architect and lived in South Dakota with his wife and three young children. But Kylie still received a Christmas card from him every year, and Trevor and his wife had sent flowers after her mother died in January.

"Hello?"

"Hi, Sarah. It's Kylie."

"Well, hi, Kylie." There was a smile in the older woman's voice, and Kylie pictured the stout brunette ambling merrily around her sunny kitchen. "How're you?"

"I guess that depends."

"Oh?"

The light turned green and Kylie stepped on the accelerator. "Matt and I broke up."

"No! Oh dear. What a shame!"

"Yeah." Kylie quickly realized she wasn't going to be able to read Allie's map and talk on her cell phone, so she pulled over to the side of the road. "After it happened, I decided I needed to get out of Basil Creek for awhile. So I'm in Chicago this weekend, and then I'm driving to South Carolina for a little vacation."

"Are you alone?"

"No. I'm staying with. . .a friend."

"Oh, well, that's good. And with all that you've been through, a little vacation might do you a world of good. I'm just so sorry to hear about you and Matt. Any chance of reconciliation?"

"No." Residue from her original anger welled up in her being. "I can't trust Matt anymore. It's over between us." She rather likened Matt's breaking his bond of trust to someone who permanently damaged his spinal cord. Once severed, there was no way to repair it.

"Kylie, I'm so sorry. What happened?"

She tamped down a swell of bitterness. "Maybe you should ask Matt." She swatted at an errant tear, wondering when she'd quit crying over Matt's disloyalty and Dena's betrayal. The tears seemed endless. She sniffed and searched for a tissue in her coat pocket.

"Kylie, I can tell you're upset."

"I am, but I didn't call to burden you with my problems. I need a favor, Sarah." Tissue in hand, she wiped her nose. "I made the mistake of not telling anyone where I was going. Now Lynellen is worried. She left a message on my cell phone. But I don't want to call the Alexanders' place because I'm afraid Matt will pick up, and I don't want to talk to him. Would you mind phoning Lynellen and letting her know I'm okay?"

"Of course. I don't mind at all."

"Thanks."

"And you call me back if there's anything else I can do, all right?"

"All right."

The conversation concluded with good-byes and well-wishes. Kylie pressed the end button on her phone and slipped it into her purse. Then she pulled away from the curb and continued her journey into the bustling heart of Chi-town.

◇   ◇   ◇

Kathryn shut down her computer in the small office at the end of the upstairs hallway, on the opposite end of the guest rooms. She'd been doing halfhearted searches for Rob and Wendy on the Internet each time she checked her E-mail. As always, her attempts proved to be futile, although several companies e-mailed her back and offered more extensive searches if she wanted to pay for it. But she didn't. She couldn't. Lee had been adamant about that.

"Any luck?"

She turned in her desk chair to see TJ walking up behind her. In his arms he carried two laundry baskets, one on top of the other, each filled with clean sheets and towels. He set them down at the doorway.

"Why, thank you for bringing up the linens. . .and, no, I didn't have any luck at all." A frown felt heavy on her brows. "It still amazes me that my children could vanish the way they did."

"People disappear every day. What's more, if Rob and Wendy changed their names, the likelihood of ever finding them is slim at best."

"Yes, I suppose you're right. But it tears me apart to think they wouldn't want me to find them—or that they wouldn't want to find me. Lee and I have a lot to be sorry for; I'll be the first to admit it. But if we could just have a second chance. . ."

"Now, Kathryn, don't get yourself all worked up. Just keep praying."

"Yes. . ." She glanced at TJ, a man about Rob's age. He'd become the responsible, caring son that she and Lee never had, and Kathryn loved him. Standing with arms akimbo, in a white, ribbed cotton crewneck shirt and black jeans, he resembled a Mr. Clean commercial with his smooth, tanned bald head and his bulging muscles. All he needed was an earring. To look at him, one might conclude that TJ was a man not to be reckoned with, for he appeared tough and hardened. But the real TJ McGwyer had a heart like a marshmallow.

Giving him a smile, Kathryn stood and stretched out the

kink in her back. "I'd better get to work. We have more people checking in this afternoon."

"Sure do. If you need any help, just holler. I'm going to see about fixing the garbage disposal. Lissa was complaining about it this morning."

Kathryn rolled her eyes. "Lissa Elliot would say just about anything to get you into her kitchen."

TJ smirked. "On the contrary, Kathryn. It's *your* kitchen. Besides, Lissa just left for the day."

Kathryn raised a brow to say she was not amused by his witticism. She'd suspected for some time now that the woman she'd hired to prepare breakfast for her guests was sweet on TJ. Of course, it was none of Kathryn's business; TJ could date whomever he pleased. But, on the other hand, there was something about Lissa Elliot that rubbed Kathryn the wrong way.

"Just be careful, TJ. You hear?"

"Of the garbage disposal?"

"No, I'm referring to Lissa."

He tipped his head back and laughed. The deep, resonating sound seemed to fill every corner of the room. "I'm fifty-two years old, Mama Chadwyk. I've been around the block a few times. I think I can handle the likes of Lissa." Striding forward, he bent over slightly and placed a kiss on Kathryn's cheek. "Besides, she's too young for me, and I've told her that."

"She's in her midthirties. Not all that young, TJ."

"It is when she's got kids at home, the oldest one being only twelve." TJ shook his head. "I've got no hankering to be a daddy at my age."

Kathryn didn't argue. She felt glad that TJ wasn't interested in Lissa; however, generally speaking, she liked the younger woman just fine. An industrious young widow with a family to support, Lissa Elliot held a part-time position at

The Light House in addition to working a full-time second-shift job as a nurse's aide. The woman professed to be a Christian and talked openly about her faith. So why the check in Kathryn's heart?

If she were completely honest, Kathryn would have to admit that it frightened her to think about someone marrying TJ and taking him away. Lee said she was becoming "controlling" in her old age—controlling because she didn't want to lose TJ like she'd lost Rob and Wendy. Kathryn hated to think her husband might be right.

"TJ, you know you're free to. . .well, to see anyone you wish."

He brought his clean-shaven chin back, looking surprised. "Of course I know that, Kathryn." Then a slow smile spread across his face and amusement sparkled from his cobalt blue eyes. "God just hasn't introduced me to the right one yet. And I'll know when I meet her. It'll be thunder and lightnin' like I never heard or saw."

Kathryn waved a hand at him. "What happened to the typical birds singing and bells ringing?"

He smirked. "It'll take more than birds and bells for me to get hitched at my age!"

"I see." Kathryn felt suddenly foolish for behaving so. . . *parental.*

"But right now, I have a garbage disposal calling my name. That's about as romantic as my life gets."

"Oh, go on with you!"

Kathryn laughed as she watched TJ leave the office. Then she turned her attention to the mounds of freshly laundered sheets and towels.

ᴊᴘ   ᴊᴘ   ᴊᴘ

It took Kylie longer than she expected to drive into downtown

Chicago and find a parking space even remotely close to Precious Things. Gathering her purse and the envelope containing Allie's letter and the old photograph, Kylie climbed out of her Outback and locked its doors. Then she began her hike toward Michigan Avenue. Reaching that street, she made a left and walked the several blocks to Blythe's shop, which was located on a side street.

Entering the small establishment, Kylie heard the little chime above the door and noted the subtle, sweet smell of jasmine incense. The aroma brought back the memory of being in this store with her mother nearly a year and a half ago. Kylie recalled the hand-painted ceramic plate her mom had purchased here. It depicted the sun over a vast body of water, and the trinket sat on Mom's bureau to this day.

Kylie closed her eyes. The reality of her mother's death still escaped her from time to time. It seemed unfathomable that she'd never hear her mother's voice or see her smile.

"Can I help you?"

Kylie looked toward the rear of the store from whence came its dark-haired proprietress. She had a willowy figure and wore denim slacks with gold embroidery over the right hip, a white turtleneck, and a matching gold and denim jacket. Her hair was short but stylishly mussed. When her dark gaze met Kylie's, recognition set in and the woman stopped in midstride.

Kylie stepped forward. She quickly glanced around, and not seeing other patrons, she felt comfortable to speak freely. "You know who I am, don't you?"

The woman opened her mouth but then closed it again.

"Your name is Blythe, isn't it?"

A cautious expression crossed her delicate features and she narrowed her gaze.

"I apologize for putting you on the spot like this," Kylie said, inching toward her, "but my mother recently died, and—"

"She died?"

Wearing a pained expression, the woman set her hand upon a nearby display table, as if to steady herself from the shock. Several glass objects on the tabletop rocked precariously, and watching them sway, Kylie felt certain they'd fall to the polished wooden floor and smash.

"I–I didn't know. . . ."

Kylie brought her gaze back to Blythe. "It was very sudden," she eked out, despite the lump of emotion in her throat. "Mom fell and hit her head."

"Oh, I'm so sorry." Blythe took several steps forward, then stopped.

Sniffing back her sorrow, Kylie reached into her purse and extracted the envelope with the photograph inside. "Last week, I got this in the mail." She held it out.

Blythe hesitated before accepting it. Examining the front of the envelope, then taking a quick peak inside, she winced and regarded Kylie again. But she said nothing.

"When I saw the photograph, I thought you looked familiar, and then I remembered seeing you here at this store. My mother took me here every year—ever since I was a little girl."

Blythe didn't reply. She stood statue-still, regarding Kylie all the while.

Clearing her throat of sudden discomfort, she continued, "But what I can't figure out is. . .if you and my mom were once friends, how come she didn't say so? Why didn't she introduce us?"

Lowering her gaze, Blythe stared at the brown envelope in her hands. It was then Kylie noticed the woman's fragile appearance, as though she were made of bone china. Odd, but Kylie hadn't ever noticed that before.

"I, um, didn't come here to upset you," she told Blythe. "I just wanted to ask a few questions. You see, I've been talking to Allie Littenberg, and—"

"Oh, that Allie!" Blythe whispered the name on a note of exasperation. Then she glanced at the ceiling before bringing her gaze back to Kylie. "What did she tell you?"

"Well. . ." Kylie sensed she'd stumbled onto a sensitive issue, but it was too late to turn back now. "Allie said that the three of you were friends and that you. . .um. . .dated my mom's brother. I wondered if you could tell me where he's buried."

"Oh, dear Lord. . . ." Blythe's eyelids fluttered closed.

Concerned, Kylie walked quickly forward. Placing a hand on Blythe's shoulder, she said, "I'm sorry. I didn't mean to cause you any pain by bringing up the past. I'm just confused. I didn't even know my mom had a brother."

When Blythe opened her ebony eyes, they were filled with such anguish that Kylie inhaled a sharp breath. . .and then she realized what a coincidence it was that Blythe had black eyes, too, like herself. Kylie had never met another person with eyes so black they concealed his or her pupils.

In the next moment, Kylie could hear Lynellen's voice as they sat in the restaurant. *Wendy doesn't really look pregnant, if you ask me.*

Kylie gasped as things began to make sense, like so many pieces of a jigsaw puzzle pressed into place. She felt her jaw slowly drop as the realization set in. She and Blythe shared the same ivory skin tone, same dark hair, and black eyes.

Kylie knew at once that she was staring at her biological mother.

"You. . ." Turning her gaze to the envelope, which she pulled from Blythe's grasp, Kylie opened it and removed the photograph. "You're pregnant in this picture, aren't you?"

"You need to leave." Blythe's lower lip trembled slightly. "My store closes at noon, and I've got an appointment in an hour. I don't have time for this conversation."

"Could I come back tomorrow or Monday? I need to talk to you."

Blythe didn't answer, and for such a seemingly delicate lady, she had a firm enough grip on Kylie's elbow as she propelled her to the door.

"Please," Kylie begged, "please talk to me. I'm confused. I need answers."

"I c—can't."

Kylie caught sight of a tear trickling down Blythe's pale cheek. Her own eyes filled. "Please?"

"You don't understand. I made a vow. . . ."

"To whom?"

Blythe didn't reply. With a hand on Kylie's shoulder blade, the woman guided her to the exit.

Stepping outside, Kylie swung around in protest, only to have the red wooden door close in her face. Next she heard the click of the dead bolt, and her heart flipped at the seeming finality. She hadn't expected such blatant rejection.

Battling her tears, she turned around and began the trek back to her car, knowing that the past few minutes had changed her life forever. But she made a vow of her own. She would be back.

CHAPTER EIGHT

A llie?"

"Come on in. I'm in the kitchen."

Closing the front door, Kylie didn't bother shedding her coat but hurried across the beige living room carpet. "Allie. . ."

"Yes?" Attired in comfy-looking dark blue sweats, Allie swung around. Seeing Kylie rushing toward her, a frown dipped her blond brows. "Are you okay? What happened?"

Somewhat breathless, Kylie took hold of her shoulders. Peering into Allie's face, she asked, "Blythe is my biological mother, isn't she?"

Allie's blue eyes widened with surprise. "Well, I—"

"Please," Kylie pleaded, "someone has to tell me the truth!"

Allie's features softened and she drew in a deep breath. "Yes, it's my opinion that she is."

"Your opinion?" Kylie felt her patience fleeing by the moment. "What does that mean?"

"I take it Blythe wouldn't talk to you?"

Kylie shook her head.

"Here, let me help you out of your coat." As Kylie unbuttoned it, Allie said, "I'll tell you everything I know, but right about the time you were born is when I stopped communicating with Blythe and Wendy. We went in different directions. But in the past few days, I've been able to put two and two together. . . ."

"Yeah, I think I've summed up the same equation."

"You poor thing." Allie cupped Kylie's one cheek and kissed the other. Then she strode off to hang up the coat.

Standing there, Kylie felt like a lost child.

When Allie returned, she paused at the stove and put the kettle on to boil. "Teatime."

Kylie couldn't help a small grin as she sat down at the kitchen table.

"Okay, what's the first thing you want to know?" Allie asked, sitting in the adjacent chair.

Kylie rummaged through all the questions swarming her brain. "Blythe was pregnant in that photograph, not my mother. Is that correct?"

"Yes."

"Why didn't you tell me?"

Allie's blue eyes darkened with sincerity. "It wasn't for me to tell."

Kylie supposed she could accept that answer. "Is my natural father Rob Chadwyk?"

"Yes."

"So that explains why people always said I resembled my mother."

"You resemble both mothers." Allie smiled.

"Very funny." Kylie sat back in the chair.

"I didn't mean to be funny. I'm serious. You've inherited Wendy's height and build, at least from what I remember of her, and Blythe's dark features."

"You're right. I have." She shook her head. "But I never saw the similarity to Blythe before. . .although, thinking back, she always kept her distance when Mom and I visited the store. I never really got very close to her, otherwise I'm sure I would have noticed her black eyes—like mine."

Kylie had always been sort of a novelty in Basil Creek, since most of its citizens had Norwegian and/or German blood running through their veins. Blond hair and blue eyes were her community members' most common features.

Like Matt's and Dena's. . .

Her heart ached. Her mind whirred with uncertainty. Kylie put her face in her hands. "I'm going crazy."

The kettle shrilled, and after giving Kylie's knee an affectionate pat, Allie stood. "I'll make us some tea, and you ask me more questions."

"I can't think anymore." Kylie's temples were beginning to throb from tension. "I thought so hard about everything on the way here from downtown Chicago that I can't honestly remember the drive."

Allie gave her an empathetic look. "I've been there myself." Dropping a tea bag into each cup, she added, "You're taking the news about being adopted amazingly well."

"I'm probably in shock."

"Yes, you probably are," Allie agreed.

"I know I upset Blythe. I didn't mean to, and I feel bad about it now. It occurred to me as I drove back here that she might face grave consequences if this thirty-year secret about me gets out."

Allie brought over the two steaming cups and set one down in front of Kylie.

"Is she married? Does she have other children?"

"Who, Blythe?" Allie shook her head. "No, she never married."

Kylie felt a shard of relief. "Blythe said she made a vow to somebody. That's why she didn't want to talk to me. She was afraid of breaking her promise."

"Had she made some sort of a pact with Wendy?"

"I don't know." Kylie toyed with her tea bag, thinking over this morning's events. "When I told her my mother died, Blythe looked as grieved as I felt sharing the news with her."

"I'll bet. It came as quite a shock to me, too." Allie waved her hand in the air. "Okay, so let me get this straight. Blythe is aware that you know she's your natural mother?"

"I think so, although I didn't come out and say I knew. But I'm almost positive she guessed it by the look on my face." Kylie thought back over their conversation. "I'm sure she guessed it. I mean, a revelation occurred right before her eyes."

"Hmm. . ."

"But she never told me where my uncle—make that my father—is buried, and I never got a chance to bring up the subject of my grandparents in South Carolina—if, indeed, they are my grandparents."

"Those are things I know nothing about."

Kylie tried to sift through the deluge of information filling her thoughts. "You said that Blythe and Rob were very much in love?"

Allie nodded.

Kylie gave her tea bag a dunking. "Somehow knowing

that gives me a little peace. I'd feel awful knowing I was the product of a rape or even a one-night stand."

"Well, you weren't exactly planned, and by God's standards it wasn't right. But, yes, you were conceived in love." Allie took a sip of her tea.

"What happened the night Rob was killed?"

Allie paused, and her gaze traveled sightlessly over Kylie's right shoulder. "It was the end of August 1968. I'll never forget it—it had to have been the hottest night of the year, both in weather and temperament. The Democratic Party met in Chicago, and over twenty thousand people showed up to protest the Vietnam War. The National Guard was called in. Cops were everywhere because riots broke out all over. I'd been waitressing at a local diner, and I was trying to get home. I got caught in the middle of a skirmish, but Jack pulled me from the crowd. That was the second time I met him. He drove me home that night. Little did I know, my friends hadn't been too far away."

"How did Rob get killed?"

"Well, there were a couple of versions to the story. Blythe said several cops beat him up with their nightsticks. The cops maintained that Rob got into a brawl with other rioters and that they were merely trying to break up the fight."

"Did Jack know Rob?" Kylie had heard their story, Jack and Allie's, last night. The tale of their breakup and reunion was a touching one.

"Jack had met him a couple of times because Rob often stayed at Blythe's house." Allie grinned. "The Oakland Park police were often summoned to the Seversons' home. As I told you last night, we were kind of a. . .a rowdy bunch."

Kylie smiled and took a sip of tea. Its warmth had a soothing effect on her, and she felt herself begin to relax.

"Jack didn't like Rob. They were opposites. Jack was a cop, a man who supported the military and our troops in 'Nam. He was part of the dreaded Establishment. Rob, on the other hand, was a charming renegade, dodging the draft and protesting the war. Suffice it to say, Rob didn't care much for Jack either."

Kylie could well imagine both men's aversion to each other. "So it wasn't until after Rob's death that Blythe found out she was pregnant with me?"

Allie nodded. "As I recall, she had wanted to keep her baby—you—at first. But back then single moms didn't have the choices they do today, and I think Blythe's parents pushed for adoption."

"Are they still alive?"

"Good question." Allie thought it over. "I'm not sure, but Jack might know. We can ask him. He and I decided we'd like to take you out for dinner tonight. . .if you're up to it."

"Yeah, I guess I am." Kylie paused to sip her tea. "It's very strange, but I know I should feel devastated by this news, and I'm not. I'm more bewildered and angry than anything. My mom and I shared everything. . .or so I had thought. Now to discover she'd lied to me my whole life. . . It blows me away. She had to have known I could handle the truth emotionally. The only reason for not telling me must be tied in with Blythe's mysterious vow."

"Or the fact she didn't want you contacting your grand-parents. I remember her saying she would never forgive them, but I'm not sure what prompted the remark."

"Hmm. . ." Kylie suddenly felt more determined than ever to meet the Chadwyks. "Well, what do you suppose the purpose was for my mother to take me into Blythe's shop every year? So she could flaunt me, like some prized possession?"

"I thought it might be so Blythe could see for herself that you were all right, loved and cared for, and that you'd become a well-adjusted person."

"I was loved and cared for, no doubt about that," Kylie said. "My dad doted on me and my mother nurtured me. My friends always said I was 'spoiled,' and I suppose that's true. But I like to think I was spoiled in a good way—if such a thing is possible."

"No brothers or sisters?"

Kylie shook her head. "Mom couldn't have kids. She had a tubal pregnancy, and the emergency surgery sort of messed up her body. We kept hoping, but no babies ever came. So I was all the more spoiled." She grinned at the memory of her dad bringing home a silver necklace with a shiny locket. He had purchased the gift for her "just because," and as Kylie recalled, that same day her mother received a diamond tennis bracelet. "My dad loved my mom. They were happy."

Allie sat back in the wooden, Windsor-back chair and held her cup between her hands. "Then never lose sight of that, Kylie. You were very blessed to have parents who loved each other—and who loved you, too."

"I'm aware of that." Kylie knew those less fortunate, like Dena, whose parents had fought all the time when she and Kylie were kids. Still, a weary sigh escaped her. "I just have so many questions. They'll eat me up inside if I don't find answers!"

"Hmm." Allie frowned as though she didn't understand.

"It's my personality," Kylie explained. "My dad used to say I should have been a detective, although I do plenty of investigative work at the library. People come in looking for things and I help them locate books and periodicals."

Allie smiled. "What are you planning to do next?"

Kylie stared into her teacup before looking over at Allie again. "I think the first thing I need to do is contact the Chadwyks and visit them in Sabal Beach. Maybe they can fill in a few blanks. While I'm gone, maybe Blythe will consider talking to me about the situation. I'll check back with her on my way home from South Carolina."

"Sounds like a reasonable plan, although I will warn you—Jack and I hope to change your mind about driving."

"Good luck." Kylie grinned and tipped her head. "So who do you think I get my stubborn streak from?"

CHAPTER NINE

Allie carried the teacups to the sink while Kylie headed for the guest bedroom with the intention of taking a nap. Allie's heart ached for the younger woman. Losing her mother, discovering her fiancé had been unfaithful, then finding out she was adopted. . .that was enough to shatter anyone's life.

Oh, Lord, I pray this turbulent time in Kylie's life will strengthen her faith.

The telephone rang just as Allie set the cups inside the dishwasher. Lifting the portable phone from the charger on the counter, she pressed the talk button.

"Hello?"

"Hey, Beautiful!"

Hearing Jack's voice, she laughed. "Is this a prank phone call?"

Jack chuckled. "Nope, sure isn't. Listen, I'm on my way over. Do you need anything?"

"Just you," Allie replied.

"You made my day."

She smiled.

"So guess who I just ran into?"

"Who?"

"Brenda."

"Oh?" Allie fought back a cringe. She could just imagine what her stepsister said to Jack. Brenda still harbored bitterness and resentment toward Allie over situations that occurred when they were in high school. Consequently, Brenda had nothing good to say when it concerned Allie.

"Apparently, she's getting laid off and she's upset about it."

"That's too bad."

"She needs a place to live."

Allie held her breath. *No, Lord, please. . .I'll take in anybody but Brenda!*

A moment passed and then another.

"Don't worry, I didn't offer her the spare bedroom—or the basement either." Jack chuckled.

"Very funny." Allie realized he'd set her up on purpose.

"And speaking of. . .where's your houseguest?"

"She's taking a nap."

"How'd it go this morning with Blythe?"

Allie quickly strode into the living room so there wouldn't be a chance of Kylie overhearing their conversation. "It didn't go well. Kylie guessed that Blythe is her biological mother, and—"

"Guessed? How'd that happen?"

"Jack, she looks just like Blythe. Wait 'til you meet her."

"Hmm. . ."

"Kylie said that Blythe knows that she knows that—"

"This is beginning to sound messy, Allie."

"I agree."

"How do you manage to get yourself tangled up in these sorts of. . .*messes?*"

Allie knew Jack's remark was made more in amazement than reprimand. "I'd like to think that it's God's hand that puts me in the middle of these. . .*situations,*" she replied, refusing to use his terminology. "And, as I've warned you in the past, this tends to be how God uses me. Just ask my church family back home."

"Back home?" There was a decided frown in Jack's deep voice. "Sweetheart, you are home. You're right where you belong."

☙ ☙ ☙

Kylie stared at her cell phone after having just heard Matt's latest message. He was sorry. He loved her. He didn't want to call off the engagement. He termed the incident with Dena "a one-time offense that'll never happen again."

But how can I be sure?

Kylie had learned this past week that just because she thought she knew a person didn't mean she really did. Her mother, Dena, Matt—the three people she thought she knew as well as she knew herself—had proven themselves disloyal. Kylie wondered if she'd ever be able to wholly trust another individual again.

But without trust, one couldn't have relationships. Without relationships, why bother even living?

A feeling of despondency crept over her soul, and Kylie wondered why she was even alive. She couldn't fathom how her present situation would ever improve. In fact, it could get worse. What if the Chadwyks behaved the same way Blythe did this morning? What if they wanted nothing to do with her?

A knock sounded on the door. "Kylie? Can I come in?"

"Sure."

Allie poked her head into the room. "I just wanted to make sure you were awake. Jack and I want to go to dinner in about an hour."

Kylie felt like telling Allie to go on without her, but she wasn't sure Allie would feel comfortable about leaving her here alone. This was Allie's home, after all, and she and Kylie had only been acquainted one week.

"Jack's son, Logan, is going to join us," Allie said with a smile. "His fiancée, Marilee, isn't feeling well tonight and opted to stay home. She's the one I told you about—the one who'd been in that awful car accident last October."

"Oh, yes. . ." Kylie remembered and nodded the rest of her reply. "What should I wear tonight? What are you wearing?"

"Something casual, a denim skirt and a sweater."

Kylie pursed her lips, thinking of the clothes she'd packed. She had brought along a pair of black slacks and a coordinating blouse and jacket that would likely be appropriate.

"I'm going to hop into the shower," Allie said. "Feel free to make yourself at home."

"Thanks." Kylie smiled as her hostess closed the door again.

Alone once more, Kylie glanced at her cellular phone, then turned it off and determined to forget about Matt—at least for the remainder of this evening.

Moving off the air mattress on which she'd been sitting, Kylie walked to the closet, where she had temporarily hung various garments. She pulled the multicolored, stylish insignia jacket from its hanger, then sauntered to her suitcase for the rest of her things. After changing clothes and brushing out her hair, she touched up her makeup. She really wasn't one to use a lot of cosmetics, but at the same time, Kylie didn't want to resemble an "unpainted barn," as her mother used to say.

Thinking of her mom, Kylie's heart twisted with grief. But she tamped down her misery, and with a final glance in the full-length mirror that hung on the inside of the closet door, she ventured into the living room to wait for Allie. Upon her entrance, she stopped short, seeing a man sitting on the couch.

He looked up from the book in his lap, and his severe expression made Kylie want to retreat. However, an instant later, he smiled.

"You must be Kylie," he said as he stood, and she guessed his height to be over six feet.

"Yes, I am."

Stepping forward, he held out his right hand. "Jack Callahan."

"Oh, right. Allie's fiancé." Kylie put her hand in his. He had a firm grip—firm but gentle. "Nice to meet you."

"Same here." He reclaimed his seat on the end of the couch, next to the side table where an ivory ginger jar–shaped lamp threw off a soft hue. "Please sit down. Logan should be here any minute."

"Thanks." Kylie lowered herself into one of the two navy wing-backed chairs near the fireplace. "Allie said that you knew my mom."

He nodded, and Kylie saw that his dark hair was tinged with gray. She thought he appeared quite distinguished. "I knew both Wendy and Blythe," he said.

She crossed her right leg over her left, then glanced down at her black slacks and brushed off a miniscule piece of white fuzz. "I've pretty much settled it in my heart that Wendy and Josh Rollins were my real parents. Rob Chadwyk may have fathered me and Blythe might have given birth to me, but they had nothing to do with my upbringing."

"You're right. They didn't."

Kylie gazed across the way and saw Jack's impassive expression; however, she could see the look of approval in his brown eyes.

"You sound like a young lady with a good head on her shoulders."

"Most of the time." She couldn't help smirking when she thought of how Matt had called her "irrational" earlier in the week. Of course, she could think of several choice names to call him right about now.

"So tell me about your mother. Last I saw her, she was holding a picket sign." Jack grinned.

Remembering the photograph, Kylie shook her head in disbelief. "That's certainly not the mother I grew up with. My mom was very conservative in her opinions. She didn't really keep up on current events and she hated politics. My dad, on the other hand, served on various committees, both local and nationwide. He was outspoken about social injustice, particularly when it concerned providing health care for the indigent. He dedicated his life to making a difference in the medical field. My mom supported his views but always kept a low profile." Kylie smiled. "She liked being a housewife."

"That's not the Wendy I once knew," Jack replied with a grin and a wag of his head. "But I'm living proof that people can and do change."

"I guess they do," Kylie muttered, examining the bare finger on her left hand. It felt odd not to wear her engagement ring. But then she reminded herself that deceit wasn't the same as change. A change of heart seemed much more acceptable.

"How did your mom and dad meet each other?"

"They met in college—at least, that's what I've been told. I was also told that my mother grew up in the La Crosse area, as did my father. I know now that's only half-true. My dad grew up there. I knew my paternal grandparents until they died, one when I was in high school and the other a few years ago. Neither one ever told me I was adopted."

"Maybe they didn't know."

Kylie shrugged. "Yeah, maybe."

"Aunts? Uncles? Cousins?"

"I have an aunt and uncle in St. Louis and three cousins. Haven't seen them in years. We were never close. Saw each other once a year while I was growing up. My mother always told me that her parents were dead and that she was an only child."

"Hmm. . . Well, it was no secret that Wendy had issues with her parents."

Kylie widened her eyes. "It was a secret to me!"

Jack gave her a rueful grin. "Did I hear Allie correctly? Your father is dead, too?"

"Yes. He died in '93 of an infection around the lining of his heart. He went quickly. It was very traumatic for my mother and me."

"I can well imagine."

"I still miss him."

"I'm sure you do. I still miss my folks." Jack's face suddenly brightened. "But I know I'll see them again someday."

"My dad and mom, too. They both had strong religious beliefs."

"How 'bout you?"

"Me?" Kylie brought her chin back, surprised at the question. "Of course I have a strong faith. I've been a Christian all my life."

Jack nodded out a polite reply, but skepticism seemed to

shadow his features, causing Kylie a small measure of discomfort. She knew there were different kinds of Christians in the world, different denominations, but she believed Jesus Christ died for everyone. To her way of thinking, everyone who embraced Christianity was under the umbrella of God's grace. However, she wasn't about to enter into a theological debate. Religion, Kylie felt, was a very personal matter and not to be discussed with people she didn't know. In fact, she'd never even talked about religion with Matt, mostly because the topic hadn't come up. Besides, they had attended the same church since infancy, except for the time Matt lived in Madison. What was there to talk about?

"Did your mother ever tell you that I led her to Christ?" Jack asked, setting his book aside and leaning forward. He rested his arms on his knees.

Kylie shook her head.

He grinned. "Wendy and I had some lively debates 'back in the day,' as Logan often terms it."

Kylie smiled.

"But a couple of months after her brother died, she started questioning things, wondering what happens after a person dies, and I was able to show her from the Bible how she could know for sure that she'd go to heaven."

"Yes, Allie mentioned something about that." Kylie shifted uncomfortably. "Although my mother told me she'd been brought up in a Christian home."

"Well, that may be." The doorbell rang, and Jack stood to answer it. "But just because someone is brought up in a Christian surrounding doesn't mean Jesus Christ lives in his or her heart."

⁂ ⁂ ⁂

While applying her cosmetics, Allie could hear snippets of

the conversation taking place in the living room. Based on things Kylie said, Allie surmised the younger woman didn't have a relationship with the Lord but merely a religion.

Oh, Lord, I don't mean to judge her. I'm only concerned for her soul.

The doorbell rang and Allie trusted that Jack would get it. Minutes later, she heard Logan's booming voice. Once she finished "putting her face on," as Jack would say, Allie headed for her guests.

"Hi, Logan," she said with a smile, entering the living room. The proverbial description of tall, dark, and handsome applied to the younger man, and he was the spitting image of his father thirty years ago.

"Hi ya, Mom." Logan strode forward and placed a kiss on her cheek.

"Oh, you're such a good boy," Allie drawled. At twenty-nine years old, Logan was hardly a "boy." However, that didn't stop her from giving him a hard time—all in fun, of course.

"Good boy? I think I've just been insulted." He pulled himself up to his full height of over six feet. "But it's my youth group's fault that I'm always thinking like a teenager."

Jack chuckled. "Guess you've got a pretty good excuse there."

Allie smiled at Kylie, who stood next to Jack, and then glanced back at Logan. "You know I love you just the way you are." She slipped her arm around Logan's waist. "I take it you've met Kylie?"

He nodded. "She was just telling me that she'd never met a youth pastor before."

"Really?" Allie lifted her brows. "You don't have a youth pastor in your church?"

Kylie gave her head a shake, and her dark hair fell over the tops of her shoulders. "I guess we've never needed one."

"Not many teenagers in your congregation?" Logan queried.

"No."

"Do you live in a retirement community or something?"

Kylie smiled and her ebony eyes sparkled with amusement. "No. We have a lot of teenagers in Basil Creek, but they don't seem to care much about going to church." She turned pensive. "They don't seem to care much about reading either."

"Kylie is a librarian," Allie informed the men.

"Oh, yeah?" Logan's face split into a broad smile. "I'll bet you'd enjoy meeting my fiancée. She's a teacher. . .or she was."

"I hope you don't mind that I told our guest about Marilee's accident," Allie said as she stepped toward the closet to retrieve coats.

"Mind? Why would I mind?"

Allie shrugged. "I just don't want you to think your future stepmother has a big mouth."

"Oh, not to worry. I love you anyway, Mom." Wearing a smirk, he took Kylie's coat and politely helped her into it.

"You mean in spite of my big mouth? Thanks a lot." She laughed.

Jack assisted Allie with her winter wrapper. "You set yourself up for that one, Honey."

"Yes, I suppose I did."

Jack glanced over his shoulder. "You two ready?"

They both nodded.

Jack's gaze returned to Allie, and he grinned. "Our dinner reservations are for seven. Looks like we'll be right on time."

CHAPTER TEN

The glass-ensconced candle flickered from the center of their cloth-covered table. Indeed, it reflected the graceful, glowing ambiance of the restaurant.

Kylie watched the flame, feeling a little amazed after just hearing Logan recount the events that had followed his fiancée's car wreck. He claimed that his natural mother, a woman he'd never known until she lay dying in a nursing home, wouldn't have become a Christian if God hadn't allowed Marilee's accident.

"Seems like kind of a cruel thing for a heavenly Father to do to His child." Kylie lifted her gaze and looked at Logan. "I mean, I would never allow my child to be injured that way. How could God allow that?"

"Sometimes He has to break us, Kylie," Jack replied as his thumb and forefinger toyed with the edge of the napkin. "The Lord can't use us until He's broken our will—kind of like breaking a wild horse. Sometimes it's a painful process." He looked up and smiled. "I sure know that from experience."

"And sometimes God has to bring us to the end of ourselves," Allie further explained, "so that we look to Him. That happened to me."

One by one, Kylie studied the three faces staring back at her. These people were very different from other Christians she knew. The way they talked so openly about God—as if He were a real person to whom they spoke in a casual way. While part of her wondered if they belonged to some weird cult, another part of her felt drawn to them. They had something she didn't, and Kylie was curious to find out what that "something" was.

"Marilee is the first to admit that, yes, God 'broke' her, but He is also at work, teaching her through the healing process and strengthening her faith." Logan smiled. "It's incredible to see what the Lord is doing in her life. You'll meet Marilee tomorrow morning—that is, if you come to church with us."

"Yeah, and if Marilee shows up," Jack added.

Kylie noted the sarcasm and frowned. "Doesn't Marilee like to attend church?"

Logan gave his father an impatient glance. "It's not that. Marilee is still recovering, and there are times when she doesn't feel well enough to go out—even if it's to church."

"Understandable." Kylie lifted her glass and sipped her diet cola.

"Did Marilee have a bad day today?" Allie wanted to know.

Logan nodded before releasing an audible sigh. Then he leaned forward, forearms on the table. "And I don't know what to do for her either. She's depressed, moody, questioning her relationship with God, questioning her relationship with me— even going so far as to try and talk me out of marrying her at times, except I know she doesn't really mean it."

"She just needs constant reassurance right now," Allie

said. "Marilee's a three-dimensional person, and that awful accident affected her physically, emotionally, and spiritually."

"I know, but it just seems like—"

Meeting Kylie's gaze, he cut himself short. "I'm talking out of turn. Forgive me. The bottom line is, I love Marilee and she's a terrific lady. We'll weather this storm together."

"Listen, you don't have to apologize to me," Kylie said, setting down her glass. "My father was a doctor, so we had three-dimensional people with three-dimensional problems calling our house day and night."

Logan smiled while Jack laughed, and Kylie marveled for the second time that night at how much alike the Callahan men looked.

Their server approached, carrying a large, round stainless steel tray. "Your dinners are ready," he said with a polite smile as he began placing dishes of food in front of them.

Noticing the waiter's blond hair, blue eyes, and the way he effortlessly handled his weighty burden, Kylie couldn't help but think of Matt. Her heart ached at the loss of her fiancé whom she loved so deeply. The pain was just as bad as the days following her mother's death.

"Logan, I need to apologize for my remark about Marilee and church tomorrow," Jack said, pulling Kylie from her musings. "That was uncalled-for. I realize it now. I'm very fond of Marilee, but I've grown somewhat intolerant of her mood swings. Still, Allie's right. What Marilee needs from us right now is love. . .and a whole lot of patience."

"Exactly." Logan smiled. "Shall we give thanks for our food?"

The foursome joined hands, a familiar practice to Kylie. She prayed along while Jack asked God's blessing on their food. *Maybe these people aren't such different Christians after all. . . .*

The following morning, Kylie dressed for church. She'd only been to a few churches in her life, all of them with her parents, and all of them similar to the one in which she'd grown up in in Basil Creek. But last night at dinner, as Logan Callahan began describing Parkway Community Church, Kylie grew more and more fascinated with the place. Its membership was larger than Basil Creek's population!

Lifting her brush, Kylie began to fix her hair. More memories of last night's dinner wafted through her mind, and she smiled, recalling Logan and his boyish charm. He and Matt would get along well.

She sighed. If only she could stop thinking about Matt!

As of this morning, he'd left two new voice messages on her cell phone. Again, he said he was sorry, and in the last recording, he stated he was worried about her and the way she had "run off."

I didn't run off, Kylie thought as she set her jaw in irritation. *I'm on a journey. This is just something I have to do. Can't he understand that?*

Kylie plaited her hair into a French braid and her thoughts wandered to Dena. Kylie's heart twisted in a mix of rage and anguish. Dena had been her best friend. The one to whom she'd told her childhood secrets. The one who said she understood even when Kylie's mother, her other confidant, hadn't. Tears filled her eyes.

Don't cry. You have to go to church in a few minutes. You'll look stupid meeting new people with red-rimmed eyes.

"How're you doing?" Allie appeared in the doorway of the guest room. "Jack's outside waiting for us."

Kylie abandoned her pity party. "I'm fine. . .and I'm ready."

Allie's lovely smile dispelled the gloom hanging over

Kylie's head. "You look so pretty." She narrowed her blue eyes. "Are those ladybugs in the design of your dress?"

Glancing down at the skirt of her black cotton-knit dress, Kylie nodded. Then she lifted a black, white, and red matching short-sleeved jacket. "And more ladybugs." She laughed. "The kids who come into the library for weekly story time get a kick out of this outfit."

"I'll bet they do." Allie's smile broadened. "You and Marilee are going to get along just fine. The two of you have a lot in common—love for books and teaching children."

Kylie replied with a polite bob of her head.

"Well, if you're ready, let's go."

Allie spun on her ivory, high-heeled pump, and following, Kylie took note of her attire. She wore an off-white, pleated skirt, one in which Kylie wouldn't dare go out in public. The narrow pleats would only accentuate her full hips. But on Allie's slender frame, the skirt hung perfectly. Completing the picture was a red silk blouse that Allie had tucked in at her narrow waist. Kylie suddenly feared she had underdressed.

"Oh, don't be silly," Allie told her after Kylie voiced her concern. "You'll see people at Parkway in various types of dress, some formal, others casual. You look just fine."

Kylie slipped her coat off the hanger in the front closet and stepped outside. The morning sunshine warmed her face, but the wind had a chill to it. Parked at the curbside with the engine running, Jack awaited her and Allie in his black Ford Explorer—the very SUV that Matt had talked about purchasing "someday."

I've got to get that guy out of my head!

Climbing into the vehicle's backseat, Kylie realized she had left her Bible at home in Basil Creek.

"Oh, don't worry," Jack assured her. "Someone will either

have an extra one or share theirs with you."

Kylie snapped her seat belt into place and sat back against the leather seat. Jack pulled away from the curb, and light chitchat ensued as they rode to church. The drive took nearly forty-five minutes, causing Kylie to wonder why Jack and Allie didn't attend a nearby house of worship.

"I'm curious," she began. "Why do you go to a church that's so far away? Oakland Park must have its share of churches."

"Our fair community has several good ones, actually," Jack drawled. "You're right. But since my son is the youth pastor at Parkway and my brother Steve and his family attend there, Allie and I figured we might as well travel the distance, too. It's another way we can support Logan in his ministry."

Kylie could understand the rationale.

Allie turned in her seat and smiled. "If you knew what a miracle it is to hear Jack talk like that. . ."

"I think I'm getting the idea." She returned Allie's smile before staring at the back of the former police officer's dark head, peppered with gray highlights. She couldn't imagine him as the gruff and ornery man he claimed to be six months ago. To Kylie, Jack Callahan seemed very sensitive and caring— and it was obvious that he was very much in love with Allie.

At last they reached Parkway Community Church, a building so large it could easily occupy two full blocks of Basil Creek's main thoroughfare. Inside the multilevel complex, Kylie was introduced to numerous people whom they passed in the hallway as Allie escorted her to one of the many ladies' Bible studies.

"Marilee?" Allie waved a slim brunette over to where they stood near the coffeepot on the far side of a room that was bigger than Basil Creek's town hall.

"Hi, Allie." A tremulous smile curved her berry-colored

lips. Dressed in a blue and burgundy floral dress and a coordinating navy blazer, her straight brown hair pulled back with an indigo bow, Marilee appeared the part of a soon-to-be pastor's wife—or at least she fit Kylie's stereotypical image.

Allie quickly folded Marilee into a motherly embrace. "How are you feeling today?" She pulled back, peering into Marilee's face as she waited for an answer.

"Oh, I'm. . .fine."

"Fine?" The skepticism in Allie's tone was unmistakable.

Marilee relented. "I'm about the same. I can't seem to shake this depression. Logan says it's a spiritual issue, but I—" She glanced at Kylie and muttered, "I suppose he's right."

"Well, don't be too hard on yourself. Just remember, about this time of year everyone in the Midwest gets the winter blues. I certainly do."

Kylie watched Marilee manufacture a polite smile. "I'm sure you're right."

Allie glanced at Kylie. "I'd like you to meet someone," she began. "This is Kylie Rollins. She's the daughter of a friend from days gone by, and she's my guest for this weekend. Kylie, this is Logan's fiancée, Marilee Domotor."

"Nice to meet you," Marilee said.

Kylie thought the reply sounded a bit aloof, and she recalled that last night Jack and Logan had mentioned Marilee's "mood swings." But was it really that? As Kylie looked into the other woman's eyes, she thought she saw two pools of deep brown sadness. But perhaps it was merely a reflection of Kylie's own mournful soul.

"Nice to meet you, too, Marilee."

"I think you two will find you have a lot in common," Allie said. She turned to Kylie. "I'm sorry to run off like this, but my Bible study is next door. We're such a big church that we divide by ages," she explained to Kylie. "As you can see, this group is much too young for me."

Kylie couldn't help a smile at the remark, and when she glanced at Marilee, she saw an amused little grin on her face, too.

Once Allie left, Marilee struck up a perfunctory conversation. "So. . .you're from Wisconsin, huh?"

Kylie nodded.

"Logan told me that he'd met you at dinner last night."

"Yes. . .and Jack and Allie were there, too." Kylie felt obligated to include the latter since she didn't want Marilee to get the wrong impression. Having known the heartache caused by an unscrupulous woman, Kylie wanted to make sure she'd never be suspected of such treachery. To drive the point home, she added, "Logan speaks very highly of you. It's obvious that he loves you very much."

Marilee smiled, then lowered her gaze. "Logan's a good man."

"Yes, he seems like it. In a way, I'm a little envious. My fiancé tended to treat me like a—a china doll," she stated, using the annoying name Matt once teased her with when they were children. "I often felt like something he'd put on a shelf and ignored, except he expected me to always be there. . . ."

Kylie willed herself to stop babbling. "Well, it doesn't matter. We broke up a few days ago."

One of Marilee's dark winged brows dipped in sympathy. "Oh, I'm sorry. I didn't realize—"

"I know. I didn't say anything to anyone except Allie and now you. And I'm not even sure why I blurted it out, other than. . ." Kylie shrugged. "I'm just going through a rough time right now. I'm one of those people who needs to talk about my problems."

"Me, too." She smiled, and Kylie noticed twin dimples, one in each of Marilee's cheeks. "My situation is totally different, but maybe we can encourage each other. I don't have many confidants."

Kylie frowned. "In this big church? I would think you'd have plenty of listening ears and shoulders to cry on."

"Logan's in the ministry here," Marilee stated in a voice that was barely audible. "He's the youth pastor."

Kylie wanted to say, "Yeah, so?" But her expression must have said it for her.

"Typically it's not wise for those in leadership to share their troubles with members of their congregation."

"Why?"

Marilee glanced around at the many ladies milling about and chatting. Obviously, she was afraid of being overheard. "Maybe we can talk later. Are you going to Steve and Nora's for lunch?"

"Yes, I think Allie mentioned it."

"Good. We can get better acquainted there."

"Okay."

Marilee glanced at her wristwatch. "Almost time for the Bible study to begin. Why don't you follow me over to where I'm sitting? I think there's an extra chair right next to mine."

CHAPTER ELEVEN

After the Bible study, Marilee Domotor escorted Kylie into the foyer of Parkway Community Church. There they were greeted by the entire Callahan clan. Allie, soon to be a Callahan herself, began introducing Kylie to Steve and Nora and their three children. As greetings and welcomes were exchanged, Marilee's gaze found Logan's. He stood just a few feet away, and she could tell he didn't know what to say for fear she'd react in some irrational way—and he was right. Marilee hated herself for her mood swings, and she knew Logan was rapidly losing his patience with her.

Or at least, he should be.

Everyone else was. Her parents were at their wits' end, and her closest acquaintances had long since given up on her.

She expelled a breath laden with regret. Marilee thought she'd give anything to turn back the clock to the beginning of October when she was still a happy, carefree, idealistic young woman in love. She'd met the man of her dreams, Logan Callahan, and she'd prayed that he'd fall in love with her and propose. At last he did. Things were perfect—maybe too perfect.

And then her car was struck from behind on the Kennedy during rush-hour traffic. The accident resulted in a broken femur and a ruptured uterine artery. The latter forced doctors to perform an emergency hysterectomy, leaving Marilee a scarred woman, physically and emotionally. Many times in the past months, she'd wished she had died on that hazy Friday afternoon. But as soon as depression threatened her, Marilee began counting her blessings. She had parents who loved her. A fiancé who loved her. The driver who'd hit her had been insured, and now she had a tidy sum in a savings account—enough to, perhaps, adopt a child someday, since Marilee couldn't conceive. Logan insisted their future looked bright. And she agreed. But, somehow, her heart wasn't in sync with her head. Inside, she felt hopeless. She was ready to give up.

Marilee closed her eyes. *Lord, I know You want me to depend solely on You. I'm trying. . . .*

Feeling someone touch her elbow, she lifted her gaze and saw Logan standing beside her. He gave her a cautious little smile, then nodded toward the sanctuary as if to say, "Time for service."

"Sorry about this morning," Marilee whispered, albeit loud enough for Logan to hear. He'd made a suggestion for a future youth activity, and she'd snapped at him in reply. The sad truth was, she'd grown weary of the youth ministry.

"No problem." He gave her elbow a gentle squeeze before letting his hand fall to his side.

Marilee bristled at what she perceived was a dismissive answer. It *was* a problem. *She* was a problem. However, she really couldn't expect Logan to discuss the matter now.

Reaching the doorway, Marilee felt suddenly very unworthy to sit among God's people. She should feel grateful to serve God by ministering to teenagers. Instead, the kids got on her nerves. Everyone got on her nerves.

She paused, then moved to let others pass. Logan made a quick side step, avoiding a collision with church members, and stood in front of her. Peering into her face, his dark brows furrowed with unspoken questions as he shifted his thick, leather-bound Bible from the crook of one arm to the other.

"What's up?" he finally asked.

"Maybe I'll just sit out here in the lobby."

"You sure?"

Marilee nodded before a tiny smirk curved her mouth. "That way when God sends the lightning bolt, it'll only strike me." She was being facetious, but that's the least she felt like she deserved.

Logan drew in an exasperated breath and crossed his eyes. Then he let his head fall back and stood there, staring up at the white ceiling tiles.

Watching his comical reaction, Marilee laughed and it made her feel better. "You poor man. I'm making you crazy, aren't I?" She sobered, wishing he'd understand—wishing she did, too! "You're engaged to a total nutcase."

He lowered his chin and regarded Marilee with warm brown eyes. "Well, I'm a nutcase, too, so we're a perfect match."

No, we're not. You're too good for me. I'm not a whole woman anymore. You deserve better.

The piteous thoughts caused Marilee's heart to constrict with anguish. She hated the idea of Logan with someone else. She loved him more than her own existence. But at the same time, she saw herself as damaged goods.

"Mari, I'd like it if you'd sit inside with me, under Pastor Warren's preaching," Logan stated gently. "There's too much distraction out here and, as the Scripture says, 'faith cometh by hearing, and hearing by the Word of God.'"

She stood there for an immeasurable amount of time, wrestling with indecision, so Logan solved her dilemma by taking hold of her upper arm and leading her through the double doors. Side by side, they walked down the center aisle of the large sanctuary to a row of seats near the front. Marilee scooted in and claimed the place second to the end. Logan set down his Bible on the seat beside her.

"I'll be back," he said, giving her an affectionate wink.

Marilee felt herself sinking into that familiar dark shell of misery—until a feminine voice suddenly plucked her from its depths.

"Where's he going?"

"What?" Marilee glanced to her right and realized that Kylie had asked the question.

"Logan. . .where's he going?"

"Oh. . .up there." She inclined her head toward the platform, then gazed in that direction and spotted Logan taking a seat in the upholstered armchair next to Pastor Warren. The choir, standing just behind the two men, prepared to sing. Marilee leaned over to Kylie and whispered, "Logan usually does the announcements."

"I see," Kylie whispered back. She glanced toward the front, then back at Marilee. "Is it okay if I share your Bible again?"

"Of course."

The choir began a soul-stirring arrangement of an old

her depression kept up. Doctors said nothing was wrong with her physically. They had "fixed" her, and they didn't seem concerned that she still needed occasional pain medication. The physical therapist said that might be the case for the rest of her life. No, Marilee's issues appeared to run deeper than the broken leg and hysterectomy resulting from her accident. But what was it?

Oh, Lord, why can't I just be happy?

◆ ◆ ◆

Kylie stood in the large, tastefully decorated lobby of Parkway Community Church feeling as though she was something of a celebrity. She'd been introduced to scores of people before the service and now, afterward, that number had doubled. Obviously, the Callahans knew a lot of people, and since Logan was the youth pastor, he knew everyone. What's more, Kylie noticed that numerous teenaged girls seemed to adore their dark-headed youth pastor. They flocked around him, chattering and giggling and reminding Kylie of Dena at that age—except these girls behaved so much younger than she or Dena ever seemed to be.

Glancing to her right, Kylie spotted Marilee standing with her back to the wall. Her brown eyes were downcast, and a pinched little frown dipped her one dark brow. Did the teenagers bother her? The girls seemed harmless as far as Kylie could see, and Logan appeared to be in control of the situation. What's more, he glanced in Marilee's direction from time to time as if keeping tabs on his fiancée's whereabouts. Kylie found herself wishing Matt had been half that attentive whenever they were out in public together. More often than not, he'd involved himself with his buddies and a competitive dart game rather than keep her company. But that hadn't bothered Kylie so much. . .until now.

Thoughts of Matt renewed the knife-twisting pain in her soul. It was hard to imagine that any amount of time would heal such a wound, just like she couldn't fathom ever recovering from the loss of her mother—and father, too. Even now, she experienced a fleeting desire to call home—as if they'd be there to answer the call. She longed to ask about all she'd heard Pastor Noah Warren say from the pulpit this morning. Kylie had never heard such a stirring, but somewhat unnerving, message about sacrifice, particularly the Lord's.

"The soul without Jesus Christ will perish for eternity," he'd said. Kylie had looked on with Marilee as the pastor read from the Bible. " 'He that believeth on him is not condemned: but he that believeth not is condemned already, because he hath not believed in the name of the only begotten Son of God.' "

Well, I believe, Kylie had mused, feeling a mite defensive. However, the next portion of Scripture proved the most troubling. Marilee had leafed through the delicate pages of her Bible until she arrived at the Book of James. " 'Thou believest that there is one God; thou doest well: the devils also believe, and tremble.' "

"You see, my friends," the pastor had continued, "the kind of belief the demons have isn't a saving knowledge of Jesus Christ, since there aren't likely to be devils in God's eternal heavenly home." Many chuckles emanated from the congregation. "But salvation comes by acknowledging one's sin and putting one's trust in Jesus Christ for forgiveness. It's a decision. Have you made your choice? Have you chosen to trust—to believe in the Savior?"

As she listened, Kylie had felt suspended in time, as if she were the only person in that huge auditorium and the pastor was speaking directly to her. Unfortunately, she'd never been given such an option before, and she wasn't quite certain she understood.

Kylie startled when someone touched her on the shoulder. A heartbeat later, she realized Marilee stood beside her.

"Are you all right?"

Kylie gave her a polite grin. "Yes. . .and actually, I was tempted to ask you the same thing."

"Why, because I look so miserable?" A rueful smile curved Marilee's mouth.

Kylie hedged, not wanting to offend her; however, "miserable" seemed an accurate description.

"I guess it's been a long winter," Marilee said on a sigh.

"That it has," Kylie agreed. "Although I think I spent the month of February in shock."

"Oh?"

Kylie nodded. "My mother died at the end of January. We were very close."

"I'm so sorry. I didn't know. Please accept my condolences."

"Thank you." Kylie managed a shaky smile.

"So you lost your mother and had a failed engagement?"

Kylie bobbed her head in affirmation. "But that's just the tip of the iceberg. My fiancé cheated on me with my best friend, and it wasn't just an accidental incident. Seems it was a calculated offense on both their parts. Then, yesterday, I discovered that I was adopted, which means my mother lied to me my whole life."

Marilee's expression of despair soon became a mask of concern. "Oh, Kylie, I'm so sorry. I. . .I don't know what else to say."

Embarrassed now for pouring out her troubles to a woman she'd met only a few hours ago, Kylie shrugged out an obscure reply.

"You know," Marilee said at last, "I think Allie was right when she said you and I have a lot in common. We do."

"Misery?" Kylie couldn't resist the retort.

"Well, yeah." Marilee wore a look of chagrin. "I was thinking more along the lines of misery loving company."

"Oh?"

Marilee nodded. "In other words, it sounds like you could use a friend just as much as I could."

CHAPTER TWELVE

Y ou're awfully quiet."

Marilee glanced at Logan, who sat behind the wheel of his maroon Mercury Sable. She studied his profile, the subtle downward slant of his eye, his perfectly shaped straight nose, and strong jawline with its permanent shadow. She thought she could gaze at him forever.

He braked for a stoplight, then looked over at her. "What're you staring at?"

"You, of course."

He grinned with satisfaction. "Is that why you haven't said more than two words since we left church? You're too busy memorizing my every feature?"

"I don't mean to deliver a blow to your ego or anything," Marilee stated in jest, "but I've been deep in thought."

Taking a hand off the steering wheel, Logan clutched

his chest. "I'm wounded."

Marilee chuckled at his antics.

"Okay, seriously now, tell me what you're so deep in thought about."

"I was thinking about Kylie Rollins. She's been through a lot."

"So I've heard."

"Did she tell you?"

Logan nodded his dark head. "Last night at dinner."

"It's sort of weird, but I feel an odd connection to Kylie. Maybe it's because we've both experienced some traumatic things, hers more recent than my car accident."

Logan pursed his lips, then looked away and stepped on the accelerator after the light changed.

"It's hard to explain, but I sense that I might be able to help and encourage Kylie. What's more, I think she might do the same for me."

"Well, I'd buy into the first part of your statement, but you'd better ask God for some quick wisdom if that's the case. Kylie leaves tomorrow for South Carolina. Apparently, she has grandparents there who she didn't know about until last week. It's my understanding they don't know about her either."

The news hit Marilee hard. "How long will she be gone?"

"Not sure. She said she took a leave of absence from work, but that's all I know."

Reclining against the headrest, Marilee turned and gazed out the window. She felt so disappointed that tears sprang into her eyes. For the first time in half a year, she'd felt God calling her to a purpose outside of Logan's ministry to the teenagers—and she had thought it related to Kylie. But obviously she'd been mistaken.

Or had she?

Oh, Lord, I'm so confused. I can't even tell anymore if it's Your voice I hear in my heart.

Within minutes, Logan parked alongside the curb in front of his aunt and uncle's house. Marilee's composure had returned, and she gave Logan a grateful smile when he'd walked around the car and opened the door for her. Since the first day she'd met him, Logan Callahan had been a courtly gentleman. One of the finest she'd ever met.

"You know," he said, leaning his forearm on top of the door, "it's really good to hear you talk about ministering to others again." A light of approval shone in the depths of his brown eyes.

"You mean because I've been so absorbed in my own pain and suffering?" Marilee instantly regretted the barb. "I'm sorry, Logan. Forget I said that."

"Okay. . ." He let his arm drop, and Marilee stepped out of the way so he could shut the door. "But would you mind telling me what brought on that remark?"

"Me. It's me, Logan. Don't you see? Every time I think God is directing me a certain way, I find out He's not. I feel like a. . .a spiritual failure. I can't even do the right thing when I want to."

"Whoa, back up. What are you talking about?"

"Kylie. I felt like God had some long-range plan for me, but obviously He doesn't. She's leaving tomorrow. And it's not just Kylie. This has happened before." Marilee swatted at a wayward tear and recalled several displaced opportunities in the past months. "I just don't feel like I have a sense of purpose anymore."

"You're part of the teen ministry. . . ."

"Those kids get on my nerves—big-time!"

There! She'd finally said it.

But instead of the disappointed frown she'd expected to see, Logan laughed. "Honey, they get on everyone's nerves. They're teens!"

The quip made Marilee grin, and she had to admit she felt relieved by Logan's reaction. For months, she imagined he wouldn't want her as his wife if he knew how she felt about the youth ministry. The teens were a giant part of Logan's life.

"You're smiling. That's better." Logan draped his arm around Marilee's shoulders as they walked across the lawn and up his uncle's driveway. "Beautiful day, isn't it?"

Marilee raised her eyes to the overcast sky. This morning's sunshine was gone. It now looked like rain. She gave Logan a curious glance. "Beautiful day?"

"Yeah." He took her hand and tucked it around his elbow. "When I'm with you, Marilee, the sun is always shining."

She rolled her eyes and laughed at his syrupy reply. But deep inside the words soothed her wounded spirit because she knew each word came straight from Logan's heart.

♪ ♪ ♪

"Kylie, it's me." A pause. "Sweetheart, I'm worried about you. Would you please call me back? I know you're upset and. . . well, you've got a right to be. I talked to Pastor Hanson after church today, and it'll make you feel better to know he gave me a thorough tongue-lashing."

Ha! It doesn't make me feel better at all!

Standing out on Steve and Nora Callahan's back deck, Kylie braved the cold wind as she listened to Matt's rambling message on her cell phone. She wondered if she should grant his request and return his call. Perhaps he'd stop pestering her if she made it clear to him that they were no longer a couple.

Without listening to the rest of the recording, Kylie pressed the delete button, then punched in Matt's phone number. Lynellen answered.

"Hi, it's me. Kylie."

"Kylie! I'm so glad you called. We've been worried sick. Where are you? Oh, wait, here comes Matt. I'll put him on. . . ."

She heard the phone being passed from mother to son.

"Ky?"

"Yeah, hi." She tried to keep all expression from her voice.

"I'm glad you called. Are you okay?"

"Yes. . .look, Matt, you have to stop calling me. We're not engaged anymore, got it? I wouldn't marry you if you were the last man on earth." She choked on the last word, and Kylie wished her voice hadn't betrayed her.

"You don't mean that, Ky; I know you too well. And I know how much we love each other, so—"

"Matt, you are such a liar. If you loved me, you wouldn't have done what you did with Dena."

"I was drunk," he said in a voice barely audible. "I don't even remember half of what occurred."

"Oh, great," Kylie replied facetiously. "I suppose you think that rights all the wrongs."

"I know it doesn't." She heard Matt sigh. "But it's no secret that when I drink, I lose my head. My friends all know it, and Pastor Hanson suggested I attend AA. Maybe he's right. Maybe I have a problem."

"You do, but it's not alcohol." Kylie felt a growing impatience with the man. "Your problem is *you*."

No reply.

"Now that we broke up, I can see how little you really cared for me, Matt. You don't know what kind of person I am or what's important to me. You don't even want to know what's in my heart. In fact, Rochelle occupies your thoughts entirely more than I ever have—and probably ever will."

"That's not true."

"Oh, yeah? What's my favorite color, Matt? What's my favorite book? Do you know what my favorite movie is?"

"Yeah, *It's a Wonderful Life* with Jimmy Stewart."

"Wrong, that was Mom's favorite movie. But I'll bet you remember all of Rochelle's favorite things."

"That's not fair. Rochelle and I were married for six years." His voice softened. "After you and I are married, I'll know all those things about you, too."

"No, you won't, because we're not getting married." A painful swell lodged in her chest. "Don't call me anymore. I have nothing more to say to you."

"Kylie, don't you dare hang up on me!"

Hearing the warning note in his voice, she hesitated.

"Kylie?"

"I'm still here."

"Good, because it's my turn. You need to hear me out. I'm not letting you go, Ky. As far as I'm concerned, we're still engaged. You gave me your heart and you can't take it back. I won't give it back. It's mine."

She willed herself to go numb, refusing to be swayed by his empty amorous words.

"And another thing. If you're not back home in a week, I'm coming to fetch you and bring you home myself. You belong here with me."

Fiery indignation caused her temples to throb. "You are the most selfish man I've ever known. If you really loved me, you'd support and encourage me. Yesterday, I found out I was adopted, Matt. Adopted. The dark-haired woman in that photograph Allie sent is my biological mother. But you don't give a flip about what I'm going through. All you can think about is you."

"What?" Matt's tone changed. "What are you talking about? Adopted?"

"It's true. My mother, Wendy Rollins, was really my aunt." Kylie didn't know why she was confiding all this to Matt. She wanted him out of her life, not embroiled in her present and future plans. "Oh, never mind. I shouldn't have even told you."

"Ky, where are you? I should be there with you. You need me."

"Yeah, like a hole in my head." A tear escaped and trickled down her cheek. "Besides, you can't leave your cows. Even they're more important than I am."

"That's not true, and deep down I think you know I love you."

"A moot point. Your actions outweighed anything you ever said to me. Good-bye, Matt."

She pulled the phone away from her ear and pressed the end button, disconnecting the call. She realized then that she was shaking, but whether it was from the cold or her battered emotions, she couldn't be sure.

Behind her, Kylie heard the sliding glass patio doors open. Seconds later, Marilee stood beside her, holding Kylie's coat.

"I didn't mean to interrupt. I just wanted to bring this out to you. You look like you're freezing."

"I am. Thanks." Kylie pulled on the mock-suede overcoat. She felt warmer instantly, but her trembling continued. "I hadn't meant to stay out here so long. I intended to make quick work out of checking messages on my cell phone. But then I returned my fiancé's call and. . .well, needless to say, the conversation went longer than I anticipated."

"Your fiancé? Does that mean you two have patched things up?"

Kylie didn't miss the hopeful gleam in Marilee's eyes. "No, I should have said former fiancé—although Matt is having a difficult time accepting reality."

"Oh?" Marilee tipped her head, and an expression of concern, laced with curiosity, crossed her face.

Kylie decided to share her feelings and her conversation with Matt. Perhaps Marilee had been right when she said they both could use a friend. However, she tried not to think of what would happen if Marilee betrayed her trust—like her mother, Matt, and Dena had. She just had to talk to someone.

"Do you really think Matt will come after you?" Marilee asked after hearing all that had transpired between them. "If you feel threatened, you could talk to Logan's dad. He used to work for the Oakland Park Police Department."

Kylie shook her head. "No. Matt's not a lunatic."

She and Marilee stepped inside the house and removed their outerwear. After hanging up their coats, they ambled into the living room where they could continue their conversation in private, since everyone else was either in the kitchen or in the den, watching basketball on TV.

"Part of me believes that Matt really does love me," Kylie said, sitting on the khaki, chenille-upholstered sofa with its multicolored throw pillows. "But another part of me is still hurt and repulsed by what he did, and if it happened once, it could happen again."

"True." Marilee lowered herself onto the opposite end of the couch. "But if Matt is truly repentant, then there's a good chance it won't happen again."

"Are you telling me to forgive and forget?"

"Forgive, yes. But I'd pray about reconciliation if I were

you. Seek God's will in this situation. Does He want you to forgive Matt and marry him, or is the Lord using this circumstance as a means of protecting you from marrying the wrong man?"

"I'd never thought of it that way." In fact, it never occurred to Kylie that God might be at the helm, guiding her life down the path of His choosing. But why would He concern Himself with her? Surely, God had bigger and more important matters on which to focus.

Didn't He?

Meeting Marilee's warm, brown-eyed gaze, Kylie sensed her new friend had the answer to this—and more.

She settled into a comfy position on the sofa. "Can I ask you a few questions?"

Marilee smiled. "Sure."

CHAPTER THIRTEEN

Allie felt pleased by how well Kylie and Marilee seemed to be getting along. They'd been locked in a deep discussion before lunch, and now, as Allie sat at the kitchen table with Nora, Kylie, and Marilee, indulging in a homemade fudge brownie, she could see a bond had formed between the two younger women.

"My oldest daughter, Veronica, is thinking of going to Northwestern in the fall," Nora said, since the subject of college had come up while a pot of fresh coffee brewed on a nearby counter. "Did you attend college, Kylie?"

She nodded, and a few ebony strands of hair escaped its French braid. "I went to the University of Wisconsin–La Crosse."

"Did you like it?" Nora asked.

Once again, she nodded. "It was close to home."

"You didn't want to go away to school?" Marilee queried.

"No." Kylie sort of smirked. "I knew I had it good at home. My dad said that with the money I saved him by not living in the dorms, he'd buy me a car. And that's what he did."

"Do you have siblings?" Nora wanted to know.

"Nope. Just me." Kylie bestowed on them a full-fledged smile. "I'm an only child. 'A spoiled brat,' as my friend Dena would say."

Her smile suddenly waned, and her gaze fell to the empty plate in front of her. Marilee slipped a sisterly arm around Kylie's shoulders. Nora gave Allie a curious glance to which Allie replied with a wink as if to say, "I'll fill you in later."

"You know, I'm really sorry you're leaving tomorrow," Marilee said. "Will you stop for another visit with us on your way back from South Carolina?"

"Yeah, maybe. . .I'd like that."

At the mention of her road trip, Allie felt that familiar plume of unease well up within her. "Kylie, have you given any more thought to flying down to Charleston and renting a car? Jack agrees with me. It's not safe for you to drive that distance alone."

Nora looked aghast. "You're not driving all by yourself, are you?"

Kylie held up her hands, palms out, as if to prevent further protests. "I am a very good driver. I've never even gotten a speeding ticket. Only one fender bender, but that wasn't even my fault."

"It's not your ability that worries me," Allie said. "I'm sure you're as good of a driver as you claim. It's the increasing number of weirdos running loose in this world that scares me senseless."

"I've got my cell phone and my AAA card."

"How's that going to save you from the crazy person who sticks a gun in your ribs as you fill up your gas tank?" Nora asked. She shook her light brown head. "Allie's right. It's just not safe for you to make that trek alone."

"I'll go."

Allie felt her eyes widen with disbelief as she turned to stare at Marilee. Shouldn't she pray about such a venture? Shouldn't she at least discuss it with Logan? "Um, Marilee—"

She seemed oblivious to Allie's beginning protest. "If you want me to ride along, Kylie, I'd be happy to. I'd love a mini vacation."

"You'd really make the drive with me?" Kylie's dark eyes suddenly shone with eagerness.

"Sure, and I'll go half with you on all the expenses."

"That would be awesome."

"I should warn you, though. I'll probably have to stop and stretch occasionally. Since my accident, my leg stiffens up on me if I'm in one position too long. And this weather is terrible for my leg. I've had to take my pain medication for the past three days."

"It doesn't make you tired?" Nora asked.

Marilee shook her head. "Kind of the other way. I feel sort of jittery. Then, again, it might be all the coffee I drank this morning."

"Well, hey, it's no problem to make pit stops." Kylie swiveled in her wooden chair. "Maybe we could take our time driving down and tour the Smoky Mountains."

"Oh, that would be so fun!"

"Whoa, ladies!" Nora leaned forward and put a hand on each one's forearm. "Marilee, don't you have a wedding to plan?"

She shook her head. "Mom's got every detail taken care of. She doesn't need me. Never has, actually." The acridity in her tone was unmistakable.

Allie lowered her gaze and broke off another chewy bite of brownie. She'd suspected for some time now that Marilee's mother stymied all ideas for her daughter's special day except her own. Consequently, Marilee had given up on the planning.

"Please forgive that last comment," Marilee said, a look of genuine repentance pinching her features. "I shouldn't have said it. My mom's been great. My wedding day is going to be one fit for a queen." She glanced at Kylie. "I think I'm really the spoiled brat."

Allie didn't miss Kylie's rueful smile. No doubt, all this wedding talk brought about a threefold ache—losing her mother, her fiancé, and her best friend.

"All's forgiven," Nora told Marilee, her teal eyes shining with sincerity. "Now back to this drive to South Carolina... don't you think you should discuss it with Logan before committing yourself?"

"Discuss what with Logan?"

Allie grinned, hearing the younger man's booming voice somewhere behind her as he entered the kitchen. From the corner of her left eye, she then glimpsed him carrying an armload of empty plates and glasses. He set his burden in the sink.

"What are you committing yourself to this time?" Logan asked on a humorous note.

"Nice going, Nora," Marilee said in fun. Twin dimples twinkled from her cheeks, and Allie thought the young lady's smile lit up the already-cheerful kitchen.

Too bad she didn't smile more often—like she used to.

Marilee stood. "Excuse me, please," she stated with a dramatic flare. "I need to enlighten my beloved of my intentions."

"Good luck." Kylie laughed. "I'll be rootin' for you."

Chuckling, Allie glanced at Logan. He stood beside the

counter with arms akimbo, and one of his dark brows was raised in question.

Marilee walked around the table and looped her arm around his. "Come on, Handsome. I have to talk to you."

He looked at Nora, Kylie, then Allie and gave them each a sheepish grin. "This doesn't sound so bad."

On that, Marilee dragged him into the other room for a private chat.

"They are such an adorable couple," Kylie said, and Allie heard the wistful note in her voice. "Logan seems so supportive of her and everything Marilee's going through."

"He is." Nora beamed in a motherly way, and why not? She had practically raised Logan. "He's a very patient man and he loves Marilee."

"Obviously." Kylie lowered her gaze and fiddled with the paper napkin on the side of her dessert plate. "I just hope that Marilee's idea about coming with me to South Carolina won't result in an argument between her and Logan."

"No," Nora said, waving one of her plump hands in the air. "Marilee and Logan never argue."

❧ ❧ ❧

"You want to go. . .where?"

"Logan, don't look at me like I've got three heads. I think this little trip will be ideal. I need to get away—"

"From who, me?" A worried frown creased his brow.

"Of course not." Marilee gave him a pleading look. She wanted him to understand. "I'm crazy about you, Logan. I'm not trying to get away from you. But I will admit to feeling weary. The expectations at church are enormous. Everyone thinks I should be perfect because I'm marrying the youth pastor, and I'm exhausted trying to pretend I'm something that I'm not."

Logan's expression softened. "You're being supersensitive. No one expects you to be perfect. You are loved by our congregation."

Lord, if this is Your will, help me make him understand.

"Logan, I'm not unhappy. I'm just. . .depressed. I know that doesn't seem to make sense, but I think it's the truth. When Nora and Allie voiced their protests over Kylie's driving to South Carolina alone, I really felt a pull to go along. Perhaps I didn't misunderstand God's prompting earlier. I can be an encouragement to Kylie. Oh, Logan, her heart is breaking with everything she's going through."

"I understand that, but what about you? You're my main concern."

"I was getting to that." Marilee drew in a breath. "Maybe I just need a. . .a vacation."

"You're going to have a honeymoon in two months' time."

Marilee smiled. "I know, and Colorado is supposed to be beautiful in June. I think our suite overlooking the mountains sounds heavenly." She sighed. "Unfortunately, I don't think I can wait that long. I need a break from life's daily grind."

Logan narrowed his dark gaze and appeared to consider Marilee's proposal for a long moment. Then he nodded, albeit subtly, and Marilee knew he was beginning to see her point of view. He knew how stifled she felt living with her parents. Her mother doted on her as though she were an infant, and although Marilee felt grateful for all the love and assistance her parents had provided since her car accident, she also felt smothered. She'd lived on her own in college, and after getting a teaching position at Parkway's Christian Day School, she'd rented an apartment with two other roommates. However, in her parents' defense, she understood how her accident had shaken them and why they felt the need to hover over her. But their suffocating protection, like the teen ministry, was chipping away at her sanity.

As if reading her thoughts, Logan said, "Your mom and dad will never go for it."

"Maybe I won't tell them." She grinned. "I'll just leave a note on the kitchen table that says, 'Bye.'"

"Marilee." There was a hint of warning in his voice. "You're starting to sound like one of my wayward teenagers."

"You're right." She held up her hands in surrender. "If I want to be a grown-up, then I have to be adult enough to discuss my plans with my parents."

"Right. So the trip's off."

"No, it's not." In that instant, Marilee decided to exercise a part of her will that she realized she hadn't used in many months. Trust. Had the lack of it been her problem all along? "Logan, if God wants me to befriend Kylie and help her through this rough time in her life and give me a bit of a respite in the process, then He'll work in my parents' hearts, won't He? Maybe He already has."

Logan pursed his lips in a way that was his habit. Then he raised his brows and nodded. In a word, he looked impressed.

Relief surged through Marilee's being. And peace—she felt at peace. *Lord, have I been trying to swim upstream all this time, when You've wanted to carry me along with the current?*

"Know what?"

"What?" Snapping from her musings, Marilee smiled up at Logan.

He returned the gesture, then stroked her cheek with the backs of his fingers. "I think I just saw a glimpse of the woman I fell in love with."

While he might have meant it as a compliment, Marilee felt shattered by the remark. She took a step backward, ignoring Logan's curious stare.

"I'll never be that same woman—the one you fell in love with." Her voice was but a whisper. "I'm not whole anymore."

Logan immediately looked stricken. "I didn't mean it like that. I was referring to your personality. The woman I fell in love with was always so upbeat and had a positive outlook on life. I saw those traits beginning to resurface." He smiled. "That's a good thing. You're on the mend, Mari."

She forced a grin, but the truth of his statement haunted her. *The woman I fell in love with was. . .*

Logan's words, as usual, had come straight from his heart. But little did he realize he'd spoken in the past tense.

CHAPTER FOURTEEN

This afternoon's gloomy clouds dissipated, and the sun made one last hoorah before it all but set on this day. Through the front, double-glass doors of the restaurant where they had enjoyed a late supper, Kylie could see only a russet shimmer, a final stand, before the blazing orb sank beneath the horizon. Glancing to her right, she caught snippets of a conversation between Nora and her daughter Veronica— something about catering—and Kylie wondered if it involved Allie and Jack's upcoming wedding reception. It had been one of the topics of conversation during their meal.

Feeling pressure on her elbow, Kylie turned and found Marilee standing behind her.

"I'd like you to meet my parents. There wasn't much time for more than a quick hello before we ate, and then you sat at the opposite end of the table." Marilee grinned. "Got a minute?"

Kylie returned the gesture. "Sure."

Marilee turned, and Kylie followed her across the dark carpeting.

"I haven't told my parents about my intentions to be your copilot yet," she said. "I thought I'd let them meet you first, and then we'll discuss the matter at home."

"Sounds like a plan." Kylie gave her new friend a smile. She hoped things all worked out so Marilee could ride along. Kylie decided she'd like the company. It would keep her mind off her own problems, if nothing else. The shock of discovering she'd been adopted was wearing off, and an indescribable emptiness had begun to take its place.

"Mom? Dad?"

The older couple stood near the table inside the restaurant. They paused and gave Marilee an expectant look.

"I realize that you met Kylie briefly before, but I wanted to give you a formal introduction. Kylie Rollins, I'd like you to meet my parents."

"A pleasure, Kylie." The woman smiled and stuck out her right hand. "I'm Eileen Domotor and this is my husband, Stan."

"Nice to meet you both."

Kylie shook Eileen's hand, noticing the woman's firm but friendly grip. She noticed again Eileen's well-tailored, two-piece outfit. Her brunette hair appeared to have been expertly styled. In summation, Kylie thought Mrs. Domotor had a sophisticated look about her.

Beside his wife, Stan nodded politely and didn't attempt to shake Kylie's hand. Instead, he pulled a white, linen handkerchief from the pocket of his dark suit and dabbed the beads of perspiration from his balding head. Kylie had to admit it was rather warm in this part of the restaurant.

"Marilee tells us you're from Wisconsin?"

Looking back at Eileen, Kylie nodded. "Yes, that's correct."

"We have friends who own property in Lake Geneva," Stan said. "Beautiful area."

"Yes, it is. My parents and I used to spend time during the summer with friends who lived near there."

Bittersweet sentiments filled Kylie's being, and she thought it would have been so much easier if her mother and father had been honest with her right from the beginning. They weren't her birth parents, but as far as Kylie was concerned, they would always be Mom and Dad. Had they been afraid she'd reject them if they told her the truth, or had they been protecting Blythe and her enigmatic vow?

"Kylie's on her way to South Carolina—Sabal Beach, to be exact." Marilee gave Kylie a smile. "She's going to visit her grandparents."

"How fun for you," Stan said, "especially since several inches of snow are predicted to fall in the Chicago area over the next few days."

Marilee expelled a weary sigh. "More winter."

"Oh, don't fret, Dear. Spring is just around the corner and so is your special day." Turning to Kylie, Eileen beamed. "I'm sure my daughter told you she's getting married in June."

"Yes," Kylie replied, "and I think Logan and Marilee make an adorable couple. They seem so perfect for each other." She smiled at Marilee.

"Indeed," said Stan, rocking slightly on the balls of his feet.

A few more minutes of chitchat, and then Allie, Jack, and Logan appeared. Soon another conversation ensued. It wasn't until forty-five minutes later that Kylie sat in the backseat of Jack's Explorer for the return trip to Oakland Park.

"So, I guess I just have to ask," Jack began. "What did you think of our church?"

Kylie saw him look at her through the rearview mirror, and she grinned politely. "It was. . .different. It's big." She felt uneasy and a bit self-conscious about going into detail.

Allie laughed. "Yes, it is. My home church in California is a quarter of the size of Parkway."

"Allie, Parkway is your home church now," Jack told her, and Kylie detected a facetious note. He chuckled. "Guess you can take the girl out of California, but you can't take California out of the girl."

"Yes, something like that."

Kylie relaxed, enjoying the easy banter. She felt glad that the couple didn't question her further. Overall, she had enjoyed her visit to Parkway Community Church. However, she planned to call Pastor Hanson and ask him about the differences in their faith, subtle as those differences may be.

Turning her gaze out the window, Kylie stared into the growing darkness. Only a week ago, her life had been mapped out with meticulous care. She'd known who she was, where she was going, and whom she'd marry.

But now she felt lost on an unfamiliar trail.

చి   చి   చి

"You're kidding, right?"

Marilee regarded her mother, who moved about the luxury condominium, putting odds and ends in their rightful places. Plush ivory carpet had been laid in every room, and each piece of furniture was of the best quality—from the baby grand piano in the living room to the oak entertainment cabinet in the den. Marilee hadn't grown up here but in a neighboring suburb. This condo had been a move toward retirement for her parents. Her father had yet to take that final step, however, and he still went to the office each morning, although he frequently finished up by noon.

Taking a seat in one of the oriental-styled, upholstered armchairs, Marilee wondered how she would ever convince her parents. At twenty-six years of age, she didn't need their permission, but she wanted it all the same. "I need a vacation, and Kylie needs someone to accompany her to Sabal Beach. This seems like a perfect solution."

"Impossible. You can't go now. I have a list a mile long that we have to accomplish before the wedding." Eileen summoned her husband for support. "Right, Stan?"

From his perch on the sofa, newspaper in his hands, he nodded. "This sounds like a half-baked decision at best. I can't believe Logan agreed to it."

"Well, he did, and the idea is not half-baked. I've given it some serious thought."

"Marilee, we have to assemble, stamp, and send off the invitations," her mother said. "Your bridal shower is—"

"I'll be gone for only ten days. My shower isn't for another month."

"But you've got an appointment next week to meet with the hairstylist and the makeup artist. You absolutely must try out your wedding-day look."

Marilee clenched her jaw in frustration but managed to sound calm. "I don't need to see a makeup artist and hairstylist. Allie said she'd do my makeup, and Beth Trier from church offered to fix my hair."

"Kind of them to offer, but they're not professionals. We want the best for your special day."

Eileen gave her an unintended patronizing smile, and Marilee felt like she was twelve again, and they were planning for her thirteenth birthday party.

"Mom, I—"

She cut herself off, realizing her mother refused to understand. Eileen Domotor had begun planning nothing short of an extravaganza since the day Logan proposed. At first, Marilee had been just as excited, happy to let her mother orchestrate the event. But now, everything seemed overdone and out of control.

"Now as far as this 'vacation' is concerned," Eileen said, "the very idea of it smacks of irrationality. Marilee, you know nothing about this woman. You only met her this morning."

"I know that Kylie is hurting right now. She's been through a lot. What's more, I sense she has a lot of questions about God, and I feel as though I can help her find answers."

"Of course you could, Marilee," Stan piped in, "if the timing were right. But it's not. You're struggling in that area yourself!"

"And the fact that you're willing to go running off to South Carolina with a perfect stranger," Eileen added, "only proves that you're. . .well, emotionally unstable."

Marilee gaped at her mother. Her words stung like a slap. *Emotionally unstable.* The insult was one thing, but what troubled Marilee most was the idea the phrase might truly apply to her.

The doorbell chimed, signaling someone in the lobby. Guessing it was Logan, since he was the only one known to show up unannounced at this hour, Marilee crossed the room to the front door. After discovering her hunch had been correct, she buzzed him up and left the condo to meet him at the elevators.

Walking through the quiet, dimly lit hallway, Marilee suddenly wished she and Logan were already married. She longed for him to fold her into his arms and kiss away her doubts and fears. But that wouldn't happen, at least not yet. Logan had set parameters in their relationship, strictures to which Marilee had agreed. He wanted to be a good example to his youth group by limiting their physical contact to the point that they would share their first kiss at the altar, after they'd spoken their vows—and not a minute before.

But sometimes Marilee didn't think she could wait that long.

Logan stepped off the elevator, still wearing his Sunday best. He saw her and, obviously, her pained expression and came to an abrupt halt.

She gave him a little smile. "I wasn't expecting you."

"Bad time?"

"No, I was just. . .well, discussing this road trip business with my parents."

"Yeah, I figured." Logan moved slowly forward. "That's why I decided to stop by. I thought that maybe you could use some backup. But if I'll only get in the way, I'll leave."

The uncertainty in his voice hurt and irritated her. Was she that "emotionally unstable" that he felt he had to tiptoe around her? Well, of course he'd be of that opinion; she'd snapped at him plenty of times in the past months. The poor man. Who could blame him for being skeptical?

"Listen, I'll just see you tomorrow."

"Wait, don't go," she said, winning over the annoyance in her spirit and replacing it with a deep regret. "I'm glad you're here." Lowering her gaze, she wished for the umpteenth time that she could erase the last six months and start over. "I'm sorry that I'm such a mess."

Logan closed the distance between them and put his arms around her, almost startling Marilee. She wasn't sure what merited this rare display of physical affection, but she encircled her arms about his waist and hugged him back. With her nose pressed into the shoulder of his dress shirt, she got a whiff of his spicy-sweet aftershave, but more, she sensed the devotion in his heart.

She lingered in his embrace for several long moments before he gave her a gentle squeeze, then released her.

"You looked like you needed a hug."

"I did, and that one meant the world to me." She stared ruefully into his deep brown eyes. "Logan, I don't deserve a guy like you."

A smirk tugged at the corner of his mouth, and Marilee knew she'd just set herself up.

"Just make sure you remember how wonderful I am in ten years when you're washing my dirty laundry."

Marilee laughed. "Okay, I will. I promise."

They began walking back to her parents' condo, and the smile slipped from his face. "You know, part of me doesn't want you to take off on this trip with Kylie. All the insecurities I've ever wrestled with seem to have resurfaced."

Her heart melted at his admission. As an infant, Logan's mother had left him. In college, he'd experienced a failed engagement. Both incidents had taken their toll on Logan's spirit. Marilee had vowed a long time ago that she'd never abandon him. But this was different. This was a much-needed retreat.

"It's just a ten-day getaway," she said as they started walking toward her parents' condo. "I'll be back."

"I know, but my brain and my heart don't seem to be communicating right now."

They stopped at the doorway and Marilee slipped her hand into his, entwining their fingers. "I love you, Logan. I want to marry you. This vacation won't change that." *And maybe,* she added silently, *I'll even miraculously turn back into the woman I used to be—the woman with whom you fell in love.*

જ્જ જ્જ જ્જ

Kylie sat on the air mattress in Allie Littenberg's guest room and stared at the numbers she'd pressed into her cell phone. At last, she pushed the send key to connect the call to Pastor Hanson. Allie was presently in the shower, and it wasn't too terribly late. The time seemed right.

"Hello?"

"Pastor Hanson? It's Kylie Rollins."

"Well, Kylie." He paused. "You've got Basil Creek fretting over you. In fact, Sarah and I were at the Alexanders' tonight for dinner, and. . .what's all this nonsense about you being adopted?"

"It's not nonsense. It's the truth." Kylie couldn't keep the sad note out of her voice. "But it's too long of a story to tell over the phone. I'll explain when I get home."

"And when will that be? Soon, I hope."

"A couple of weeks. By the end of March."

"Hmm."

"Pastor, I visited another church today and I heard some things I've never heard before. That's why I'm calling you. I need to ask you some questions."

"All right."

Kylie thought about what Marilee had asked her at lunchtime today. "Pastor Hanson, if you died tonight, would you be 100 percent certain that you'd go to heaven?"

A pause. "Well, yes. . ."

"How do you know?"

Another slight hesitation. "My soul is secure because I believe that Christ died to pay the debt of sin, incurred by mankind. He rose from the dead and is seated at the right hand of God the Father Almighty."

Kylie grinned. Spoken like a true preacher. "Yes, that's the same thing I heard at Parkway Community Church. But I guess I hadn't given my eternal destination much thought until today." She hesitated for an instant and glanced at the colorful pamphlet Marilee had given to her earlier. She lifted it from where it lay next to her sleeping bag and stared at the passage in which Jesus said, "Ye must be born again." On the back page, a brief "Sinner's Prayer" had been printed. While simply stated in print, salvation seemed a complicated matter.

"Pastor Hanson, when did you get, um, born again?"

"That's a very personal question."

"It is?" Kylie felt the weight of her frown creasing her brow.

"Yes, but since you're like a daughter to me, I'll answer it. I asked Jesus to save me after Sunday school one day when I was about ten or eleven."

"I've heard those terms 'saved' and 'born again' a lot today. Why haven't I heard them before?"

"Perhaps you weren't paying attention."

Kylie had to grin, hearing the lilt of amusement in her pastor's voice. But her heart felt heavy and troubled. "You know, I don't think I've ever had that kind of religious experience. I've believed all my life that Jesus Christ is God's Son. But this morning I saw the passage in the Bible about the devils believing in Him, too."

"Yes, except the devils have swallowed Satan's lies and believe they will be as gods—their own gods. On the contrary, it takes a heart of humility to cry out to be saved. I'm sure you're a Christian, Kylie. You've always been such a good girl."

Somehow that didn't pacify her. "Is Matt saved?"

"I trust he is."

"One wouldn't know it from *his* actions." Kylie couldn't keep the sarcasm from her tone.

"You're referring to what happened between him and Dena, aren't you? Well, I don't blame you for being angry. I would be, too. But all I can say in Matt's defense is that Christians make mistakes, too."

"Mistakes?" Kylie couldn't believe how her pastor trivialized the incident; however, she realized he might only know a portion of what really happened. "Pastor Hanson, if it had been only a mistake, I could forgive Matt—Matt and Dena both. But what occurred was more than that. It was sheer treachery on their parts."

"Christians are just as prone to sin as anyone else."

"Are you sure Matt and Dena are even Christians? Have you ever asked them? Did they tell you about a special time in their lives when they got saved? I never had such a conversation with either of them, and Matt was my fiancé. . .and Dena, my best friend!"

"Kylie Rollins, I am called to preach the gospel, but I cannot do the Holy Ghost's work and change a man's heart—and neither can you." There was a harsh ring of defensiveness in his voice. "The wheres, whens, and hows of an individual's faith are none of our business. Those specifics are between a person and God!"

Her cheeks burned with embarrassment and sorrow. "My apologies. I didn't mean to challenge you. I'm just looking for answers. The Christians I've met here are very open about their faith. It's more than an outward display. It's a part of them. They talk about it, and—"

"Every shepherd has his own way of caring for his flock, and it's only natural that his flock follows his example." An edge in his voice remained. "I prefer subtle evangelism to pulpit pounding. I preach God's Word; then I let God do the rest."

Time to end the call. That much rang in her soul loud and clear. "Okay, well, thanks for your time." Kylie felt close to tears. She had wanted her pastor's sympathy, not his reproof. "Sorry I phoned so late."

"Not a problem. Call anytime." Pastor Hanson's voice immediately lost its brusqueness. "But I think Matt's right to worry about you. I'm a little concerned myself. You sound like you're at the breaking point."

Kylie laughed. "I'm beyond the breaking point. I'm broken. But Allie and Jack both told me that sometimes God has to break a person. That's where I am right now. I see the writing on the wall. The scales have fallen from my eyes." She grinned at the hyperbole. "See, Pastor, I was paying attention on Sunday mornings."

"I'm worried about you, Kylie," he reiterated. Obviously, he hadn't found her facetiousness amusing in the least. "I think you should come home and seek some professional counseling. You have a lot of stress in your life right now."

He thinks I'm nuts. The realization alarmed her, but she refused to reveal it to another man who didn't understand— and who didn't want to. "I'm fine, Pastor Hanson. Really. I'm fine. Give my love to Sarah, and let Lynellen know that I'm all right. Good-bye."

With that, Kylie ended the call and pushed herself to her feet. Then she went to find Allie—the only person in the world who took her seriously.

CHAPTER FIFTEEN

Allie listened as Kylie relayed what transpired during her phone call with her pastor.

"To make matters worse," Kylie said, "I think he's taking Matt's side, and he's labeling me another irrational female."

"Hmm. Well, 'irrational' is an easy excuse a lot of men use when they're too impatient to understand and deal with female sensibilities."

"Just curious. . ." Kylie cocked her head to one side. "Does Jack understand female sensibilities?"

Allie laughed. "He's getting better. But I can't be too hard on him. He's functioned in a man's world for decades. I'm really the first woman, other than his mother, that he's opened his heart to."

A wistful-looking grin curved Kylie's lips. "That's rather touching."

"I think so." Allie returned the smile. "Remember, Kylie, the Bible tells us that with God all things are possible. That's my life's verse, and I hung onto it all through my stormy marriage. But, getting back to the irrational business, many people don't consider the spiritual aspect of their circumstances." Noticing Kylie's confused expression, she continued, "Take your situation. I think everything happening to you is part of God's road map, if you will, for your life. He's leading you on this journey, Kylie, because He loves you and He wants to be the Lord of your life. But you never would have left your comfort zone if He hadn't shaken things up a bit."

"A bit?" Kylie chuckled. "God shook things up a lot!"

Allie laughed and stood from the armchair in which she'd been sitting. Walking to the fieldstone hearth, she tossed an artificial, papered log in the fireplace and struck a match. Within minutes, a cozy, golden hue lit up the room, and Allie reclaimed her seat. She had a hunch this conversation between herself and Kylie would go on into the wee hours of the morning.

"I think there are people," Allie said, "who misinterpret God's refining fire as emotional instability. When God works in our hearts, it affects how we think, which in turn affects how we behave. So to see you questioning things and seeking out the truth about your heritage might seem 'irrational' to those who have known you all your life."

Kylie nodded, her expression tight and pensive. "I agree. But before I go one step farther, I need to be sure I'm a Christian." Her dark gaze met Allie's. "Will you help me?"

Odd, Allie thought. *Since Kylie's mother had made a decision for Christ, wouldn't she have made sure her daughter heard the same truth and had the same chance to decide for herself?*

"I mean, what do I do?"

Allie smiled. The young woman in the adjacent armchair sounded like the jailer in the Book of Acts who asked Paul and Silas, "What must I do to be saved?" Allie decided to answer in the same manner.

"Believe in the Lord Jesus Christ and you'll be saved. It's as easy as that." Standing, Allie walked over to one of the end tables and retrieved her Bible. She knelt before the chair in which Kylie was sitting and turned to the Book of Romans, where she'd penned in what was commonly known as "the Romans Road to Salvation." Allie hoped Kylie would take that path tonight.

"May I show you a few verses? They might be very familiar to you. First, Romans 3:23: 'For all have sinned, and come short of the glory of God.' " Looking up at Kylie, she asked, "Would you agree with that passage? We're all sinners?"

Kylie seemed to weigh her reply.

"Sin is a harsh word, isn't it?" Allie said. "Maybe it would help if I were to define what I mean by sin," Allie said. "The textbook definition for sin is 'a willful transgression against a known law of God.' That's just a fancy way of saying sin is knowing something is wrong and choosing to do it anyway; or knowing something is right and choosing not to do it. If this is the case, do you know anyone on earth who can say they've never sinned? Anyone?"

Kylie smiled and shook her head.

"We're all sinners. Agreed?"

"Agreed."

Allie nodded and moved on to the next verse. "Romans 6:23 states, 'For the wages of sin is death.' " Bringing her gaze back to Kylie, she added, "God is a holy God, and where He is, sin cannot dwell. Because of our sin, we forfeited the chance to gain entrance into heaven and share eternity with

Him. The payments we deserve by our sinning—the wages we earn—are spiritual death and eternal separation from God. If we hope to have eternal life beyond this physical existence, we somehow have to rid our lives of the stain of sin. But, how? No matter how hard we try, you and I can never pay the high price required to buy ourselves a pure heart again. But Someone stepped up and paid that price for us, then turned around and gave us a priceless gift. Read the next part of this verse."

Sliding the Bible onto her lap, Kylie read, " 'But the gift of God is eternal life through Jesus Christ our Lord.' "

"Do you believe Jesus Christ is the only begotten Son of God?"

"Yes. I've always believed that."

"Okay, well, I've always believed in airplanes. As a kid, I saw them in the sky. I'd see them on TV, taking off and landing. But it wasn't until I actually boarded one and sat in my assigned seat that I put my trust in that aircraft to take me to my destination." Allie grinned. "That's probably a poor illustration compared to what Jesus did for us on the cross, but the principle is similar."

Kylie smiled. "I get it."

"Okay, on to Romans 5:8," Allie said. " 'But God commendeth his love toward us, in that, while we were yet sinners, Christ died for us.' Here the apostle Paul is saying that Jesus didn't die for righteous souls, He died for sinners. . .and who's a sinner?"

"Everyone."

"Correct. So that means everyone is in need of salvation. It doesn't matter what church a person attends or how much money he has or what his social standing is—everyone needs to be saved." Allie flipped over to Romans 10:13. "The next question is, how can anyone be saved? Here's our answer. 'For whosoever shall call upon the name of the Lord shall be saved.' Kylie, that means anybody. No matter what an individual has in his or her past, he or she can be saved. Now, I'll let you read verse nine."

Kylie took the Bible. " 'That if thou shalt confess with thy mouth the Lord Jesus, and shalt believe in thine heart that God hath raised him from the dead, thou shalt be saved.' "

"Do you believe that, Kylie?"

"Yes."

"Have you ever confessed your sins to Jesus and asked Him to forgive you?"

Slowly, she shook her head. "I don't think so. I mean, the knowledge has always been there. I just never. . .boarded the airplane."

Allie couldn't help but chuckle. "Do you want to?"

After a moment's deliberation, she nodded.

ॐ   ॐ   ॐ

The next morning, Marilee phoned early to say she was coming along. Kylie felt elated that she'd have companionship on the way to Sabal Beach. She and Marilee seemed to get along well, and they laughed about everyone thinking they were wacky for dashing off to South Carolina. At least they were going crazy together. But Allie had made a good point: They would need a place to stay, nutty or not, and it might prove unwise to wait until the last minute to make hotel reservations. So Kylie phoned the Hampton Inn in Charleston and booked a double room. Then she worked up her nerve to contact the Chadwyks. This seemed as good a time as any to e-mail the older couple and ask to stay in their bed and breakfast, at least for a few nights.

Seated at Allie's kitchen table, Kylie opened her notebook

computer and began creating her post. She wanted to be direct, and yet she didn't want to shock the Chadwyks, nor did she want to divulge the sad news of her mother's death. As difficult as it might be to tell them face-to-face, Kylie deemed it the best way to notify them of the fact. She had no idea if the pair knew Rob had been killed. Regardless, Kylie decided she wouldn't divulge that in an impersonal E-mail either.

Finally, reading over her letter, she hoped she had accomplished her goal.

Dear Mr. and Mrs. Chadwyk,

I'm writing because I have reason to believe we're related. I recently discovered that I was adopted and that you might be my grandparents. My adoptive mother's first name was Wendy, but it turns out she was really my aunt. Just days ago, I learned my biological father was Rob Chadwyk, my mother's brother. My biological mother's name is Blythe Severson, who, at this time, refuses to discuss the matter with me. I hope she'll change her mind. In any case, the news of my adoption has been quite a shock to me, as you can imagine.

I am on my way to South Carolina for a ten-day vacation, and I wondered if I might stay at The Light House for at least part of the time so we can meet and so I can find out if what I suspect is true. I can provide you with photographs, which may substantiate my claim. I hope you'll agree to speak with me. Please e-mail me with your reply.

Sincerely Yours,
Kylie Dawn Rollins

P.S. I have a friend traveling with me.

hymn called "O Teach Me What It Meaneth," and Marilee wished she were up there singing, too. This was one of her favorites, and the words and melody combined always spoke to her heart—or used to. She had once been a part of the music ministry here at Parkway. God-honoring music was a vital part of her life. But since her accident, the song in her heart seemed to have diminished note by note.

"O teach me what it meaneth:
    Thy love beyond compare;
The love that reaches deeper
    Than depths of self-despair.
Yes, teach me till there gloweth
    In this cold heart of mine,
Some feeble, pale reflection
    Of that pure love of Thine."

The stanza plucked a familiar chord in the depth of her being, but then Marilee's gaze came to rest on Jill Binion in the alto section, and the harmony in her spirit went awry. Jill had been her roommate and friend, but a couple of months ago, she publicly predicted that Marilee would ruin Logan's ministry if she didn't stop feeling sorry for herself.

Lord, no one understands. . . .

The choir reached the last stanza, and Marilee felt close to tears.

"That was really lovely," Kylie said, leaning over the armrest between the two seats.

"Yes."

Unfortunately, Marilee's sullen spirit prevented her from enjoying the song, largely because she believed what Jill had said was true. She would likely damage Logan's ministry if

∽ ∽ ∽

It was late Monday afternoon before Kathryn had a chance to check her E-mail. She sat down in the far corner and booted up her computer. At last, she accessed her inbox and saw that her cousin Tabatha had sent a post, announcing the date of this year's family reunion. Next, she waded through several humorous forwards from friends before one particular E-mail caught her eye. It had been sent from someone with the screen name "librarylady." Curiosity prompted Kathryn to open it, and as she took in the message, her heart began to pound. A granddaughter! In all her surprise and nervousness, she had to read the post three times before she understood that Kylie was Rob's daughter, although Wendy had raised her.

"Lee!" She shrieked. "Lee, come quick!"

Within moments, he appeared in the hallway behind her. "What is it?"

TJ had answered her cry as well. "Are you okay, Kathryn?"

Slowly, she turned in her desk chair and faced them. "You're not going to believe this," she said, feeling stunned herself. "We have a granddaughter. She's coming to visit."

∽ ∽ ∽

By dusk on Monday, Kylie and Marilee had driven as far as Lexington, Kentucky. They found a hotel, one with an indoor swimming pool at Kylie's request, unloaded their luggage into their room, and then drove off in search of a restaurant. They ended up at Cracker Barrel. Since it was a national chain, both women knew what to expect.

"You look really tired," Kylie said, noticing the shadows beneath her new friend's brown eyes.

"I am. I didn't sleep well last night."

"Because of the argument with your parents?"

"Partly that, yes." Marilee took a sip of her diet cola before continuing. "Hey, look, I'm sorry I complained for the first one-hundred-and-fifty miles of our trip. My parents mean well, and I know they love me. My accident was, in some ways, more traumatic for them than for me."

"You don't have to apologize. I did my share of griping today." Kylie squeezed the lemon into her iced tea. "I practically told you my life's story."

Marilee perked up. "Oh, I enjoyed hearing every word. You didn't gripe at all."

"Okay, so we're even." Kylie grinned.

Marilee smiled back. "Just for the record, I wasn't complaining about Logan either. He's a wonderful guy."

"Yeah, but he's still a guy and they have faults, too. No one's perfect." Kylie shook her head. "Marilee, relax. You didn't sin or anything, if that's what you're thinking. You're fine. So stop apologizing."

"All right." Marilee appeared properly chagrined.

"So what do you want to do when we get back to the hotel? Go swimming, then watch a movie?"

Marilee nodded. "Sounds good."

"What kind of movies do you like? I enjoy watching what Matt calls 'chick flicks.' *While You Were Sleeping* is one of my favorites."

"Oh, mine, too!" Marilee chuckled. "Logan and I laughed when we saw that film because the hero's got the same last name—except he spelled Callahan a different way."

"That's right." Kylie smiled. "Well, you're lucky Logan would watch it with you. Matt refused. I have to go to 'chick flicks' with my girlfriends. But I'll have you know, I sat through *The Terminator* with him."

Marilee scrunched up her nose in distaste. "I never saw

that one. Don't care to either. Not my thing, I guess."

"Mine either. Trust me."

Marilee laughed.

"My mom and I went to a lot of movies together. My parents were my best friends, and after my dad died, my mom and I grew even closer. I was perfectly happy to go out to dinner with Mom on Friday nights while most of my friends, Matt included, went to the Red Rocket Lounge and listened to some amateur live band."

"Have your feelings for your mother changed at all now that you know you were adopted?"

Kylie pondered the question. "No. I guess not. Knowing my parents, they just wanted to shield me from the hurtful truth. Although I'll know more if Blythe will ever agree to speak with me. It could very well be that my parents were honoring her wishes."

"True. It's great that you're not harboring any bitterness."

"How can I? As I think over my life, I've been given everything I wanted. I had a happy childhood. I was well taken care of. I loved my parents and they loved me. I know so many who were much less fortunate than I."

"Perhaps, but don't you think it's unwise to compare your situation with someone else's?"

"Maybe. But I've had the past two days to think about everything, and as shocked as I was at first, as betrayed as I felt initially, I honestly can't find it in my soul to be angry with my mom and dad."

"You're a better woman than I am, Kylie Rollins."

She rolled her eyes. "You know what? You need to develop some backbone." She smiled, hoping to encourage Marilee, not chasten her. "Not everything bad that happens is your fault or a result of some. . .some sin you accidentally committed."

"I know that." Marilee's color heightened, indicating her embarrassment.

"And I don't ever want to hear you say or even imply again that Logan is too good for you. That's absurdity. He loves you, and you're just as 'whole' right now sitting across from me in this booth as you were six or seven months ago."

A rueful expression crossed her face. "Kylie, you don't understand. . .and how could you? You can have children."

"Well, we're assuming I can. I've never tried. What if for some reason I can't conceive? Will my husband love me any less?" Kylie took another drink of her beverage and narrowed her gaze. "He'd better not or he'll face the wrath of Kylie."

Marilee chuckled. "I admire your tenacity."

"Maybe some of it'll rub off on you."

"Yeah. That might not be such a bad thing."

Kylie laughed just as the server appeared carrying their dinners. She felt relaxed and. . .happy for the first time in so very long.

When their waitress walked away, Marilee suggested they pray. Bowing her head in reverence, Kylie knew this trip was what she and Marilee both needed. They weren't just headed to Sabal Beach; they were on the road to healing.

CHAPTER SIXTEEN

Kylie towel-dried her hair after a refreshing dip in the hotel's swimming pool. She and Marilee were delighted to find they had the pool to themselves. Apparently, there weren't many guests with penchants for doing laps at this particular hotel on a Monday night.

Stepping out of the bathroom, Kylie overheard snatches of Marilee's telephone conversation.

"I'm feeling fine, Logan. Tell Mom and Dad to stop worrying. Kylie stopped every couple of hours and we stretched our legs, and tonight we went swimming here at the hotel. It did wonders for my leg and hip. Maybe that's what I need in my life. Swimming."

Kylie grinned and sat down on one of the two double beds in their room and pulled her notebook computer onto her lap. She turned it on and waited for Marilee to finish up so she could plug into the phone line and check her E-mail. Having forgotten her cell phone in the car, Marilee opted to use her calling card and save herself a trip back outside.

"I'm sorry to hear Carolyn McGregor has the chicken pox. That's one of the worst things that can happen to a sixteen-year-old girl." Marilee chuckled at Logan's reply. "I love you, too. Yes, I'll call you tomorrow night. Promise. Bye."

A whip of jealousy stung Kylie. She wished she had a fiancé as dependable and trustworthy as Logan Callahan. And, in that very second, Kylie both loved and hated Matt. She missed him, but at the same time, she wished she never had to see him again. Odd, how the boundaries between one feeling and the other suddenly blurred.

Marilee hung up the phone, and Kylie padded across the dark carpet and plugged in her computer. She hoped to see a message from the Chadwyks, and she sent up a quick prayer of thanks when she wasn't disappointed.

Dear Kylie,

My husband, Lee, and I would be happy to speak with you. Give us the dates that you will be in town, and we'll reserve a room for you here at The Light House. I'll look forward to your arrival.

Respectfully,
Kathryn Chadwyk

Kylie finished reading the E-mail and felt discouraged. It wasn't a warm and fuzzy letter as she'd imagined. On the contrary, the post sounded stiff and formal.

However, it wasn't enough to deter Kylie completely. She clicked on the reply button and wrote:

Dear Mrs. Chadwyk,

*Thank you for writing back to me. My friend
Marilee and I will be in Charleston tomorrow night.
We have reservations at the Hampton Inn for the next
six days. I am aware that what I previously stated must
have come as a shock. So if you would rather Marilee
and I didn't stay at The Light House, I could meet you
and your husband for lunch at your convenience.*

~Kylie Rollins

❧   ❧   ❧

TJ didn't like it. He didn't like it one bit. "We know nothing about this girl. She could be anything from a fortune hunter to a murderer to a petty thief. I vote we hire a PI to check her out."

"Doesn't sound like we've got that much time," Lee said, a frown creasing his tanned forehead. Having just returned from an afternoon's round of golf, he still wore his khaki pants and a yellow polo shirt. "She'll be in Charleston tonight."

"We could run some sort of background check on her," TJ said. "There must be a Web site we can log onto that'd help us out."

"You think so?" Kathryn asked. In a navy skirt and printed blouse, she'd draped a red cotton sweater around her shoulders to stave off the cool sea breezes that blew in through the opened door.

TJ shrugged. "The way I see it, it wouldn't hurt to find out."

"I agree," Lee said.

Kathryn stood and began pacing back and forth across the colorful blue, yellow, and white geometrical rug in the sunroom, an ominous expression on her age-lined face. "But Kylie knew Wendy's name. She said Rob Chadwyk was her father. . . ." Kathryn paused in midstride and whirled to face the men. "Did either of you notice that Kylie used the past tense when referring to them?" Her gaze lingered on her husband. "Oh, Lee, what does that mean?"

"I guess we'll find out soon enough."

"Look, we can't just open our home and our hearts to this woman." TJ felt a tad hypocritical as those words tumbled from his mouth. Where would he be today if the Chadwyks hadn't offered him a job and taken him in? His history included a stint in 'Nam, and after returning to the U.S., all the fighting and killing over there hadn't made a lick of sense to him. For years, drugs and alcohol numbed his confusion. To top it off, he'd had a police record a mile long. Thus, he was in one sorry state that day he arrived in Sabal Beach and stumbled onto the Chadwyks' doorstep.

But this situation was different.

"Kathryn, your searches on the Internet might've opened you up to all kinds of scams. I tried to warn you about plugging in personal information."

"And I heeded that warning," Kathryn said, lifting her chin like a defiant child.

TJ grinned.

"Besides, Kylie says she's bringing pictures that might prove we're her grandparents." A pained expression crossed her face, and TJ noted the faraway look in her eyes. "Grandparents. . ."

Feeling like he had to protect these precious people, he stood from the armchair in which he'd been sitting. "Look, I'll see what I can find out about Kylie Rollins."

"TJ, that's unnecessary. I know you have other plans today."

He tried to give Kathryn an assuring smile. "I'd drop

anything to help you out. You've been more of a mother to me than the woman who carried me in her womb and attempted to bring me up." TJ shook his head, disgusted with the memory. "She did a lousy job raising me and my two brothers, one of whom is dead, as you know, and the other's in jail. But that woman sure could raise a ruckus on a Friday night at the corner tavern." He looked at Lee. "And you've already heard the horror stories about my dear ol' daddy."

Lee reached out and touched TJ's forearm. "The past is dead and gone, Son."

"Right." He met Lee's gaze with a sure and steady one of his own. "So maybe we should just keep it that way."

తు తు తు

The next morning, Kylie and Marilee set out early. After reaching Knoxville, they selected the route through the Smoky Mountain National Park which led them into the small, tourist towns of Sevierville, Pigeon Forge, and Gatlinburg. They couldn't help but stop and behave just like. . .tourists. Almost immediately, they discovered Governor's Crossing, a unique structure housing twenty-five outlet stores. Then they found the Mountain Mall and spent a couple of additional hours shopping. Next Marilee wanted to tour the Thomas Kinkade Gallery, while Kylie had fun nosing around neighboring knickknack stores. Finally, after a satisfying lunch, they climbed back into Kylie's Outback and hit the road. By late afternoon, they entered North Carolina.

As Kylie drove through the Great Smoky Mountains, she felt awed by the surrounding beauty. She understood now how the mountains got their name as she witnessed the defining "smoky" appearance in the distant peaks. Flowers bloomed along the winding highway, and the buds on the trees had opened to the warm sunshine. While it was still largely winter in Wisconsin and northern Illinois, it was most definitely spring in this part of the United States.

"I'm glad we decided to drive through the Parkway," Marilee said after they'd stopped to admire the view at one of the many lookout points. The warm afternoon wind tousled their hair. "Might not be the quickest way to the Atlantic, but I'll bet it's the most scenic."

"How could anyone doubt there's a God in heaven after seeing a sight like this?" Kylie stared out across the deep, tree-studded valley and rested her gaze on the mountainous horizon.

"It's been my experience that a good many people believe in God. They just refuse to believe their sin nailed Jesus Christ to the cross—and He allowed it to happen in order to fulfill His Father's perfect will."

Kylie grinned and glanced over at Marilee. "You're going to make a terrific pastor's wife. You can write his sermons for him."

They shared a laugh, then stood and ambled back to the car.

"Sorry. I didn't mean to be preachy back there," Marilee said as they continued driving through the picturesque scenery.

"Oh, you weren't. And to tell you the truth, I'm sort of envious of you. . .and Allie, too. You're both so confident about your Christian faith, and it's obvious you try to live it out. So talking about it is like everyday conversation for you."

"Yes, I suppose it is."

"Like the Bible study we did together this morning. I think I learned more in that hour at breakfast than I have in a host of Sundays."

"Kylie, have you ever thought about changing churches

once you get back home? Logan can give you a list of good Bible-believing churches in your area."

"I don't know." Kylie wasn't comfortable with that idea. She'd been a member of her tiny rural church all her life. "Maybe the problem hasn't been with Pastor Hanson all these years, but with me. Now that I'm sure I'm a Christian, I'll probably get more out of his sermons."

"Well, that may be true. The Lord may want to use you in your present congregation."

"I hadn't really thought about it like that before. But I can't imagine God using me."

Marilee grinned. "I think we all feel that way—undeserving. And we are. But that's why it's so cool when the Lord does use us. I know that when He uses me to minister to another person, it strengthens my faith and gives me a. . .a reason for being."

Kylie smiled. "See, you're going to make one terrific pastor's wife."

Marilee didn't reply for several long moments. But finally she spoke in a soft voice that plucked a wistful chord in Kylie's heart. "You don't even know it, but God is using you already."

∽ ∽ ∽

TJ paid one hundred and sixty-five dollars to have a background check run on Kylie Rollins. He'd found a secured Internet site recommended by lawyers, politicians, and high-profile businesspeople. The site reported within eight hours, and TJ had learned Kylie was from Wisconsin, she paid her income taxes on time last year, and she was employed by Basil Creek's Public Library, part of the La Crosse County Federated Library System. As for a criminal past, Kylie Rollins didn't have so much as a speeding ticket on her record. Learning the information put TJ's mind at ease. But, as of last night,

Kylie hadn't checked into any of the Hampton Inns in Charleston.

The news disturbed Kathryn when she heard it the next morning at breakfast. "I didn't get another E-mail from her. I hope she didn't change her mind." Kathryn picked at her grapefruit. "Perhaps I was too curt in my initial reply. But I wanted to be careful." She shook her head. "I remember Wendy often accused me of—"

"Kathryn, stop it," Lee said in a stern but gentle tone. He folded the newspaper and set it on the edge of the block-glass tabletop. "No sense in blaming yourself if, indeed, Kylie had a change of heart."

TJ set his large hand over the older woman's fragile one. "Kathryn, it could be Kylie is sharing a room with her friend, and they registered under that friend's name. Or it could be they just didn't check in yet."

"Marilee. That's her friend's first name," Kathryn said with a hopeful look. "Check for a Marilee."

"I will. I'm going to do some calling around again this afternoon."

"Good." Worry clouded Kathryn's hazel eyes, and she pulled her pink bathrobe more tightly around her. "I pray nothing dreadful has happened to her. . .them."

TJ sat back in his chair. "We've got to keep in mind that God's in control here. I, for one, tend to forget that fact."

"We're all guilty of it," Lee said with a grin. He glanced at his wife. "Relax, Kathryn. God's taking care of this situation."

She looked from Lee to TJ and back to Lee again. She gave them each a resigned smile. "Seeing as I'm outnumbered, I guess I have no choice, do I?"

"None," TJ quipped, rising from his seat.

Gathering his dishes, he carried them from the breakfast

nook into the kitchen, where Lissa Elliot busied herself with food items and carried them into the dining hall where the guests of The Light House were offered a scrumptious buffet.

"Teej," she said, running his name together on one sweet note, "I could use some help. That family out there is eating me out of house and home!"

He glanced at his wristwatch. "Well, the good news is they've only got another hour of chow time."

Lissa gave him a withering look and TJ laughed. He didn't mean to be cruel, but he wasn't about to get caught in her domestic web like an unsuspecting fly. Kitchens were dangerous places for single guys—especially when inhabited by persistent widow spiders like Lissa.

Depositing his dishes in the sink, TJ nodded out a goodday greeting and left. As he made his way to the shed, he almost wished he could warm up to Lissa. He had his lonely times, and she was pretty enough to keep him company: blond hair that was cut into a sassy style, trim figure, ocean blue eyes that beckoned him, and an amusing pink pout whenever he refused.

Lord, she's just too young for me and she's got those kids. . . .

Fatherhood, and for that matter, becoming a husband, scared TJ more than the most ominous storm he'd ever chased. He had this nightmarish vision of damaging another person's psyche—like his dad had damaged his, his siblings', and even his mother's. Sure, things were different. TJ was as similar to his dad as the sand was to the sea. TJ had been saved by grace, but his father had died in his sin, despite TJ's best efforts to share his faith with the perishing old man.

Nevertheless, a passage from the Old Testament Book of Numbers haunted TJ. "The Lord is longsuffering, and of great mercy, forgiving iniquity and transgression, and by no means clearing the guilty, visiting the iniquity of the fathers upon the children unto the third and fourth generation."

While TJ understood that he fell into the "forgiven" category, he also couldn't get past the part about God "visiting the iniquity of the fathers" on their offspring. In a word, TJ felt cursed when it came to being a spouse or parent. Therefore, he figured he'd better not press the issue. Unlocking the aluminum shed door, TJ opened it and extracted his toolbox. He shook off thoughts of Lissa Elliot and everything associated with her. There were plenty of things around The Light House to keep him busy today, including playing private eye this afternoon. He'd focus on digging up information on Kylie Rollins.

And after that, who knows? he thought, strolling back to the house. *Maybe a good storm will be on the horizon.*

CHAPTER SEVENTEEN

I figure we'll get to Charleston by noon tomorrow," Marilee said, plopping onto one of the beds in their hotel room in Asheville, North Carolina. "This has been so much fun."

Kylie grinned. She couldn't agree more. They'd lost a day's travel time, but it had been worth it. "I want to tour the Biltmore Estate before we leave in the morning." She lifted the brochure that she'd picked up in the hotel's lobby. "Listen to this. The place was built in 1895 by George Vanderbilt, and it's got thirty-two guest rooms, a billiard room, an indoor gymnasium, and a bowling alley." Kylie glanced up. "Can you believe it? There are two hundred and fifty rooms total. All that in one house!"

"Just think about how many missionaries that man could have supported if he'd scaled down his mansion a bit."

Kylie laughed. "It does sound rather obscene, doesn't it?

But I've got to see it anyhow."

Marilee smiled and crawled into bed. "Well, in that case, we'll be lucky if we reach Charleston by sunset."

"Who cares?" Kylie said, reaching for her cellular phone. "We're on vacation."

"Good point."

They shared a smile while Kylie turned on her phone to check for messages. She didn't know why she bothered since the only person liable to call was Matt. But, just in case some unforeseen emergency had occurred, she decided she'd best make the effort.

"You have three unheard messages," the computerized voice told her.

Kylie listened, and just as she suspected, Matt had phoned.

"Hi, Ky. Just called to say hi. . ., and, um. . .well, Pastor Hanson said you phoned him Sunday night, asking all sorts of questions. He's worried about you, too. I feel like I might have driven you over the edge or something, and I'm just sick about it."

Kylie glanced at Marilee. "Matt thinks I'm nuts now, too."

Marilee yawned. "Call him back and tell him we shopped all day so you feel sane again."

Laughing, Kylie strained to hear the end of Matt's message.

". . .said he'd take care of things here so I could drive down to Chicago to be with you."

"Oh, no. . ." A frown pulling at her brow, Kylie quickly pressed the end button and dialed Matt's number. It rang four times, and she almost disconnected by the time he picked up.

"Good," she said, "you haven't left. Don't come to Chicago. I'm not there."

"Kylie?"

"Yeah." She tried to tamp down her bitterness, but it didn't work. "Were you expecting someone else?"

She heard Matt's indignant sigh and reminded herself not to react. Any show of emotion would fuel the ideology that she was unstable and that she needed him. Well, she wasn't. . .and she didn't!

Now if only she could prove it.

"Sorry about that, Matt. My remark was uncalled-for." Kylie finger-combed her hair away from her forehead. "Listen, I'm calling to tell you I'm fine and there's no need to worry." She forced a softer inflection into her voice. "But don't drive to Chicago. Like I said, I'm not there. I'm in North Carolina. I'm on my way to meet the Chadwyks."

"Yeah, that's what Dena thought you might be doing."

A rush of anger rose up in Kylie so fast it took her breath away.

"And don't get the wrong idea. I haven't spoken a word to her," Matt quickly added, as if perceiving Kylie's thoughts. "I actually haven't spoken more than a couple of sentences to Dena since. . .well, you know. Since that incident in January."

Kylie felt suddenly nauseated.

"She's been talking to Mom. They're both worried about you. . .just as I am."

"Don't worry. I'm fine." However, she felt anything but fine as unshed tears threatened to choke her. "And, Matt, please don't call me anymore. I start feeling better and then I hear your voice, and it's as if my wounds get ripped open all over again."

Silence filled the airspace.

"Bye, Matt," Kylie said at last. She meant each syllable from the bottom of her heart.

She ended the call and stared at her phone with misty eyes.

"Oh, Kylie. . ." Marilee threw off her bedcovers and came

to sit beside her. She draped a sisterly arm across Kylie's shoulders. "I know you're hurt. I would be, too. You're not 'unstable' or 'irrational.'" Marilee paused to give her a little hug. "You're a woman, and we have a right to our emotions."

With a sniff, Kylie turned to look at Marilee.

She returned an embarrassed little smile. "Guess I need to take some of my own advice, huh?"

A grin escaped Kylie. "My mom used to say, 'It's hard to see the picture when you're inside the frame.'"

"True. . ."

Kylie sniffed and Marilee reached for the Kleenex box. She set it in Kylie's lap, and they sat in an amicable quiet for the next few minutes.

"I'm really glad you came along on this trip," Kylie finally said. "Everyone might think we're nuts, but the irony is that we're on the road to healing."

"You're absolutely right." Marilee withdrew her arm. "Feeling a little better?"

"Yeah." She stood and put the tissue box back on the bed-side table.

After tucking herself back into bed, Marilee grew pensive for several long moments. "Kylie?"

"Hmm. . . ?"

"Ever think about forgiving Matt?"

"Sure. I forgave him the night he told me about him and Dena. But I can't forget what he did. I'll never forget it!"

Marilee propped herself up on one elbow. "But don't you see? You may not be able to forget, but you can forgive and put the offense behind you—just like God puts our sins as far from Him as the east is from the west."

"Well, He can do that because He's God." Kylie shook her head. "I can't."

"Why?"

"Because, like you said, I'm a woman, entitled to my emotions," she quipped. "Besides," she added, growing serious again, "for me to overlook what Matt did would mean I'd have to slip right back into the person I was before. . . Basil Creek's librarian, Matt Alexander's fiancée, Dena Hubbard's best friend. . .and the Rollinses' daughter. Unfortunately, that woman doesn't exist anymore."

"No one understands more than I do. Since my accident, I'm not the same. But I'll bet Matt's not the same guy he was a couple of weeks ago either. Don't you see, Kylie? Here's your opportunity to show him Christlike love and win his heart forever. Dena's, too, for that matter."

Kylie tossed her a look of mock exasperation. "Maybe I'm not so glad you came along after all."

With a long dramatic sigh, Marilee turned over, her back to Kylie. "Okay. I'll shut up."

Kylie laughed. "Logan would be proud of you if he knew how much preaching you've been doing."

"No, he wouldn't. He'd say I give up too easily."

"Lucky for me."

They chuckled, and it wasn't long before they were giggling like schoolgirls.

৶ ৶ ৶

TJ pulled his favorite tan Stetson off his bald head as he ambled into the Hampton Inn to inquire about Kylie. The Chadwyks hadn't heard a word from her since Katherine got the E-mail Monday night. Since no one seemed to want to divulge much information over the phone, TJ decided to make a personal stop.

Approaching the registration desk, he noticed the female clerk looked no older than seventeen, slim build, short brown hair, and red-framed glasses. She appeared the studious type, quiet and intelligent, and after TJ handed her his business card and relayed a sketchy version of the situation, she was eager to help.

"Our records show Ms. Rollins revised her reservation, and she's arriving tonight," the girl said, checking the computer. "But she hasn't shown up yet."

"Thanks. Mind if I hang out in the lobby for awhile?"

"No, go ahead."

TJ grinned. "Any chance I could buy a cup of coffee?"

She smiled. "Help yourself, Mr. McGwyer. We serve fresh coffee day and night." She pointed to the long back counter in the far side of the lobby.

TJ dipped his head in a gesture of gratitude. "Good customer service skills."

"Thanks. Maybe you could let my boss know so I'll get a raise."

"Good head for business, too." TJ grinned. "Sure, I'll let him know."

"Her." The young lady produced a business card and slid it across the registration desk. "My boss is a female."

Holding the card between two fingers, TJ saluted before plunging it into his shirt pocket. Then he set off to find the coffee. What he hoped to do was catch a glimpse of Kylie Rollins and maybe even talk to her—find out her true intentions. However, TJ had to admit that after reading Kylie's first E-mail, the one she'd initially sent Kathryn, he now suspected the younger woman merely wanted to find her roots, a rather popular practice. Plus, the recent discovery that she had been adopted might have prompted Kylie's search—assuming she'd told the truth in her E-mails.

But for now, TJ resigned himself to waiting.

Two and a half hours later, the local news came on and TJ watched it on the lobby's television set.

"This is your news for Thursday, March 23, 2000," a deep male voice announced, followed by the broadcast's dramatic theme music.

TJ yawned and decided to hang around until after the sports. Twenty minutes later, he wished he'd remembered that segment always came at the end of the newscast.

He stood and stretched, preparing to take his leave. Then, just when he'd abandoned the idea of meeting Kylie and her friend, two women entered the hotel. One wore a denim jumper and the other, blue jeans and a striped T-shirt. They were both dark-headed, but the one in the jeans had hair so black it shone blue. Setting down their luggage, the ladies muttered something to the clerk before taking off in the direction of the rest room.

Mustering his patience, TJ reclaimed his seat in the lobby. He lifted the newspaper he'd already read so as not to appear conspicuous and kept his gaze on the hallway leading into the bathrooms. It seemed like another half hour before the women exited. But when TJ got a good look at the gal with the ebony hair, there was no longer a doubt in his mind that she was a Chadwyk. He'd seen enough pictures of Rob and Wendy to know that Kylie Rollins resembled her father.

Slowly, TJ stood and made his way over to the registration desk. "Excuse me, are you Kylie Rollins?"

It was as if Snow White herself turned to face him, ivory skin and jet-black hair. "Yes, I'm Kylie Rollins."

TJ extracted one of his business cards. He didn't want to come across as too forward; however, he sensed Kathryn would have apoplexy if he returned home without her granddaughter. It was so blatantly obvious that Kylie's claim was true. And if she had pictures. . .

Oh, Lord, when I said I'd like a good storm, this wasn't exactly what I had in mind. TJ sensed Kylie's arrival would stir up the past but good.

Kylie accepted his proffered card, read it, and looked back at him. "Oh. The Light House."

"I work for the Chadwyks. We'd like it if the two of you would stay with us." He looked at the hotel clerk and grinned. "No offense."

The friendly clerk of hours ago had been replaced with a no-nonsense older gent who now glared at TJ. "There's a fifty-dollar cancellation fee because—"

"I'll pay it," TJ cut in before his gaze returned to Kylie. "What do you say?"

"Um. . ." She turned to her friend.

The other woman shrugged, but her concern was evident on her face.

"I'm harmless, and you'll be perfectly safe at The Light House."

The women exchanged glances once more, and TJ wondered what he could say to win their trust. "If you'd like to give the Chadwyks a call to verify who I am, you're more than welcome to do so."

Kylie's dark eyes narrowed and she scrutinized him so hard that TJ nearly grinned. "I don't know. . . . " She turned to her friend. "What do you think, Marilee?"

"I'm okay with it, and we could always call Jack on the way to make sure things are cool."

Kylie whirled back around and glanced at TJ. "We have a friend who's a cop. So if you're not who you say you are, we'll find out."

TJ wanted to laugh at the implied threat. But the sad fact

was, if folks searched his background the way he had investigated Kylie's, they'd get an eyeful of his blemished past.

"Well, ladies, I have to be honest with you," TJ said, leaning his elbow on the desktop. "If your friend the policeman runs a check on me, he'll find I have a record a mile long. Now, I don't mean to frighten you, but I wasn't always the guy I am today. I'm a law-abiding, churchgoing citizen now, although I wasn't until ten years ago, when the Chadwyks hired me." He nodded, indicating the clerk. "I'm willing to pay the cancellation fee if you two would like to stay at The Light House. I know it would please your grandmother, Kylie. But if you're uncomfortable, stay here. You can always meet the Chadwyks another time."

"I sensed from our last correspondence that Mrs. Chadwyk wasn't all too thrilled about meeting me."

"You're referring to her E-mail in reply to yours?"

"Yes."

"You couldn't be more wrong there. Kathryn Chadwyk has been thinking of nothing except meeting you for the last two days. She did mention that she was trying to be careful with her reply until we could find out more about you. She's been doing searches on the Internet, hoping to locate either Rob or Wendy, and as you might know, there are tons of scams on the Net." TJ purposely dropped names in an effort to prove himself honorable.

Kylie regarded him askance. "How can you be certain I am who I say I am?"

TJ couldn't hold back a chuckle. "One, I paid to have a background check run on you, and two, I've got a set of good eyes. I can see you're a Chadwyk. Now, what's the word, Miss Rollins? You and your friend staying, or are you coming with me?"

She looked aghast. "You ran a background check on me?"

TJ gave her a single nod. "Can't be too careful in this day and age. Now what's it going to be?"

After a brief hesitation, she turned to Marilee. Something passed between them that TJ couldn't define. But at long last, Kylie accepted the invitation.

"Good," he muttered, pulling out his wallet from the back pocket of his jeans. He handed the clerk a fifty. "I've been sitting here so long I feel like a piece of petrified wood." Replacing the leather billfold, he picked up the women's suitcases and headed for the hotel's front doors. "Follow me, ladies."

ↈ   ↈ   ↈ

Kylie had little trouble staying close behind TJ McGwyer's dusty gray Chevy Silverado. The vehicle was much larger than Matt's, but of late Kylie had a loathing for all pickups, no matter what shape or size they came in. Of course, she knew it wasn't the truck's fault its driver had been a drunken fool one cold January night. Still, association was a powerful phenomenon.

"Mr. McGwyer reminds me of that wrestler who's now the governor of Minnesota," Marilee said. "What's his name? Hulk Hogan?"

"No, Silly! That's Jesse Ventura." Kylie started laughing only to realize her stomach muscles were sore from all the carrying on she and Marilee had done all day. "Ohhh," she sighed, "don't get me started again."

"I won't. I promise. You need to watch the road."

"I am. Don't worry."

Kylie noticed that when roads were crowded or dark, or if there was a lot of construction taking place, Marilee became anxious. She admitted her nervousness was due to her accident, so Kylie made sure she slowed down and used more care than usual.

As they left Charleston behind, the road grew narrower and streetlights fewer and farther between. It was obvious that they drove across inlets, and either sides of the highway looked like great black holes. The lights of Charleston were but sparkling gems on a dark, velvety horizon.

Minutes later, they came upon a sign announcing their entrance into James Island. They drove through the small town and soon passed eateries that offered fresh crab and shrimp specials.

Slowing at an intersection, Kylie recalled one of TJ's remarks, and it began to haunt her. He had made mention of "Kathryn" trying to locate Rob or Wendy. Kylie assumed that meant her grandparents didn't know both their children were dead. *Which means I have to tell them.* Her heart took a dive.

"Marilee, will you pray? Pray for us. . .for me and meeting the Chadwyks. Pray that I'll know how to answer all the questions they must have."

"Sure. I'll do it right now." Marilee bowed her head in reverence. "Dearest, most precious heavenly Father, Kylie and I turn over our hearts and minds to You. We love You, Jesus. We worship You, and we long to bring honor and glory to Your name with everything we say and do."

Kylie prayed along but continued to concentrate on her driving. Until yesterday, she'd never known someone could pray while performing other tasks—such as maneuvering an automobile down a mountain road.

"Lord, You said that if any person lacks wisdom, he or she should ask. So we are asking now that You give Kylie wisdom as she meets her grandparents for the very first time.

We ask that You open the Chadwyks' hearts, and give all of us Your peace. We thank You for what You have already done and for what You will do in the days to come. In Jesus' name, amen."

A comforting warmth spread through Kylie's body, like smooth hot cocoa on a cold night. She somehow knew right then that God had heard their prayer. "Thanks, Marilee. I feel less nervous already."

Less than a minute later, they drove by a sign that read:

Welcome to
SABAL BEACH
The Edge of America

CHAPTER EIGHTEEN

Kathryn hurried to get dressed after TJ called from his mobile phone. She'd been in bed, nearly asleep, when she heard the news. "Your granddaughter is following me as we speak," he'd said, "and, Kathryn, there's no question about it. She's a Chadwyk."

"Oh, merciful Father. . ."

Kathryn rushed to the bathroom and brushed out her hair. Then she made her way downstairs to find her husband. She sent up a prayer of thanks that she didn't stumble down the wooden steps and break a hip in her haste.

"Lee. . . ?"

"Out here."

She raced through the kitchen and opened the sliding door that led out to the deck. The acrid smell of burning tobacco immediately tickled her nostrils. "Lee, what on earth are you doing? I thought you gave up cigars once and for all."

"I did. But I suddenly had a hankering for a smoke." He glanced at her and grinned. "Besides, if revered theologians like Spurgeon and Moody could enjoy a good cigar, so can I."

"Yes, well, the health risks weren't known back in Spurgeon and Moody's day."

"Darling, I'm nearly eighty years old. I should be concerned with health risks at my age?" He chuckled.

Expelling a weary sigh, Kathryn lowered herself into the adjacent lawn chair. "TJ's bringing Kylie here tonight."

"I know. I heard. I was on the extension when TJ called."

"Is that what triggered your urge to smoke a cigar?"

After expelling a puffy white plume, Lee sighed. "Might have been."

"Are you scared to meet Kylie?" Kathryn rubbed the knees of her white slacks. "I am."

Lee didn't answer at once. It was as though he had to think about it. "Scared to meet Kylie? No. But I'm scared to face the past. I have this raw pain in my gut that this girl's going to unlock plenty of secrets—secrets that were hidden away in the decades. I don't know if I'm man enough to handle them. . .or her. I'm too old."

"God doesn't give us more than we can handle." Kathryn reached out and placed her hand atop his.

"If Kylie Rollins behaves anything like Rob or Wendy, she's ten times more than I can bear."

Kathryn sat back in her chair, realizing Lee had just spoken her innermost fear. As though it were yesterday, she could still recall her last conversation with her daughter. Wendy wouldn't say where she was calling from, but she made it clear she would never forgive Kathryn and Lee for not giving in to her demands. She said she and Rob were "broke" and "hungry." She said they'd been living on the street. But Kathryn had been just as determined as Lee to demonstrate "tough love" to their spoiled children.

Who would have thought she and Lee would never see them again?

"Perhaps Kylie will become our mediator. Maybe we'll finally be able to make peace with Rob and Wendy, although. . ." Kathryn suddenly recalled how Kylie used the past tense when referring to them in her E-mail. Moreover, she didn't understand the whole adoption story. "Oh, Lee, maybe we should hope for the best but expect the worst."

He drew deeply on his cigar, then exhaled. "My thoughts exactly."

Kathryn wrinkled her nose. "Put that dreadful thing out, will you? You're going to smell like tobacco, and what kind of Christian testimony is that when you meet your granddaughter for the very first time?"

Lee grumbled but did as she asked.

The sound of car doors opening and closing below suddenly reached their ears.

"Lee, they're here."

"Yes, it would seem so."

He stood and Kathryn followed suit. Together they walked into the house and into the entry hall just as TJ opened the front door and led two young ladies inside.

Kathryn pressed her lips into a polite smile. "Welcome to The Light House."

Her guests returned tremulous smiles.

"Kathryn, Lee," TJ nodded to each one, "I'd like to introduce Marilee. . ." He paused.

"Domotor," she quickly put in.

"Marilee Domotor and Kylie Rollins."

"Nice to meet you both," Lee said.

"Yes. . .nice to meet you." Kathryn's gaze went from the slim brunette on the right to the raven-haired woman on the left. Lifting her fingers to her lips, Kathryn tried to quell her surging emotions. TJ hadn't been joking when he said Kylie was a Chadwyk. She favored Lee's side of the family, with her sturdy build, round face, sculptured cheekbones, and full lips.

"Hi," she said, her dark eyes moving from Kathryn to Lee. "I can see that my mom resembled her father."

"Resembled?" Kathryn couldn't stand the suspense a moment longer. "Please, tell us about Wendy. Where is she?"

"I'm going out to get the luggage," TJ announced.

"I'll help," Marilee added in spite of Kylie's frown.

Then, after only the three of them remained in the hallway, Kylie looked back at Kathryn and Lee. She edged forward while a worry line marred her brow.

"I really didn't want to start things off like this," she began. "I'm sorry to be the one to tell you, but. . .well, um. . . my mom died at the end of January. She had an aneurysm, the result of a fall in which she hit her head."

Tears sprung into Kylie's eyes.

"It still seems a little unreal to me. I miss her. . . ."

"I—I'm sure you do. . . ." Kathryn's mind tried to grasp the facts. *Wendy. Wendy's dead. This is my granddaughter. My own flesh and blood. My granddaughter. . .and she's mourning her mother. My daughter.*

In two great strides, Kathryn reached her. She wrapped her arms around Kylie. "There, there, dear heart. I know the sadness you feel."

Kylie returned the embrace, and a piece of Kathryn's heart miraculously healed.

Pulling back, Kathryn cupped the younger woman's face,

so strange, yet so familiar. She realized then that tears were sliding down her own cheeks.

"I'm sorry I had to be the one to tell you," Kylie repeated.

"Of course you had to tell us," Kathryn replied gently. "We needed to know the truth. All these years. . ."

Kathryn glanced at Lee. His expression was indecipherable.

Looking back at Kylie, she asked, "What about Rob? Do you know about him?"

She nodded. "I was told that he died in 1968—before I was born. He never even knew I'd been conceived. His sister— my mother, Wendy—adopted me. My biological mother was one of her best friends."

Kathryn's heart felt like it had been wrung out to dry. Her children were dead.

But hadn't they been dead to her for years? She'd just never known it.

"I'm sorry," Kylie said again, this time in a strangled little voice.

"No need to be sorry, young lady," Lee told her, stepping closer. He touched Kathryn's shoulder.

Kathryn sidestepped, and reaching out, Lee took his granddaughter's hand and gave it a pat. The sight caused Kathryn to smile.

"What matters now," Lee said, sounding a bit choked up himself, "is that we've found each other."

A smile sliced through Kylie's sorrowful expression. Lee grinned in spite of his suddenly misty gaze, and Kathryn sensed at once that her granddaughter's visit would be more blessing than backlash.

∽   ∽   ∽

Marilee awakened and allowed her gaze to roam the brightly colored bedroom. Last night she'd been so tired and the lighting had been so dim, she didn't have an opportunity to appreciate the decorations for which this room had been named—the Birds 'n' Blossoms Room. But this morning, with the sunshine streaming in through the semisheer yellow draperies, Marilee got an eyeful. Pretty little birds of various colors, shapes, and sizes had been stenciled over a light blue wall. Nearer to the floorboards grew a painted garden of multihued flowers. The artist had even included a fat tabby cat hiding behind a patch of lilies.

Smiling, Marilee tossed off the bedcovers and rolled out of the double bed. A bathroom had been built in the center of the birds and blossoms, and on the other side of it was Kylie's double bed. This one room really felt like two.

Showering and dressing, Marilee grabbed her Bible and peeked at Kylie, who still slept soundly. Marilee sent up a prayer of thanks that last night's initial meeting had seemed to go well between Kylie and her grandparents.

Lord, let them form a precious bond. They need each other. They're family!

Marilee strode out onto the veranda, which faced the Atlantic Ocean. She thought of how much Logan would appreciate this view. He loved water, and he would most likely gaze out over the ocean and think up some activity for the youth group.

She smiled, swallowing a laugh, and suddenly a song filled her heart. How long had it been since she sang praises to her King?

Too long, her soul seemed to reply.

Marilee hummed the melody, recalling Charles Wesley's lyrics from centuries ago. She'd been part of the choir at Parkway Community Church for years and had sung this hymn numerous times. "Jesus, lover of my soul. . ."

TJ walked out of the house and headed for the shed where he kept his tools. If Lissa Elliot broke that garbage disposal again, he might be tempted to curse. Couldn't she get it through her head? He wasn't interested in becoming her. . . *kitchen aide!*

TJ headed down the wooden walkway but didn't get far before he heard singing. He stopped and cocked an ear. The woman had a nice voice, and her song's soulful melody made him want to forget his chores and listen awhile. Stepping off the walkway and onto the beach, he looked up to catch the identity of the vocalist. He spotted Kylie's friend, Marilee, standing at the porch rail, pouring her heart out in song. By the expression on her face, this was obviously an intimate moment between her and God, and TJ felt embarrassed for eavesdropping.

Good thing she never saw him.

But oddly enough, that sweet song did wonders for his sour heart, and it somehow reaffirmed that he'd done the right thing in bringing both Kylie and Marilee to The Light House.

Unlocking the shed, TJ pulled out his toolbox. Maybe now he'd even have the strength to be polite to Lissa, and he found himself praying for exactly that on the way back into the house.

After a satisfying breakfast of scrambled egg casserole and an English muffin with butter and jelly, Kylie went for a walk along the beach with Marilee. The Chadwyks were busy with their bed and breakfast guests, and TJ was trying to fix something in the kitchen sink. It seemed a good time to stay out of everyone's way.

As they strolled down the shoreline, Kylie stole a glance at Marilee. Wearing a red cotton printed skirt and a white scoop-neck T-shirt, she appeared so carefree. A gentle wind tousled her hair, and her barefooted prints disappeared in the cool sand.

"You look happy," Kylie remarked, smiling.

"I am." Marilee smiled back. "I had a wonderful time with the Lord this morning, and then Logan and I had a terrific conversation. . .sort of like it used to be. . .before my accident."

"Glad to hear it."

Kylie meant every word. But, at the same, sharing Marilee's joy caused her to long for Matt and the way things "used to be." He hadn't called again since Monday night. Perhaps it finally sunk in; their relationship was over.

Too bad Kylie's heart couldn't seem to grasp that fact. In spite of what he did, she still missed him. She thought about him all the time and often had to remind herself that they weren't a couple anymore.

"I know who you're thinking about," Marilee said, her smile transformed into a smirk.

"You should have been a rocket scientist," Kylie quipped.

At Marilee's quelling glance, she laughed, picked up a stone, and tossed it into a wave. In many ways, Marilee reminded her of Dena, and despite her ex-best friend's traitorous behavior, Kylie missed her, too.

"You know, I think something's seriously wrong with me. I should hate Matt and Dena, but I don't."

Marilee didn't reply.

Kylie heaved a sigh. "But I'm sure all those negative emotions will come once I'm back home and I have to see them every day. Basil Creek isn't very big. Dena works at the only bank in town, and Matt. . ."

Kylie could only imagine how incredibly wounded she'd feel if he found someone else and remarried—especially if that "someone else" turned out to be Dena.

And then there was the house she'd grown up in and lived in to this day—the house that would never again be a home without her mother there.

The mother whom Kylie loved and missed so terribly.

The mother who, in actuality, had been her biological aunt and who never told her she had grandparents in Sabal Beach, South Carolina.

Kylie blew out a frustrated breath. "My life's a mess."

Marilee placed a sisterly arm around her shoulders. "I can relate."

"I know." Kylie turned and stared into Marilee's warm brown eyes. "So where's God in all of this. . .mess?"

An expression of chagrin shadowed Marilee's face. "He's where He's always been. It's just, well, to borrow your mother's saying, 'It's hard to see the picture when you're inside the frame.'"

Kylie churned out a curt laugh. "Yeah."

Then Marilee suddenly brightened. "Turn around. Look. It's awesome."

At her friend's insistence, Kylie pivoted, her heel digging into the soft sand. She gazed dead ahead, and there in the sky, poking through patches of clouds, were rays of sunshine, streaming down to the sparkling blue gray ocean below. The sight reminded Kylie of a picture she'd seen in a book of Bible stories for children, and somehow it seemed to answer her question.

God hadn't ever been very far away.

CHAPTER NINETEEN

"What a morning!" Kathryn exclaimed as she sat down at the table for lunch. "Problems and complaints everywhere." Sliding the blue linen napkin onto her lap, she smiled at Kylie and Marilee. "But I have the entire afternoon free so we can get acquainted."

"Let's pray," Lee said from his place at the head of the table.

As Kathryn listened to her husband ask the blessing on their food, she offered up her own prayer for wisdom in the following hours as she got to know her granddaughter.

Granddaughter. The word felt both foreign and fantastic on her tongue. *Granddaughter!*

When Lee finished praying, TJ's hearty "amen" bounced off the dining room walls, making Kathryn chuckle.

She glanced at Kylie. "Do you have brothers or sisters?"

The young lady shook her head. "My mom had trouble conceiving. I was told she'd gone through surgery for an ectopic pregnancy when I was an infant. It hindered her from having children."

The two abortions Wendy had as a teenager probably didn't help matters, Kathryn thought as she took a bite of her croissant filled with crab salad. But she wouldn't tell Kylie those ugly particulars. Had Kathryn been a Christian back then, she would have never allowed Wendy to go through with the murderous procedures. Unfortunately, she'd signed the papers, admitting Wendy to the hospital where the abortions had been performed—two years apart.

And that was only a couple of the many things Kathryn regretted about her parenting.

"From what I know about my biological mother, she never married and had kids," Kylie said. She smirked and glanced at TJ. "Didn't your background check on me give you all this information?"

"Nope." He didn't even miss a beat. "I only learned the basics and that you're not a fugitive."

"Hmm. . ."

"Please don't be insulted about the background check," Kathryn told her. "We live in a wicked day. TJ was only trying to protect us. He's like a son to us since. . ." Her voice trailed off and she lowered her gaze.

"No problem. I understand."

"Tell us about yourself, Kylie," Lee said.

"Well." She dabbed the corners of her mouth with her napkin, then sat back in her chair. "I've always been told that my dad attended Rush Medical College and my mom went to the University of Chicago. That's where they met— Chicago. I believe it's true, but not the part about my mom going to college. From what Allie's told me, that wouldn't have made sense. Mom wouldn't have been old enough."

"Who's Allie?" Kathryn asked.

"A friend of my mom's when they were teenagers. I'll get the old faded photograph."

Standing, Kylie excused herself and returned minutes later with a brown envelope in her hand. She offered it to Kathryn, who opened it and pulled out a black-and-white glossy. Seeing Wendy on the far right, holding a picket sign, Kathryn's trembling fingertips went to her lips.

"My biological mother is on the left," Kylie explained. "Allie and Jack are in the middle, and my mom—or aunt, if you will—is on the right."

"Yes, I see that. It's Wendy, all right." Kathryn handed it to Lee.

"That's where all the controversy comes into play," Kylie said. "The Wendy Rollins I knew would have never protested in public. . .in that outfit. My mother was a conservative Christian woman who lived a quiet life as a homemaker in a rural community."

"Sounds to me like she was a woman who didn't want to get found," TJ said. "She never worked outside the home?"

Frowning at his remark, Kylie shook her head.

"I think I see what you're getting at TJ," Lee said with a pondering expression. "If Wendy wasn't employed, she never had to file taxes, and it wasn't until the late 1980s that everyone in the same household was required to put a social security number on tax returns. Before then, you only had to list the members of your household by name." Lee looked at Kathryn. "That's why our private investigators couldn't locate Wendy. But if we would have tried to find her ten or fifteen years ago, we might have been successful." He sighed.

"By then, we'd given up."

Kylie appeared confused, so Kathryn gave her an assuring smile. Lee passed the picture back to Kathryn. She handed it to TJ.

"Our children ran away from home," Kathryn explained for her granddaughter's benefit. "Wendy was only seventeen. But Rob was her hero, and since he was determined to dodge the draft, she decided she'd dodge it right along with him."

With her elbows on the table, Kylie pressed her fingertips against her temples. "That so totally does not sound like my mom."

Kathryn watched as Marilee leaned over and put a comforting hand on Kylie's shoulder.

"But it explains why she wanted to adopt me after Rob was killed—if he was her 'hero,' I mean."

"Have you any idea how Rob was killed?" Lee asked, and Kathryn could hear constraints of emotion in his voice.

Kylie looked up. "Allie told me he died in a riot during the National Democratic Convention in 1968."

"Oh, Lord, have mercy!" Lee muttered, putting his face in his hands. "I watched it all on TV, saw it on the news, the convention, the protestors outside the convention hall. I never imagined my son was killed on the same streets being filmed."

A heartbeat later, Lee stood and left the room. Kathryn looked at Kylie, whose ebony eyes had filled with tears.

"I'm sorry," she eked out.

"Don't be, Dear." Kathryn reached across the table and grasped her hand. "It's not your fault." She paused, tears filling her own eyes. "It's ours."

Kylie's features softened.

"Did Wendy. . . ?" Kathryn removed her hand and sat

back. "Did she ever mention us to you?"

"No." Kylie gave her head a little shake. "I was told my mother's parents were from the La Crosse area, but that they'd died when I was a baby."

Kathryn tried to not show how horribly wounded she felt inside. But what had she expected? Wendy said she'd never forgive them. Apparently, she hadn't.

"Miss Rollins, I can see a resemblance to your natural mother," TJ said. "She's this lady right here?"

He pointed to someone in the picture—someone beyond Kathryn's line of vision—and Kylie nodded.

"She's a beautiful woman. Have you met her?"

"Yes. She owns an antique store in Chicago called Precious Things. But she has refused to speak with me about the photograph, about my mother, and about me."

"Antiques, huh?" He grinned. "I like antiques."

Kathryn rolled her eyes. "I should hope so. You live with two of them."

Laughter filled the dining room, and Kathryn knew TJ had accomplished his goal. He couldn't abide doom-and-gloom atmospheres—unless, of course, they were associated with a thunderstorm.

✽ ✽ ✽

After lunch, Kylie went out to her car and fetched the photo albums she'd brought from home while Marilee opted to take a nap. While Kylie sensed her friend was trying to be polite and allow her some time alone with the Chadwyks, she had to admit that a couple hours of sleep did sound rather tempting.

Reentering the house, Kylie walked through the entry hall, kitchen, and then headed for the sunroom. There she found TJ and her grandparents waiting for her.

Seeing her approach, TJ immediately stood and took the

numerous volumes out of her arms. "I would have gone out to get these for you," he said on a note of light admonishment. "A little girl like you ought not be carrying such a heavy load."

"Little girl?" Kylie had a good laugh over that remark. "I don't think I've ever been called 'little.' I was always the tallest, biggest girl in my class, up until about my junior year in high school when most of the boys passed me up. Even then, I was the largest girl."

"Wendy was that way, too," Kathryn said from her place on a settee with mint green floral cushions.

"Well, Miss Rollins, you're little compared to me," TJ remarked, depositing the photo albums on a large, square coffee table.

"We're all small compared to you," Lee quipped.

Kathryn laughed and patted the seat beside her. "Sit down, Kylie. I'm eager to hear all about you."

By now, Kylie had determined that her grandmother was a classy lady, from her professionally coiffured hair and manicured fingernails to her fashionable attire. Today, she wore a yellow T-shirt over a pair of stylish plaid capris. White canvas tie-ups covered her feet.

At her grandmother's bidding, Kylie crossed the room and lowered herself onto the settee. Next, she reached for an album, pulling it on top of her knees.

"This is the first one. Here's my mom and dad, Wendy and Joshua Rollins. In this picture, Mom's holding me."

She handed another photo album to her grandfather, who sat on the couch, positioned to her immediate right. TJ sat across the way in a cushioned wicker chair that creaked beneath his bulk.

Kylie handed him a book, too. "My parents were wonderful people. My dad was a doctor and worked in our local clinic and at the hospital in La Crosse. Sometimes if people in our community were too poor and couldn't afford medical insurance, my dad treated them for free. My mother, as I mentioned earlier, led a quiet life. She and my dad were very happily married. I never once heard them argue. Although," Kylie added with a grin, "I'm sure they did. Both my parents had strong opinions about things, but they also loved each other more than they valued their views. My dad was crazy about my mom—to the point where it was sometimes embarrassing to me." She laughed and her audience smiled. "Dad pampered and spoiled 'his girls,' as he called us, and my mother was one of my best friends, more so after Dad passed away."

No one uttered a word, and the pages illustrating Kylie's life continued to turn in strangers' hands. But she was more than happy to share her memories. She treasured them and enjoyed talking about her past.

As the afternoon wore on, Kylie relayed stories of her birthday parties, Christmas Eves, school plays, high school dances, prom nights, graduation, miscellaneous college functions, and her graduation from the University of Wisconsin–La Crosse. Kylie tried not to wince each time she glimpsed a picture of herself and Dena together, and she'd purposely left the last three photo albums at home. They contained a slew of photos of her and Matt. How could she have been so wrong about him?

Kylie pulled herself out of that painful remembrance. All her other memories were fond ones.

"As you can see by these photo albums, my mother was extremely organized. Our whole house is organized. Well, except for the attic and the garage. Those areas are still crammed full of stuff. Mom and I always meant to get to them and clean them out."

"I just wish that Wendy would have allowed us to be a part of her life," Kathryn said wistfully. "Hers. . .and yours, too."

"That's the part I don't understand," Kylie confessed. "On the other hand, I can't help but believe that she and my dad would have never deceived me if it weren't for some bigger picture that I'm just unable to see at this point in time."

"She must have hated us," Kathryn said, a tear slipping down her age-lined cheek.

"I don't know about that, Kathryn." TJ slapped closed the album in his hands before returning it to the stack on the table. "As I think about it, Kylie's very name seems a contraction of yours and Lee's. Ky—lie. Maybe Wendy didn't hate you at all. Maybe she wanted to patch things up, but like your granddaughter said, there was a reason she couldn't—a reason we don't know about." He paused before adding, "Yet."

Kylie laughed. There was something quite charming about Mr. TJ McGwyer.

Lee sat forward on the couch. "Thank you, Kylie, for sharing these pictures with us. You've painted a lovely picture of our daughter—one I would have never imagined." His nut brown eyes turned misty. "When I thought about all that might have become of Wendy, I envisioned a—" He stopped himself. "Well, let's just say it was nothing good."

"My mom was everything good," Kylie countered, "and I loved her so much." Tears sprang into her eyes, and her grandmother placed a comforting hand over hers. "That's why I can't understand why Mom would lie to me—unless she had a really, really important reason for it."

"Might that reason lay with your natural mother?" Kathryn asked.

"I think so."

Kathryn removed her hand. "Do you think. . . ? Well, this

is difficult for me to ask and yet I must."

"What is it?" Kylie felt her brows draw together in a curious frown.

"Do you think your natural mother knows where Rob is buried and. . .and what happened the night he died?"

"Kathryn, those details are better left unearthed. Just like Rob." As he spoke, Lee's fine white hair danced on the gentle breeze blowing in off the ocean.

"I have to know, Lee."

"Blythe has the answers to our questions," Kylie stated, her gaze lingering on her grandmother's face. "I'm sure of it. But she made some sort of promise. . .and I intend to find out to whom. I'm not going to rest until I know the entire truth. Unfortunately, Blythe has underestimated my stubborn streak."

TJ chuckled and stood. "This little gal sounds like someone else I know." He cleared his throat. "Kathryn."

"You spoke my very thoughts, TJ," Lee said, smirking at his wife.

Kathryn draped an arm around Kylie's shoulders. "My dear, it seems you have inherited my inquisitive nature."

"Is that good or bad?" Kylie smiled as she asked the question.

"All depends," TJ answered. "But if you two are going antique shopping in Chicago, I want to come along."

Kathryn looked taken aback and Lee laughed. "Why on earth would you want to do that?" Kathryn asked.

"Yeah, I gotta hear this one," Lee drawled.

A slow smile spread across TJ's face. "You aren't the only ones with 'inquisitive natures'."

CHAPTER TWENTY

W hat do you think?" Kathryn glanced over at her husband. He sat behind the wheel of their Avalon as they drove the distance back from church the next morning.

"Kylie is everything I could ask for in a granddaughter. I agree with you. We could grow to love her very easily."

"Yes, and that's why I don't want her to leave. Oh, Lee, she told me how alone she feels since Wendy died. And now that her engagement is off, her sense of loneliness has doubled." Kathryn's heart ached for the younger woman. "She's been through so much. She's lost so many important people in her life."

"You said Kylie promised to think about our offer. All we can do is pray that she accepts."

Kathryn sighed. "You're right."

She had been awake half the night, asking God to make

Kylie want to stay in Sabal Beach. However, she knew she prayed out of selfishness. The plain truth was, Kathryn didn't want her granddaughter to live so far away.

Yesterday, she had taken Kylie and Marilee shopping on Market Street in Charleston. The weather had been sunny and warm—much like it was today. They'd had a lovely time, and Kathryn felt she connected with her granddaughter, especially after they stopped for tall glasses of lemonade and Kylie spilled the whole sad story about her fiancé and best friend. Kathryn had been able to offer up advice—for which Kylie seemed appreciative.

Odd how in just a matter of days she had accomplished with Kylie what she'd never managed with Wendy.

They'd formed a relationship.

Lee's cell phone rang, drawing Kathryn from her thoughts. She grinned, finding it amusing that Lee still needed his "toys." The sleek cell phone he kept in his shirt pocket was only one of the many gadgets he continually acquired.

"Hi, TJ. . .no, I don't see a problem with it. But let me check with the boss." Smiling, Lee sent Kathryn a quick glance. "Seth Brigham is in town and TJ wants to invite him to The Light House for lunch. That okay with you?"

"Of course. It'll be delightful to see Seth again." She'd always liked that young man.

Phone to his ear once more, Lee relayed the news. "We'll see you back at home."

♪   ♪   ♪

Kylie fanned herself with a bulletin as she stood in a shady part of the asphalt parking lot adjacent to the red brick church. She listened to the conversation going on between Marilee and Lissa Elliot, whose children played on a nearby swing set. Kylie half wished she'd left with her grandparents. She felt uncomfortable in the escalating humidity and longed to kick her shoes off and change clothes. But since TJ had given her and Marilee a lift this morning, the Chadwyks assumed he'd drive them back, and they'd taken off before Kylie could catch them.

Glancing over her shoulder, she saw that TJ was still socializing with a small cluster of folks. One of them was a man named Seth Brigham, to whom Kylie had been introduced before this morning's service began. From what she'd gathered, Seth and TJ had been friends for years, and seeing that Seth had just returned to Charleston on business, he'd been invited to The Light House for lunch.

As if sensing her stare, Seth's toffee-colored eyes met hers. He smiled, and Kylie, feeling totally embarrassed, smiled back before she turned away. She hadn't meant to gape at the man, and she didn't want him to get the wrong idea. She wasn't interested in him.

Or was she?

Seth was a nice-looking guy, and after being introduced, he had seated himself beside her in the pew. For the next hour, Kylie had inhaled the scent of his woodsy cologne. She wished she knew the name of it; she'd buy Matt a bottle.

Why do I keep thinking about Matt? It's over between us.

"Ladies, are you ready?"

Kylie felt herself straighten at the sound of TJ's commanding voice. Discovering that he'd served in the military came as no great surprise to her. Each time he belted out a question, no matter how polite, Kylie felt like saluting.

Bidding Lissa a hasty good-bye, Kylie and Marilee traipsed along a row of cars until they reached TJ's Silverado. TJ, attired in tan trousers and a navy jacket, was in the process of opening the truck's doors to let some of the inside heat escape. In front of her, dressed in an olive green suit, Seth opened the door for Kylie.

"Thanks," she muttered, stepping up and into the cab's backseat. Seth assisted her with his hand beneath her elbow, and Kylie imagined she was no graceful sight, climbing into the pickup in a dress and heels.

"All set?"

Kylie gave Seth a nod.

Another smile and he closed the door.

Next to her, Marilee fastened her seat belt. Kylie did the same while TJ started the engine. Seth hopped into the front passenger seat, and before they'd reached the first intersection, Kylie could feel the vehicle's air conditioner cooling off the cab.

Seth twisted around. "TJ tells me you ladies are from the Midwest."

"That's right," Marilee replied in her usual sweet tone. "I'm from Illinois and Kylie's from Wisconsin."

Seth bestowed on her another charming smile, and Kylie thought he was all the more handsome at a closer distance. His hair was the color of polished mahogany, and with the severe way he pulled it back and banded it in a short ponytail, he appeared the artsy type. Kylie started wondering about his occupation.

"So how'd you two become friends?" he asked.

"It's a long story," Marilee said, casting a glance in Kylie's direction.

"Well, I like stories." Seth chuckled, and the friendly sound caused Kylie to grin.

"Actually, we only met a week ago. I decided to drive here to South Carolina to meet my grandparents, the Chadwyks, and I stopped in Chicago to collect information from a past friend of my mother's. Marilee and I met through that friend; she decided to ride along with me, and. . .here we are."

Seth narrowed his brown-eyed gaze, obviously digesting the information. TJ laughed from behind the wheel.

"We're well aware of the fact it sounds a bit. . .crazy," Marilee added, smiling all the while. "But the truth is, Kylie and I have never felt more rational in our lives."

"That's right." She laughed at the sight of Seth's gaze ping-ponging between her and Marilee.

"Doesn't sound crazy to me." He looked over at TJ. "Does it sound crazy to you?"

"No, but I'm not the best judge of crazy."

"You've got a point there." Seth smirked before sending Kylie a charming wink.

"What kind of business are you in, Seth?" Curiosity finally got the better of her.

"I'm a programmer for Hinkman and Haas, an upscale men's clothing store. We've got locations in thirty of the USA's fifty states with our headquarters here in Charleston. But since I wrote our new Y2K program, it's up to me to work out any bugs in the system."

"So how did you and TJ become friends?" Marilee asked, turning the question around on him.

Touché, Kylie thought as a grin tugged at the corner of her mouth.

"TJ and I go way back. Way, way back."

"Well, not that far back."

"Almost ten years." Grinning, Seth moved to glance at Marilee, then Kylie. "I went to CSU—that's Charleston Southern University for you Yankees."

Kylie rolled her eyes at Seth's teasing, complete with its thick Southern drawl, and TJ hooted.

Seth turned back around, facing the dashboard, and continued. "I was in my senior year, and all the students were encouraged to do volunteer work. So every Saturday night I'd help out a pastor who was running a church—well, I wouldn't exactly call it a 'church.' It was an old storefront that served as a place where people who didn't feel comfortable in traditional churches could go and still hear the Word of God."

"I was one of those people," TJ said. "And even though I've got a good twenty years on Seth, we've been good buddies ever since. If it weren't for him and the Chadwyks, I'm sure I'd be dead or in jail right now."

Kylie felt impressed. She'd heard how TJ had become a Christian and about the kind of man he'd been beforehand. To learn that Seth had played a role in TJ's transformation was incredible. What's more, she suddenly realized how many committed Christians God had put in her own pathway in just a very short time. It was no coincidence. Kylie was certain of that much.

But now what did God have planned for her future?

After a bit more chitchat, TJ pulled his truck into the carport of The Light House and the four passengers exited the vehicle. Kylie immediately heard the squawks of the seagulls and smelled the salty spray off the ocean. Palmetto trees lined the street, and their thick, long green leaves waved in the warm breeze, as if welcoming her home.

Home.

Kylie felt like she didn't have one anymore, although her grandmother had invited her to move here to Sabal Beach, and Kylie promised to consider the offer. She had a feeling it wouldn't be difficult to adjust to life on this beautiful, tranquil island. It wasn't even a half hour's drive into Charleston, and Kylie felt certain she'd be able to find employment there, if not here at The Light House.

But is that what she wanted?

Is that what God wanted?

After ascending the front stairs, TJ led the small group into the foyer. Smiling a greeting, Kathryn beckoned them into the living room. Seeing that her grandmother still wore her Sunday best, Kylie decided against running upstairs and putting on her blue jeans.

"Please make yourselves comfortable," Kathryn said in her naturally hospitable tone. "Lee is on the back deck grilling chicken. It'll be done soon. I thought I'd serve it up with the homemade vegetable soup that Kylie and Marilee helped me prepare last night."

"We didn't do much," Kylie admitted.

"Why, yes, you did. I abhor peeling carrots and potatoes, so you and Marilee were a godsend."

Kylie smiled as she sank into a floral upholstered armchair.

Seth shed his suit jacket and lowered himself onto the matching couch. "Are you a good cook, Kylie?"

She shrugged, wondering where his question was headed. The inkling fluttering in her stomach said he shared her "interest."

But how could she even think of a new romance when, in her heart, she still felt engaged to Matt?

That's ridiculous. I'm not engaged. It's over between us. . . .

"I have a feeling Kylie has superb culinary skills," her grandmother clucked like a mother hen.

Shaking off thoughts of Matt and her broken engagement, Kylie pushed out a grin. "Well, I don't burn things too often."

"Oh, you. . ." Kathryn closed the distance between them and leaned over to kiss the top of Kylie's head. "I'm so glad you're here."

Kylie smiled—genuinely this time. "I'm glad, too."

Marilee had seated herself at the shiny oak baby grand piano, which jutted out from the far corner of the room. She played a soft melody that seemed to pluck both a sad and familiar chord in Kylie's heart. She'd heard the melody before, although she couldn't think of where.

"I'm going to check on our lunch," Kathryn declared. "I see TJ's out on the deck with Lee. I imagine the chicken is almost ready."

She walked off, and Kylie began to feel Seth's scrutiny.

She glanced at him and he grinned.

"So," he began, sitting back on the sofa, "is there a lucky guy waitin' for you back home in Wisconsin?"

Her inkling hadn't been wrong.

Meeting Seth's stare, she had to laugh. The guy got right to the point.

"I. . .um. . .was engaged, but we. . .broke up."

Seth winced. "Sorry to hear that."

"Thanks. What about you?" Kylie asked right back.

Seth didn't appear unnerved in the least. "Nope. No one special, although God's blessed me with a lot of friends."

"Girlfriends?"

An embarrassed grin curved his narrow, but nicely shaped, mouth. "Some girls, yeah."

"As in a girl in every port?"

He laughed. "Hardly!"

Marilee ceased her piano playing. "What are you two talking about?"

"Seth and his travels," Kylie explained. "He's got a woman waiting for him in every city."

"Urrrnt," Seth replied, sounding like a game-show buzzer. Then he shot a throw pillow at her.

Kylie made the easy catch. However, in that moment, she decided she liked Seth Brigham.

Turning her attention back to Marilee, she asked, "What song was that you were playing, and where have I heard it before?"

"It's called "O Teach Me What It Meaneth." It's an old hymn set to new music, and our choir sang it last Sunday."

"Oh, right." Kylie remembered now.

"This song has become very special to me."

"How so?" Seth wanted to know.

Marilee took a few moments to think over her response. "I guess it sums up what I feel in my heart. A prayer in the form of a song."

"Sing it for us." Crossing her leg, Kylie allowed herself to grow comfortable, anticipating the impromptu concert. She'd heard Marilee sing along with the radio on their trip here or in the shower at the hotels. No doubt about it: The woman possessed an incredible singing voice.

Turning back to the piano, Marilee played a short introduction before she sang.

"O teach me what it meaneth:
    That cross uplifted high,
With One, the Man of Sorrows,
    Condemned to bleed and die!
O teach me what I cost Thee
    To make a sinner whole,
And teach me, Savior, teach me
    The value of a soul.

O teach me what it meaneth:
    That sacred crimson tide,

The blood and water flowing
    From Thine own wounded side.
Teach me that if none other
    Had sinned, but I alone,
Yet still Thy blood, Lord Jesus,
    Thine only, must atone."

Kylie's soul was stirred as she listened, and the sharp reality that Jesus had suffered and died for her—her!—suddenly sliced through her being. The Lord wasn't some impersonal God, as unapproachable to the average person as the president of the United States. Jesus Christ truly was, as Marilee often said, a "personal Savior." It surprised Kylie that it had taken so long for her to understand that incredible piece of truth.

"O teach me what it meaneth:
    Thy love beyond compare;
The love that reaches deeper
    Than depths of self-despair.
Yes, teach me till there gloweth
    In this cold heart of mine,
Some feeble, pale reflection
    Of that pure love of Thine."

Marilee played a brief interlude, then continued in song.

"O teach me for I need Thee;
    I have no hope beside,
I am the 'chief of sinners,'
    For whom the Savior died.
O Infinite Redeemer,
    I am so full of sin,

Thy grace alone can reach me;
>Thy love alone can win. . . .
Thy grace alone can reach me;
>Thy love alone. . .can. . .win."

Marilee finished and a reverent hush filled the living room.

"That was beautiful," Kathryn murmured from the doorway.

When Kylie looked across the way, she saw that her grandfather and TJ stood at the entryway also. They appeared as awed as Kylie felt.

"Thank you." Marilee rose from the piano bench, looking abashed.

Kylie, on the other hand, felt proud of her friend. "You're going to make a terrific youth pastor's wife."

The spark that lit up Marilee's gaze could have rivaled the afternoon sunshine. "Thanks. I needed to hear that."

"You've set your mind on marrying a pastor, eh?" Seth asked, a confused frown marring one of his thick, dark brown brows. Marilee flashed her engagement ring at him, and Seth replied with an, "Ah, I get it."

Smiling, Kathryn moved forward into the room. "Let's continue this discussion in the dining room, shall we? Lunch is ready."

CHAPTER TWENTY-ONE

A llie, should we take our coffee outside and sit on the deck?"
"Sounds good to me." She wrung out the dishcloth
and wiped off the counter while Nora poured two mugs of
steaming coffee.

"We've been abandoned for college basketball, so we
might as well enjoy this beautiful spring day."

Allie laughed. "Every Sunday afternoon it's the same thing.
Your kids disappear." She glanced at the ceiling and counted on
her fingers. "Veronica goes upstairs to do her homework. Rick
and Rachel pal around with Logan, Steve, and Jack, who
become immersed in whatever game is on television. You and I
get kitchen duty. . . ." She sighed dramatically. "We should be
used to this drudgery by now."

"Ha! A woman's work is never done, remember?"

Allie tossed the dishcloth into the sink. "Well, it's done for the next few hours, anyway."

"Amen to that."

Smiling, Allie followed Nora out to their octagonal deck that overlooked a spacious backyard. The treetops were a pale green as their tiny buds began to blossom.

"I never liked spring," Nora confessed. She took a seat in one of the colorful padded armchairs scattered about. "The grass is brown, there's garbage and dead leaves in the bushes, and everything's muddy."

"Illinois's spring is like California's winter," Allie remarked, taking a sip of her coffee.

"Are you going to be able to adjust?"

Allie drew in a deep breath as she thought about it. There were so many things she missed about her home in Long Beach; however, she hadn't given up her idea of talking Jack into keeping her condo. If she knew she had somewhere to escape when the winter blues struck, Allie felt certain she could make Oakland Park her permanent residence.

"You're taking an awfully long time to answer my question, Allie. I'm getting worried."

She laughed and looked over at her brunette friend with the teal eyes. She set her hand on Nora's forearm. "Not to fret. Jack is well aware of my attachment to California. But I love him, and I know I can be happy wherever God wants us—even if it's here, as I'm certain it is for now."

"Good. I'd hate to lose you. You've become like a sister to me."

"Oh, you're sweet. . . ."

The two women clasped hands, like a brief sisterly hug, and then the patio doors opened. Both Allie and Nora twisted around to glimpse the intruder.

"Mom, Rick won't let me have a turn on the computer," Rachel whined. As the youngest, she often felt indignant over something her older siblings did or didn't do, and she typically felt left out.

"Rachel, your father is in the same room as the computer. Why didn't you tell him?"

"I did, but he wouldn't listen."

"Well, your uncle Jack has always been your hero. Why didn't you tell him?"

The pixie, who resembled her mother, pouted. "Uncle Jack is talking to someone at the front door."

"Oh?" Nora cast a curious glance at Allie.

She shrugged.

"Who's at the door?"

"Some lady. She's crying."

"Uh-oh." Allie stood, and just as she turned toward the patio doors, Logan stepped onto the deck.

"Hey, Allie, Colleen's here. She's upset about something. Can you come in?"

"Of course."

Allie followed Logan into the house. Her heart raced at the mention of her dear stepsister's name and the word "upset" in the same sentence. After thirty years, she and Colleen Strobel had been reunited, and they made it a point to meet for lunch at least twice a month so they could keep up on each other's lives. Allie's younger stepsister, Brenda, on the other hand, wanted nothing to do with her. The word "forgive" was not in Brenda's vocabulary. Worse, she seemed to blame Allie for every bad thing that happened in her life, including a failed marriage, a factory job from which she recently got laid off, and two arrests for driving while intoxicated. But Colleen had a tender heart and sensitive soul—the complete opposite of her younger sister.

Reaching the small hallway, Allie saw that Jack had placed an arm around Colleen's shoulders as she cried into the ragged tissue she held in her hand.

"Colleen, what's wrong?"

She glanced up, and Allie noticed the relief that washed over her features. "Oh, Allie. . .it's terrible."

"What, Honey? Tell me." She looked at Jack and noticed his somber expression as she put a comforting arm around her sister's waist.

"It's Brenda," Colleen choked out. "She overdosed on tranquilizers and alcohol. She. . .she's not going to make it. I heard the para. . .paramedics say that."

"Did you find her?"

Colleen nodded. "In our basement."

Allie's heart began to melt with compassion. Brenda had moved into Royce and Colleen's finished basement as temporary living quarters until her house sold and her divorce was final.

"Did they take her to Oakland Park Memorial?" Jack asked.

Again, Colleen nodded. "After the ambulance pulled away, I stopped at your apartment, Jack; then I went to Allie's house, and when I didn't find you guys there, I came here." She convulsed with sobs. "I hope it's okay. I didn't mean to bother you."

"You're no bother. Of course, you're no bother!" Allie blinked back her tears and looked at Jack.

"What can I do to help?" Logan asked.

"You can pray, Son. Brenda's not a Christian. She's flat-out denied the Lord Jesus."

Logan winced. "I'll be praying. You can count on it."

"We'll all be praying," Nora said.

Jack's dark gaze returned to Allie. "Let's go," he said, motioning toward the front door with a bob of his head.

Allie ran to fetch her purse, blowing Nora a kiss on the way out. Jack was helping Colleen into his Explorer by the time Allie reached the curb.

"Where's Royce?"

"Don't know." Jack assisted her into the backseat so she could be with Colleen.

"Royce is at a basketball game," Colleen informed them both. "Ironically, he's with Dave and the two boys."

Brenda's two teenaged sons. Allie recalled meeting the "boys" once and only briefly. Throughout all the ugly divorce proceedings, they had taken their father's side—and no one could blame them. Brenda's reasons for severing her twenty-year marriage to Dave Perkins were petty. She was "sick of him." She thought he was a "loser" and a "sofa spud."

Dear Lord, please give Brenda one more chance. It's not Your will that any should perish but that all would come to repentance. Lord, You are the God of second chances. I'm living proof of that. . . .

Allie felt Colleen's head come to rest on her shoulder. Allie opened her eyes and took her sister's hand, giving it an affectionate squeeze.

"Are you praying, Allie?"

"Sure am."

"Good, because if anyone has a special 'in' with God, it's you."

Allie couldn't help a slight laugh, and from her vantage point, she saw Jack's grin.

"Anyone can have an 'in' with God. It's not only for the elite or privileged."

"Yeah, otherwise you know where I'd be," Jack interjected. "I'd be there, too."

"I know, Allie." Colleen sat up and peered at Jack. "I know. The two of you have told me before. But, right now, if you'll keep praying, I just know Brenda will be okay. . . ."

⁂ ⁂ ⁂

The noon meal stretched out into the early part of the afternoon as everyone stayed at the dining room table and lingered over coffee and dessert. The topics of conversation ranged from Marilee's rapidly approaching wedding to Seth's latest computer software challenge to TJ's last storm-chasing encounter; and each time Seth looked in Kylie's direction, she felt herself warming to his attentions.

The discussion finally came around to how Kylie found her grandparents.

"I must confess to being leery about the meeting," Lee said, his rheumy eyes coming to rest on Kylie's face. "I expected the worse, I'm afraid. But I am pleased to have discovered I couldn't have been more wrong."

"I'm glad you feel that way." Kylie gave her grandfather a smile. "I'm pleasantly surprised myself."

"That's one of the most touching stories I've heard in a long time," Seth remarked. "The 'finding each other' part is really cool."

Kylie looked across the table at him, and he stared into her eyes in a way that made her want to melt all over her grandmother's polished parquet flooring. Had Matt ever looked at her like that?

Finally, she had to tear her gaze away from his out of sheer embarrassment. If she could see Seth's interest, so could everyone else.

She took to studying the napkin in her lap—the one

she'd been fidgeting with for the last forty-five minutes.

"That must have been devastating for you to learn you were adopted after all this time," Seth remarked before forking a piece of chocolate cake into his mouth.

"I'm not devastated." Kylie looked up. "But I am confused. I want to know why. Why was it—or is it—such a big secret?"

"You might never find out," TJ said. "I have a thousand similar questions about my family and my past, and God revealed to me that I'll know the answers in His due time—which may be when I get to heaven."

"Guess that's true with a lot of things in life," Lee stated.

TJ stood and stretched. "Well, I'm ready for some college basketball. How 'bout you, Lee? Seth?" He rubbed his palms together. "Final Four."

Kylie grinned. Back home Matt was probably planted in front of the TV watching basketball, too.

"I think I'll pass on watching the game," Seth replied. "Too nice a day." He looked at Kylie. "Say, how about taking a walk?"

Before she could answer, TJ walked over and gave Seth a friendly whack on the back. "Have fun."

"Hey, thanks—and thanks for inviting me to lunch." He rose and smiled at Kathryn, then Lee.

Kylie's grandfather wore an ear-to-ear grin as he walked around the table to shake Seth's hand. "Glad you could join us."

"Entirely my pleasure."

"Yes, so I've noticed." After glancing at Kylie, Lee chuckled as he left the dining area.

Marilee quickly excused herself, saying she had to call Logan. But as Kathryn gathered up the coffee cups and saucers, she imparted a tight smile, and Kylie clearly saw her grandmother's look of disapproval.

"What do you think, Kylie? Wanna take a little stroll?" Seth held up his hands as if in surrender. "I'm an honorable man. You have nothing to fear. Besides, I know TJ would tar and feather me if I behaved as anything less than a complete gentleman."

"I don't doubt your integrity, but, well, I don't know," Kylie hedged, watching her grandmother leave the room. "I'm wearing these shoes that aren't very comfortable for walking." She stuck her foot out, displaying one black, high-heeled pump.

"Hmm. I suppose I could watch a bit of the basketball game while you change."

Kylie arched a brow. "Could I really ask you to do such a thing?"

He gave her a feigned look of contrition. "I suppose I can suffer for a little bit while you change."

Laughing, Kylie gave in. "Okay. I'll be right back."

While he headed for the den, Kylie took off for the kitchen to find out what her grandmother could possibly object to in a man like Seth Brigham.

※　※　※

Kathryn stood at the kitchen sink and chastened herself. She shouldn't feel anything but happiness for Kylie. Perhaps the young woman was on the brink of a new relationship, one that would heal her heart and enable her to grow into a strong Christian. But instead, all Kathryn could think about was the possibility of losing the granddaughter who'd walked into her life less than a week ago.

Oh, God, how can I be so selfish?

"Mrs. Chadwyk?"

Kathryn whirled around to find the object of her thoughts coming toward her. "That has to stop, young lady." She smiled as she administered the light scolding.

Kylie appeared embarrassed. "Sorry. . .Grandma Kathryn."

"When I was a girl, people called me Kate."

"Grandma Kate?" She nodded. "That has a nice ring to it."

"Yes, it does." It was a "ring" Kathryn never thought she'd live to hear.

"Well, Grandma Kate, I have a question for you." One of Kylie's dark brows dipped into a frown, and Kathryn knew her well enough to realize that what she was about to ask was something along a more serious vein.

"What is it, Kylie?"

"I wondered if you'd tell me what you have against Seth. Should I be more careful? I mean, if there's something I need to know about him, I wish you'd warn me."

"And I would, Kylie. Of course, I would." She drew in a breath, knowing she owed her granddaughter an apology. "Kylie, please forgive this old lady for her interfering ways. We all have our struggles, and mine is insecurity. I'm terribly afraid of losing the people I love. So I try to hold onto them with all my might." She smiled. "On the other hand, I'm wise enough to realize that I have no right to control what others do or don't do. God Himself doesn't impose upon us in that way. How dare I?"

Kylie looked confused. "Are you saying that you see Seth as some kind of threat?"

"As hard as it is to admit, yes. I mean, if you marry him, Kylie—"

"Marry him? Grandma Kate, he just wants to go for a walk!" Kylie laughed and simultaneously shook her head and rolled her eyes.

Kathryn felt a bit put out that her confession had become such a joke. But then her granddaughter's next sentence pierced her very soul.

"You sound just like my mother. Why do you think I'm almost thirty-one and still single? You two have a lot in common. I've noticed it before."

"I–I don't know what to say. I suppose I owe you another apology. You're right. Seth's invitation hardly mirrors a marriage proposal. As for your mother and I being alike. . . Well, I never saw us having a similar bone in our bodies. We didn't think the same way either. Whatever I advised or instructed, Wendy did the opposite."

Folding her arms, Kylie leaned against the kitchen counter. "I didn't rebel. I don't know why, other than I loved my mom and I knew it wouldn't be right if I went against her wishes. Maybe I'm just too docile, although I had it pretty good at home." She shrugged.

"You and Wendy are very different people. That's what makes us individuals." A smile pulled at Kathryn's lips. "Go for your walk with Seth, if that's what you want to do. The afternoon is quickly slipping by."

"You're right about that. But I wondered if—"

"Ahem. . ."

She stopped, hearing Seth clear his throat. Kathryn looked across the room to see the young man standing in the doorframe.

"Those don't look like walking shoes to me," he said, gazing at Kylie's feet.

Kathryn noticed the blush that crept up her granddaughter's neck and colored her cheeks with a lovely shade of pink.

"I was just on my way upstairs. . . ."

"Well, I've got a better idea." He winked at Kathryn, and she shook her head at him, the sassy boy. "TJ says there's an art exhibit in Charleston—says I can borrow his truck, since my car is still in the church parking lot. Want to go?"

"Um, yeah, sure."

Kathryn detected the hesitation and presumed it stemmed from Kylie's recent broken engagement. She wondered once more if this little outing with Seth would do Kylie a world of good.

"Great, let's hit the road," Seth stated, wearing a grin. "Gotta be back in time for the evening church service."

"Have fun, you two."

"Thanks, Grandma Kate." Stepping forward, Kylie placed a quick kiss on her cheek.

Kathryn returned to her dishwashing. *Wendy did a fine job, raising that girl. . . . Does that mean I might have done something right raising Wendy?*

CHAPTER TWENTY-TWO

The art exhibit was held in the elaborate gardens of one of Charleston's oldest plantations. Walking along the crowded pathway, Kylie decided the blooms equaled the masterful oil paintings, charcoal sketches, and watercolors.

At last, she and Seth reached the end of the display. They ambled up the pathway to a refreshment stand, where Seth purchased two glasses of lemonade. Finding a shady spot on the wide stone ledge below some thick green hedges, they sat down.

"It's a beautiful day," Kylie remarked.

"Sure is." Seth took a swallow of his beverage and inclined his head toward the vast display. "What did you like best out of all the artwork we saw?"

Kylie took a moment to think over her reply. "Hmm. I guess I'd have to say I liked the painting of that old, dilapidated Victorian house and its falling-down outbuildings; then in the distance there's a view of a bulldozer and cement truck building new homes, maybe a subdivision. I thought that painting was both sad and powerful."

"Really? Guess I didn't see it as sad, just necessary in life. The past has to be torn down before the future can be erected."

"But that house represented days gone by—like this plantation behind us. It represented an era, one that needs to be preserved for future generations."

"Can't live in the past. Even this plantation has been updated with modern conveniences, like—" He grinned. "—indoor plumbing."

Kylie could see his point, although she wasn't sure she agreed with it. "I think the old is worth hanging onto and saving."

"Sometimes—and sometimes not. The past can be a detriment to others and a hindrance to their growth and productivity."

"Are you referring to slavery here in the South?"

"I am. Now, granted, for historic purposes, slave quarters have been preserved, but no one is forced to live in them anymore—thank God."

Kylie thought about her mother and wondered if her perspective of the past had mirrored Seth's. Allie had suggested it, and indeed, her mother may have set out to build a new life and torn down her old one—the one that included Kylie's grandparents.

Seth finished his drink. "Are you a nostalgic person, Kylie Rollins?"

Given her thoughts just now, she had to laugh. "Yes, I

suppose I am. I work in a library. I'm around history all day long."

"Ahh. . ."

"What about you? Are you nostalgic?"

"Not at all. I'm more goal-oriented. A plotter and a planner. Always looking ahead."

"Where are you from?"

"Indiana."

"What? You're a Yankee just like I am?" Kylie shook her head. "And here I thought you were a Southern gentleman."

"I'm a transplanted Yankee." He chuckled. "My folks, on the other hand, still live in a little nothing town in Indiana called Casper."

"Can't be smaller than Basil Creek."

"Wanna bet?"

They shared a laugh.

"Did you live in town or outside of town?"

"In—that is, if you can call it a 'town.' Us boys used to throw baseballs from one end of town to the other with little problem."

Kylie smiled. "What did your parents do for a living?"

"Dad was a truck driver and Mom stayed home. I grew up in a three-bedroom house, and there were four boys and three girls."

"Are you serious? I grew up in a three-bedroom house, but I was an only child."

Seth grinned and his amber brown eyes lit with mischief. "And I suppose you're going to say you always wanted brothers and sisters, eh? Too bad we didn't know each other back then. I would have gladly given you a couple of mine."

Kylie chuckled and, again, she felt drawn to Seth.

"Okay, now I'm going to get nosey," he said with a

charming grin. "You can let me know if I'm out of line, but I can't help asking. . . . What happened that caused you to break off your engagement, or did your fiancé break it off?"

"I broke it off because Matt's a cheat and a liar."

Seth pursed his lips and lifted his brows. "Guess that's a good reason." He paused, his gaze meeting hers. "Do you still love him?"

At the pointed question, the air seemed to leave her lungs. She looked down at the plastic cup in her hands. "Emotions don't just go away because a situation has changed." She lifted her head. "Yeah, I still love him."

"Any hope of reconciliation?"

"I'm not sure. Matt and I would have to start all over because I'm a different person now than I was before, and I don't think he wants that. Matt wants to pick up where we left off and I don't."

"Hmm. . ."

Kylie had to smile at Seth's pensive stare into his empty cup. She wondered if he'd lose interest in her now that he knew the ugly particulars of her life.

And to think that only a month ago, she'd lived a nearly perfect existence—

Or at least she had believed she did.

♫ ♫ ♫

Allie sat beside Colleen in the family room, just behind the main waiting area of the emergency department. Inside the ER, the well-trained staff of professionals was attending to Brenda. Allie couldn't imagine the outcome. A nurse had already informed them that the type of medicine Brenda ingested caused kidney and liver damage when taken in excess. The fact that Brenda was unconscious when Colleen found her meant the pills had already begun to penetrate her nervous system and vital organs.

The door opened and Allie, Jack, and Colleen looked up, expecting to see a doctor, nurse, or social worker. Instead, Logan sauntered in and sat down in a nearby chair.

"Any news?"

"Not yet," Jack replied.

Allie noticed the grim set of his mouth and knew he antici-pated the worst. Oftentimes, it seemed Jack had witnessed too much on the police force to think positively in crisis situations.

"Aunt Nora says she and Uncle Steve are praying. The kids are, too."

"That's great." Colleen attempted a smile. "Prayers are appreciated. The more, the better."

"Would you like me to lead us in prayer right now?"

Colleen's eyes filled with tears.

"Go ahead, Son," Jack said, sitting on the edge of his chair, his hands folded, his head bowed.

Allie did the same.

"Oh, Lord, You are the Giver of life. No one departs this earth without Your say-so. We ask in Mrs. Perkins's case that You intervene and spare the life she tried to end herself, apart from Your perfect will. You are the Great Physician, Lord. There's nothing too hard for You. Mrs. Perkins's soul is of much more worth than her physical body, and it's no secret that she doesn't know You. Please give her another chance to accept You as the Way, the Truth, and the Lord of her life. We ask this in Jesus' name. Amen."

Colleen broke down and began to sob. Allie put her arm around her stepsister's shoulders and held her while she cried.

Several minutes later, a blond man with military-short hair stepped into the room. He wore pale green scrubs and a white jacket.

"Hi, I'm Dr. Mason." He shook hands with everyone and introductions were made. "Well, we've got her stabilized, but she's not good," he stated, referring to Brenda. "In fact, we want to transfer her to Northwestern Memorial because we're such a small hospital. We really can't give her the specialized care she's going to need in the days ahead—and that's assuming she makes it."

"So it's still touch-and-go?" Jack asked.

The slim doctor replied with a solemn nod. "I don't want to mislead you or give you false hopes. It really doesn't look good."

ॐ ॐ ॐ

Later Sunday night, Kylie checked her E-mail while Marilee phoned Logan. Normally, she only "checked in" with Logan once a day, but Allie's stepsister attempted suicide today and Marilee wanted to get an update.

"Lord, please don't let that woman die," Kylie muttered under her breath, and she launched her Internet program. Pastor Ludington and the entire congregation of Seaside Baptist Church had prayed for Brenda Perkins in the evening service. Now, as Marilee said, they just had to "wait on the Lord."

Kylie scanned her inbox, noting several messages from the Book Lovers Loop she had joined. They read a novel each month and then discussed it via E-mail. Kylie found that it was a fun way to meet people from all over the world.

Suddenly she saw Lynellen's E-mail address, "lcalex," and clicked the tiny envelope pictured to the left.

Dearest Kylie,

I hope this note finds you doing okay. We have had a lot of rain here—supposed to be snow, but the temps

*warmed up. I used my key to get into your house to
make sure everything was closed up and dry. I always
did that when you and your mom went on vacation, so
I figured I'd do it again. I hope you won't be angry
that I let myself in without asking you. I was just trying to help.*

*Matt is really feeling bad about everything. I know
it's all his fault, but as his mother, I need to say on his
behalf that we all make mistakes. Dena has been coming
over here a lot. We've been having some deep discussions
about things.*

Kylie stopped reading long enough to wonder if those
"deep discussions" included Matt. She envisioned him sitting at the kitchen table with Dena and his mother, drinking a cup of coffee and talking about how "irrational" Kylie
had been acting.

*Dear God, take this jealous feeling away from me. I broke off
our engagement. Matt's no longer committed to our relationship. . .
and neither am I.*

So why do I constantly feel like I am?

Kylie read the remainder of Lynellen's message, which
was really more of the same, although she closed with, "Matt
and Dena say hello."

A sick feeling dropped into the pit of Kylie's stomach,
like a brick into a shallow pond. Dena wanted him. She'd
said so. What if she won his heart now that Kylie wasn't
around?

*Then, obviously, he was never meant to be mine in the first
place!*

Looking back at the post, Kylie strengthened her resolve
and clicked the reply button.

Hi, Lynellen,

Thanks for checking the house for me. That was really thoughtful of you. I'm having a nice time here with my grandparents. They're wonderful people. I went to an art exhibit this afternoon in Charleston. It was held in the gardens of a beautiful restored plantation. I think I could get used to being a Southern belle. In fact, my grandparents have asked me to move in with them. I'm thinking about it. Please say hi to Matt and Dena for me.

Love,
Kylie

After sending the E-mail, Kylie realized she'd been clenching her jaw. She forced herself to relax at the same time Marilee walked in from the balcony where she'd been talking to Logan on her cell phone.

"Well, Brenda's still alive but just barely. Our prayers accomplished that much, anyway."

Kylie smiled, feeling hopeful. "We'll keep praying."

"Yep."

A light *tap-tap-tap* sounded at the door.

"Come on in," Kylie called.

The knob turned and Grandma Kate peeked in. "A gentleman's on the telephone for you, Kylie."

"Who is it?" Alarm shot through her when she thought it might be Matt.

"It's Seth." Her grandmother grinned. "Who else?"

She walked away, allowing the door to remain open.

Kylie began to fret. She and Seth had shared a lovely outing today, after which he had kissed her good-bye. Kylie wanted to handle things with grace and tact, but Seth was moving a little too fast for her.

"What do I do about that guy? I can count the dates I've had in my life on one hand. I'm not exactly Miss Experience where men are concerned."

"That's not a bad thing, so don't apologize." Marilee sat on the end of one of the beds. "Do you like Seth?"

"What's not to like?" Kylie signed off her computer. "But I guess I'm still hung up on Matt. It's getting better, I think, but I don't know if I'm ready for another relationship quite yet—if ever."

"Makes sense. It's only been a little more than a week since your breakup."

"Or my breakdown." Kylie smiled at her own pun.

"Yeah, that, too."

"So what do I do?"

Marilee paused to think it over. "I think I'd be completely honest with Seth about where you're at emotionally. I'm sure he'll respect your position on things, and maybe he'll back off a little."

"I've already been honest with him about Matt and me."

"Oh." Marilee laughed. "He's rather the persistent type, isn't he?"

"I'd say so. Although, I have to admit, Seth was perfect this afternoon. Nice, friendly, not pushy at all. It was an enjoyable time. I really do like him."

"Then just take it one step at a time—and encourage him to take it one step at a time, too."

Before she could reply, her grandmother's kind but reproving voice wafted in from the hallway.

"Kylie, it's not polite to keep the man waiting."

"She is so much like my mother," Kylie muttered, half-amused and half-amazed. "That was totally my mom just now."

Standing, Kylie left the room to take her phone call. She

strode down the hallway to where the Trimline model sat on her grandmother's desk next to the computer.

"Hello, this is Kylie."

"Hi, it's Seth. I think I can arrange to get off work tomorrow. Want to spend the afternoon together? I thought maybe we could tour the Battery."

His forthright manner made her laugh.

"What's so funny?"

"You." Kylie cleared the amusement from her throat. "You sure don't beat around the bush." It had taken Matt a half hour to ask her out the first time.

"Beating around the bush doesn't accomplish a whole lot. Can I pick you up about one o'clock?"

Kylie laughed again. She'd never, in all her life, met a man so blunt and outspoken. In a way, it was refreshing. In another way, Kylie found it hilarious.

"What do you say?"

"Sure, it sounds fun."

"Great. I'll see you tomorrow."

"Okay. Bye, Seth."

Hanging up the phone, Kylie walked back to her room, chuckling to herself. She had to admit, she suddenly looked forward to tomorrow's outing.

CHAPTER

TWENTY-THREE

The next morning, Kylie and Marilee sat on the warm sand beside the ocean with their Bibles opened in their laps. Above them, the sky was as blue as a robin's egg, and the sun's rays cut the chill in the breeze off the water.

Kylie listened as Marilee read today's devotional, followed by the first nine verses in the eleventh chapter of the Book of Isaiah. When she finished, Marilee explained each verse, beginning with the lineage of Jesus Christ and how the Old Testament prophesied Christ's coming, which was fulfilled in the New Testament.

"You know, a lot of things are beginning to make sense to me," Kylie said. "I've spent half my life in church, but I've never really understood God's Word."

Marilee gave her an understanding smile. "It happens."

A shrill whistle disrupted the peaceful hour, and when the ladies glanced back at The Light House, they saw TJ waving at them.

"Phone call for Kylie," he hollered, his voice echoing down the beach.

"Must be Seth." Marilee grinned, and Kylie didn't miss the teasing gleam in her friend's brown eyes.

Standing, she brushed the sand from the seat of her jeans and walked across the beach to the wooden walkway that led up to the house. When she reached the top, TJ handed her the portable phone.

"Who is it?"

"What? Do I look like your secretary?"

Kylie feigned a scathing look and grabbed the phone out of his large hand.

TJ chuckled and reentered the house.

"Hello?"

"Ky, it's Matt."

She froze.

"Mom printed out the E-mail you sent her last night so I could read it. What's all this craziness about moving to South Carolina?"

"Craziness?" Leaning on the wooden railing, Kylie stared out over the Atlantic. She thought of her Bible study this morning, her new friends, and her grandparents. "Matt, I've never felt more sane in all my life."

"So you're serious?"

"I'm seriously considering the idea, yes."

"You are, huh? Does that mean you don't love me anymore?"

His words were like daggers in her heart.

"You know, Kylie, when you said you loved me and said

you'd marry me, I took that as a forever kind of thing. It never occurred to me that in two weeks' time, you'd have such little regard for our relationship."

"Two weeks is pretty good, considering it took you one night." Kylie was amazed at how calm she felt. Maybe she was just numb.

"I made a mistake."

"A big one."

"Okay, I made a big mistake."

"And you lied to me."

"I didn't lie; I just didn't tell you the whole truth."

"Same difference."

"Kylie, I didn't want to hurt you more than I already had."

She didn't reply. He'd hurt her more than words could ever express.

"Honey, I'm so sorry. A million times I'm sorry, and I swear I'll spend the rest of my life making it up to you."

She ignored the apology. It seemed so lame. And in that moment, the painting she'd admired yesterday flashed across her memory. In a way, she felt like that old Victorian house. Were there bulldozers in her future, ready to tear down the past and build a new future?

"Kylie, are you still there?"

She opened her mouth to reply, but then the phone line went dead. Kylie realized Matt probably thought either she had hung up on him or they'd gotten disconnected. Pressing the off button of the portable phone, she wondered if he'd call back.

She wondered what she'd say to him if he did.

❧ ❧ ❧

Allie spent most of the night at Northwestern Memorial. Royce, Colleen's husband, had arrived, as well as Brenda's

"Hang in there, Allie. I'll get you home as soon as I can."

"Thanks." She yawned. "I don't know how you're staying awake."

"Practice. All those years of double shifts are paying off." She grinned.

As they drove away from the medical complex and down the quiet, early morning streets, Allie couldn't keep her eyes open and finally just gave up. She thought of Brenda and their blended family back in the late 1960s. She recalled how her younger stepsister pestered her until she screamed and how Brenda swiped her sweaters and earrings and wore them to school as if the items were her own. Ugly arguments ensued after Allie discovered the offenses.

Too bad I didn't know You back then, Lord. Too bad I was so absorbed in myself that I couldn't even find it in my heart to be kind to a kid who probably looked up to me in some way.

"Quit beating yourself up, Allie."

"What are you talking about?" She opened one eye, glanced at Jack, and closed it again. She felt embarrassed that he'd guessed her thoughts.

He laughed. "You know what I'm talking about."

Allie couldn't hide her grin. She marveled at how well Jack knew her. They'd first met when she was seventeen and he was a rookie cop with the Oakland Park Police Department. She'd run away from home after her mother died. Jack and his partner apprehended her at the Seversons' house.

"Remember Brenda's reaction the day you brought me home from Blythe's place? My dear sister was as glad to see me as I was to be back in my stepfamily's house."

"Yeah, I remember. And you know what? Brenda never really changed from being that smart-mouth junior high kid."

"You'd think college would have matured her."

"You'd think."

"She and Dave met in college, huh?"

"So the story goes."

Allie chanced another look at Jack when he stopped for a red light. As if sensing her stare, he turned her way and winked. Funny how she could still see that charming rookie cop in him after thirty-some years.

The light changed, and Jack pressed on the accelerator. "My personal philosophy about Brenda and Dave is she had lofty aspirations for him and he never quite measured up. When money got tight, Brenda got a factory job that paid a lot better than most professional positions she qualified for with her degree. She got stuck in a rut and so did he. They both sort of stayed there. Brenda felt disappointed in Dave, and he felt disappointed in himself. The disappointment led to depression. He became an unmotivated sofa spud, and well, she's in the hospital on life support."

"How sad and all too familiar, I'm afraid."

"Sadder still is that Dave's a decent guy. If Brenda would have encouraged him instead of putting him on the chopping block and making mincemeat out of him, he probably would have surpassed her expectations."

"Well, let's not forget it's a two-way street there, Jack."

"I know, I know. And I suppose all this speculation is irrelevant, anyway, given the circumstances. But just before Logan left tonight, he said something hopeful. He told me this tragedy could be turned into triumph if even one soul gets saved."

"How true."

A wave of peace suddenly washed over Allie. Peace like a river—one that would carry her through the night.

∽   ∽   ∽

Seth arrived for Kylie at one o'clock sharp. From the window in the front room, she watched as he approached the door, wearing khaki slacks and a maroon short-sleeved polo shirt. The day was a balmy one with temperatures in the high seventies. But not being one to wear shorts because of her fair skin, Kylie put on a cotton royal blue pantsuit whose top had short sleeves and flattering button side tabs at the waistline.

Her grandmother answered the door while Kylie collected her purse.

"Have fun," Marilee said with an encouraging smile.

"Thanks." Kylie returned the gesture. "You, too. . .and, listen, thanks for agreeing to take my grandmother to the grocery store. Did you see the look of relief on my grandfather's face when you said you'd do it?"

Marilee waved her hand in the air as if to say it was nothing. "I'm happy to go shopping with your grandmother."

"Kylie?"

Grandma Kate's voice beckoned her to the foyer, where she and Seth stood.

"What time do you think you'll be home, Dear?" Kathryn asked, reaching out and straightening Kylie's collar.

She suddenly felt like a teenager again. "Do I have a curfew?"

"Oh, honestly, Kylie!" After an indignant cluck of her tongue, she let her hands fall to her sides. "Of course there's no curfew."

"Just checking." She sent Seth an amused grin, then kissed her grandmother's petal-soft cheek. "See you later."

As she left with her date, Kylie glimpsed the injured expression on Grandma Kate's face and felt badly for teasing the sweet woman whom she was quickly beginning to love.

But at the same time, she realized how difficult it would be to move into the Chadwyk household and have her grandmother continually fussing over her. As close as she'd been to her own mother, Kylie had won her independence by the time she'd turned eighteen. She wasn't about to lose it at age thirty-one.

Kylie snapped from her musings when Seth opened the door on the passenger side of his sleek, black Camaro. She slid into the front seat and clicked her seat belt into place. Next, she noticed the sunroof had been opened. Seconds later, Seth climbed in behind the wheel.

"Ready?"

"Ready."

Seth took off but deliberately squealed his tires as they passed TJ, who was on the side of the house, cutting back some brush. After an annoyed look, TJ waved. A few blocks later, Seth braked for a stop sign and flashed Kylie a charming smile. "How and when did you get saved?"

She felt taken aback by the question, but then she told herself she shouldn't be so surprised by this man's straightforwardness. Just last night it had touched off a veritable giggle-fest in her and Marilee's room—although that wasn't uncommon for the two of them.

On a very serious note, Kylie began to share her testimony of faith, beginning with the faded photograph Allie Littenberg had sent. By the time they reached Charleston and parked in a public lot, Kylie had divulged her shattered hopes and dreams and her disillusionment with those she'd always trusted the most.

Seth killed the engine. "God is obviously growing you up fast. I mean, you're a new baby Christian, and look how far you've come already. I think the Lord's got special plans for you, Kylie." He opened the door and crawled out of the sports car. "Those plans might even include a displaced Yankee from Indiana."

"Wh–a–at?!"

He closed the door on her incredulous reply, and as he walked around to her side, Kylie began to laugh. . . .

And she hardly stopped all afternoon.

CHAPTER TWENTY-FOUR

"Seth, I've decided you're a lunatic," Kylie said as she traipsed up the steps to her grandparents' front door.

He followed her. "Well, only when I want to make a lasting impression."

"I'd say you accomplished that goal."

He expelled a dramatic sigh. "Now if I could just be as persuasive when I'm introducing my new software."

"I didn't say you were persuasive. I said you're a lunatic."

"If the end result is the same, I'm rejoicing!"

Another peal of laughter escaped from Kylie. She'd smiled so much today, her face hurt.

They stopped at the door.

"I had a wonderful time today."

Kylie nodded. "Me, too."

He leaned against the outer doorframe, and beneath the soft glow of the porch light, Kylie could see his eyes regarding her with earnest intent.

"How 'bout those ribs?"

Ribs? Kylie frowned. But then she realized what he meant. "Oh. Dinner. Yeah, the ribs were great. But now I can't eat for the next week."

"Aw, sure you can."

The small talk was causing Kylie to feel nervous. She lowered her gaze.

"Say, listen, I want to get serious for a minute here."

Kylie tried not to grimace. *Oh, please, Lord, he's not going to propose already, is he?* At this point, she wasn't sure what to expect from this guy.

Seth came toward her and set his hands on her shoulders. "I really like you, Kylie Rollins. I like you a lot. You're fun, you're pretty, but most of all, you're honest. An honest woman is hard to come by these days."

Kylie found that rather hard to believe.

As if divining her thoughts, he went on to explain. "I'm a thirty-four-year-old unattached male and that makes me fair game, if you will, in the dating scene—even in Christian circles. There are a lot more single women than men out there, and these women want husbands."

"Oh, you poor man. My heart breaks for you." She laughed.

"I'm not trying to be funny. Ask TJ. He feels my pain."

Kylie didn't feel sorry for him one bit.

"Anyway, my point is this—I feel totally comfortable around you. I don't feel pressured to make promises I can't keep."

"I hope you don't make promises you can't keep."

"I don't, Kylie, and I want you to be able to trust me." Earnestness came through in his voice. "I know you're struggling with that right now."

"I sure am."

"Okay, well, here's the deal. I'd like to see you again, but I want to be sure it fits into God's plan for my life and isn't just something I want. What I mean is, you know from experience how painful it is to give your heart away, only to have it smashed to smithereens."

Kylie swallowed the unexpected lump of emotion that formed in her throat and managed a nod in reply.

"Well, I don't want that for either one of us. So will you pray about our relationship?"

Kylie gave him a small smile. "Yes, I will. I like you very much, Seth."

"The feeling's mutual."

Seth's hands went from her shoulders to around her waist. Leaning forward, he kissed her in a way that was both passionate and polite. When it ended, Kylie wished it hadn't. It hadn't been like Matt's kisses, but she'd enjoyed it just the same.

As if reading her mind, Seth told her, "Maybe I'll be able to make you forget that guy. . .what's his name again?"

"Who?" Kylie teased. "I haven't a clue who you're talking about."

"Know what? You're also great for my ego." He kissed her cheek. "Hopefully, I'll see you tomorrow. I'll put some pressure on TJ to invite me over for supper or something."

"I don't think you'll have to press too hard."

"See you tomorrow."

Smiling, Kylie watched Seth to his car, then she opened the front door and entered the house. All was quiet, except for strains of a television program coming from the den. Kylie strolled in that direction and found TJ stretched out on the large area rug.

"Hi."

He tipped his head back and looked at her upside down. "Hi. Have fun?"

"Had a blast."

"Good. Seth's a great guy."

"Yes, he is."

"So where'd you eat dinner?"

"Sticky Fingers."

"Some of the best ribs in all of South Carolina."

Kylie grinned. "So I found out."

"Did you see the Battery?"

"Uh-huh, it was awesome. We took a carriage tour—horse and buggy, the whole works. I found it interesting that many of the homes in Charleston were actually built sideways."

"Right." TJ stood and stretched. "It was due to some tax law about the number of square footage facing the street equaling the amount of money owed to the city."

Kylie nodded.

"Well, time to hit the hay. You want to watch TV, or should I shut everything off?"

"Oh, you can turn everything off. Thanks. I'm going upstairs."

TJ inclined his head ever so slightly. "Well, then, g'night, little girl."

Little girl? She rolled her eyes. "Good night." As she ascended the stairs, she wondered if he'd waited up for her. Nice of him, if he had.

Kylie opened the door to the Birds 'n' Blossoms Room and found her roommate pacing the dark green carpet and wearing an anxious expression. She noticed Marilee's limp immediately.

She narrowed her gaze. "Are you okay?"

Marilee shook her head and tears filled her eyes. "I think I overdid it today. But I took a couple of painkillers, so I should be feeling better soon. The only problem is, my depression has come back."

"Well, as long as you know it's the medicine making you feel that way, you can handle it, right?"

Marilee froze. "What did you say?"

"I said, as long as you know it's the medicine—"

"Kylie!" Her brown eyes widened with realization. "I don't believe it! You just hit the nail on the head!"

Kylie set down her purse and began to undress. "What are you talking about?"

"The pain medication. It's what's been causing my depression and mood swings."

"Probably. I mean, you've been fine all week."

Marilee turned pensive. "I haven't taken any pain medication all week. I haven't had to. We swam at the hotel and made stops to stretch during the day. My leg and hip have been fine. . .until tonight."

"There's your answer," Kylie said, grinning. "See, it's not you—never has been."

"I've got to call Logan." Marilee rushed to fetch her cell phone off the dresser beside her bed. "I talked to him about an hour ago and I started to cry. That, of course, got him upset." She hurried for the patio. "Kylie, you're a genius."

She shook her head. "It was kind of a no-brainer."

While Marilee chatted with Logan, Kylie changed into her nightshirt and padded to the bathroom. She removed her makeup, washed her face, and brushed her teeth and hair.

Minutes later, Marilee walked in, since Kylie had left the door ajar. Brown pill bottle in hand, she dumped its contents into the toilet and flushed it down.

"They're gone, Logan," she said, her cell phone to her ear.

Marilee left as fast as she came, and Kylie chuckled in her wake.

Leaving the bathroom, Kylie crawled into bed and mentally rehashed the last ten hours she'd spent with Seth. She'd gotten so lost in her daydream, she didn't even hear Marilee come in off the veranda.

"Everything's all right."

"What?" Kylie extracted herself from her pleasant thoughts. "Oh. . .good, I'm glad." She then recalled the grievous situation with Allie's stepsister. "Hey, how's Brenda doing?"

"There's no change. She's on life support. Logan said her family will probably have to make some decisions soon."

Kylie winced. "That's awful. I'm really sad to hear that."

"Yeah, me, too. Kind of adds to my doldrums." Marilee sat down on the edge of her bed.

"Why didn't God answer our prayers?"

"Well, it's not over yet. But if the Lord doesn't heal Brenda, I guess it's because it's not His will. It's kind of like our parents when we were kids. We'd ask for things, and most of the time we'd get them, but sometimes we didn't. It's the same with our heavenly Father."

Kylie wondered over her reply—until Marilee changed the subject. "Logan asked when I was coming home, and I told him we planned to leave the day after tomorrow. Is that correct?"

"Yes. I figured we'd head out Thursday right after breakfast."

"Sounds good." A smile spread across her face. "Logan must have said he missed me four times during our phone conversation. Isn't that sweet? I miss him, too."

"That is sweet. You guys are a cute couple." Kylie meant every word. If ever two people belonged together, it was Logan and Marilee.

"Thanks." A hint of a blush pinked Marilee's cheeks. "And speaking of. . .tell me all about your day! I want the details."

Kylie grinned. Her turn to blush. Nevertheless, she sat up, crossed her legs, and began to relay her better-than-perfect date with Seth Brigham.

"So we promised to pray about our relationship."

"That's a good start."

"But how will I know if it's right or wrong?"

"God will show you."

"How? Writing on the wall? In the sky?"

Marilee laughed. "Maybe. God can do anything. More realistically, He'll use people. He might even use Matt and Dena. . .and your pastor back home."

Kylie put her face in her hands. "Oh, Marilee, I am so dreading the return home. I don't want to go back. When I see Matt, my heart will break all over again, and when I see Dena, I'll want to scratch her eyes out." She looked up and laughed. "Some Christian I am."

"Kylie, Christians are as fallible as anybody else. I'm proof of that."

"Ha. You're about as close to perfect as they come."

"Thanks." A hint of a smirk tugged at Marilee's mouth. "But you just said it yourself. 'Close to perfect,' meaning I'm not. And that's true. Just for the record, I'm far from 'close.'"

They sat there, deep in thought and regarding each other as the seconds ticked slowly by.

Then Marilee stood. "I want to show you a Scripture verse that just came to mind." She found her Bible and returned to the end of Kylie's bed, where she sat down again. She leafed through the delicate pages of the Book until she found what she was looking for. "Here it is. First Corinthians 10:13."

After reading the verse aloud, Marilee explained, "Nothing you're going through is odd or unique. Others have experienced the same things, and God doesn't give us more than we can handle."

Marilee closed her Bible. "You don't have to dread going home, Kylie, because your heavenly Father will go with you. He won't let anything happen to you that you can't deal with. When the darkest hours fall, He'll even make a way for you to escape." Tears pooled in Marilee's eyes. "He did it for me, and He used you."

"Me?"

Marilee nodded. "I was sad and depressed, wondering what was wrong with me, wondering how I could ever be a pastor's wife in my miserable state. But then you walked into my life and allowed me to come on this little getaway. . .and you even figured out the very thing that triggered my mood swings." She sighed and a look of relief washed over her features. "I can finally get off the emotional roller coaster that was threatening my sanity as well as my relationship with the man I love."

"No kidding? I did all that?"

Marilee nodded. "No kidding!"

Kylie rode a wave of exhilaration at the mere thought of being one of God's instruments, used to help another Christian.

"And you know what that's called, Kylie? Ministry."

❧ ❧ ❧

Kathryn lay awake in the darkness of her bedroom, listening

to Lee snoring softly beside her and the female voices talking and laughing in the next room. Apart from Lee's snoring, the noise didn't bother her, but rather it consoled her. This part of The Light House was alive again, where before it had merely existed.

Just like herself.

Turning onto her side, Kathryn tried in vain to squelch the troubled feeling she had over Kylie's return home. She admitted it was largely her own selfishness that didn't want her granddaughter to go; however, it was also a concern about Kylie. The poor dear had no one now and many important decisions to make.

Lord, I want to help her, but I don't want to be controlling or overbearing.

Kathryn sighed.

"You having trouble sleeping, Honey?"

"Mm-hmm. . .I keep thinking about Kylie."

"You don't want her to leave, do you?"

"No. But I don't want to smother her either."

Lee rolled over and gave her hip an affectionate pat. "You're doing fine. Just fine." He yawned.

Kathryn remembered her granddaughter's remark about having a curfew. "I'm not so sure."

"Hon, she's known us a week. Give it some time."

Moving onto her back once more, Kathryn strained to see her husband in the darkness. "Time is not on our side, Darling. You might feel like you're fifty on the golf course, but—"

"All right. All right. Point taken."

Kathryn laughed softly.

Several moments of silence lapsed.

"I do have a concern—"

Kathryn noted the seriousness in her husband's tone. "What is it?"

"Well, before you three ladies went shopping Saturday, I had a bit of a chat with Kylie. She mentioned feeling uncertain about handling some of Wendy's outstanding affairs. Before the breakup of her engagement, Kylie thought her fiancé could help her, but apparently she's not so sure about reconciling with him."

"Yes, I know. . .and it bothers me. Remember how stubborn Wendy was? She had a way of hardening her heart. If you crossed her once, she'd write you off like a bad debt."

"Wendy was a child when she left us, Kathryn. Sounds like she became a beautiful person."

Kathryn turned in his direction. Her throat constricted with unshed emotion. "Then why didn't she contact us?"

"Because in her mind, we were still those hard-nosed parents who practiced tough love on her and Rob. We wouldn't help them when they called and asked for money, and she blamed us for Rob's death—as if his life might have been spared if we'd wired them two hundred dollars." He expelled a disappointed-sounding sigh. "As if a few bucks would have solved their problems."

"Oh, Lee, maybe we should have. . . ."

"No. We did what we thought was best at the time."

Kathryn wiped her eyes with shaky fingers. She had shed so many tears over this situation that she was surprised to find she had any left.

"On a lighter note," Lee said, "TJ thinks the two of us should drive back with Kylie. She's alone and she needs us. We can finally be grandparents to her. Now I know it's kind of a long trek, but it might be nice." He yawned again. "I s'pose we could fly, although I started thinking that if we stopped in Chicago with Kylie when she drops off Marilee, we could—"

"Find Rob's grave," Kathryn cut in, swallowing her sadness. Hope swelled in her heart. Her thoughts were way ahead of him. "Oh, Lee, let's do it! TJ can run The Light House."

"Of course he can, but don't you think we ought to pray about it, then discuss the matter with Kylie first?"

Kathryn let out a long, slow breath. "Yes, of course. I am forever putting the cart before the horse, aren't I?"

"No." Lee gathered her into his arms. "You're just a. . .a passionate woman." He nuzzled her neck.

"Oh, for pity sakes, Lee, stop that nonsense!"

He chuckled. "Guess I feel fifty in more ways than just golf."

Grinning, Kathryn rolled onto her side again and Lee pulled her up next to him. Snuggling in the warmth of her husband's embrace, she felt herself grow drowsy. Minutes later, Lee began to breathe heavily. He'd fallen asleep again. . . and Kathryn knew she wasn't far behind him.

CHAPTER TWENTY-FIVE

Shafts of morning sunlight whittled their way through the white metal blinds of the intensive care waiting area. The doctors were making their rounds, and a team of them had just been in to see Brenda. They spoke to Dave and Colleen afterward—giving them a most depressing report.

Allie glanced at Logan, who stood in the far corner of the room. He seemed to be having an in-depth conversation with the Perkinses' two sons, Kirk and Brett. She was grateful that Logan felt led to minister to the young men. If anyone could put a senseless tragedy into perspectives that teenagers understood, it was Logan Callahan.

Allie's gaze shifted to her left. Standing several feet away, Jack and Royce spoke in hushed tones with Brenda's husband,

Dave. The poor man had to render the kind of decision people hoped and prayed they'd never have to make—whether or not to remove their spouse from life support. In Brenda's case, her major organs had failed and there was very little brain activity. Allie felt heartsick imagining her stepsister slipping closer and closer into a Christless eternity. Of course, for all Allie knew, Brenda could have become a believer some time in her forty-five years of life. But it didn't seem probable. Allie couldn't nor wouldn't judge. She could only speculate.

If only God would do an amazing miracle, she thought, like when He rained down fire to consume the sacrifice, the wood, the stones, and the dust, which Elijah had drenched with water beforehand. When the people saw it, they said, "The Lord, he is the God."

Oh, Father, Colleen and Royce, Dave and his sons—they need to see that You are God!

"Allie?"

Snapping from her reverie, she glanced at Colleen, who sat beside her on the sofa.

"You're tired, aren't you? I can tell. If Brenda knew how many hours you've spent here at the hospital, I think she would have finally seen the sort of big sister you really are."

Allie pushed out a smile for Colleen's sake. "I wish we hadn't parted on such unpleasant terms. Even at Christmas, when I ran into her at Dominick's, she gave me such a scathing look when I said hello."

"I know, but Brenda has been so angry and unhappy. . . well, for years. She thought walking away from her marriage was the cure, but it wasn't." Colleen paused and glanced at Dave before bringing her brown-eyed gaze back to Allie. "I think Brenda had this disillusionment of suddenly being twenty years old again once she filed the divorce papers."

"How sad."

"Kind of a midlife crisis, I guess."

"A crisis, for sure."

"Ladies." Jack waved them over.

They stood, and Colleen grabbed Allie's hand. They both sensed what was coming.

"I. . .I guess it's best if. . ."

Tears leaked from Dave's hazel eyes, and Allie's heart went out to the rotund man with dark brown hair. True, he wasn't Hollywood handsome, but in the past few days, Allie had learned that Dave Perkins was a regular teddy bear.

What's more, he really loved his wife.

"I've given this matter a lot of thought," Dave began again. His two sons and Logan had joined their intimate circle. "If Brenda did wake up, she'd be a vegetable."

"Mom would hate that," her oldest son, Kirk, muttered. A strapping young man, he'd inherited many of his father's features.

The youngest, a definite mix between his parents, nodded in agreement.

"So, I think we should pull the plug." Dave's voice broke. "That's what she wanted anyhow. She wanted to. . .go."

Allie winced and looked at Jack. They exchanged sad glances.

"I've heard of people living on life support for decades," Royce said, running a hand through his auburn hair. "That's hardly quality of life. It's existing at best."

"God didn't intend for people to live on life support, did He?" Dave looked at Logan.

"That's a matter of perspective, I guess," Logan replied, his dark brows puckered in a solemn expression. "But my feeling is no, He didn't. I believe heart and lung machines, respiratory equipment, and all that are a means to sustain a person's existence until he or she recovers. They're not a way of life."

Allie glanced back at Dave, who looked suddenly relieved of a weighty burden.

"I think we're doing the right thing," he said.

His sons agreed.

Jack clapped Dave on the back, an obvious act of support.

Colleen sniffed and pulled a shredded Kleenex from her pocket. "Well, if we're going to do this, let's get it over with. . . ."

✿   ✿   ✿

While Marilee checked out The Light House's honeymoon suite, thinking she'd like to change her plans for after the wedding, Kylie sipped her morning coffee and listened to her grandparents' proposal. They wanted to follow her back to Wisconsin in their car.

"It's a long trip," she warned them.

"Oh, I think we're up for it," Lee said. He smiled and took a bite of his scrambled eggs.

Kylie noted her grandfather's outfit and thought he looked quite dapper in his pale yellow polo shirt, which was tucked into the waist of a pair of navy blue pleated trousers. He and TJ had already been golfing. There was no question in Kylie's mind; her grandparents were in very good shape for their age. The trip wouldn't be difficult for them.

"If you'd rather we didn't go, Dear, please say so," Kathryn put in. She had been out for her morning walk, had showered, and changed into blue-and-white-checked shorts and a white T-shirt. "We don't want to interfere or be an imposition."

Kylie felt an embarrassed smirk tug at the corners of her lips. "I wasn't so much thinking you'd be imposing or inter-fering. I was remembering what a mess I left in the house."

Laughing, Kathryn waved a hand at her. "That lived-in look is in style."

"That's good. My house is definitely 'lived in.' " Kylie grinned and mulled over the idea of hosting her grandparents. Her thought process gave way to a measure of comfort. "You know, I think I'd like having you two around. Too bad you can't stay forever." Apart from her volition, her eyes grew misty.

"Oh, Kylie. . ." Kathryn touched her arm. "Are things really that bad for you back home?"

Her first reply was an uncomfortable little shrug. Then she said, "I've been dreading my return because I know it means I'll have to face Matt and Dena again."

"You still have feelings for the young man?" Kathryn asked.

"Feelings? Sure I do. But if you're asking do I still love Matt. . ." Kylie sighed. "I guess I do. It's like I told Seth. Emotions don't disappear just because the situation has changed."

"Very well said."

"Is Matt a Christian?" Lee queried.

"I'm not sure. We never really talked about our faith because there was no need. Matt and I attended the same church since we were kids, although he lived in Madison for a number of years when he was married to Rochelle. I don't know what church they attended—if they did."

"Is he divorced?" her grandmother asked.

"No."

Kylie then relayed the entire story about how Rochelle and baby Jason were killed.

"How tragic," Lee said, shaking his head as a somber frown puckered his white winged brows.

"Sometimes I think Matt never really got over her—them.

But I've come to realize he probably never will." Kylie took another drink of her coffee. "Therein lies another dilemma. Can I live with Rochelle's shadow hanging over my head for the rest of my life—that's assuming Matt and I reconcile?"

"Kylie, can this old man give you some advice?"

She smiled at her grandfather. "Sure, but I can't promise I'll take it."

"You owe me no promises. I simply want to help."

"All right."

"You have many, many issues to sort through. They're hidden things that have only now come to light. But God has used them already to lead you to Him, and I believe He will continue to use them to direct your future. For instance, this hurtful situation with Matt—could it be it's not God's will for you to marry this man?"

Kylie peered into her coffee, her heart breaking for the umpteenth time. "Yes, I suppose God may not want me to marry Matt. Marilee and I have discussed that at great length."

And it's no accident that God gave me a friend like Marilee at this precise point in time.

"Kylie, I said all that to make a point," Lee continued. "Be careful you don't make decisions out of the Lord's will. You'll live to regret them. Trust me. I speak from experience."

Kylie replied with a grateful smile. "I want my life to be what God desires, but I wish I had all the answers—now."

Lee chuckled. "You're off to a great start."

"We would love to help you through this trying time, Kylie," her grandmother said. "We want to be part of your life."

"I want that, too," Kylie replied. Those words had come straight from the depth of her soul. With her mother gone, her relationship with Matt unclear, she needed people in her life upon whom she could depend. Like Allie, Jack, Marilee, Logan, TJ, and the Chadwyks—they all seemed worthy of Kylie's trust.

Glancing from Kathryn to Lee, she grinned. "You're welcome to follow me back to Basil Creek. I'd love to have you stay in my home."

Just then, TJ walked into the breakfast nook. "Am I interrupting?"

"Not at all," Kathryn said. "Please join us."

Kylie watched him pull out a chair and sit down. "My grandparents are coming to Wisconsin for a visit."

"I think that's a fine idea." He grinned at Kathryn, then Lee, before looking back at Kylie. "I heard a rumor that you're moving in with us soon."

"That's not for sure. I'm still. . .praying about it. I want to be sure it's. . .God's will."

"That's my girl!" Lee exclaimed with a broad smile.

She smiled back. *My girl.* She suddenly felt like she belonged, and in that very moment, she loved her grandparents.

"Well, here I thought maybe you'd take Lissa's job," TJ muttered under his breath but loud enough that everyone around the table could hear.

Kylie caught his good-natured wink just before Kathryn swatted him on the arm with her linen napkin.

"TJ, you should come to Wisconsin, too," Kylie said. "We get some pretty intense thunderstorms and our share of tornados."

"Hmm. I'll have to keep that in mind when I plan my next vacation."

Kylie laughed, then spotted Marilee walking through the kitchen and heading in their direction. Wearing pink-and-white printed capris and a pink sleeveless sweater, she appeared relaxed and comfortable. That awful anxious feeling from last night had dissipated; she'd told Kylie so earlier, and she finally felt like herself again.

"Well, Marilee," Kathryn said, "did you enjoy your tour of the honeymoon suite?"

"Very much." She glanced at Kylie. "Have you seen it yet?"

Kylie replied with a shake of her head before popping the last of her English muffin into her mouth.

Marilee's gaze returned to Kathryn. "May I show her, Mrs. Chadwyk?"

"Go right ahead. We didn't have guests last night, so all the rooms are vacant. No need to worry about disturbing anyone."

After wiping her hands on the white linen napkin, Kylie followed Marilee upstairs and down a long hallway, opposite TJ and the Chadwyks' private quarters. At the end of the corridor, they paused and Marilee unlocked the wood-paneled door.

"Prepare yourself."

Kylie grinned. "Okay."

Marilee opened the door. Inside, the spacious room had ivory textured wallpaper, and matching valances hung across the tops of the row of windows that overlooked the street. The bed had an antique white, lacy canopy and a creamy satin comforter. At the opposite end of the suite were patio doors that opened to a private veranda.

"Can you believe this hot tub?" Marilee asked after they'd stepped outside. "Logan'll sit there," she planned aloud, indicating the side of the Jacuzzi closest to the house, "so he can stare out over the ocean, and I'll sit here, so I can stare at Logan."

Kylie rolled her eyes, but she had to admit, the way the

spa had been built into the natural wood deck was, in a word, awesome.

"And the view of the ocean. . ." Marilee cast her gaze out over the sea and expelled a dreamy-sounding sigh. "It's so peaceful, and Logan loves being by the water. I think he'd enjoy a week's vacation here instead of the Rockies."

They reentered the room, and Marilee closed the sliding glass door.

"Matt wouldn't be very impressed," Kylie said, touching the devotional that lay on the bedside table. It was titled *Daily Devotions for Newlyweds*. Looking back at Marilee, she added, "He would rather be in the mountains. The Grand Canyon would be just his style."

"Did you hear yourself?"

She hadn't, but now that Marilee brought it to her attention, Kylie realized what she'd just said.

"When you think of marriage, you still think of Matt. I mean, am I wrong to assume the thought of sharing this suite with Seth, for instance, never entered your head?"

"Marilee!" Kylie felt her face begin to flame, although peals of giggles escaped her. "I can't believe you said that!"

"I'm merely pointing out the obvious."

"Well, thanks for nothing. I'm very much aware of the obvious." Kylie sighed and felt the smile slip from her face. "I just don't know what to do about it." She hadn't heard from Matt since yesterday morning, and that fact both relieved and worried her. On one hand, Kylie didn't want to talk to him, didn't want to hear any more of Matt's lame excuses. But on the other, she imagined her ex-best friend determined to console him—and succeeding. The thought left her insides a jumble of anger and sorrow.

Marilee moved forward and put a sisterly arm on her

shoulders. "Kylie, you don't have to do anything, and you don't have to fret." She smiled and her brown eyes shimmered with sincerity. "Your heavenly Father has it all worked out."

❧ ❧ ❧

As Brenda Perkins lay dying, Logan read to her from the Bible and explained God's plan of salvation. At first, Allie saw his attempt to witness for Christ as pointless, but then the Lord reminded her that He is able to reach anyone at any time—even a soul who hung precariously between earth and eternity.

"Well, I think I've said what I needed to," Logan announced, standing from where he'd been sitting on the edge of Brenda's hospital bed. "Please allow me to encourage you all to take a turn and say your good-byes."

No one moved for several long minutes. The quiet in the room seemed to roar in Allie's ears.

Finally, the youngest Perkins boy ambled over to his mother's bedside. "Bye, Mom," Brett said, his voice breaking. He touched her hand, then whirled around and walked back to his chair. Setting his head in his hands, he cried and his broad shoulders shook with each sob.

Allie blinked back the tears that filled her eyes.

Logan put his hand on the boy's back, a silent gesture intended to comfort and console.

Brenda's oldest son went next. He stared at her for a long minute, then in a shattered voice, he asked, "Mom, why'd you do it? Why? You could have been happy if you'd just tried. We're not bad kids. I know of a lot worse."

"Whoa, hang on a second, Kirk." His uncle Royce stood and walked over to the young man. "This has nothing to do with you."

"It has everything to do with me. Me and Brett and Dad.

Mom thought we ruined her life. Look at her. Is this a mother who loves her family?"

Logan got up from his chair. "Kirk, your mom wasn't thinking of anyone but herself when she overdosed. Suicide is the ultimate act of selfishness."

"But she could have had so much more. What was so wrong with our family that she left Dad?"

"My mother did something similar," Logan said. "When I was eighteen months old, she put me down for my afternoon nap, then took off, emptying the joint checking and savings accounts before she drove out of town. She left my dad with nothing but a baby to care for. What kind of mother does that? Was it my fault?"

Kirk frowned. "No. Of course not. You were just a baby."

Logan nodded. "Exactly. But I only recently came to terms with that truth. I carried the weight of guilt with me for twenty-eight years. Finally, I met my biological mother and she admitted it wasn't anything I did. She simply despised her circumstances and wanted desperately to change them. Unfortunately, she learned too late that she'd gone about it the wrong way, just like your mother."

Dabbing her eyes with the balled-up Kleenex in her palm, Allie gave Jack's hand a squeeze.

He squeezed hers back.

Kirk glanced over his shoulder at his mom before bringing his gaze back to Logan.

"Forgive your mom," Logan advised in a soft, compassionate tone, "and pity her. She will soon face the Lord and, at the name of Jesus, the Bible says, every knee will bow and every tongue confess that He is Lord. How simple. He's the Answer. The Way, the Truth, and the Life. Not a handful of pills. What's more, I imagine Jesus Himself will reveal to your mother the magnitude of her selfish act."

Kirk appeared to be mulling it over.

"Let me put it this way," Logan added. "Think back on a time when a teacher, a coach, or your principal reamed you out. Now imagine a reprimand like that coming from a holy, almighty God."

A slight wince shadowed the younger man's face, and Allie could tell he understood.

Logan crossed the room and sat down while Kirk looked back at his mother. Then, he turned slowly around and moved closer to her bedside. He reached out and touched her limp hand before walking back to his seat on the other side of Logan. Allie's heart went out to the young man.

Colleen walked over to Royce, who still stood at Brenda's bedside. Together they said their farewells.

"Allie, did you want to say something?"

She shook her head. "I don't think Brenda would want to hear from me."

Colleen disregarded her excuse and waved her over. "This is more for you than her, Allie. Come here."

Jack let go of her hand, and Allie took that to mean she ought to do as Colleen bid her. Standing, she strolled across the room. She glanced down at her stepsister, lying so peacefully that one could imagine she was only asleep. Her red hair splayed across the pillow, and her face appeared unnaturally puffy.

Allie didn't know what to say. Last time she and Brenda exchanged words, it was an ugly scene—the very night of Marilee's car accident, in fact. Since then, they'd seen each other here and there, in the supermarket, the department store, but Brenda always ignored her. It had always been that way, ever since her father married Allie's mother, bringing them together as sisters.

"I'm so sorry, Brenda," Allie eked out. "If I have any regrets about my return to Chicago, it's that you and I never made peace."

"Don't feel bad," Dave said, coming up behind her. "She and I never made peace either. The last words Brenda spoke to me were so bad, I couldn't repeat them in this company."

Allie grimaced, sensing the man's pain as he came to stand next to her.

"Dad, it's not your fault like it's not my fault," Kirk told him.

"I guess I know that." Dave stared down at his wife. With a shaky hand, he touched her hair, then her cheek and gown-clad shoulder. "But it hurts just the same. Try as I might, I never could make her happy, and this here's the end result."

"Dave, don't be so hard on yourself." Allie touched his forearm.

He seemed oblivious to the remark. "I loved her the best I knew how."

"Of course you did," Colleen said. "No one disputes that."

Leaning forward, he kissed Brenda's forehead. Then straightening, he spun on his heel and left the room.

Allie met Jack's gaze briefly as he followed Dave.

Then, after telling Brenda good-bye, she made her way back to the cold, hard, uncomfortable folding chair and continued the waiting game, along with the rest of her family.

CHAPTER

TWENTY-SIX

After two days of traveling, Kylie pulled up to the high-rise in which Marilee and her parents lived.

"We're here." A mixture of relief and sadness filled her. She felt weary of driving but hated to relinquish her new-found friend.

Marilee gathered her things, stuffing her cell phone into her purse. "Dad said he'll come to the door and help with my luggage."

"Okay." Kylie opened her door and climbed out of the car.

Marilee did the same. "Are you sure you and your grand-parents won't stay with us? Mom and Dad would love it. So would I."

Kylie shook her head. "We're all tired. We wouldn't be very

good guests." Her grandparents had stopped and already checked into a hotel right off the highway. Grandpa Lee had called her on her mobile phone to say he'd gotten adjoining rooms.

"I plan to hit the sack early."

"You could hit the sack in my apartment right now."

"Thanks, but no. Besides, you've got that funeral to attend tonight, and my grandparents are eager to visit Precious Things in the morning."

"Have you decided whether to go with them?"

She nodded. "I won't go into the shop. If Blythe sees me, she won't talk to my grandparents. I'm pretty certain of that. So I'll walk up and down Michigan Avenue and shop to my heart's content. I plan to find a bookstore or two."

"Oh, you'll definitely find bookstores." Marilee grinned.

With the hatchback opened, Kylie pulled the suitcase from her car while Marilee collected her shopping bags.

"I'm going to miss you, Kylie. Keep in touch. I'll do the same."

"I will. I already promised, and I keep my word."

Marilee smiled and squinted into the late afternoon sunshine. "I'm dying to know if Seth e-mails you again tonight. He's quite a character."

"You're telling me!" Kylie couldn't suppress a laugh just thinking about the post he'd sent her yesterday. She'd read it aloud to Marilee last night in the motel room they shared, and both women went into hysterics.

"You know, he probably sent that same E-mail to a dozen women."

"Oh, I doubt it. When he came over for dinner Tuesday night, he seemed genuinely interested in you—and you seemed interested, too."

"I know," Kylie said, feeling a bit disgusted with herself. "I guess I succumbed to his charm."

Marilee laughed. "He cracked me up when he came right out and said he's looking for a wife. Talk about being straight-forward. Wow!"

"Yeah, but I can see his point. He's thirty-four; he's sick of traveling; he wants a family, a home."

"Sounds like husband material to me." Marilee raised her brows conspiratorially.

"Yeah, well, I thought Matt was 'husband material.' Remember?"

"I remember." Any trace of humor disappeared from her face. "Keep me informed of the latest details, okay? I'll be pray-ing for you. And, speaking of charming. . .here's my dad."

Seeing their approach, Mr. Domotor opened the door for them and relieved Kylie of his daughter's heavy suitcase.

"You girls look no worse for wear." He gave Marilee a one-armed hug. "Have a good time?"

"Wonderful time," Marilee said.

Kylie silently agreed with a smile.

"And you're sure you won't stay with us?" Stan Domotor asked. "We've got plenty of room."

"Thank you, but my grandparents are already checked into the hotel."

"You know how to get back there, right?" Marilee asked.

"You've given me terrific instructions. But if I get lost, I've got my cell phone."

Opening her arms, Kylie hugged Marilee good-bye. Remorse gripped her heart, but she told herself they'd see each other again. If not before, then at Marilee's wedding.

And there was always E-mail.

As she drove back to the hotel, Kylie marveled at how

fast she and Marilee had bonded. Their friendship had formed instantaneously, and Kylie felt sure it would be one of those relationships that would last forever. She might have lost Dena as a friend, but God gave her Marilee.

Slowing at an intersection, Kylie grinned, recalling the laughs they'd shared last night. Thinking of Seth's E-mail soon caused her to remember the Internet post Matt sent her, followed by the message he'd left on her cell phone this morning. Kylie hadn't returned either. She really didn't know what to do. What would she say when she saw him? What would she say to Dena?

Lord, Marilee and my grandparents say I should place all my cares in Your hands and leave them there. I'm not sure how to do that. Will You help me? Kylie smiled. *I think maybe You already have!*

৩ ৩ ৩

The next morning Kathryn fussed with her outfit in front of the bathroom mirror. She felt nervous at the thought of entering Blythe Severson's shop. What if the woman somehow recognized her and Lee? *But, of course, that notion is ridiculous,* Kathryn scolded herself. *I wouldn't even recognize my own picture from thirty years ago!*

She smoothed on a subtle shade of lipstick, deciding it would have been polite of Ms. Severson to notify them of Rob's death. Couldn't she have dropped them even an informal line or an anonymous note?

Well, who knows what Rob told her about us? Perhaps she thought we were monsters.

Lee knocked on the door. "You coming out anytime soon?"

"Be right there."

"It's ten minutes after eight. Kylie's waiting for us in the restaurant downstairs."

281

Kathryn opened the door. "For goodness sakes, Lee, beauty takes time."

He grinned at her retort.

Together they left their hotel room and rode the elevator to the lobby. The restaurant was a tiny dinerlike place with only six booths and four tables, so it wasn't hard to find Kylie.

"You look so pretty today," Kathryn said, admiring the red-and-white-striped sweater her granddaughter wore. The temperatures were quite different here in the Chicago area, compared to those in Sabal Beach. "I like the way you did your hair."

"Thanks, Grandma."

Kathryn smiled, noting she'd left off "Kate" from her name. That could only mean they were growing closer.

Tears of joy sprang into Kathryn's eyes, causing her granddaughter's gaze to narrow in concern.

"You'll have to forgive this old lady," she explained, taking a seat beside her husband. "I have these spells from time to time. You might see tears, but in my heart, I'm really rejoicing."

"You're thinking about Rob this morning, aren't you?" Kylie took a sip of her coffee. "I'm sure this is very difficult for you."

"That's part of it. . .and, yes, it is difficult, although I didn't think it would be."

Lee said nothing, as was his usual way whenever he felt particularly troubled.

The waitress appeared and filled Kathryn and Lee's white ceramic cups with a rich-smelling brew. She took their orders, then hurried away and disappeared behind a swinging aluminum door.

"Have you heard anything from your former fiancé?" Lee asked.

Kylie nodded. "He's angry with me because I won't return his calls or E-mails." She took another drink of coffee. "But I really don't know what to say."

"Hmm. . ."

"What about Seth?" Kathryn couldn't help asking. "Have you heard from him?"

"Yeah. . ." Kylie's cheeks suddenly grew pink. "We chatted on-line for a couple of hours last night."

"The Internet is an amazing invention, isn't it?"

"I'll say," Kylie agreed.

"You have two men vying for your attention," Kathryn remarked. "That must make you feel special."

Her dark eyes clouded over. "On the contrary, Grandma. The way I feel today, after hearing Matt's message on my cell phone, staying single is awfully appealing."

"What did he say to upset you?" Lee wanted to know.

Kylie blew out a weary breath. "I would rather not talk about it."

"Very well. That's your prerogative."

"No offense, Grandpa."

"None taken, my dear."

Kylie pushed back a wayward lock of her jet-black hair. "It's really the same old song and dance, just a different tune."

"I see." Lee gave her a smile before sipping his hot coffee.

The waitress appeared with their food, and as they ate, they exchanged small talk. Once they finished, they paid for their meal and returned to their rooms, packed up, and checked out of the hotel.

In the parking lot, they synchronized their watches and planned to meet at a restaurant that Marilee suggested. Then they climbed into their respective cars and began the drive into the city.

Following the directions Marilee had sketched out yesterday afternoon, Lee maneuvered the vehicle onto the Northwest Tollway. Kylie was right behind them, and Kathryn found herself marveling over her granddaughter's courage, yet fretting over the young woman as well. *Lord, at Kylie's age, I had two small children to care for. . . .*

"What are you thinking about?"

Kathryn turned to her husband. "Oh, I was just remembering back to when I was thirty. Rob must have been five and Wendy three and a half." She laughed. "Remember how Rob used to imitate John Wayne? Wasn't that the cutest thing?!"

Lee chuckled. "Yeah. . ."

"He loved to pretend he was a cowboy. You know, all these years I sort of thought he was out West somewhere."

"Well, he was west of Sabal Beach." Lee made a turn onto another stretch of expressway. "TJ and I logged onto the Internet several nights ago, and we started doing searches on the 1968 Democratic National Convention. Those were the days of Abbie Hoffman, Jerry Rubin, and Tom Hayden, part of the 'Chicago Seven' who went to trial for inciting riots during the convention."

"Oh, yes, I'm beginning to recall." Kathryn shook her head. "That was a lifetime ago."

"Our son was in the thick of things."

Remorse washed over her. "So it seems."

Lee grew quiet, and Kathryn sensed he was privately mourning Rob's death. It was a journey, she knew, that he preferred to make by himself.

They reached Michigan Avenue and found the side street on which Precious Things was located. After parking, they walked down the sidewalk until they came to the small store with a fire-engine red wooden door. Opening it, a bell jangled as they stepped inside, and Kathryn smelled sweet incense, which tickled her nostrils until she rubbed her nose.

"Hello, may I help you?" A small-framed woman about Kathryn's age rose from where she'd been sitting near the cash register. With her dark hair cut short and brushed forward around her face, she reminded Kathryn of a recent picture she'd seen of actress Suzanne Pleshette.

"We're just here to browse," Lee said.

"Oh, of course, go right ahead."

Kathryn followed her husband farther into the quaint little shop. They meandered around tables whose surfaces displayed an array of antique perfume bottles in various colors. Kathryn remembered her mother having similar bottles on her bureau. Several feet away, Lee paused beside an old Federal-style dresser to look at a brass clock. He picked it up and examined it.

"Oh, that's a new piece. My daughter found it in a Dumpster outside one of the big hotels here in Chicago." The woman walked out from behind the counter. "She found this lovely oak chair in the Dumpster, too. It's amazing what people throw away, isn't it?"

"Yes, it is." Kathryn wondered if this was Blythe's mother.

"And look at this. . .what a sweet little French Provincial chest of drawers. You wouldn't believe it, but it was on the curb waiting for the garbage collectors. My daughter scrubbed it up and put a new coat of varnish on it, and—"

"Your daughter?" Lee asked.

"Yes, Blythe Severson. She owns this store." The woman smiled. "I'm just filling in this week while she's on a much-needed vacation."

Kathryn's hopes plummeted, and she suddenly realized

how much she'd been looking forward to finding some answers about Rob.

"This entire shop is filled with things that Blythe's collected over the years. She goes to rummage sales and people give her sets of dishes for a dollar. Like these over here. . ." The woman walked across the store and lifted a lime green cup and saucer. "At first glance, this set looks quite. . .well, ugly. But if you turn the pieces over, you'll see they're stamped with an insignia that makes them quite valuable. Of course, Blythe could give you the details."

Lee smiled and began to inspect some photographs and paintings hanging on the wall, while Kathryn examined a pair of cut-glass candleholders on an adjacent tabletop.

"How long has your daughter owned this store?" she asked.

"Hmm, let's see. . .must be at least twenty-five years." The woman chuckled, and the lines around her dark eyes multiplied. In that very moment, it occurred to Kathryn that Kylie had another grandmother.

Did this woman know about Kylie?

Suddenly the thought of sharing her newfound granddaughter was unappealing.

Oh, Lord, I'm a selfish woman, aren't I? As if in reply, Kathryn's heart affirmed that she was just human.

"My daughter has always collected. . .things," the woman continued. "Finally, our basement got so full, my husband, God rest his soul, told Blythe she had to get rid of her stuff. That's when she opened this store."

"Quite enterprising of her," Lee remarked.

"Oh, yes, it was always her dream to run an antique store."

"Well, it would be a pleasure to meet your daughter sometime. Perhaps we'll stop back here again. We'll likely pass through Chicago on our way home."

"Where are you from?"

"South Carolina."

"Oh, really?" The woman smiled once again. "I thought I detected a Southern accent."

Lee chuckled, then glanced at Kathryn in a way that made her understand he wanted to leave.

"Thank you very much for your time," Kathryn said.

"Oh, yes, of course. Come back again."

"Thank you." Lee gave her a perfunctory nod, and then Kathryn turned and walked out of the store, her husband right behind her.

Stepping onto the walk, Kathryn pulled her jacket more tightly around her and looked at Lee. "What do you think?"

"I think we'll have to stop by in a week or so."

"Hmm."

Lee grinned. "I doubt Kylie will mind if we hang around in Basil Creek that long." He glanced over his shoulder at Precious Things. "I have a feeling it will be worthwhile to make another visit here and speak with Blythe. In fact, I think Kylie ought to come with us."

CHAPTER TWENTY-SEVEN

A magnificent sunset, arrayed in colors of gray and magenta, was painted across the horizon as Kylie maneuvered her car up the gravel driveway of her home in Basil Creek, Wisconsin. After extracting her stiff body from behind the wheel of her Outback, she felt the spongy ground beneath her feet and realized it had recently rained. Seconds later, her grandparents' Avalon pulled up behind her. As they exited their vehicle, Kylie watched them stretch, then glance around and take in their surroundings.

"Charming place," her grandmother stated at last.

"Thanks, only I had nothing to do with it. Dad bought this house when I was born—or so I've been told—and it's got almost three acres of land surrounding it."

husband, Dave, and their sons. Allie felt so sorry for those three men. They looked sort of lost and helpless, particularly Dave, although he didn't utter more than a few words. His sons didn't say much either, in spite of Colleen's attempts to engage them in conversation.

Then, just before dawn, Jack insisted they leave and catch a couple of hours of sleep. Exhausted, Allie readily complied.

"I feel like I'd probably antagonize Brenda, anyway, if she suddenly regained consciousness."

Jack replied by putting an arm around Allie's shoulders as they walked through the quiet hallway, heading to the parking structure.

"I wish she didn't hate me so much."

"Allie, that woman wasn't happy, period. It wasn't you. It was her. We're all created with a God-shaped hole in our hearts, and Brenda tried to fill hers with everything else except Him."

"Please don't talk in the past tense." Looking at Jack, she saw his puzzled frown. "You said she had a God-shaped hole in her heart."

"Sorry."

"You don't think she's going to live, do you?"

"I don't know, Allie. I wish I had the answer, but I don't. What I do know is that if Brenda does pull through, she'll likely need dialysis the rest of her life because—well, you heard the doctor."

"Yes, I did." Allie recalled how he'd said Brenda's kidneys were damaged. "But I still don't want her to die."

"I know you don't."

The automatic glass doors opened, and Allie and Jack entered the covered parking structure. Allie rested her head against the shoulder of Jack's leather jacket as they walked to his vehicle.

Kylie felt proud of her home as she led the Chadwyks down the walkway toward the back door. She remembered that today was the first of April. If her mother were still alive, she would look forward to tending the flower beds and arranging for Matt to bring over his till and turn over the vegetable garden. They'd plant in another month—that is, if Mom were still here.

Sometimes her death still seemed so surreal.

Unlocking the door, Kylie led her grandparents into the back hall, then the kitchen. She'd left dishes in the sink and on the table, but Lynellen must have placed them in the dishwasher for her. The simple white appliances were nothing like the industrial-sized stove and refrigerator at The Light House. Lissa told Kylie that a daytime soap opera star and her husband often stayed at the elegant seaside B & B. But this home was very simple—and very country.

Kylie took her grandparents upstairs and showed them into the third bedroom, which often served as the guest room. Two single beds protruded from one wall, an oak nightstand between them. On the opposite wall stood a large oak dresser, and an old piano bench sat beneath a set of windows that looked out over the yard.

"I know this bedroom is only about a third of the size of—"

"I'm sure we'll be very comfortable," Lee cut in.

Kathryn agreed.

Kylie felt relief wash over her. Her father had made a nice income, one that she and her mother lived off of even after his death. But being a general practitioner in a small town wasn't the same as being a brain surgeon in a big city.

"I'll start carrying in our luggage," Kylie said. "Then I'll whip up something for dinner." She grimaced, thinking of her sparse food supply. "But I might have to make a quick flyer from the friendly greeter. They headed toward the pharmacy area first, where Kathryn found what she was looking for, and then they made their way to the food section.

"I pretty much need everything," Kylie said, picking up a bag of prepared lettuce and tossing it into the cart.

"Kylie, did you see the price? Goodness! That salad mix is much too expensive."

Laughing, she put the lettuce back on the shelf. "I don't often look at prices, Grandma. That's my problem. I'm an impatient grocery shopper. Now, my mom, on the other hand, snipped coupons and watched for sales all the time."

"Perhaps all those years of dragging her to the grocery store with me paid off."

"Must have. My dad was like I am. He walked in, grabbed what he wanted, and checked out."

Kathryn shook her head. "Men are allowed. Lee and TJ are a bit like that, too." She took in a deep breath. "All right now. Let's begin again. What's on special today?"

Kylie gave in to her grandmother's thrifty shopping habits and settled on pushing the cart behind her. It was almost like being with her mother.

"Aunt Kylie!"

At the sound of a girl's voice, she swung around to see twelve-year-old Amber Hubbard staring back at her. Without a second thought, Kylie pulled Amber into a bear hug. She had a hand in raising both Dena's kids through the years, and Ryan and Amber considered her an "aunt" from the time they could talk.

Then reality began to set in. "Is your mom here?"

Amber shook her curly auburn head. "No. Me and Ryan are with Dad this weekend."

"Oh."

"He's buying Ryan some shoes." Amber held up a case of soda pop and a box of microwave popcorn. "I was sent to get the important stuff."

Kylie laughed before making introductions.

"Oh, yeah, I heard Mom say something about you visiting your grandparents." Amber gave Kathryn a smile before turning back to Kylie. She pushed the sides of her thick hair away from her face. "Hey, look at this. Mom finally let me get my ears pierced. I got them done last night."

"Well, that's all you're getting pierced," Kylie said with a teasing grin. "Understand? And no tattoos either."

Amber smiled and wiggled her backside in a sassy way as she walked off. The girl had her mother's thin frame and long legs, which were all the more noticeable in the blue jeans and pink sweater she wore this evening.

Kylie resumed shopping with her grandmother, but her mind was miles from the bread and dairy aisle. *Amber doesn't know about the falling-out between Dena and me. I'll miss those kids if I completely sever my relationship with their mom.*

"What about breakfast tomorrow? Should we pick up some of this raisin bread? Lee loves it. He says it makes great toast."

Kylie nodded, only half listening. She wondered what Dena was doing tonight since Todd had the kids. Was she with Matt?

Molten hot rage twisted itself around Kylie's heart. She clenched her jaw, imagining what she'd do if she caught those two together. Suddenly the term "crime of passion" no longer lay beyond her realm of comprehension.

Lord, I have to get over this. What am I going to do? I can't keep feeling this way. It's not right. It's not Your way.

As her grandmother gently set a dozen eggs into the cart,

Kylie heard God's voice speak to her troubled spirit. It wasn't an audible voice, but she knew it definitely belonged to her heavenly Father.

"Forgive them."

I have forgiven them.

"No, you haven't. Not like I forgive."

Kylie recalled Marilee reading something from the Psalms, something about God putting our sins as far from Him as the east is from the west.

If I do that, Lord, Matt and Dena will think everything is okay. They'll think our relationship is just like it used to be, and it's not. I am a different person.

"You obey, and I will take care of the rest."

Kylie blew out a breath, and the gesture caught her grandmother's attention. "Tired of shopping? We're almost finished."

Kylie couldn't subdue the laughter that bubbled out of her. "You sound just like my mom."

❧ ❧ ❧

Lee and Kathryn Chadwyk headed for bed shortly after ten o'clock, but Kylie wasn't tired. Thoughts of Matt and Dena continued to haunt her, and the idea of talking to them and letting them know all was forgiven was gaining merit. She'd mentioned the topic at supper tonight, and her grandfather said forgiveness was a decision—not a feeling. It also set a person free from the kind of heartache bitterness caused.

Kylie marveled at the concept.

Okay, I'm deciding here and now to forgive. I forgive my mom for lying to me. I forgive my dad. Tears filled her eyes as she sat alone in the silent den. *I forgive Matt. Did she mean it?* She wanted to mean it. *I forgive Dena, too.*

"Now you need to let Matt and Dena know."

Standing, Kylie wanted to obey what she believed was God's command, but she wasn't sure how she'd broach the subject. On the other hand, she figured she would find at least one of two at the Red Rocket Lounge connected to the bowling alley in town. The place offered live music on Saturday nights and was the local hot spot. Dena liked to hang out there. It wasn't Kylie's favorite place, but Matt took her there sometimes and ended up playing pool or throwing darts with his friends.

Deciding to check it out, Kylie went into the bathroom and fixed her hair. She touched up her makeup, then smoothed on lip gloss. In the dining room, she located her purse and pulled out her keys and a ten-dollar bill. She stuffed the money into the front pocket of her blue jeans as she made her way to the back hall. Yanking her jacket off one of the colorful plastic hooks, Kylie quietly exited the house and walked to her car.

As she drove into town, she prayed like never before. She envisioned the worst-case scenario and asked God to keep her heart free of malice and vengeance. She tried to remember that the Lord had already taken care of everything. All Kylie had to do was forgive. . .but maybe it could wait until tomorrow.

She almost turned her vehicle around, but the prompting to continue onward was undeniable.

Parking in the bowling alley's lot, Kylie walked around the building and entered through the lounge's door. Inside, the music was deafening, and as her eyes adjusted to the darkness, she saw several people she knew. Tom Frees and Greg Onikan, two of Matt's buddies, sat at the bar. They glanced her way and Tom waved.

Kylie waved back just as Greg slid off his barstool and approached her.

"Is Matt with you?" he yelled in order to be heard above the band.

Kylie shook her head. "I thought he'd be here." She had to repeat herself before Greg heard the reply.

"No, he's not here yet. Might be soon, though." He leaned on her shoulder, and Kylie smelled his beer-tainted breath. "You're his fiancée; you should know where Matt is."

Kylie gave him an irritated look and pushed Greg's hefty body away from her.

He laughed.

"Is Dena here?"

Greg nodded his balding head and pointed to the front where the dance floor was located. Kylie smiled her thanks and headed in that direction, where she soon spotted Dena, rocking to the band's lively beat. It appeared her partner was Russ Bettinger—a very married man and one old enough to be Dena's father. But it wasn't as if they were slow-dancing, so Kylie wondered if perhaps it wasn't such a great offense after all. Although, if Russ were her husband, he'd be in big trouble!

Finding a vacant stool at the bar, Kylie sat down, hoping to catch Dena's eye. Finally, the song came to a close, and Dena moved to speak with Russ. Her gaze suddenly found Kylie's, and Dena froze. She gaped in surprise, and Kylie couldn't help smiling at her friend's astonished expression. Slowly, Dena stepped forward, forgetting all about her dance partner.

She stood there, her midsection even with Kylie's knees, just as the band announced a break. The lights in the Red Rocket Lounge grew brighter, and people flocked to the bar.

"Do you still hate me?"

"No." Kylie stared at the woman who'd been her best

friend all her life. "I forgive you."

Swallowing hard, Dena's eyes misted over. "Are you waiting for Matt?"

Kylie shook her head.

"Then let's get out of here and go someplace where we can talk."

Kylie hesitated. Did she really want to "talk" to Dena? Was that necessary to put what she did with Matt as far away as the east is from the west?

Dena didn't wait for a reply. Grabbing Kylie's wrist, she dragged her off the barstool and back through the crowded lounge. The aisle to the exit was so jammed that Kylie wound up stuck in the throng and began conversing with Larry Cravitts, Terry Dunlap, and Megan Winters—all people with whom she'd gone to high school. It wasn't long, however, before Kylie realized that Dena, who'd been right in front of her, had disappeared.

"Yeah, you can sure lose people in this place," Larry said after Kylie relayed the situation.

The man was as thin as a reed with a stubbly jaw that, oddly, made him appear attractive. He'd never married, a fact that caused him to be a prime target for single women—all except for Kylie, who had long ago decided Larry wasn't her type. But that didn't mean they couldn't be friends.

Kylie gave him a wave after deciding to continue toward the front door.

Nearing the entrance, Tom caught Kylie's arm. "Hey, I just phoned Matt and told him you're in here dancing with every fella in the place." Tom hooted. "He hung up on me. Think he's mad?"

Kylie pulled her arm out of his grasp. "Matt knows better than to listen to you when you're drinking."

Tom laughed again. "Guess you're right about that."

Kylie gave him a look of disgust. She'd never been drunk, although she would admit to tipsy. However, consuming alcohol hadn't ever been her idea of having fun, and she'd always found drunken behavior unbecoming of anyone—man or woman alike—Matt and Dena included.

As if on cue, the petite blond caught Kylie's jacket sleeve. "Where have you been? Come on."

They left the bar, and Kylie felt like she reeked of cigarette smoke. "You know what, Dena? I hate that place and I'm never stepping foot in there again."

Dena glanced at her as they walked down Main Street. "Why?"

"Because. . ." She attempted to put her feelings into words. "Because that environment hurts people." Kylie thought about Tom's lie about her "dancing with every fella in the place." Tom meant it as a prank, of course. He'd never injure Matt on purpose. Tom was one of Matt's best friends. But once intoxication set in, it seemed there was nothing sacred.

Not even an engagement.

Oh, Lord, I'm having trouble with this forgiveness stuff. . . .

"Hey, want to go to my place and talk? The kids are with their father tonight, so—"

"I know. I saw Amber in Wal-Mart. She said you finally agreed to the ear-piercing deal."

"Yeah, she caught me at a weak moment."

Kylie grinned as they turned into the parking lot. She reached for her car keys, preparing to unlock the door.

"So, should we go to my place? We can order a pizza."

"Your place is fine, but I'm still full from dinner. My grandmother made grilled cheese sandwiches, and I heated up tomato soup to go with them."

"Your grandmother?" Dena looked shocked. "What grandmother?"

"The one from Sabal Beach. She and my grandpa followed me back here. They're staying for a couple of weeks while I decide what to do about. . .everything."

"What's everything? You're not breaking off your engagement, are you?"

"Dena, I broke off my engagement the day I left for South Carolina. I threw Matt's ring at him. Almost nailed him with it, too." Kylie waved her left hand in front of her friend's face, wiggling her naked ring finger.

"You threw Matt's ring at him. . . ? I didn't know that." Beneath the dim streetlamps, Dena appeared aghast.

"I've discovered I have a very bad temper."

"You only discovered that now? I could have told you that a long time ago!"

Kylie feigned a dubious glare. "Very funny."

"Seriously, Ky, I think Matt will be devastated if you break up with him."

"Didn't you hear me? It's a done deal. The question is, can we or will we reconcile?"

"Then reconcile. Matt needs you."

"But what about what I need?"

"Spoken like a true only child, selfish brat."

"Knock it off, Dena." Kylie leaned her back against the car door, feeling fed up with having her birthright thrown in her face for the millionth time. She hadn't asked to be an only child. "Look, I'm a very different person than I was two weeks ago. I learned I was adopted. My mother was really my biological aunt."

"Yeah, that I heard. Lynellen told me."

"My grandparents want me to relocate and move in with

them. They're in their midseventies, and they want the three of us to spend as much time together as possible."

"Kylie, are you crazy? You can't leave Matt. He loves you. Do you know what I'd give to have a man love me the way Matt loves you?"

"Yeah, I know," Kylie said, pushing off from her car. "Our friendship."

CHAPTER TWENTY-EIGHT

Sitting in the backseat of her grandparents' sedan, Kylie relayed last night's events while they rode to church.

"Forgiveness sounds like an easy thing to do, but it's not. I'm finding that out." She toyed with the strap of her black purse. "Marilee told me when we forgive, we should put the transgression as far from us as the east is from the west." She looked up as they passed the Wylers' farm. "Last night, I told Dena I forgave her, but then I flung the incident in her face again. She got insulted and stomped off, and we never did talk."

"Forgiveness is a difficult command, all right," Lee said from behind the wheel. "Just like love."

She arched a brow. "Love is a command? I thought love was a feeling."

"Well, there are sentiments that come with love, certainly," her grandmother said. "But feelings can change from day to day. Love has to be based on something much more solid than tingles and shivers."

Kylie grinned at the terminology.

"So if you decided to forgive Dena, then do it and don't let anger get in the way," Lee advised. "Give that emotion to God instead. He can handle it." He chuckled. "I tell ya, if Kathryn poured out all her feelings on me, I'd be a broken man."

Kathryn laughed and playfully swatted at his arm. "Honestly, Lee, you say the silliest things."

Watching them, Kylie rolled her eyes. Her grandparents were the cutest couple she'd ever known—next to her parents, of course.

"Okay, Kylie, which way do I turn now?"

She gave her grandfather directions to church, praying with all her soul that Matt wouldn't be there. Couldn't the Lord give him the twenty-four-hour flu? She didn't feel ready to face Matt. If last night was any indication, she had a lot more to learn about forgiveness before she could bestow it on him.

Forgiveness is a decision, she reminded herself.

They reached the tiny white clapboard church with time to spare before the service began. Lee parked in the gravel lot, and the sunshine trickled through the treetops overhead as they walked to the sanctuary.

"After the service, I'll show you where my parents are buried."

"We'd like that," her grandpa replied.

Stepping inside, they were met by the Hansons, and Kylie made introductions. Sarah Hanson, Pastor's wife, enfolded Kylie in a snug embrace. "We've missed you," she said. Then she held Kylie at an arm's distance. "I think you've lost some weight."

"Boy, did you say the right thing!" She'd done nothing to watch her weight, and this morning her skirt barely zipped. "I think I ate my way through the last ten days."

They all smiled, but Sarah insisted Kylie looked slimmer.

"Please don't get your eyes checked," she quipped as she and her grandparents slid into a pew, located about halfway up. Kylie sat on the far end, her grandfather on the other on the aisle side, and Grandma Kate in between them.

Folks passing in the aisle stopped to say hello, and Kylie, in turn, introduced the Chadwyks. Most were shocked to learn she had grandparents, but Kylie made the explanation short, and no one pressed them for details.

Then Lynellen Alexander walked in and exclaimed over Kylie's return. She met the Chadwyks with polite enthusiasm and began to make small talk. Just as Kylie wondered if Matt had come with his mother, she felt someone slip into the pew beside her—very close beside her. She knew it was Matt. She could smell his aftershave.

Lord, why couldn't he have gotten the flu?

"Forgiveness is a decision, just like love."

With her heart banging like the drums in last night's band, Kylie slowly turned around. But before she even got a glance at him, Matt leaned across her in a familiar way and stuck out his right hand. "A pleasure to meet you, Mr. and Mrs. Chadwyk."

Part of Kylie wanted to push him away, and another part of her rather enjoyed the physical contact—brief as it was. He sat back and stared at her. She met his penetrating sapphire blue gaze. But she didn't read the expected anger in his eyes, nor worry, nor fear. Instead, an unfaltering determination shone from their depths.

"Welcome home."

"Thanks."

"Guess we have a lot to talk about." Matt's voice was barely audible.

Kylie bobbed out a reply and looked down at her Bible, resting in her lap. Matt set his hand on hers, and soon his calloused palm had enveloped all but the tips of her fingers. Kylie strained against the urge to cry. If love wasn't a feeling, then what was the emotion called that swelled in her chest right now, threatening her next breath? It couldn't be remnants of a broken heart. . . .

Could it?

જ્જ   જ્જ   જ્જ

Marilee couldn't help smiling. She was rejoicing. God had renewed her perspective. Even as she stood beside Logan in the back of Youth Group Hall while another member of the youth staff presented the Sunday Morning Challenge, her nerves weren't jangled. She didn't feel she had to run to the adult sessions for cover.

Thank You, Lord. The last ten days did wonders for my spirit.

Marilee sent up another prayer, this time for Kylie. She wondered how her new friend was faring in Basil Creek. Marilee planned to phone her this evening and catch up.

"Logan!"

The whispered call came from the doorway, and when Marilee glanced over, she saw Jeanne Young motioning for him. Logan crossed the room, and reaching the older woman, he exchanged a few words with her. Then he waved for Marilee.

Standing, she strode to the entranceway where she heard Mrs. Young say, "Someone told me she's your sister, although she looks Hispanic."

"My half sister, perhaps." Logan turned to Marilee. "There's a woman upstairs asking for me. Apparently, she's upset."

They headed down the hall toward the elevator.

"She's more than upset, Pastor Logan," Jeanne said. "She's hysterical. Crying. Shaking like a leaf. I put her in your office."

"Thanks a heap."

Logan's dry sense of humor earned him a chuckle from Jeanne and a grin from Marilee.

"You don't know what she wants?" Logan queried, serious once more.

"No. All I understood was she's your sister and needs to talk to you."

Logan looked at Marilee and shrugged. "Guess we'll find out soon enough."

Marilee accompanied Logan to his office, where they found Patrice Rodriguez waiting for them. Tall with long, reddish-brown hair, Patrice was Logan's younger half sister. He'd only met her six months ago after their mother died, and contact between them had been sporadic at best. Another half sister, Kelly Acevedo, had moved to Oklahoma, where she had relatives. Neither had wanted much to do with their brother, the youth pastor.

"Patrice. What's up?"

She stopped her pacing long enough to stare at Logan through misty brown eyes. "Oh, Logan, I've got issues."

He closed the door once Marilee had entered the office.

"Hi, Patrice. Remember me? I'm Logan's fiancée, Marilee Domotor. You and I met briefly when Logan and I came to your door and invited you to our Christmas program."

"That's right. Yeah, nice to see you again."

"So, what's going on?" Logan asked again.

Patrice began relaying the whole story in rapid-fire Spanish.

"Whoa, senorita," he said with a grin. *"No comprendo Espanol."*

"Sorry. When I'm upset, it's just comes out."

"No problem," Marilee said. "But why don't you come over here and sit down? Get comfortable."

"No, I can't sit. I'm too nervous."

Marilee and Logan exchanged wondering glances.

"Okay, this is what's happened. I was living with my boyfriend—"

"The guy whose dad is a lawyer?" Logan asked.

"No, no. I broke up with him after Thanksgiving last year. This is another guy. Jamal Higgins. He's a bartender downtown. We moved in together in January. But a month ago, we broke up. Jamal's new girlfriend, Idora, moved in, and since I didn't have anywhere to go, they let me stay— even though Idora and I can't stand each other."

Marilee grimaced, marveling at how easily sin tangled up lives.

"Well, then I found out I'm pregnant," Patrice continued. "I'm just about four months along. Idora is furious and kicked me out. Jamal gave me money and told me to get an abortion. I made the appointment, and Kelly said I could live with her in Oklahoma, but I had to get out there on my own. Jamal gave me money for that, too. So this morning I show up at the clinic—"

"No! You didn't kill your baby, did you?" The words were out before Marilee even realized she'd spoken them.

Logan reached for her hand and pulled her into the chair beside him.

Patrice's dark eyes filled with unshed tears. "No, I didn't

have an abortion. I couldn't go through with it. I kept think-ing of you," she said to Logan, "and how our mother had wanted an abortion, but she gave birth to you and now you're such a nice person. You're a pastor here at this big church." Patrice shook her head. "No, I didn't kill my baby. I couldn't. But now what do I do? Jamal will want his money back, and I spent half of it on airfare I can't use. I have no place to go because Kelly told me she doesn't want a kid around. She has a good job and a decent boyfriend. There's no place in her life for her pregnant sister. I don't have any money, and. . .and I don't want this baby!"

Well, I do! Marilee's heart screamed. She whipped her gaze at Logan, who gave her hand a gentle squeeze as if warning her not to react.

Patrice broke down and sobbed.

"You did the right thing," Logan told her on an encour-aging note. "God will bless you for choosing life for your unborn child."

"Hey, if this kid turns out half as good as you, it'll be worth it."

"Well, I'm flattered you think so." Logan smiled. "But now let's think through your dilemma."

"You can stay with me," Marilee blurted, but then she realized her parents wouldn't appreciate having an unwed, unemployed pregnant woman hanging around their upscale condominium. Despite their deep-rooted faith, Marilee's folks still kept up with the proverbial Joneses and cared what the neighbors said.

She looked at Logan, her eyes pleading for an alternative.

He took the hint. "I don't think that'll work, Mari. You're still recovering from your car accident."

"Accident? Oh, that's right," Patrice drawled. "You were

in a serious wreck the weekend Mom died. Are you okay?"

"Much better, thanks." Marilee stood and grabbed the Kleenex box off Logan's desk. She handed it to Patrice, then put a comforting arm around the woman's shoulders.

"How 'bout Allie?" Logan suggested. "Patrice, you know Allie. She was at our mother's funeral. She's the one who worked at the convalescent center."

"Blond hair, blue eyes. . .that Allie?"

Logan nodded. "She'll take you under her wing in a minute. Allie is the ultimate mother hen. She'll see to your needs and give you a place to stay, at least temporarily. How 'bout I go find her and ask?"

Patrice nodded. "I s'pose it's worth a shot."

Once Logan left the office, Marilee turned to Patrice. "Can I get you some coffee or a soda? Water? Anything?"

The woman shook her head, and the multiple gold hoops in her earlobes tinkled.

Marilee worked her lower lip between her teeth while she thought over what she wanted to say. "Patrice," she began at last, "I haven't prayed about this, nor have I discussed the matter with Logan, obviously; and I must do both. But, well, I just have to ask you something."

The woman turned to Marilee with an expectant look.

"Would you ever consider letting Logan and me adopt your baby?"

"Adopt?" A puzzled frown furrowed Patrice's brow.

Marilee nodded. "I can't conceive since my accident. I was forced to undergo an emergency hysterectomy. This baby you're carrying might be the closest I'll ever come to raising Logan's flesh and blood."

"You can't have children?" Patrice repeated, the tears continuing to stream down her cheeks. She dabbed at them with a tissue. "A hysterectomy? But you're so young."

"It was either the operation or bleed to death."

"Oh, yeah, in that case, I'd choose the hysterectomy, too. But look at it this way; now you don't have to worry about getting pregnant. Lucky you."

"But don't you see? Children are a special gift from God. I wanted babies. Logan's babies."

Patrice took a moment to digest the information. Then she lifted her chin and hardened her gaze. "You might want to know that Jamal isn't white and I'm part Hispanic, so this kid," she said, pointing to her belly, which was well concealed beneath her blousy, printed shirt, "isn't going to be your average Caucasian. You still want him?"

Momentarily thrown off guard, Marilee's brain whirred to form a reply.

Unfortunately, Patrice mistook her silence as a form of condemnation. "Yeah, that's what I figured." She made a move toward the door.

"No, wait. Yes, I still want him—or her. Race doesn't matter to me. You just caught me by surprise, that's all. Please. . ."

Marilee coaxed Patrice into a chair in front of Logan's desk. "God doesn't look at skin color. He sees the heart. The soul. I do, too. Or at least I try to." She smiled and knelt beside Patrice. "I'm far from perfect, and I didn't mean to offend you. Will you forgive me?"

"What's to forgive? You're not the one homeless and pregnant." More tears gushed from Patrice's dark eyes. She put her head in her hands. "But I am!"

❦ ❦ ❦

"Kylie, we have to talk."

"I know, but not now." She pulled her arm free from

Matt's hold. "I promised my grandparents I would show them Mom's grave."

"Fine. But how 'bout afterward you bring them to the house. We'll have lunch, and you and I can discuss things."

"Um. . ." She glanced over her shoulder and saw that her grandparents were conversing with Lynellen and the Morrisons, another older couple. Looking back at Matt, she knew she couldn't put him off forever. "All right. If my grandparents aren't too tired, we'll come over for lunch. Do you want us to pick something up on the way? Dessert?"

"Sure." He smiled and leaned forward until his forehead touched hers. "You know I love you, Kylie."

Her heart flipped with emotion. But was it love?

He straightened, narrowing his gaze. "You're still angry with me, aren't you?"

"I–I guess not. No. I made a decision to forgive you and Dena in the same way God forgives us. That means putting the incident as far from me as the east is from the west." She raised her arms and shoulders. "Can't be angry if all's forgiven, right?"

Matt's eyes sparkled with mischief. "And I forgive you, too, for not returning my calls. Brat."

He chucked her under the chin as though she were a little girl, and suddenly Kylie feared their relationship was settling back into the same niche as before. But that would never work. Kylie needed to know things between them were different. What guarantee did she have that Matt wouldn't cheat on her again? What if, next time, things went further than necking in the cab of his truck?

"What's wrong?" The smile slipped from Matt's face.

Kylie sighed and forced a tremulous little smile. "I guess we have more to talk about than I first realized."

Not waiting to hear Matt's response, she turned and walked down the steps to the walkway on which her grand-parents stood. After saying their good-byes, the trio ambled into the cemetery. Tall pine trees surrounded the century-old acreage, and headstones of various shapes and sizes marked the resting places of souls that had passed on from this life to the next.

"Here we are," Kylie said at last. "This is where my mom is buried." Crouching, she reverently slid her fingers across the marker's rough, granite edge, and a swell of remorse lodged in her throat. "I miss her so much. I miss them both."

Grandpa Lee put his hand on her shoulder.

"I never thought I'd stand at Wendy's grave," Kathryn muttered. She hunkered down beside Kylie. "It hurts so much to think she never gave us a thought, didn't wonder how we might be getting along, didn't care."

Kylie couldn't understand it either.

No one spoke, and the only sounds came from chirping robins and distant car doors slamming shut as the last of the church members took their leave.

Finally, Lee said, "So much of what happened when Rob and Wendy were young was brought on by their own rebel-liousness. I refuse to take the blame simply because I tried to be a good parent."

Lifting his hand from Kylie's shoulder, he pivoted and started toward the parking lot.

"I have to agree, Kylie," her grandmother said, standing.

"I won't argue the point."

With her grandmother's hand in the crook of her arm, Kylie guided her from the cemetery. They reached the car and climbed inside. Lee had already started the engine.

"Matt wants us to come over for lunch," Kylie blurted as

run to the grocery store first."

"I can come with you," her grandmother offered.

Kylie smiled. "That'll be great."

The three of them ended up carrying in several loads each. Kylie made sure she was the one to haul suitcases upstairs, afraid the strain might harm her grandparents. As she set her grandma's piece of luggage on the piano bench, she marveled at how quickly the Chadwyks had found a place in her heart.

Back downstairs, Kylie showed her grandfather into the den, where she turned on the TV. Lee selected one of the national news magazine shows and settled comfortably onto the sofa. Kylie put on her jacket as her grandmother pulled on her coat; then the two left for the store.

"The one in town closed at six," Kylie said as she pulled onto the highway. "We'll have to go to the super Wal-Mart. They just built on a grocery store."

"Fine with me. I need to pick up a few things in their pharmacy department, anyway."

"You're not sick, are you? Is Grandpa? I know it was a long drive from Chicago."

"No, no, Dear, there's nothing to fret about. Your grand-father just has some arthritis in his knee. I think the cold weather caused it to act up. He asked me to pick up some of that deep-heating cream."

"Oh, okay."

Kylie drove out of Basil Creek, and ten miles later, they reached the large discount store. The well-lit lot was swarm-ing with patrons, but Kylie managed to find a parking spot. Then she and her grandmother strolled to the mammoth, sliding-glass front doors.

Inside, Kylie grabbed a cart while her grandmother took a

she fastened her seat belt. It seemed a good time to change the subject. "I told him we'd come if you two weren't tired."

"It's fine with me," Kathryn said, glancing at her husband. "Lee, what do you think?"

"Well, I'm starving. So if there's food at the Alexanders' place, I'm game." He seemed to have shaken off his melancholy.

Kylie grinned as her grandfather backed out of the parking space. The gravel crunched beneath the weight of the car's tires.

"I offered to bring dessert, which means, Grandpa Lee, you'll have to make a pit stop at Dee Dee's—it's the grocery store in town."

"Sure 'nough. Just tell me how to get there."

Kylie directed her grandfather into town, and while he and Kathryn waited in the car, she ran into the quaint food store and purchased a blueberry pie and vanilla ice cream. Returning to the Avalon, she instructed her grandfather on how to get to the Alexanders' dairy farm.

"Oh, my!" Kathryn exclaimed. "I can't recall the last time I visited a farm. How many cows does Matt have?"

"About fifty or sixty, I think."

"Does he name each one?" Lee wanted to know.

"No, Grandpa." Kylie laughed. "But Matt calls all his heifers 'Bessy.' Original, eh?"

"Sounds like a Wayne Newton song." After humming a few bars, he began to sing. "Bessy the heifer, the queen of all the cows."

"Oh, Lee, you're dating yourself again." Kathryn chuckled. "Get with the times."

Kylie saw her grandfather grin in the rearview mirror while she laughed.

"Does Matt have pigs and chickens, too?" Lee asked.

"No, just cows. They're his 'girls,' and they keep him plenty busy. Trust me. But he does grow some crops. Corn, hay, and soybeans, for cow feed mostly, and oats and wheat, which he'll sell for a profit later in the year."

"Is this the kind of life you want, Kylie?" her grandmother asked. "Farm life?"

"Sure. I've grown up in the country. Farming is nothing new to me, although I'll probably keep my job at the library."

Looking out the window, a little sigh escaped her. She talked as though she and Matt were engaged again. Except, she couldn't see herself married to anyone else.

Kylie shook herself. "Grandpa, make a left turn right up here."

He slowed down. "Here? This dirt road?"

"Yes." Kylie fought to quell her sudden reservations. "It leads to Matt's house."

❧   ❧   ❧

"Of course she can stay with me!"

"Allie. . ."

She felt Jack's hand squeeze her right elbow.

"We're getting married in three weeks. After that, we'll be gone for a month. This is not the time to take in a houseguest."

"Dad, I'm sure we can find somewhere for Patrice to go until she figures out what to do with her life—and her baby. But in the meantime, she needs a place to stay."

Allie turned to Jack. "It's just temporary, Honey."

His dark gaze slid from Logan's face to hers, where it narrowed in a way that made Allie know he was none too pleased with the situation. She gave him a pleading look and watched him melt like ice cream on the Fourth of July.

Jack shook his head. "I'm such a sap where you're concerned, Allie." He glanced at Logan. "I'm in big trouble."

"Join the club." Logan grinned and placed his hands on his hips. "So what do you say? Should I tell Patrice she can move in with Allie. . .temporarily?"

"Yeah, but stress the temporary part," Jack groused.

Allie laughed. She couldn't help but find her fiancé's somewhat grumpy ways loveable and utterly charming.

Perhaps she was the one in "big trouble."

"Okay, I'll relay the message." Logan's arms fell to his side. "Oh, and will you keep Marilee and me in prayer? I can already tell that she's entertaining thoughts of adopting Patrice's baby. Patrice said she didn't want the child, but she could always change her mind."

Jack rubbed his jaw, looking troubled. "Oh, boy."

"Yeah, my sentiments exactly."

"Well, first things first," Allie told the men. "Logan, let Patrice know she's welcome to stay with me *temporarily*." She tossed a glance at Jack. "And we'll prayerfully take it one step at a time from there."

"Sounds good, Mom."

Shaking her head at the wisecrack, Allie watched Logan take off through Parkway Community Church's large lobby.

"The Christian life is so exciting, isn't it?"

"Yeah," Jack replied in a deadpan tone. "I can hardly wait to see what happens next."

"Stop being such a grouch." Grinning, Allie slipped her arm around his elbow. "Look what God's done in just the past few days. He used Brenda's death as a means to reach Colleen, Royce, and Dave and his two sons. They were in church this morning!"

Jack nodded. "I'd like to believe Brenda's death wasn't in vain."

"Exactly my point." Allie gave his arm an affectionate squeeze and smiled up into his eyes. "Now just think of what the Lord might do with Patrice's situation!"

CHAPTER

TWENTY-NINE

"So that was the last time we heard from Wendy," Kathryn explained to the Alexanders.

The blueberry pie Kylie had bought sat untouched on the beige woven place mat in front of her, and she wondered if her grandmother had become upset as she rummaged through the past. Kylie hoped not.

"Over the years, we hired investigators," Lee said. "But they never found anything, probably because Rob was dead and Wendy married, changed her name, and moved to Basil Creek."

"You'd think they would have found something." Matt's expression revealed his disbelief.

"Twenty years ago, we didn't have the Internet, Matt."

He glanced across the dining room table and met Kylie's stare.

"It was a lot easier for people to disappear back then," she added.

"It's not as simple to find someone who doesn't want to be found as you might think," Lee said.

"I suppose so." Matt's wooden chair creaked beneath his weight as he sat back on it. The look on his face said he still wasn't convinced. But he grinned at Kylie and gave her a wink.

She smiled, marveling at the effect he still had on her. But if he weren't so charming, she'd like to be angry with him for challenging her grandparents. Why was he being so contrary?

"It's amazing to me that Wendy hid Kylie's adoption all these years," Lynellen remarked, taking a sip of her decaf coffee. "Wendy and I were close friends. You'd think the secret would have come out."

"Yes, one would think so," Kathryn agreed. "But Wendy was always a very private person. She hid things well."

"Like the marijuana she'd stashed in that round plastic body of the mirror on her dresser. The top was just screwed on." Grandpa Lee shook his head. "We wouldn't have ever discovered the drug, except the day we were moving into The Light House, the mirror fell and cracked apart. There inside lay a plastic bag of decades-old weed."

"Yes, and it wasn't easy explaining that to the movers," Kathryn put in, massaging her temples.

"I can't believe it," Lynellen said, looking somewhat amused. "That's not the Wendy I knew and loved. Although she did have an underlying spark of stubbornness, determination, and drive. Everyone wanted Wendy on her committee."

Kylie smiled before glancing down the long table to the end where her grandmother sat. She looked peaked. "Grandma, do you have a headache?"

"Oh, I'm fine, Dear." She put her hands in her lap, but Kylie could see the strain around her grandmother's eyes.

Kylie stood. "I think we should go home."

Matt's gaze widened at the announcement.

As if reading his thoughts, she asked, "Could we put our discussion on hold for an hour or so? I'll take my grand-parents home and come back."

"Sure. Not a problem." His features relaxed. Then he stood as well. "Anything I can do to help you, Mrs. Chadwyk?"

Kathryn appeared embarrassed by all the attention and shook her head.

"It's been a rather long day," Kylie explained to Matt and Lynellen. "Especially after all the driving we did this week."

"Amen to that!" Lee rose from his chair. "Excellent meal, Mrs. Alexander. Thank you."

"Oh, please, call me Lynellen, and you're quite welcome. It's been such a pleasure talking with both of you."

"Likewise." Lee regarded his wife with furrowed brows.

He helped Kathryn to her feet, alarming Kylie. Her grand-mother never seemed like a frail individual before; however, at the moment, she resembled a delicate flower, withering in the elements.

Oh, please, Lord, don't let anything happen to my grandma Kate. I just found her. Please don't take her away now!

Kylie rushed to her side. "Are you okay?"

The older woman touched Kylie's cheek. "Darling, I'm fine. I suffer with these nasty headaches from time to time, and I feel one coming on. After a little nap, I'll be as zippy as ever."

Mom went to bed and never woke up. The memory caused Kylie to panic. She looked at her grandfather, who must have seen the worry reflected in her eyes.

He put a hand on her shoulder and gave her an assuring smile. "Would you mind fetching Kathryn's purse and coat for me?"

"Of course not." Kylie did as he'd asked, then bid a hasty good-bye to Matt and his mother.

"Whoa!" Matt caught her by the wrist as she rushed past him. Pulling her close to him, he whispered, "I wish you'd fawn all over me like you do your grandma."

Kylie felt that familiar sting of aggravation. "I used to. But you always regarded me as a. . .a china doll, something you put on the shelf and forget about."

Matt pulled back as if she'd spit at him. "What? China doll? Where'd you get that from?"

"From your stupid nickname for me when we were kids. Matt, can't you see? Someone else always takes center stage with you—memories of Rochelle, your friends, even your cows. But not me."

"That is so not true! The only person I've thought about for the last two weeks is you! A lesser man would have given up by now." He softened his voice. "But I love you, Kylie. I wish you'd believe me."

They stared at each other, and Kylie wondered if perhaps she'd misjudged him. He had a point about a lesser man giving up. She had done everything in her power to turn Matt away, from breaking their engagement to disregarding his phone calls. But he hadn't thrown in the towel. She had to credit him with that much.

"Okay. We'll talk more after I get my grandparents home," she promised.

He grinned. "Hurry back."

Matt leaned forward to kiss her, but Kylie turned her head so his lips met her cheek. It was a reflex and nothing more, and it surprised Kylie as much as it insulted Matt.

"Sorry, I–I just have a lot on my mind right now." The excuse sounded flimsy even to her, but Kylie hoped it would suffice. Her emotions were in such a tangle that she didn't know what she felt toward Matt anymore.

She left the house, still mentally sorting through the rubble of their relationship. But one look at her pale grandmother, so wan in the front seat of the car, and Kylie's inner alarm bells went off.

On the way home, she sat forward and kept a hand on her grandmother's shoulder.

"You're so sweet to fret over me," Kathryn said. "But this will pass, you'll see. Right, Lee?"

"That's right."

"I know, but the image of Mom's grave is so fresh in my mind. . . ." Kylie's eyes filled with tears. "I've lost so many people in my life. I don't want to lose either of you now, too!"

Lee raised his hand and Kylie took it.

"You're a fine young lady, Kylie Rollins," Lee said. "I'm blessed to have you for a granddaughter."

"Even though I'm a worrywart?" she asked with a sniff.

"Can't be any worse than TJ," Kathryn said, a smile in her voice. Her eyes were closed as she relaxed against the headrest.

Kylie smiled and wondered what TJ would think about Matt. He'd probably like him. Next, she wondered what her grandparents thought of him.

"I'm sorry about the way Matt behaved at lunch. I hope you don't think he was rude for challenging some of the things you said."

"Nonsense. I think Matt was trying to protect you," Lee replied. "You should have seen TJ's reaction when Kathryn announced we had a granddaughter. He immediately assumed you were a little gold digger. The only problem is, Kathryn and I don't have any gold." He chuckled.

Kylie grinned, and her grandfather released her hand. He slowed at an intersection, and Kylie directed him to turn right. He did.

"Like TJ," Lee continued on, "Matt was making sure we are who we claim. I didn't take any offense to that. Did you, Kathryn?"

"None at all."

Kylie sat back in the seat and considered what her grandparents had said. "If Matt was protecting me, I should be glad. So why did it bother me?"

There was a pause from her grandparents before Lee replied. "I think that's a question only you can answer, Kylie."

She thought it over, speculating at how she'd come to such a conclusion. She stared out the window. "All I know is I don't want to be treated like a child or like a woman who doesn't have a brain in her head. I want to be. . ."

"Matt's equal."

"Yes! Thank you, Grandma." She bolted forward just then and had to laugh. "Grandpa Lee, you just missed the turn and passed right by my house."

He slowed and made a U-turn on the lonesome highway, running parallel to the Rollinses' property. Afterward, he maneuvered the car up the driveway and parked.

Kylie helped Kathryn out of the Avalon. The sound of the car doors slamming shut echoed through the budding treetops. Once inside the house, Kylie assisted her grandmother up the stairs and into her room. After taking some medicine, the older woman stretched out on one of the twin beds. Kylie covered her with a cozy quilt.

"Shall I get you an ice pack for your head?"

"Oh, no, that won't be necessary."

Lowering herself onto the bed, Kylie regarded her grandmother. "Are you sure there's nothing I can do for you?"

Kathryn opened one eye. "You are as parental as I am. Now you know where you get it."

"Oh, good grief." Kylie grinned.

"You're a woman who needs lots and lots of children."

"At my age? I'll be thirty-one in seven days."

"We'll have to celebrate."

Kylie grinned. "I'd like that."

"You seem very healthy. I'm sure you've got plenty of good years ahead of you in which to bear children."

"Aren't you forgetting something? I need a husband first."

With her eyes closed, Grandma Kate smiled. "Matt loves you. I can see it in his face when he looks at you. As much as I want you to move to Sabal Beach, I can envision you settling down here."

Kylie sighed. "I don't know, Grandma. Something's wrong between Matt and me, but I can't put my finger on it."

"You don't love him?"

"Well, I do. . .I did." Kylie shook her head. "I don't know."

"Perhaps you're still angry with him."

"I don't feel angry. In fact, I sort of feel like I love Matt, but it's not like it was before."

"Hmm. . .well, you're different now, Kylie. You're a Christian. Maybe that's the difference you're sensing. So can this old woman give you some advice?"

"Sure." Kylie couldn't help the smirk. "But you know my take on advice."

A tight grin pulled at Kathryn's lips. "You're not obligated to follow it. I realize that much. But I would like to suggest that before committing to Matt again, you make certain he's a believer. The Bible warns Christians not to marry those who aren't saved."

"Don't worry, Grandma," Kylie said in all seriousness. "That's one of the many topics Matt and I have to discuss."

"Yes, but it's probably the most important one."

"I understand."

Kathryn patted her hand. "You're a good girl—a credit to your mother's parenting skills."

"She was my friend as well as my mom."

Glancing around the bedroom, Kylie felt nostalgic and began to tell her grandmother the story of how she and her mother went on a binge one summer, painting walls and rearranging furniture.

"We ordered these curtains from JC Penney," Kylie said, looking at the printed material above the windows. "I never liked them. Mom got her way that day. But I suppose it doesn't matter. I've got to sell this place, and if Matt and I do end up getting married, Lynellen wants a new mobile home built near the apple orchard on their farm."

When there was no reply, Kylie gazed down at her grandmother, realizing the bedtime tale had put the older woman to sleep.

Smiling, Kylie quietly inched her way off the bed, then made her way downstairs. She found her grandfather in the living room, relaxing in a chair and reading a portion of the thick Sunday newspaper.

"Grandma's asleep, and I'll be back in a little while."

He looked up, smiled, and waved.

Walking through the kitchen and back hall, Kylie left for Matt's.

As she drove to his house, she prayed for the right words to say and the right questions to ask. She tried to imagine how Allie or Marilee would handle this situation. She thought about everything Allie had told her about her first marriage. Kylie didn't think she'd ever be able to put up with an abusive husband.

Or an unfaithful one.

Kylie pulled into Matt's driveway. *I wish I knew beyond a shadow of a doubt that what happened once will never happen again.*

Suddenly, she hit the brakes when Dena's white van came into view. Kylie felt almost violated to see it there, parked next to Lynellen's faithful old Buick.

"I forgave her," Kylie reminded herself as she steered her car the rest of the way up and parked. She spoke aloud, as if doing so would permanently affix the words to her heart. "I'm not mad about what happened between her and Matt anymore. It's as far from me as the east is from the west."

Then why am I shaking?

Unbuckling her seat belt, Kylie steadied herself and got out of her car. She headed for the house, but Dena's shrilly laughter carried on the breeze, and it didn't take long to realize it came from the barn.

Feeling sick, Kylie made her way in that direction, trying desperately not to think the worst. But in spite of her efforts, she clenched her jaw and balled her fists. Several yards away from the barn's wide entrance, she stopped. Did she really want to see what was going on inside? An image of Matt and Dena together forced Kylie to place a hand on the fence post and collect her wits. She heard Dena's giggles again and made out the words "oh" and "darling," although the syllables in between were inaudible.

Paralyzing heartache kept her standing still for an immeasurable amount of time. But then, realizing that she was about to sob, Kylie forced her legs to walk to her car. She climbed in, started the engine, and peeled out of the driveway as if demons were on her tail. Tears streamed down her cheeks as she hit the highway. She stomped on the accelerator and raced with the wind.

As angry as she felt, however, she eventually heeded her common sense and slowed down. She didn't want a speeding ticket. Matt wasn't worth it. If that's the kind of guy he was, a two-timing jerk, then God sure had answered her prayers and showed her that piece of truth. Her worst fears had been realized. The worst that could happen had happened.

Oddly, Kylie felt a measure of relief.

It was over.

༺ ༺ ༺

Kathryn awoke to pounding. Where was it coming from? She opened her eyes and peered at the iridescent face of the clock ticking beside her bed. The time told her she'd been sleeping for two hours.

More pounding. *What on earth. . . ?*

She pulled back the quilt and sat up. Her headache was gone. *Thank You, Jesus!* Padding to the doorway, she heard a man's voice downstairs, then her husband's response. It appeared Lee had the situation, whatever it was, under control.

Walking to the bathroom, Kathryn freshened up before making her way to the first floor. She was surprised to find Matt Alexander standing in the kitchen, talking with Lee; however, she disliked the weighty expressions on the men's faces.

"What's going on?"

"I'm sure everything's fine," Lee began. "There's just been a bit of a misunderstanding."

Matt groaned and hung his head back. "I can't believe it."

"Believe what? Where's Kylie?"

"That's what Matt wants to know, but she isn't here."

"She was supposed to be at my place," Matt said. "We had planned to talk about. . .things. But between the time that Kylie dropped you two off and drove to my farm, Dena stopped over with her kids. She'd just picked them up from her ex-husband's place. I don't know if you're aware of all that's happened in the past. . . ?"

"We're aware," Kathryn said.

Matt looked chagrined and lowered his gaze for an instant before forging ahead with his explanation. "There's nothing between Dena and me. Nothing. She only came over today because Mom had promised Ryan one of our kittens since it's his birthday tomorrow."

"All right," Lee said. "So what happened?"

"Well, we were all in the barn, Dena, her children, Mom, and me, when we suddenly heard a car's tires squealing and spitting gravel. When we walked out of the barn, we saw Kylie's car barreling down the driveway." Matt raked his hand through his blond hair. "I couldn't believe it. I knew she'd jumped to conclusions and raced off. I panicked. My first wife was killed in a car accident, so I was scared Kylie would end up in a ditch, hurt—or worse. I went after her, but she was driving like such a maniac that she was long gone by the time I turned onto the highway."

Kathryn put her fingers to her lips. "Oh, my soul! How long ago was this?"

"A couple of hours. I've looked everywhere for her. I drove past here a dozen times but didn't see her car, so I knew she wasn't home. She never parks in the garage. It's so full of junk. . . ." Matt waved his hand at the unnecessary details. "Dena's been riding around with her kids, searching for her.

Mom's been trying to call her. I have, too. Finally, I realized I needed to get both of you involved in case Kylie—"

The telephone rang.

A grin tugged at the corners of Matt's mouth. "In case she calls."

"Maybe that's her now." Kathryn turned on her stocking-footed heel.

"Don't tell her I'm here," Matt said. "She'll probably hang up."

Kathryn strode into the hallway, where she plucked the receiver from the wall phone. "Hello, Rollinses' residence."

"Grandma?"

"Well, hi, dear heart. I wasn't sure if I should answer your phone or not." She motioned to the men that it was, indeed, Kylie on the other end.

"I was hoping you'd pick up. Is your headache gone?"

"It completely vanished. Where are you?"

Matt came in close to listen.

"I'm at a coffeehouse in La Crosse. I'll be home in awhile. I just didn't want you and Grandpa Lee to worry."

"A coffeehouse in La Crosse?" she repeated for the benefit of the eavesdroppers. "What are you doing there?"

Matt lifted his gaze and smacked his palm against his forehead. Kathryn was hard-pressed not to grin.

"I'm drowning my sorrows in French vanilla cappuccino. Oh, Grandma," she lamented, "it's over between Matt and me. He's a cheat and a liar."

"Are you sure, Dear? Matthew seems like such a nice young man." She glanced at the alleged perpetrator, noting the remorse in his blue eyes.

"Find out which coffeehouse she's at," he whispered.

"Where did you say you were again, Kylie?"

"I'm at a coffeehouse near the university. My old stomping ground."

"I see." Kathryn thought her granddaughter's voice sounded so down and discouraged. "Well, I can tell you're upset. Would you like Lee and me to meet you somewhere, and we can have dinner? You can tell us all about what happened."

Kylie sniffled. "That would be nice."

"Where shall we meet?"

"How 'bout Lexi's? It's a wonderful Italian restaurant. Can you find a pen and piece of paper? I'll tell you how to get there."

"All right. Just a moment." She covered the mouthpiece. "I need a pen and something to write on."

Matt went to fetch the items, returning within seconds.

"Go head, Kylie."

Kathryn wrote down the directions, trying to ignore Matt, who practically breathed down her neck as he strained to see the information. She finally shooed him away.

"At what time should we meet?"

"Um, how 'bout in an hour? That'll give you time to get ready, and I'll finish my coffee."

"How long will it take us to get there?"

"Only about twenty minutes."

"That should be fine. And, Kylie, please don't cry anymore. Everything will work out. You'll see."

"Thanks. You're right. Matt's not worth a single one of my tears."

"Well, I didn't mean it quite that way, but. . .oh, never mind. We'll see you in a bit."

Kathryn hung up the phone. Matt stood ready and eager to take off for La Crosse and find Kylie.

"Which restaurant?" he asked.

"I'm afraid you can't be privy to that information," Kathryn told him.

"What?" Frowning, Matt brought his chin back in surprise.

"I can't allow Kylie to think I betrayed her." Kathryn glanced at her husband. "We can't betray her, Lee."

"I agree. That's happened to Kylie far too many times in the past. No offense intended, young man." He turned to Matt. "We'll talk to Kylie over dinner tonight and perhaps—"

"No. 'Perhaps' isn't good enough." Matt straightened to his full height, towering over both Kathryn and Lee with sparks of determination in his eyes. "I've been on my knees every night since all this started, begging God for another chance with Kylie."

"Are you a Christian, Matthew?" Kathryn asked. Now seemed the perfect time, since he'd brought up the subject.

"Of course I'm a Christian." His blond brows sloped in confusion.

"I'm glad to hear that." She smiled. "When did you get saved?"

"Um. . ." He glanced at Lee, then back at her. His discomfort was obvious.

"Forgive me. I didn't mean to put you on the spot. It's just that Kylie recently made a decision for Christ, and—"

"She did?" Now his brows went up in complete surprise. "You mean, she wasn't a Christian before? I thought she was."

Kathryn had to grin. It seemed he understood.

"I accepted Christ when I was in high school, but I sort of pushed aside that part of my life when I was in college and even after I got married. I didn't mean to. Just got busy, I guess. It wasn't until Jason, my son, was born that my mother talked to Rochelle about the Lord and she believed." Matt rubbed his jaw before his hand moved to the side of his head, and he pushed his hair back. "She's in heaven today, but no real thanks to me. Guess my faith is an area that gets neglected except for Sunday mornings. Although," he added as a hopeful gleam sparked his gaze, "I have started attending a men's Bible study in La Crosse. I've only gone once, but I promised Pastor Hanson I'd be faithful to it for at least the next eight weeks in lieu of my. . .mistake last January. I thought I had a drinking problem, but maybe it's just something between God and me that has to get worked out."

"Either way," Kathryn assured him, "the Lord is ready and able to help you."

"I know. And I sure need His help now." Matt shook his head and raised his eyes upward. "I can't believe what happened this afternoon!"

"Son," Lee began, "maybe it wasn't wise to allow Dena to come to your farm today."

Matt expelled an exasperated breath, and Kathryn thought he looked as miserable as Kylie had sounded on the telephone. She felt sorry for him, on one hand, but defensive of Kylie on the other.

"I didn't think it mattered if Dena was there today, since she and Kylie were together at the Red Rocket Lounge last night. I thought they patched things up."

"That was Kylie's intent, but I don't believe her conversation with Dena went as she planned."

"Well, that's not going to happen with me. I want to look Kylie full in the face," Matt said on a passionate note, shaking his finger with purpose, "and I want to tell her what she heard or saw this afternoon—or what she thought she saw—wasn't what really happened. I have witnesses! But, in all due respect, Mr. and Mrs. Chadwyk, if you tell her, Kylie will think you've swallowed my lies, and she won't believe you either. I know this woman probably better than anyone. The truth has to come from me."

"Lee, what do you think?" Kathryn tipped her head. Matt's reasoning sounded quite logical.

Rubbing the back of his neck, he thought it over. "Well, Matt, I guess I can't stop you from following us to the restaurant, now, can I?" He let his hand fall to his side. "It's a free country."

A slow smile spread across Matt's face as he comprehended the plan. "Yes, Sir. It certainly is."

CHAPTER THIRTY

N ice night," Logan said, leaning on the wooden rail of the balcony. "I think spring has finally arrived."

"Don't be so sure. This is northern Illinois in April. We're supposed to get a blizzard next week."

"Hey, great idea, Mari. We'll take the teens snow tubing!"

"Oh, yeah, that'd be fun."

With lifted brow, he glanced at her. "Did I hear you correctly? Did you say 'fun' when I mentioned snow and teens?"

She touched her forehead. "I guess I did. Maybe I have a fever."

Logan laughed. "Hey, great comeback."

"Thanks." Smiling, she wrapped her sweater more tightly around her and stared out over the city lights. One thing about her parents' condo—it had an awesome view.

"It's good to have you home. I think that vacation did wonders for you."

"It did."

"On a serious note, I thought things went well today. Great to see the Perkinses. And I was really glad they came to lunch at Aunt Nora's."

"The Sunday afternoon family gathering is growing."

"Sure is, and now Patrice has been added to the membership list."

"I was amazed when she decided to come back to the evening service."

Logan agreed. "I was just as amazed. But Allie sort of laid down the law. No alcohol, drugs, cigarettes; Patrice has to find a job, at least part-time, and she has to attend church."

Marilee's eyes widened with surprise. "Tall orders. Did she agree?"

"Uh-huh. A miracle, wouldn't you say?"

"Yes, but then again, the woman is desperate."

"True, but Mari, I think she also knows she's safe with us. . . with Allie. That's why she showed up at church this morning, asking for me. She was seeking refuge, and she found it. Now we just have to pray she finds Christ."

"Absolutely."

Logan wrapped his arm around Marilee's shoulders. "And we'll keep praying about adoption, okay?"

"Okay."

Marilee wanted to drop the subject—and fast. While she desired nothing more than to adopt Patrice's precious child, she was scared to get her hopes up only to have them dashed. Better, she decided, to focus on becoming Logan's wife. He'd never had a mother dote on him, so Marilee planned to make up for lost time.

"Logan," she said, snuggling against him, "I've made up my mind that whether we adopt or not, you're always going to be my favorite child."

"Hmm, and just what are you implying?"

"Ah, that you're a kid at heart." Marilee grinned.

"Right." He gave the back of her neck a playful squeeze.

Laughing, Marilee suddenly remembered the pictures she'd taken of her vacation and the honeymoon suite at The Light House. "Logan, come inside. I want to show you something."

He followed her into the living room and sat on the sofa. Marilee ran to her bedroom and grabbed the photos off her dresser and made a speedy return.

"I wondered if we could change our honeymoon plans." She handed Logan the pack of glossy three-and-a-half-by-fives, then lowered herself onto the designer-print up-holstered couch. Leaning her shoulder against his arm, she described each scene as he looked through the small stack.

"The Chadwyks said we could stay for free. They want to help our ministry. I told them that wasn't necessary. We can pay our way, but they insisted."

"Wow, look at that ocean."

"Ten miles of beach," Marilee said, purposely tempting him. She knew how much he liked water. "Windsurfing, golfing, biking. . .private hot tub outside the honeymoon suite."

Logan glanced at her, his brown eyes alight with interest. "I wonder if we can get our deposit back from the other place."

"We can, because if we act now we'll be giving more than thirty days' notice."

"Sold." He handed her back the pictures.

Smiling at her success, Marilee slid them back into the cardboard package. "I'll make the phone calls tomorrow."

Logan let out a long, slow breath. "Just one problem."

"What's that?"

"It's two months before we get married. Two whole months. Do you know how long two months is? It's sixty-one days, according to my calendar. I could die waiting for sixty-one days."

Marilee grinned and saw her mother enter the room just as Logan finished his feigned tirade.

"Logan, wait on the Lord and be of good courage," Eileen Domotor quipped. "Marilee and I have a kazillion things to do in two months. I don't know how we'll get them all done."

"I told you we should have eloped," he whispered.

"Yeah, and I should have listened," she whispered back.

"I heard that," Eileen replied in a sing-song voice.

They shared a chuckle before Marilee lowered her gaze. It was then that she noticed Logan's rumpled white shirt. He'd ditched his jacket and tie even before they had climbed into his car and headed here to Marilee's folks' place. It occurred to her that Logan's little-boy charm had resurfaced. She hadn't seen him act so carefree and, yes, even silly, since her accident. It awed her when she realized how much of an impact she had on his ministry, his life. . .his very being.

Her depression had brought him down, too. But that was over now. God had used a very special new friend and sister in Christ to uncover the source of her blues. For that, Marilee would always be grateful to her heavenly Father for sending Kylie Rollins into her life.

With a comfortable little sigh, Marilee put her stocking feet up on the coffee table. "Hey, Logan?"

"Hmm?"

She smiled. "It's really great to be home."

Kylie's emotional storm had blown over, and now all she felt was a firm resolve as she sat in Lexi's waiting for her grandparents. The place was dimly lit and red linen cloths graced each tabletop. Classical Italian music wafted through the overhead speakers, and the effect was a comfortable, somewhat romantic ambiance.

Unlike the coffeehouse, where the music was as gyrating as the espresso.

Even so, this afternoon while she sipped her frothy brew, Kylie had prayed and really felt the Lord gave her the answer to go. Go to Sabal Beach and live with her grandparents. Maybe only for the summer. Maybe for a year. Maybe for the rest of her life. But the duration wasn't the issue. Her existence in Basil Creek was. She had to leave. The small town wasn't big enough for Matt, Dena, and herself.

Her cell phone rang, and Kylie dug it out of her purse. She peered at the number on the illuminated screen but didn't recognize it.

"Hello?"

"Kylie, how're you doing? It's Seth."

She grinned. Of all the times for him to call her. "I'm doing rotten. How 'bout you?"

"Whoa! Bad time? Want me to call back?"

"No, it's okay. I'm actually not quite so rotten anymore."

"What's going on?"

Taking a deep breath, Kylie relayed events occurring this afternoon, hoping she wasn't talking so loud that every patron in Lexi's would hear. "It hurts because Matt still means a lot to me. I mean, I loved him enough to say I'd marry him. But obviously I can't marry a guy I don't trust."

"I wouldn't advise it, that's for sure."

His reply was the confirmation she'd needed. "What's more, I still have unfinished business with my biological mother. I need to talk to her. I need some answers."

"Understandable. So are you moving to South Carolina?"

"Yes."

"Great."

The smile in his voice made Kylie laugh.

"Tell you what, I'll even drive up and help you move. I've got some vacation time I should use by the end of the year or else I'll lose it."

Kylie was touched by the kind offer. "I couldn't ask you to drive all the way up here to help me."

"Well, then, it's a good thing you didn't ask. Besides, TJ and I came up with a great plan."

"Uh-oh." Grinning, Kylie toyed with her place setting. "Let's hear it."

"TJ's going to ask the McKenneys to move into The Light House for a few weeks. Todd and Laura McKenney are a younger couple who often run the place while the Chadwyks are gone and TJ is away."

"Hmm." The idea was gaining merit. "If you and TJ came up to help me move, that would take an awful lot of strain off my grandparents, not to mention save me some money."

"Our thoughts exactly. And then there's Marilee's wedding you wanted to attend. You'll need an escort." He cleared his throat.

Kylie smiled. "That's really nice of you, Seth. Let me think about it. I'll talk it over with my grandparents."

"Why the hesitation, Kylie?"

Hearing the seriousness in his tone, the smile slipped from her face. "Look, I'll be honest. You're moving kind of fast for me."

"Okay, that's fair."

She expelled a sigh of relief. "Thanks for understanding."

"No problem. So when do you want TJ and me to come up?"

Kylie laughed. "Seth, you are so crazy!"

At her exclamation, the young man at the next table turned to give her a curious glance.

She lowered her voice. "Excuse my outburst, Seth. I'm kind of wired. I drank two large cups of cappuccino this afternoon."

"French vanilla?"

"You got it."

"My favorite. Now, I'm looking at my calendar. . . ."

Kylie started laughing again. The guy just didn't give up.

Suddenly Kylie spotted her grandparents in the doorway. "Sorry to cut you off, Seth, but I've got to end our call. My grandparents are here."

"No problem, Kylie. Keep in touch, okay?"

"Okay."

"And, listen, I'll be praying for you." He sounded sincere. "I'm sorry about what happened with Matt. I know you're hurt."

"Thanks. I am. But things are looking up."

"Bye, Kylie."

"Talk to you later."

Her grandparents reached her table just as Kylie ended her call.

"Well, I'm relieved," Kathryn said. "You don't look half as upset as I expected." She removed her coat, draped it over the back of her chair, and sat down.

"That was Seth on the phone. He called and lifted my spirits."

"Seth Brigham?" Lee's white bushy brows drew together.

"Yep."

"Hmm. . ."

Kylie saw her grandparents exchange glances. "What's wrong? Shouldn't I talk to Seth?"

"Well, Matt might not appreciate it," Kathryn said.

"Grandma, it's over between Matt and me."

"Dear heart, there's been a terrible misunderstanding. . . ."

As her grandmother spoke those words, Kylie saw Matt enter the restaurant. "No way! Did you guys set me up?"

Lee put a hand on her forearm. "No, not exactly. We would never do anything to hurt you. Matt followed us here. He wants to explain, and, Kylie, there's nothing on God's green earth that was going to keep him from having his say."

She fought to quell her surging emotions. "Sure. That's fine. Let him have his say."

Matt slowly approached the table. Reaching it, he nodded a tentative greeting. "Kylie."

She returned it. "Matt."

"Um. . ." Leaning forward, he put his hands on the table. "Ky, you jumped to conclusions today. Dena was in the barn with me, yes. But so were her kids and my mother. They'll testify to that. It's Ryan's birthday tomorrow, and Mom said he could have a kitten for a gift."

She felt her jaw drop, and she thought over what he said. April third. Yes, tomorrow was Ryan's birthday. Kylie recalled hearing "oh" and "darling," and she supposed Dena could have been exclaiming over a cat.

"If I falsely accused you, Matt," Kylie replied, swallowing a good portion of her pride, "and it seems I did, I'm sorry."

He gave her a skeptical stare. "Yeah, that was sort of. . . too easy."

"Matthew, please sit down," Kathryn said.

He did, and Kylie almost laughed at his guarded expression. Almost.

"Matt, I've prayed about this, and I've decided to move to Sabal Beach with my grandparents."

"What?!"

At his loud reply, every head in the house turned.

"Shhh."

"You can't be serious!"

"Kylie, don't make a decision like this when you're upset," Kathryn exclaimed.

She looked from Matt to her grandmother. "I wasn't upset when I made my choice. Don't you want me to move in with you anymore?"

"Of course I want you to, Silly!" Kathryn clasped Kylie's hand and gave Matt a guilty look. "But this young man loves you."

Kylie slid her glance across the table to Matt. "Deep in my heart, I think I love him, too."

"You think?" The muscle worked in Matt's jaw.

"He's a Christian, Kylie," Grandma Kate added.

"That's good. We'll see each other in heaven." She matched his unwavering gaze. "But here's the problem. Love isn't everything. It's only the beginning. It's like that seed you plant in the ground, Matt, and out of it comes the harvest. Something good was growing in our relationship, but it has withered and died. It's no more."

Irritation crossed his features. "Kylie, I made one mistake." He held up his forefinger. "One. Today, you made the mistake."

She raised one brow. "It's not the same, I assure you. But, listen, it doesn't matter because I'll continue to jump to conclusions. It won't be limited to today. Every time I see your truck and Dena's van in the parking lot of Dee Dee's, I'll jump to conclusions."

"That's ridiculous."

She ignored the retort. "If you're late coming home some-day, I'll jump to conclusions again. Matt, don't you see? The bond of trust between us has been severed. Trust was the life-line keeping our love alive."

He stared at her for a long while, and it was obvious to Kylie that something undefined chipped away at his anger. "Can't we try again?" His Adam's apple bobbed, and his blue eyes filled with the same deep sorrow Kylie felt in her heart. "Love's a pretty strong seed."

"That's true, Dear," her grandmother said. "It is."

Kylie thought it over but felt no inner peace at the idea of patching things up with Matt. "I–I don't know," she stam-mered. "I really feel like I need to move to Sabal Beach with my grandparents. I'll be safe there. I'll be able to sort out things and heal there. Maybe it'll be good to put some dis-tance between us for more than just ten days."

"Listen, Kylie, get a grip," Matt said. "Absence does not make the heart grow fonder. It makes the heart forget. If you move away, you'll find someone else. . .and so will I."

His subtle threat didn't rile her in the least. In fact, Kylie had thought about it already. "If we find 'someone else,' then we were never supposed to get married in the first place."

Exasperated, Matt threw his hands in the air.

The waitress appeared, handing them menus. Matt stood and noisily pushed in his chair.

"You're welcome to stay and have dinner with us," Lee said.

Matt glared at Kylie. "No, thanks. I lost my appetite."

She watched him leave the restaurant, yanking open the

door as he went. She felt awful for hurting him, but she didn't know what else to do. Everything she told him, she felt in her heart. Everything she said was true.

Her grandfather cleared his throat. "Kylie, my dear," he said, eyeing the menu, "you sure know how to make it tough on a guy. But I'm proud of you."

She peered at him askance. "Why? I'm not proud of me at all. I hate the fact I hurt Matt. But I really believe I obeyed God."

"And you did it with dignity," Grandpa Lee said. "But if Matt is as serious about you as he seems, this won't be the last of him. You know that, don't you?"

Kylie felt emotionally stronger with each passing moment. "Whether I see him again or not, it's all in God's hands now. I don't have to worry about anything. He's taking care of it all."

"Yes, He is."

"Kylie, do I even dare to hope that you're serious about moving in with us?"

She turned to her grandmother and smiled. "I'm very serious." She paused, thinking about what a move like that meant. "I just have one question."

"And that is. . . ?" Kathryn grinned.

"Will you help me pack?"

"Of course."

"You don't know what you're getting yourself into. Mom saved *everything*."

"Sounds like someone else I know," Lee muttered, glancing at his wife beneath raised brows.

"Oh, honestly, Lee!"

Kylie chuckled. "Seth told me that he and TJ will make the drive from South Carolina to help."

"Mmm, yes, I suppose the McKenneys can run our place

while they're gone. What do you think, Lee?"

"If they're available, it's fine by me."

"I understand that's the plan," Kylie said. She began to make a mental list of things to accomplish. "I'll have to put the house up for sale."

"Are you sure you want to do that?" her grandfather asked. "You grew up in that house."

Kylie pushed several strands of ebony hair off her face. "True, but the people I loved and who lived with me there are gone. It makes me sad to be in that house by myself. It's not a home anymore."

Lee reached over and patted her hand. "I understand."

"We could have an estate sale."

"Great idea, Grandma."

"Oh, this'll be so much fun!"

"You're looking at the queen of rummage sales," Lee informed Kylie.

"Well, I have had a few in my day, you know."

A soft laugh slipped through Kylie's lips as she pondered the menu. For the first time in a very long while, she felt free. Free from anger and bitterness—and even sorrow. She'd forever miss her parents and the relationships she had shared with Matt and Dena. But God had given her a set of grandparents to love, new friends who cared about her and prayed for her, and a bright future that shone into eternity.

And to think it all started when Allie sent that faded photograph. . . .

Would you like to offer feedback on this novel?

Visit www.barbourbooks.com

or write to:

AUTHOR RELATIONS
P.O. Box 719
Uhrichsville, OH 44683

ABOUT THE AUTHOR

ANDREA BOESHAAR has been married for twenty-five years. She and her husband, Daniel, have three adult sons. Andrea attended college first at the University of Wisconsin–Milwaukee, where she majored in English, and then at Alverno College, where she majored in Professional Communications and Business Management.

Andrea has been writing stories and poems since she was a little girl; however, it wasn't until 1984 that she started submitting her work for publication. In 1991 she became a Christian and realized her calling to write exclusively for the Christian market. Since then Andrea has written articles, devotionals, and over a dozen novels for **Heartsong Presents** as well as numerous novellas for Barbour Publishing. In addition to her own writing, she works as an agent for Hartline Literary Agency.

When she's not at the computer, Andrea enjoys being active in her local church and taking long walks with Daniel and their "baby"—a golden Labrador-Retriever mix named Kasey.

What readers are saying about *Broken Things*. . .

Broken Things. . .is what Christian fiction should be.

C.R.

I happened to pick up a copy of your book *Broken Things*. . .and passed it on to a friend. It has ministered to her in ways I never thought possible. Thanks for sharing your wonderful gift of writing with us—I cannot wait to read *Hidden Things*.

S.K.

Outstanding! *Broken Things* is a wonderful story of how God uses people and situations from our past and present lives to bring us back to Him and to restore in His time and his way those tattered and torn relationships.

S.M.

What a fantastic read! I enjoyed it from front to back.

J.M.

Broken Things is an inspiration! I have endured many rough spots in life and have to admit that reading this [book] put it all in perspective for me.

D.F.

It was good to read about broken hearts and relationships being mended. I'll be looking for the next book.

V.C.

This is a wonderful story, and so masterfully written. You had a perfect blend of everything—great story and story elements.

Y.L.

Very interesting story and very well written. The faded photograph theme is a great way to tie a series together. I will look forward to reading the next one.

C.T.

Broken Things

Favorite **Heartsong Presents** author Andrea Boeshaar takes us into the world of a woman who courageously faces the failures of her past when she finds a faded photograph of the Chicago cop she once loved. . .but left. When Allie Littenberg returns to make amends for broken relationships of more than twenty years earlier, she finds she is not the only person who has changed. Instead of the tender beau she'd left, Jack Callahan has turned into a bitter man, angry at a God who failed him. Can God use Allie to minister healing in Jack's shattered life and broken family?

ISBN 1-58660-756-1

Available wherever books are sold.

PRECIOUS THINGS

The Faded Photographs series—Book Three

It all started with a faded photograph and an invitation to restore relationships of decades ago. But Blythe has buried her past and moved ahead. . . that is until the daughter of the one man she loved and lost appears asking uncomfortable questions. Now this successful antique dealer is suddenly forced to undergo her own emotional and spiritual excavation. Amid the trauma, will she find precious treasures of love and faith?

ISBN 1-59310-065-5

Coming May 2004.